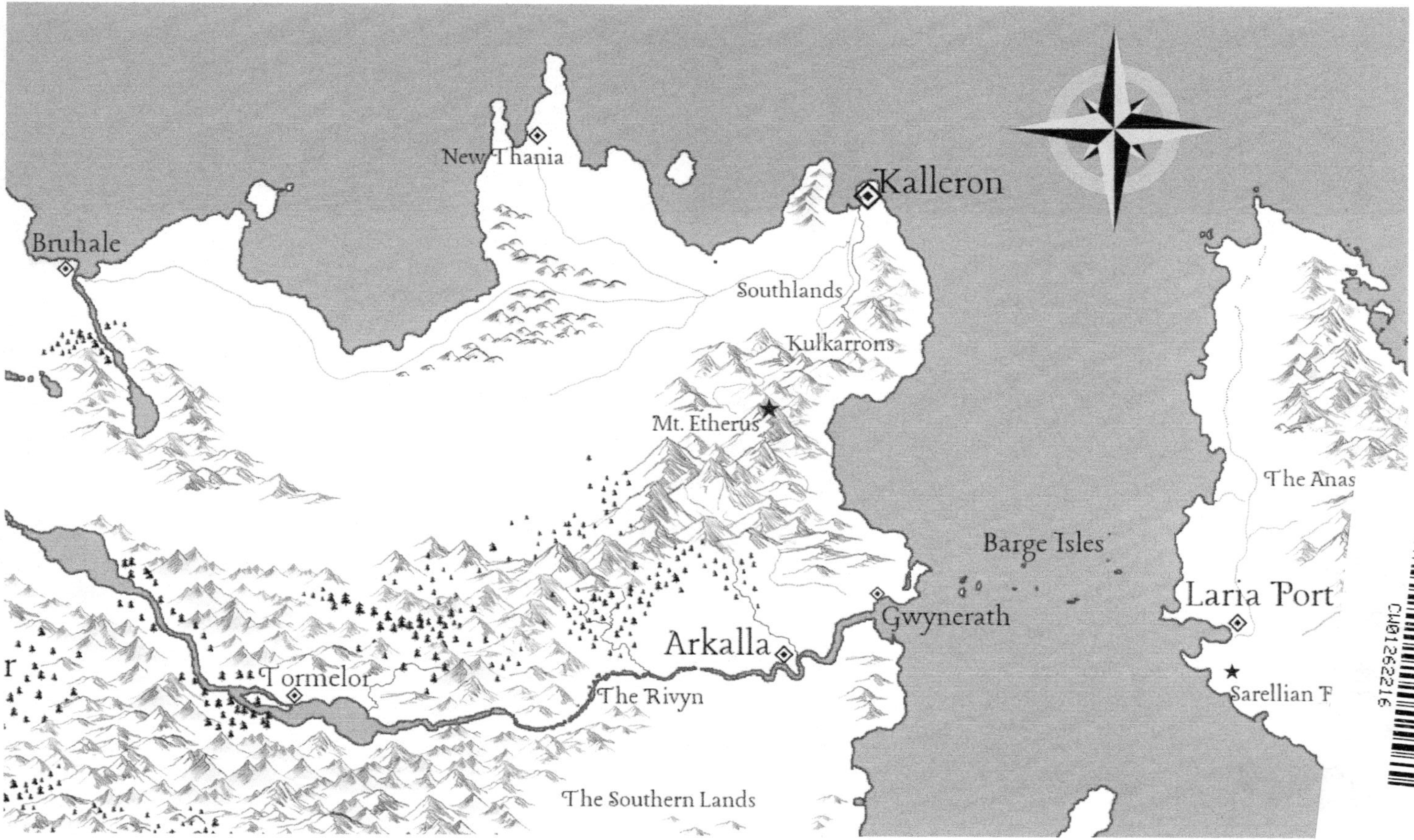
New Thania
Kalleron
Bruhale
Southlands
Kulkarrons
Mt. Etherus
Barge Isles
Laria Port
Gwynerath
Arkalla
Tormelor
The Rivyn
The Southern Lands

Melody & Majesty

KALLERON Book I

James D. McEwan

Melody & Majesty: Kalleron Book I by James D. McEwan

Published by James D. McEwan

Website: jamesdmcewan.com

Copyright © 2023 James D. McEwan

All rights reserved. No portion of this book, including cover artwork, may be reproduced in any form without permission from the publisher, except as permitted by U.K. copyright law. For permissions and contact info visit: jamesdmcewan.com.

ISBN: 978-1-7391270-4-6

This is an original work of fiction. Names, characters, places, and incidents either are the products of the author's imagination or are used fictitiously. Any resemblance to actual persons, living or dead, fictional entities, or places, is entirely coincidental.

Cover concept and titles by James D. McEwan. Kalleron map designed with Wonderdraft.

Front cover text and jacket design were created using Canva.

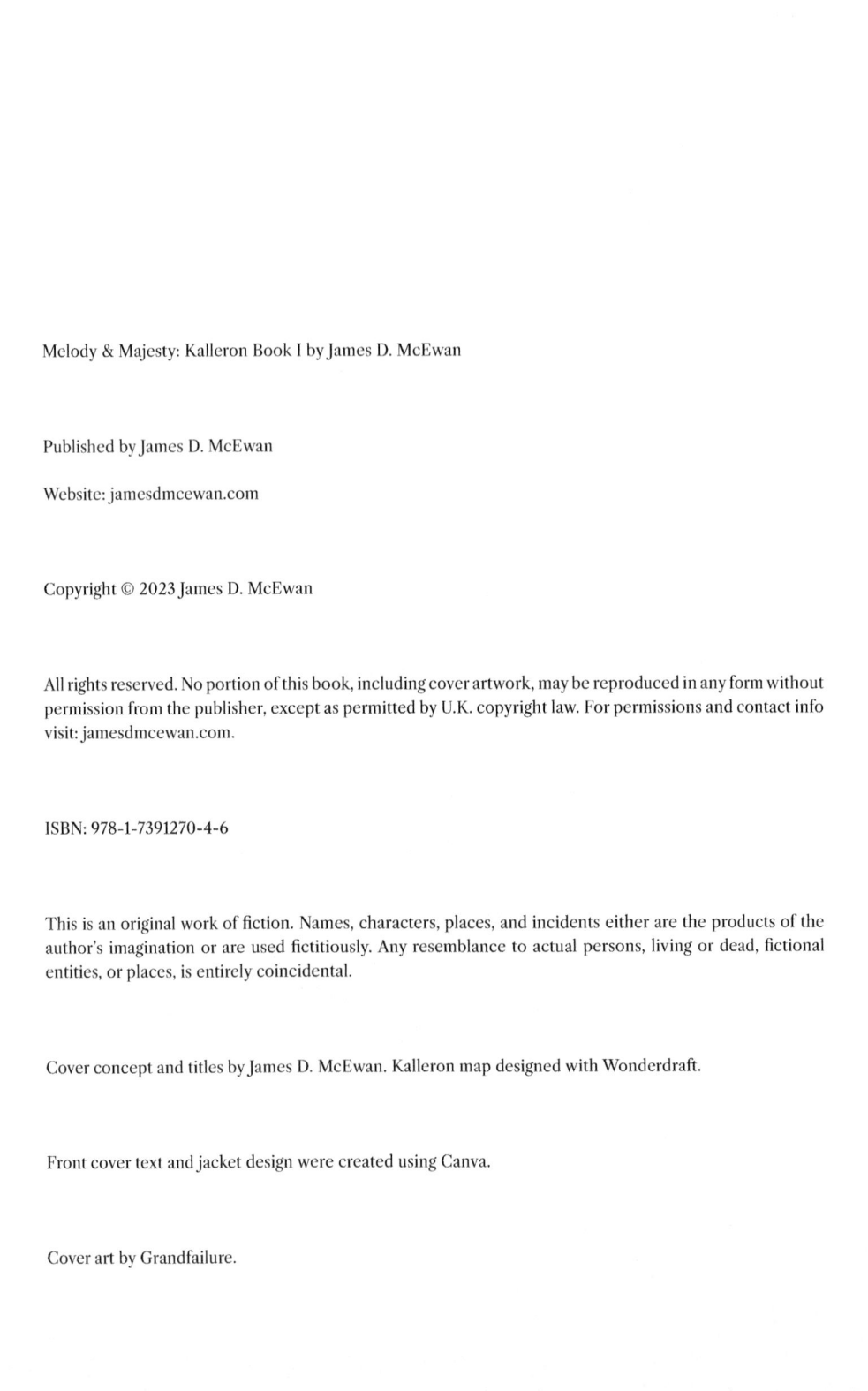

Cover art by Grandfailure.

To Carolyn.

You've given me genuine support from day one, and I've always valued your feedback—even if my reactions can be a little prickly. It is telling though, that no matter how petulant I might first appear, I return to the work and iron out the creases. Thank you for keeping me on track.

And a special thanks to Julia & Matt for their independent reviews of Hammer & Glass. Your positive comments on the writing style guided a complete, line-by-line edit of Melody & Majesty. I hope this story doesn't disappoint.

Chapter I

Argan was often silent. Never quick to judge, nor fast to temper; the giant Bruhadian stared back at Shadow. A wrinkle in his dark brow, he huffed and put down the leg of ham.

'Did you go too far?' he asked.

Shadow shrugged. He wasn't having a crisis of conscience; he was content with his behaviour, though he was curious about his friend's perspective. 'Did I? You think?'

'You broke his jaw,' Argan said with emphasis. 'His jaw, Shadow—you broke it.'

A statement of fact; it wasn't even an answer, at least not a good one. Shadow hadn't posed the hardest question to his statuesque acquaintance. A simple matter of property. The necklace had been legitimate loot from the last voyage. There was a saying among thieves: What's yours is mine, and what's mine is my own. Though it was rare that he'd trust his own profession. Regardless, the plunder of the glittering jewellery hadn't been the issue. It was the brazen reaction it had provoked.

Shadow raised a finger to Argan, recalling the egregious offence. 'He ripped it from my neck. Called me a back-alley kiss-coin.'

Argan's frown remained.

In a whisper, Shadow said, '*Kiss-coin*. Me?'

The Bruhadian shrugged. With another sigh, he said, 'Shadow, it was Hoydai, and you were wearing...'

'Wearing what?'

His frown relenting, Argan rolled his eyes. 'It was a woman's necklace. You stole it from the innkeeper's mistress.' He turned his huge palms upwards. 'And it *was* Hoydai.'

'Yeah, but the diamonds looked good on me.' Shadow pointed to where the necklace ought to be. His fingers tracing his neck, he rued not grabbing it back. 'That jealous lowlife had no right!'

Argan's stare was accompanied by a slight shake of his head, but his features remained blank. Shadow had long puzzled over the frequent silences and his rare, often prophetic words. Though now, Argan seemed content to pick at his leg of ham. It had been a challenge to pin down his origins. Shadow had tried to speak of it with his captain, Petra. All she would agree was that it was probable he was from Bruhada's disbanded Royal Guard. No more would she discuss; not while they were the crew of the *Melody of the Sea*; a ship of second chances and new life. Royal Guard? Had to be with that impressive bulk. Not to mention the aura that Argan emanated. Although the Bruhadian had never shown aggression, Shadow knew there was a storm lurking beneath the calm. Beware the unwitting fool who pushed Argan over the edge, although to Shadow's knowledge, no man or woman had managed such a feat. He picked at the cured meats on his platter and tried to recall how many times he had tested Argan's patience.

He squinted at the Bruhadian. 'If a toss-pot innkeeper from Kalleron said that you looked like a...'

A sudden commotion arrested his flow. Shadow turned his head, scanning for the source. *Honourhome*, the preferred haunt in cold Laria, was awash with customers, and the chaos of conversation and laughter was an audible soup; a background stream of fluctuating noise that could wake the dead. Larian traders had come home from the continent with their wares from Gwynerath, and Kallerye entrepreneurs sought contracts with outcast Rotynians; Honourhome was where merchants established jovial bonds before the ruthless bartering began.

Shadow, standing tall and craning his neck, turned his attention to the excited chatter that was separate from the business and banter. Under the iridescent mosaic ceiling of crushed shells and ornate hanging lamps, he found the commotion. Visible through fleeting gaps in the crowd, the source of the disturbance came as no surprise.

'It's only bloody Petra,' he said, turning to Argan.

The Bruhadian didn't take his eyes off his food. 'In trouble?'

Shadow didn't think so. His captain was being dragged by her hair across the floor of the inn, but it didn't cause him concern. He'd seen worse. The assailant, dressed in red and black leathers, had the rough attributes of a Kallerye pirate; a lower breed of scum than the nominally more respected Rotynians. Shadow grinned; what the idiot didn't know would surely deliver the evening's entertainment.

He moved to join the melee, but a solid thud slamming down on his shoulder stopped him in his tracks. He turned, throwing a wild punch at his aggressor.

His fist found Argan's open palm. A feeble child slapping a prize bull. Shadow hesitated, his anger floating behind a veil of wonder. It was the smallest things that defined the enigmas of life; insights that delivered more understanding than any historic tome, or a bard's rambling song of heroes. Royal Guard he might be, but how, in the name of the bloody gods, did the big Bruhadian move so fast?

Argan lowered his arm. 'Easy, Shadow.'

A nod toward the captain. 'But, Petra!'

'Let's just watch the show from afar, eh?' He motioned to the tankard on the table. 'Beers and brawls, and you don't have to spill a drop.'

Conflicted by the urge to fight and his desire to drink, Shadow huffed. Argan was right. Petra could take care of herself. It would be a good show. Lifting his tankard but remaining on his feet, Shadow gazed with anticipation at what wonders might unfold.

A hazy rainbow passing overhead; it should've been pretty. Vibrant colours and candlelight. A charming sight spoiled by circumstance; Petra's hands holding firm to her assailant's wrists, fearful he might pull out her hair. A struggle to think. How had it all started? She and Felicitra, seated in a cosy booth, enjoying a carefree evening. Keen for the crew to relax and enjoy the comforts of her native Larian hospitality. *Honourhome* was a reliable port in any storm; a reputable inn with excellent fare. Perhaps it was the dratch? Felicitra had brought a bottle ashore, paid the innkeeper a steep corkage. Given him more to turn a blind eye. Few inns north of Shaddenhyne tolerated the erratic effects of the hallucinogenic toxin. Yes, blame the dratch. Though it still didn't explain the undignified drag across the hard wooden boards. Too much thinking.

Enough!

Petra clawed at her captor's wrist, her nails digging deep into flesh; a soft popping sensation as she found the tissue beneath.

A howl. Not hers.

Freed at last, Petra spun on her rear and rubbed her scalp with both hands. A furious massage to dismiss the painful itch of her unceremonious escort.

'You bloody cow!' yelled the...

'Pirate?' Petra said. 'A bloody Kallerye pirate?'

Clutching his bleeding wrist, he stared at her. The grimace on his face, the spittle from his mouth; Petra presumed she had his attention, if not his respect. She didn't care for the latter.

The pirate was seething. 'You almost cut my fucking vein!'

Petra squinted at the simpering fool. 'I missed? Damn.'

He lunged. A downward arc from his flying fist; Petra crumpled under the impact. Calloused knuckles connecting with her cheekbone sent a judder through her skull, but she didn't wince or yelp. Though she regretted drinking the bloody dratch. The spirit appeared to alter the flow of time; the strike hitting home before she saw it coming. Shadow's wise words came to her frazzled mind: Nothing beats a boozy fight, but only an idiot swings on the green stuff.

'Whoops,' she said as her body lurched; the floorboards sliding past her bleary gaze.

Where the hell was he going? Wherever it was, she wasn't. Petra lashed out with the heel of her boot. Three strikes missing their target; the pirate yelled something lost to the thudding in her skull. Frustration creeping in, Petra rued the command given to her crew. They all knew not to help; petite she may be, but she wasn't a delicate princess. She could handle herself. One of the *Rules of the Melody*: an order given was an order obeyed. Too many damn rules, Petra thought; her head bumping against the leg of a table. One last kick.

A solid contact; another howl of pain. Free again and scrabbling away from the pirate, Petra shook her head, tried to find her focus. She had to get to her feet. The bloody dratch playing tricks; she was already upright. So too was the pirate, storming toward her with a fresh limp. But Petra had a secret. Deep within her soul, the red mist was rising. How many times had it come to her aid? A few seconds of instinct to banish the fugue. Shaky but assured, she dropped low and pulled the dagger concealed within her boot. The pirate was almost on top of her. Petra swung the blade and side-stepped the charge with a drunken twirl, the dagger ruffling the hair on the nape of his neck when a voice rang out.

'PETRA, NO!'

Her grip loosened on the command, and the blade scraped the pirate's flesh. A signature drawn in blood; her mark would remind him of his mistake. Silver glinted in the air as the rainbow reflections of the tiled ceiling spun to the floor. In near silence, the clatter was a crash.

Felicitra. Her voice. A siren without compare to bring the world to its senses. Honourhome quelled. A dumbfounded pirate, and Petra sanctioned. From the crowd, a group of thugs dressed in red and black came for their friend. Arms around their shoulders, he limped away, never looking back. Petra turned to Felicitra, fearful of a scolding.

The hand that was raised fell softly on her cheek. 'Petra, my love. You can't kill your way out of everything.'

What could she say? What defence did she have? 'You brought the damn dratch.'

Felicitra laughed. 'Oh, we're blaming the alcohol now?' Her gaze reached beyond Petra. Nodding, she continued. 'Not even Shadow starts a fight on that.'

The cornered wolf becoming a little lamb, Petra hung her head. She recalled what had started the fight. 'I heard him talking at the bar. To his mates. Said what he was going to do... to you. I saw red.'

'As you command your own, Petra, you know I can take care of myself.'

It was a truth Petra understood. Felicitra's voice was her rapier. Her wit was her shield. If they failed, and they rarely did, then the wickedly sharp *sesuri* concealed under her steel bracelet was her failsafe. It wasn't the piercing stab that settled wayward tempers; it was the sedative herb packed into the hollow point.

'Come on,' Felicitra said, 'let's get you to bed.'

'All right.'

The night was young, but Petra didn't relish the attention of the crowd. The chatter and gossip she expected. It was the questions on the lips of the crew, the doubts in their minds that gave cause for concern. Had their captain lost a fight? She peered across the floor, sought her friend at the far side. Between moving silhouettes, she saw him. Separated by the crowd, Shadow was staring back at her. A wide grin on his face. Petra frowned, unsure if he would see her silent question. Lost to the resurrected noise of Honourhome, the shape of his mouth spelled reassuring words. A wink and a raised fist to seal the praise.

You had him.

Petra smiled, and taking Felicitra's arm, she left the pleasures of Honourhome behind.

Away from the crew, concealed behind her stateroom door, Petra had no need for courage. As Felicitra dabbed the graze on her cheek, the alcohol stung as though the barb of a Tormelorian wasp.

'Ouch!'

Felicitra raised a manicured eyebrow. 'Ouch?'
Petra frowned. Nodded.
'How do you do it?' Felicitra asked, standing from Petra and placing her hands on her hips. Illuminated in the candlelight, auburn hair fell across her shoulders in waves of dark fire. Her piercing blue eyes were Noctyrne's light dancing on the ocean crests. A tall woman, hailing from the Valley of Seven Cities in Tormelor, Felicitra was the one-in-a-million lover of which stubborn hearts could only dream. She was a song for bards; a melody for the soul. Petra still wondered what fates had smiled upon her the day their paths had crossed.
'Do what?' she said.
'This.' Felicitra leaned forward and dabbed Petra's cheek.
Another sting. Petra winced without protest.
'I see you. As human as your crew. You bleed as they do; love as they do. You lose fights as they do. Yet...' Looking to her palm, at the astringent-soaked ball, Felicitra shook her head. 'None of them sees this. Why?'
Sobered by the fight and the freezing walk to the *Melody*, Petra frowned. 'I've told you countless times. I'm their captain; I need to be stronger than all of them.'
Felicitra laughed.
'What?' Petra asked.
Felicitra raised her hand, bringing the delicate cotton swab closer to Petra's face. 'I doubt Argan would wince at this.'
'Not in public, perhaps.'
'Shadow?'
Petra's grin widened. Shadow, how she loved him for the fool he was. 'He'd cry like a baby. You'd not even get near him with that.'
Felicitra laughed again. It was a beautiful sound. 'You're probably right. But your outward face; what you show the world. Do you really feel it needs to be so...?'
'So, what?' Petra wanted to know what word Felicitra would hesitate to use.
'Invincible.' Felicitra frowned and shook her head, pacing backwards a single step. It felt as though a mile. 'Because you're not. Nobody is. Not us, at least.'
In the centre of her stateroom, the most beautiful woman in Petra's world stood naked but for a sheer cotton nightdress. The contours of her perfect body highlighted in the candlelight; she was an artwork rendered real by unknown gods. Yet Petra found her gaze drawn to Felicitra's feet.
'My father,' Petra said. 'I've told you this.'
Feet moving closer, the lover kneeling down; Felicitra's hand reached to lift Petra's chin. 'You're not your father.'

Petra reached to hold Felicitra's wrist. 'More than people know.'

'But he was...'

'Everything to me.'

It comforted Petra that Felicitra remained close. The discussion wasn't new; it wasn't pleasant. She thought repeating it might push her away. Perhaps it was true what they said of the Tormelorians. If they had the patience to build seven cities; then they must have had the patience of the gods. It was a quality Felicitra had in abundance.

'I know my father wasn't a good man. But he was to me. I was all he had, and he gave me everything a man of his nature could. Taught me everything he knew.' She lifted her gaze. 'When they finally came for him; when they set eyes on me...'

The glow of Felicitra's face dimmed. A sadness to replace the joy. Petra thought she might rise to her feet, but those loving hands came to her face, held soft against her skin. 'I know. I know.'

Secure in that cradle, Petra lost herself in Felicitra's blue eyes. She fought to control the emotion of the wicked memory. 'They had me. Almost.' Nodding. It was becoming harder to fight the tears, but she continued. 'My father. The wealthy trader. Noble benefactor. The alderman. Corrupt to his rotten core. But none of them knew his truth. My father; the murderer. Killed more men and women than I knew. And I hated him, Felicitra. I hated him until that day. Hated how strong I had to be; how strong he asked me to be. But that day he showed me his true face.'

Petra recalled the day her father's squalid empire had come crashing down. And though in the years after she had tried to find who had betrayed him, the answer had always eluded her. Whoever it was, they had brought despair to her life.

Felicitra's touch gave Petra the confidence to relive the memory. 'Like rats, they swarmed through the mansion. Scurrying like degenerates. They took everything, no matter its value; they came to rip his legacy apart. As far as they were concerned, I was just part of his empire. Barely thirteen, I was nothing to them but property. Something to take. I couldn't count the hands that were on me. So many, clutching and clawing, and I thought...'

Felicitra's finger moved to Petra's lips. 'I know. And I'm sorry I brought it up. You don't need to go over it again.'

Given fortitude by her father's ghost, Petra brushed the hushing finger from her lips. Thinking of that moment, of what wicked men might steal from innocence, a fire rose within. A fierce flame to burn away the fears.

'A murderer came to me that night. Stopped the horror. My father, come screaming as the Wind herself. A furious gale of anger. I can see it as clear as yesterday.' She looked at Felicitra, a frown offered to her lover. 'I don't know how he broke free, but he appeared among them. A knife in hand. As many times as I've told you, Felicitra, my father had uncanny strength. The blood of strangers rained down on me that evening. My father—the heroic monster. But there were too many to overpower, and I think he knew his fate. I scrambled away from it all, his last words sticking in my mind: *Run, my sweet girl, run.* I can see his face, even now; his wide smile to see me flee.' Petra held tight to Felicitra's hand; she wanted her lover to know the truth. 'A weak man wouldn't have saved me. No normal man could have stopped them from taking what they wanted. It took just one murderer to stop a dozen rapists. It showed me—I knew what I had to be to survive.' Petra leant forward and kissed Felicitra. She remained close, sharing the air they breathed. 'Only you get to see the sweet girl my father knew.'

Felicitra nodded. 'All that happened; what your father did. That's why you have such affection for Shadow.'

It was so obvious; how could she not have seen? Shadow, in almost every way, was the embodiment of her father. A love of vice and violence; but a man so loyal to Petra that many thought them lovers. As her father had done, she knew Shadow would risk all for her. As would she, for him.

Petra sighed and nodded. 'I can't imagine how stupid I look. I never thought of it like that.'

'It's not stupid, Petra. Even I can see the worth in Shadow. He's an acquired taste, certainly; a rough diamond, definitely.' Felicitra's hand cupped her cheek. 'But perhaps the only one to keep you safe? When I'm not around, of course.'

Petra smiled. 'He is... unique.' Another kiss for Felicitra. 'But even he doesn't see what I want you to see. I am me, only for you.'

Felicitra wriggled free of her grasp. She stepped to the door and turned the latch. Graceful steps carried her across the wooden boards. Not a single creak came from the polished timber planks. One by one, Felicitra extinguished the lamps. As darkness enveloped the room, her voice came as a messenger from the gods.

'Then be mine tonight, Petra. Be all of you.'

Chapter II

Laria. Petra's homeland was a contradiction. A frigid and hostile place; it's people and towns were warm and welcoming. The Anastra, a range of rugged and vertiginous peaks spanning the eastern horizon, dominated the island. The mountains had a profound effect on the Larian climate; a perpetual winter experienced in all but the western coastal fringes. On the edge of the Larissian Sea, Laria Port experienced a milder cold season. A shallow valley with steep sea-cliffs sheltered the capital, sparing Petra's favoured city from the worst of the elements. Despite that relief, Petra was quick to remind her crew that a refreshing chill was the best they could hope for.

With the Anastra obscuring the sun's ascent, the harbour languished in shades of ochre, and the western sky was dark in the Larian dawn. A breeze ruffled the canvas on the Melody of the Sea, and on deck, clasping a warm brew of *Ouhla*, Petra stared westward. Beyond the Larissian Sea, Kalleron was a divergent and dangerous world, fractured by politics and conquest. She had sailed to many places over the years, learned what was, and what was not, profitable territory. In the southern Free Lands, the pleasure capitals of Shaddenhyne and Hoydai were an excess of vice and opulence. Separated from the continent by the Rivyn, a vast and wide river, Petra regarded the Free Lands as a world apart from northern Kalleron. Hoydai, preferred by her crew, was a lush green paradise in the far south. The ancient city provided a relaxed sense of decay. Shaddenhyne, in the east, was a poor mimic of its cultured neighbour. Its vice was too vulgar; the pleasures less sweet. Even though it had a long and storied history, Shaddenhyne had, in Petra's opinion, embraced too much of the modern age.

On the far western coast, Drohendrir and its northern neighbour, Dreyahyde, nestled among dense forests of pine. And though the route was long, Petra's seasonal voyage to Dreyahyde had become a ritual. There, the finest artisans saw to the *Melody's* repairs, and her crew could relax without fear of Kalleron's reach.

Petra sighed, visualising the world beyond the horizon. All of those cities and the scattered towns and settlements lay south or west of the Rivyn. They all found solace in the ward of Water; the boundary of the elemental Earth. Petra's world was a human domain; a place of love and hate, laughter and tears. But it was also *theirs*. Ambivalent yet powerful creatures that existed without reason and moved without thought. Water, Wind, and Fire appeared disinterested in mortal affairs. Unseen, untouched; these demigods could well be myth. Petra had learned early in her life, however, that there was one elemental whose presence was altogether more frightening.

The northern city-state, from which they named the continent, was as no other in the world. Ruled by Kalle, the Immortal, his consort was the elemental Earth. Infamous for her genocidal deeds, the Terrible Queen of Kalleron was a weapon wielded with impunity. Far removed from the elemental's earthly reach, Laria was a sanctuary. And although it had never caused her concern, Petra couldn't draw her gaze from the world beyond the horizon. What Felicitra had told her this morning had chilled her to the core. Beyond the Larissian Sea, the King had staked his claim on another nation, and the Queen's power was rising.

Petra heard familiar footsteps and turned to greet her lover. Felicitra came close, a kiss offered to her cheek. A kiss goodbye.

'Petra, you know I have to go.'

'Why didn't you tell me last night?'

'And spoil the moment?' Felicitra shook her head. She appeared amused; inconsiderate, given the circumstances.

'What can possibly bring a smile to your face?'

'It's not pleasure. A cruel joke, perhaps.'

'A joke?' A spark of hope rising within; Petra lifted her head. 'You think the news isn't true?'

Felicitra raised her hand; a gentle grasp on Petra's shoulder. 'No, it's true. We both know it. Kalleron has given Arkalla ample time to respond. The Seer's faith is unshakable; he would never relent to Kalle's demands.'

A frown to respond, Petra shook her head. 'Then why the humour?'

'The Rivyn. It's her boundary. If only they had built Arkalla on the southern bank; they would be safe.'

Petra recalled the city. A proud and beautiful place. Pretty white buildings, often coloured with accents of amber and green, nestled among sculpted stone towers capped by golden spires. Arkalla, the capital of Arkallon, had long opposed Kalle's claim over the northern swathe of the continent.

'I don't understand,' Petra said. 'Is the Seer so blind?'

'Belief is a blindfold to some.'

'But Tormelor, Thania. Even Bruhale. Can he not see what will come?'

Felicitra sighed. 'None of them had faith in the new gods. The Seer has Arkana; Arkalla, if we must move with the times. He truly believes his god will save his people. How can Arkana let the greatest city built in his honour fall to a heathen Queen?'

'It is foolishness. Madness, even. He is condemning his own.'

'Perhaps.'

'What of the soldiers?' Although she asked of them, Petra knew they would offer no resistance to the march of the Queen.

Felicitra raised her eyebrows; a cynical smile on her face. 'The Seer doesn't need an army; he has his god, remember? Local militia and justices are all Arkalla requires.'

Petra shook her head. 'It will be dangerous, Felicitra. I can come with you.'

'You know my business. I must travel alone to Gwynerath. Then onto Arkalla.' She turned and paced to the stateroom door, nodding for Petra to follow.

Petra hesitated. A sombre mood had descended. Felicitra's invite wasn't for pleasure. 'Inside? Why?'

'For your ears only. You understand?'

Not a lover's words; they were pragmatic. Not a surprise coming from Felicitra's lips. The crew knew little of her true calling. Petra presumed they thought her a travelling diplomat of sorts; often appearing in the company of town elders. Few had ever questioned her affairs, perhaps because of the rules under which they sailed; Petra's commandment that forbade interrogation. Once aboard, and part of the crew, your past was your own. Only Shadow had questioned Felicitra's presence, and Petra had told him all she could without breaking her bond to Felicitra. Anxious of what would come, Petra entered the stateroom and closed the door behind.

'Cult business?' she asked.

'Not directly. But my father is too poorly to travel. The runner who came yesterday told me that people are already leaving. They don't trust the Seer's faith.'

'And what of your father?'

Felicitra smiled; it seemed ill at ease on her troubled face. 'I had warnings of this eventuality—of the Seer's defiance. We've tried to make him see sense, but it doesn't take a network of spies to see the endgame.' She drummed her fingers on Petra's wide desk. 'I've hired help for my father. Though I'll need to oversee his evacuation myself. Trust is a rare commodity in these delicate moments; too many profiteers and cut-throats waiting to take what isn't theirs.'

Petra questioned the need for privacy. 'Everyone has family somewhere, Felicitra.' She gestured to the confines of the stateroom. 'Why did you need to speak in here?'

'Because of this.' Felicitra removed a letter from the drawer in the desk.

'What's that? And how did it get there?'

'I put it there yesterday. I've been carrying it for a while; wasn't sure when to show it to you.'

'Show?'

Felicitra inhaled and clicked her tongue. It was one of her rare tells; a trait to betray her anxiety. Petra understood that whatever came next wouldn't be sweet roses and delicate perfume. She leant on her prized darkwood desk. Something solid to steady the nerves.

Holding the letter toward her, Felicitra said, 'If I don't come back, you...'

'You bloody will come back!'

Felicitra paused; she kept the letter floating between them, giving it a gentle shake. 'If I don't...'

Grim thoughts in her mind, Petra shook her head. 'Put it back in the drawer.' She nodded to the desk. 'You can do what you want with it when you return.'

Felicitra, her grip tight on the letter, stared at Petra.

'The drawer,' Petra said.

'You're a stubborn bitch. You'll not relent, will you?'

'I'd sooner burn that, than take it from your hands. I've no interest in what it says, not if it requires your absence to say it. You'll come back, and you can read it to me over a glass of wine and candlelight. We'll laugh at how you made such a drama about this. Understood?'

With a sigh, Felicitra placed the letter in the drawer. She appeared to hesitate before pushing it closed. It shut with a gentle thud of the solid Drohendrian timber. 'You understand I have no desire to stay in Arkallon?' She pointed at the desk. 'One day, Petra, if the time comes, you'll open it? Promise me.'

With the letter and whatever sombre message it contained hidden from view, Petra accepted Felicitra's request without fear of loss. 'I promise. I'll listen to whatever it says... when you read it to me.'

'You'll truly not give up, will you?'

Petra shook her head. 'Not for you.'

'Then, when you hear my voice, you'll listen?'

'Always.'

'Good.' Felicitra appeared content, although her focus drifted back to the letter secured in the drawer.

Good. It was strange how it sounded. Final. Perhaps the atmosphere; the talk of a dangerous journey ahead. How better to be prepared than to ask Felicitra more?

'So, tell me, if I'm forbidden to travel with you and your secretive friends; your mission to Arkalla, to your father; give me all the details. Reassure me of your safety and how easy this will all be. I've no wish to wait here and fret like a child.'

Felicitra moved around the desk and stood before her, reaching for Petra's hands. 'We wouldn't want the crew to see that now, would we?'

'While you travel, I can go back to being as cold as ice.'

Nodding to the outside, Felicitra smiled. 'In Laria, ice is relatively warm.'

Petra leant in, kissing her on the lips. 'Shut up. Now, your journey: tell me your plans and of when you'll return.' A pause, a thought. 'Do I need to make room aboard the Melody for your father?'

Chapter III

The light filtering through the porthole was a shade past morning. As good as any time to surface from slumber. Shadow huffed and rolled from his bunk, dropping with a thud to the rug beneath. Once a lone grey wolf from the forests south of Dreyahyde, the beast had picked the wrong supper. It had pained Shadow to slay such a magnificent animal. He had tried to ward it off. But animals were stubborn; as dumb as humans. Its loss was his gain. Shadow ruffled the wolf's misshapen head and rose to his feet. Was the Melody at sea? The hull lurching to the side. A headache to navigate his position; a glance through the glass to see the bay of Laria Port. Calm waters. Yet the cabin rolled under his feet. Shadow smiled. A sure sign he'd had a good night; though he'd need to ask the others if that was so. The memory was cloudy as ditch water. One thing was clear: he had to find Petra; she would have the *aryll* extract to ease the thudding in his skull. Throwing his heavy dark cloak around his naked frame, he stumbled to the deck.

'Petra?' Shadow tapped on the stateroom door. No answer. He repeated his call, more insistent. 'It's cold out. Need a favour.'

'She's not aboard.'

Shadow turned his head; a glance over his shoulder. 'Argan. Morning. Afternoon. Whatever... where is she?'

The Bruhadian, moving heavy barrels back and forth across the deck for no apparent reason, pointed to the dockside. 'She's seeing Felicitra off.'

'Off?'

Argan nodded.

'Off where?'

Argan shrugged. Of course, he wouldn't know. Never appeared interested in the affairs of the crew. Perfect for the Melody, even before he knew the rules. Shadow peered at Argan's barrels. 'You moved the water?'

The Bruhadian pointed port side and continued with his inefficient behaviour. Shadow stared a while longer. 'If I do that,' he asked, 'will I get as big as you?'

Argan chuckled, but gave no reply, and continued his pointless endeavour. Secrets, Shadow thought. Secrets for everything. Familiar with Argan's preference for quiet, Shadow took no offence and paced to the barrel. He removed the lid and cupped his hands, dousing his face with a mixture of frozen slivers and biting cold water. With his cheeks tingling, he drank some of the fresh elixir and replaced the lid. A nod to Argan, who didn't appear to notice, and Shadow stepped to the gangplank and onto the dockside.

Petra wasn't hard to find. She cut a lonely figure standing at the end of the boardwalk. She held her favoured white fur tight to her shoulders. Once the luxurious pelt of a Larian mountain ox, the cloak suited the captain. She was as hardy as the rugged beast. An easterly wind had rolled in, and Petra's silver-coloured hair flicked and danced in the breeze. Shadow winced at the chill; wondered how long Petra had been alone. An awkward image floated in his mind. He tried to push it away. Poetry wasn't to his taste, but she looked as though a princess sent from the very heights of Etherus. Perhaps even a queen; a cold and lonely queen.

Without invite, he came to her side. 'Petra.'

Her attention on the tall ship leaving port, Petra returned his greeting. 'Shadow.'

'Is that...? Argan mentioned something about Felicitra?'

'She's bound for Gwynerath; then onward to Arkalla.'

'Gwynerath? Why're we not...?'

'It's not trade, Shadow. It's personal.'

'Oh.' Shadow didn't understand the relevance. Gwynerath was a good place to be. On the eastern fringe of Arkallon, nestled under the Kulkarron mountains, there was wealth and pretty things aplenty. 'But why are we not sailing ourselves? You say she's going to Arkalla? We could slum it uptown on the coast. Wait for her. Somewhere warm.'

A long exhalation of her breath floated into the icy air. He waited for her words. None came. 'Petra?'

'Of all the crew, Shadow, you know more than most. Felicitra's got business to attend, and it's her business alone. She'll do it her own way, as she always does. You know how it is.'

He did. But there was rare unease in his captain's voice. A lack of confidence that nibbled at his curiosity. It would be wrong to pry, but what else could he do?

'You're pissed?'

'No.'

'Then... then what, Petra? C'mon on, you can tell me. You know I'll not care, and besides, I'll forget about it anyway. Something's up. That's clear, even to me. Get it off your lovely chest.'

Petra turned to face him. A cut on her cheek shining nicely.

'Ouch. That's gonna bruise,' he said. 'That from last night?' He reached up, intent on poking her wound. Petra slapped his hand away with a sigh.

'Felicitra brought some dratch.'

Shadow grinned. These moments were rare; a chance to revel in Petra's foolishness. His own bloody captain drinking the green stuff. 'You picked a fight, and you were drunk on that insidious venom? Did you have visions?'

Petra shrugged. 'Of sparkles and rainbows, aye. Seemed a good idea until it wasn't.'

He patted her shoulder; a reassuring tap. 'We've all made that mistake at some point. Live and learn, they say.' Shadow glanced to see the tall ship fading from view. He frowned, recalling Petra's tone. 'So, what's actually happening here?'

She turned to face him; anxiety in her eyes. 'The Queen. She's been sent to destroy Arkalla.'

Shadow, seated in Petra's stateroom, recalled the reason he had sought her.

'You still have some aryll?'

Pacing back and forward, Petra pointed to a small ceramic jar on one of many wooden shelves. Books, trinkets, and other oddities from around the world decorated her modest cabin. As far as Shadow could tell, a new collection appeared after every voyage, the stacks of shelves growing larger each year. Rising from his plush chair, a leather padded seat complimented by well-rounded arms swathed in soft fabric, Shadow retrieved the vessel and returned. He stared at his agitating friend.

'You'll wear a hole in your timber.'

Petra glared.

Shadow pulled the lid from the bright blue jar. 'Your huffy-eye powers don't work on me; remember, I'm a moron. I don't take hints.'

With a sigh that was a little too dramatic, Petra moved to her desk and slumped in her chair. She pointed across the darkwood at the aryll in his hand and scrunched up her face. 'Does the wee boy need a pick-me-up?'

Her familiar tone had returned. The blunt-force Petra that was better suited to his hangover. Not the moping sop. Shadow was happy to engage with his prickly friend. He put a hand to his cheek. 'Did the silly little girl bang her pretty wee face?'

That glare again. But Shadow saw the cracks; a grin beginning to form. 'There she is!'

A sigh of capitulation carried her words. 'Oh, fuck off.'

'Seriously though, last night, I wanted to step in. I think Argan stopped me.'

She shrugged her slender shoulders. 'When don't you want to step in? Probably for the best. I like Honourhome. Don't think murdering patrons would hold us in good stead. Felicitra's better at keeping the peace.'

Shadow, munching on the aryll root, tried to recall the specifics. The herb could work wonders for hangovers. 'Didn't you pull a knife?'

'Pah!' Petra swished her hand through the air. 'Details.'

Another thought. Perhaps not for now. Yet somehow, it came out. 'I've never seen you lose a...'

Her rebuke was swift. 'I didn't lose anything.'

Hands raised; Shadow offered an apology. 'I mean, it was a fleeting thought. But seeing your ass being dragged across the floor... well, it's not like you.'

'Dragged? Oh, you're mistaken. I lost a gold coin; was looking for it when my foot got caught on some pirate's boot-buckles. A freak occurrence.'

Shadow rolled his fingertips on the table. He drummed out his dissatisfaction with her feeble lies. 'Oh, really?'

Petra smiled and rolled her eyes. She smacked her lips. 'He was an asshole, and I wanted to kill him.'

'That's more like it.'

'Another good night in Honourhome.'

Shadow thanked Petra for the aryll and placed it back on the shelf. He remained there, browsing through her curiosities. 'Arkalla, then. You mentioned the Queen.'

'Arkalla hasn't accepted Kalle's terms. It's been months of negotiating.'

Shadow had scant interest in the politics of Kalleron; he had long detached his mind from such futile thoughts. Though he preferred its climate, skirting the coast, sailing on azure waters with the warm ocean breeze; it beat freezing his backside off in Laria. Although, however hard he tried to ignore the affairs of the mainland, it was impossible to ignore the legend of the Queen.

'So, Kalle makes good his threat?'

'Felicitra believes so.'

'Well, how bad can that be?' Shadow shook his head. 'It's just one woman.'

Petra frowned. 'I thought it was me that knocked my skull.'

'No, they knocked it for you. But what d'you mean?'

'You said just one woman.'

Shadow thought the aryll might not be working. Or was Petra being awkward? 'Aye. The Queen; one woman? It's a bloody myth; a metaphor. I mean, everybody knows there's no scary queen. Kalle sends her with his army.'

'A metaphor? She's *Earth*. The elemental.'

He waved away her nonsense and shook his head. 'Not a chance. That's all Kalle's deception. He sends in spies to spread fear; people flee the city. Then the Queen comes along, all drama and theatre, and they make it appear like she's an elemental. It's all tactics, Petra. Clever Kallerye magic—smoke and illusion—to scare the idiot masses. I should know, I used to be one of them.'

Petra raised an eyebrow. 'You really don't think she's real?'

How could he? It had to be a ruse. There was no magic in the world; just fanciful fables to justify the evil that men did. He shook his head, scowling at the thought. 'She'll be a witch at most; an impotent bloody pot-stirrer. Everyone's scared of a witch, right? I bet my balls there's a massive army behind her; all cannons and siege weapons. Tucked out of sight. Kalleron has engineering and ingenuity on its side. They don't need an elemental. They just need the myth. To rule by fear.'

Silence. Petra appeared to be absorbing his words. She sighed and nodded. 'I'd prefer that to be true. I admit, nobody but Kalle can know for certain. He leaves few survivors.' Another pause, as though her mind was reorganising ideas. 'It would certainly make things easier for Felicitra.'

'Why'd she go? At least, what can you tell me?'

'No intrigue there; her father's in Arkalla. Too poorly to move. She's gone to get him out.'

Shadow pictured the journey. A couple of days to sail to Gwynerath, more on an unfavourable wind. It was easily another one or two to reach Arkalla on horseback. 'How long until the spooky Queen, arrives?'

Petra shook her head. 'Felicitra wasn't certain.'

'If Kalleron's got forces on the move, Arkalla would see them from afar. The Kulkarron signal beacons would be lit up like Larastra's Day. If they're not burning, there'll be plenty of time to get there and back safely.' Shadow smiled, thought of the leisure time. 'We can settle in.'

'There's still danger over there.'

'For Felicitra?' Shadow pictured Petra's lover. A woman capable of taming the Melody's captain; she had inner resources few possessed. 'I'd not worry about her. I'd say she's even tougher than you. She'll be back in a week.'

Petra's expression remained troubled, but she forced a smile to her face. 'One week?'

'One week.' He squinted, pinched his fingers in a circle. 'Or so.'

Petra clapped the desk. 'Well, we can use the time to patch up what's not been patched.'

'Aww... what? Can't we relax?'

'One week's far too long for leisure, you lazy Kallerye dog. Set a schedule for the crew. Let Argan work in the cargo hold; he's precious about his box.'

Argan's box. It was a massive chest. A strange thing to request to bring aboard. He had paid Petra a sizeable bounty in gold to stow it in the hold. But once inside, it was subject to the rules.

'You've never asked him?' Shadow asked.

Petra shook her head. 'I trust Argan and whatever his cargo is.'

'Never peeked?'

A pause. Petra grinned, but said nothing.

'You sly cow!'

She was quick to react. 'Oh, no. I never peek. But it's heavy; bloody heavy. I wanted it moved to the midline for balance. I couldn't budge it.' Petra's gaze drifted; a squint of her eyes, a slight shake of her head. 'When he brought it aboard, he carried it without effort. I couldn't move the crate one damn inch. Had to ask him, and he pushed it like it was full of lambs' wool.'

'He *is* strong.'

Petra touched her cheek. 'Yes, he is.'

'Probably armour? In the box?'

'For a horse, perhaps. If there was even a breed big enough to carry him.' She paused and clapped her hands. 'Get moving, Shadow; you're stalling today's chores. Divvy them up as you see fit.'

Shadow stood, bowing with a melodramatic flourish, and turned to the door. His hand on the latch, Petra called out.

'And Shadow, put some bloody clothes on. Your arse is like a little peach when the wind catches that cloak.'

Chapter IV

Gwynerath, Arkallon's eastern harbour. As distant from Laria Port as it was from the city of Kalleron, the coastal town was a world of its own. Felicitra disembarked onto the dockside and peered at the terraced steps. Built into the cliff, the tiered town was a rainbow of colour; a harmonious mis-match of architecture and culture. Tiled roofs and stone walls sat alongside wooden cabins topped with bundles of thatch. As varied as the buildings, the people milling around had come from far and wide; traders coming to profit from the close bond shared between Laria and Arkallon. Above all the bustle, seabirds flew in constant patrols, ready to swoop down and snatch discarded foodstuffs; sometimes stealing shiny trinkets and fleeing to the sky.

To be lost in the atmosphere was a typical response; Felicitra gazing all around and taking in the ambience of an Arkallian summer evening. In the air, spices and herbs floated in pungent cascades. The sounds of lazy guitar strings and soft-popping drums complemented the scene.

Felicitra startled as a hand fell upon her shoulder. She turned, smiling to see a familiar face. 'Larimer!'

A handsome man with a crop of black hair, Larimer was a frequent contact for her Arkallian dealings. Once a captain in Kalleron's army, his disdain for Kalle's greed had brought him to the cult. He wore a simple blue tunic wrapped around his body, but Felicitra knew he would carry a weapon underneath. Not a man to cross, but a man to trust; Larimer was a welcome sight in these troubling times.

'Felicitra, take it all in,' he said, gesturing to the colourful view. 'It'll all be gone soon.'

'I can see it already.' She understood the meaning of his words. Gwynerath was the closest port to Laria, and refugees would soon flood the picturesque terraces. Among them, she and her father would be a drop in the ocean. There were hints of distress already visible. One too many boats jostling for position in the water. Smugglers on the harbour wall, ill-fitting among the cheerful crowds, were searching for desperate fares.

'Still no Petra?' Larimer asked.

She shook her head. 'It wasn't an easy decision. I want nothing more than for her to be by my side. If my heart wasn't involved, I'd still value her protection.'

'You've spoken of her with such devotion. It puzzles me; from everything you say, she seems a perfect recruit.' He gestured to the void where a feisty Larian ought to be. 'Yet... she eludes you?'

'She has crew. They are family. I wouldn't ask her to give that up.'

'If she trusts you, she would surely remain anonymous. What better ally than a civilised and dependable pirate? Or is that a contradiction?'

She smiled. His words defined Petra without insult, though Felicitra considered her a trader of opportunity. 'One day, she'll be ready. When she is, I'll ask her.'

Larimer peered at the clifftop. 'As usual, Gwynerath's evenings start early, but the sun will be above the horizon for a few hours. We can get you on your way now, or perhaps some rest. Start at dawn?'

'Tonight. Haste is essential. Horses?'

'Not Stars, but close enough. Most of the stables have sold their best to the wealthy fleeing Arkalla. We have three mounts, one for you, two for the escort.'

'And you? You're not coming?'

Larimer grimaced an apology. 'Kastane's orders. Needs me near Etherus.'

'Etherus? I didn't think the plans were in place.'

His nod was emphatic. 'No other reason to be there.'

'When?'

'Once I have you on your way to your father, I've to head into the Kulkarrons. I'll be back and forth between here and there, figuring out what our friend in Kalleron has planned for us.'

'How are they getting inside?' Felicitra imagined the challenges. The Etherus weapons complex near the peak of the Kulkarrons was a fortress. Not considering the hostile environment, it was well-guarded and remote. 'Are you going inside?'

Larimer pursed his lips and shook his head. 'You know Kastane's paranoia starts with his own plans. I only know what I need to know. I'm just a runner for now.'

'You think we're truly ready?'

'We've tried how many times? Four, five? Lost how many people? This time feels different. His secrecy betrays a confidence. I think the infiltration has already started.' Larimer was quick to raise a finger. 'Just my opinion. No facts.'

Felicitra wondered if the Queen's threat was coincidence? Etherus, known for its plumes of black smoke tainting the highest peaks, offered an incredible prize. Kalleron's sorcerers, engineers with exquisite talent and intelligence, had long-served a higher purpose. Rumours circulated they had achieved the impossible; they had captured the essence of the Wind. They had created a weapon, a tantalising taste of elemental power. It was yet to be shown to the world. Some warned it was propaganda, and in some circles of the Kallerye court, Felicitra understood the work wasn't in favour. To them, it was blasphemy. Another elemental weapon would not sit well beside Kalle's singular power. For the cult, though, it would offer a great deal. She wanted to know more, but she had her own immediate problems to overcome.

'I wish you well with that, Larimer.'

'To the horses, then?'

Felicitra nodded, glanced back at the ocean, and followed Larimer into the crowds of Gwynerath.

Felicitra and her escort followed the Rivyn west to Arkalla; a single stop required to rest the horses. They had proven hardier than she expected for a mixed breed. Areya, a female mercenary from distant Drohendrir, appeared just as robust. She had already travelled far before arriving at Gwynerath. She was bright and cheerful, though her partner, Hestra, said little during the travel. A diminutive Bruhadian, he stood a shade taller than the average Kallerye man. He rarely spoke, although when he did, his conviction to the cause appeared absolute. Dressed as civilians, their weapons concealed behind unfussy, drab tunics, they had travelled onward, reaching the city at dawn. Arkalla, settled on the northern bank of the Rivyn, sat on a large and fertile plain. The Kulkarron mountains loomed far to the north; the glacial rivers flowing through the foothills painting nature's canvas with azure and verdant hues. Lush meadows, deciduous woodlands, and fields of crops surrounded the city; all nourished by the waters that flowed into the Rivyn. Arriving a day and a half after leaving Gwynerath, Felicitra was tired but eager to keep moving.

As they approached the walls, she noted the new battlements built along the northern front. It had only ever served as a token defence, but Arkalla had since expanded the feeble barrier outward and upward. Lighter shades of stone sat on top of weathered blocks. The fresh faces of cut masonry lacked the ornate detail of the worn surfaces beneath; rough edges and careless tooling marks contrasting with the timeless and intricate design. Not yet complete, the new wall spanned hundreds of yards.

Areya said, 'Will it hold?'

Felicitra craned her neck to look as she rode under the main arch. 'Against soldiers? Possibly, for a while.'

'Against the Queen?'

She didn't think so; speaking her thoughts to Areya.

They rode down Arkalla's historic avenue, where fruit-bearing orange trees lined the cobbled and picturesque thoroughfare. Quaint townhouses with elegant balconies looked onto the street. Ivy climbed the walls and flower baskets hanging under colourful shutters swayed in the gentle breeze.

Areya leaned in and said, 'You think she's as real as they say?'

About to answer, Felicitra raised a hand, pulling her horse to a stop.

'What is it?' Areya asked.

'It's morning.'

'Yes?'

'Where is everybody?'

The city appeared abandoned, not a soul in sight. The bright coloured shutters were closed over most windows. It appeared as though the city had forgotten to wake. Near the centre, the towering golden spire above Sinder's temple cast a plume of grey smoke into the sky. The beacon burned from dawn to dusk; a marker for weary travellers to follow. Arkalla was open to all.

'What can you see?' Areya asked.

Felicitra, staring south toward the central square, thought she saw a shape. Hundreds of yards away, in front of the massive statue of Arkana, there was movement. 'Let's ride on.'

As they travelled to the square, they passed silent houses and shops without trade. The elegant spires, clustered around the centre of the city, were glinting under amber fire; the sun beginning to break over the eastern horizon. As they neared the statue of Arkana, the noise became clear; the movement recognisable.

'Is that the Seer?' Areya asked.

It was. The Seer of Arkallon; preaching to a small crowd of onlookers. Fretful faces and anxious eyes peered at their leader, some staring upwards at their god. It was an ugly statue. As tall as a mansion house, they had rushed the effigy's construction. When Kalle's intent had become apparent, the Seer had ordered the old and modest statue removed and this new grotesque had appeared almost overnight. Of plaster, and painted a gaudy yellow, it was incongruous with

Arkalla's aesthetic. Felicitra thought it was a desperate act. A delicate hand raised against the executioner's sword.

The Seer was telling people to go back to their homes. His words were as honey; his oration warm and reassuring as any golden dawn. Arkana would prevail. The city would not crumble under a heathen Queen and her army of sub-human degenerates. They would be vanquished; Arkana would repay their faith with glory. God would swallow the enemy whole; the rivers would rise and fall upon them, sending their bodies to the Rivyn. Cheers of nervous praise returned from the crowd, voices speaking with uncertainty, repeating a mantra as though it might become real. Arkana would save them. Arkalla would prevail.

'I've seen enough,' Felicitra said. 'Let's get my father.'

Away from the square, Areya said, 'The Seer; he's persuaded the city to stay?'

'It seems so.'

'Kalle hasn't changed his orders. His Queen, and whatever she commands, is coming.'

Felicitra nodded. It had taken her by surprise—the power of faith. Arkallon had once idolised the elementals. A strange thing, to have piety for the immortals. They were not gods. They were more real; more distant. Yet Arkallon, bolstered by a new way of thinking, had adopted a human god. The roots of this religion grew from a rebellious sect which had appeared many centuries ago. Arkalla's wealth had increased, and its growing trade brought glory and culture to the city. For many, it seemed God had spoken. Reward followed faith. The elementals had never shown such generosity. They were aloof and cold creatures. It was easy to walk away from such callous indifference and embrace a new spiritual path.

Felicitra said, 'This place has flourished for more than a century. All under the gaze of their god. I've seen other nations and their ways. Some have gods that appear vengeful. Others worship despair.' She waved a hand at the pretty buildings; to the fruit-bearing trees lining every street. 'This is what Arkana brings.'

'But... you don't believe, do you?'

'If I had to believe in one; it would be Arkana.'

'Then, perhaps the Queen will finally find her match?'

Felicitra shook her head. 'I said, *if I had to believe*. I cannot believe. Not with what I've seen over the years.'

'Oh.' Areya appeared disappointed.

'Do you have a god?'

'In Drohendrir, we pay our dues to the forest. I'm not sure if a god speaks to us, but I know the wilds do. The animals and their kin share our spirit. But we have room for other meaning.'

'I understand.'

Hestra, quiet until now, raised his voice. 'Their god will not save them.'

The Bruhadian faith was unique. They hadn't worshipped the elementals, but they had built their culture around them. Legends of stone, and prophecies of kings. The narrative wasn't hindered by the Bruhadian physiology; strong and enduring. Felicitra's dealings with Kastane and his cult had given her ample insight into the world of a once great nation. It was ironic; the threat of the elemental Queen's coming had brought Bruhada to its knees. Decades ago, having defeated Kalleron's ruthless General Te'anor, Bruhada's legendary King Baza'rad, had fled to an unknown exile. Many had thought it a humiliating disgrace. Felicitra and others knew it had been the only way to save his people. Pondering the moment, she thought of the Seer.

To Hestra, Felicitra said, 'There is power in faith.'

'There is no power other than the elementals. It is folly to believe otherwise.'

'Then you think Arkalla is truly doomed?'

Hestra pointed back toward the effigy of Arkana. 'If they hadn't lost their way; they would know what comes. This city should be empty. Left for Kalle's plunder. With hands we can lift stone and build again. We can't resurrect the dead from their shattered bones.'

Chilling words. A drop of ice down Felicitra's spine. She shivered, her thoughts returning to her mission. With a nod to Hestra and heels digging into her mount's flank, she moved with haste to her father's house.

Beneath green and slatted shutters, neat flower boxes added a rainbow of colour to the grey masonry of a three-storey townhouse. A tall chimney puffing white clouds into the air capped a red-tiled roof. In a recessed arch, on a single-cut piece of dark timber, an inscribed plaque hung above a bronze ring. The inscription told of an older time, to the place from where her father hailed. *Seven Valleys.*

Areya pointed. 'Your father's house?'

'Yes.' Felicitra smiled. More than a few years had passed since she played as a child on the cobbled streets, plucking fruit and hopping across the gaps in the stone. Time had aged her body and mind, but the place remained the same.

'Pretty,' the mercenary said.

Felicitra nodded, dismounting and moving to the door. She paused, and turning to Areya, asked, 'The others?'

'Others?'

The smallest cloud of doubt crossed Felicitra's mind. 'My father is ill. There should be a wagon for him.' She turned and scanned the street, seeking for signs of other cultists. 'Where is it? Where are they?'

A creak from the door; Felicitra swivelled around. Joy in her heart, she was expecting to see her father's kindly face. It was another that greeted her. Her soaring spirits crashed to earth.

'You!' she said to her brother.

'Felicitra,' he said, not so much a greeting as a confirmation.

Touran's presence brought anxiety to the fore. What was he doing here? An Arkanian zealot, his faith was absolute. Felicitra's mind returned to the Seer; his command to the loyal.

'Father?' she asked.

'He is safe.'

Touran's stance was defensive, his body shielding the door. Felicitra looked to the street. A step taken toward her brother. 'Touran. A wagon. Did a wagon come?'

'I sent it away.'

Her stomach lurched; a hole carved within. Felicitra struggled to stay in control of her rising anger. 'How long?'

'Long?'

Another step to her brother; Touran inching the door closed. She asked, 'When did you send it away?'

'Last night. It is long gone. I told them we had no need of it. Arkana will help us.'

'NO!' Felicitra stormed toward Touran, pushing hard against the door and slamming it into his face. He fell backwards, and Felicitra rushed across the threshold of the house.

'Felicitra?' It was Areya calling.

She looked at the mercenary and cursed under her breath. 'You should go.'

'Go?'

It was over. The wagon had been their only chance. Her father could not ride. His body was brittle; she couldn't risk hauling him over a horse's back, let alone journey across hill and meadow. There was a bed within the wagon; Felicitra had organised herbs and medicine for the journey. Without those simple things, her father would perish.

She gestured to the empty street. 'I needed the wagon. We saw nothing on the way in. All transport has already left. Larimer spoke of the lack of horses; the wealthy buying their passage away from here. We don't have time to arrange anything else. Leave while you can, both of you. I won't abandon my father.'

Areya, taking a step forward, was halted by Hestra's hand. He bowed his head to Felicitra. 'You are sure you cannot come?'

'A promise I made myself. I'll not leave him. If he can't travel, nor will I.'

'You understand what will happen?'

A sigh from Felicitra. A realisation of the irony. 'When she appears, I'll finally know her truth. Perhaps there is hope yet?'

Hestra stared. If she sought reassurance, his eyes gave none. Empty and cold.

A sudden thought. Of Petra in Laria. Safe across the sea. Felicitra moved her hand to her belt and removed the leather purse. She tossed it to Areya. 'With haste to Laria Port.' Pointing to the pouch, she said, 'That will cover all costs plus more. Find the captain of the Melody of the Sea. Tell Petra of this. Tell her...' She paused. Words from the heart were so difficult to say. The letter. Petra had promised to read it. 'The letter. Tell her she will find my voice in the letter. She will understand.'

Areya nodded, although she appeared confused. Hestra, giving one last bow, pulled her away. Without looking back, the two mercenaries mounted their horses and, slapping the riderless beast on it's flank, they fled Arkalla.

Felicitra turned, ready to berate Touran, who was rising to his feet. Scorn on her face and bitter words on her lips, a thrum of footsteps sounded from the wooden steps. She forced a smile; her nephew and niece were stampeding down the stairs. How they had grown.

'Jonna, Jadebloom!' she said, greeting them with open arms, and though her embrace was real, her joy was not. A gentle lie for the children; Felicitra kept her despair hidden from view. Was it not insult enough that Touran had stranded her father? He had brought his children, too.

'Father said we will see a great day,' Jonna, in his tenth year, said.

Jadebloom, three years younger, pulled away from Felicitra. 'Have you come to see the Reckoning, Auntie Felia?'

Her composure strained, Felicitra maintained her cheerful lie. 'Reckoning?'

Touran spoke, his voice grating on her nerves. 'To see the heathen Queen repelled. Kalleron's heresy laid bare.'

Her stare focusing on Jadebloom; Felicitra held the girl by her shoulders. A reassuring squeeze given to the innocent child. 'Yes, Jade, I've come for the Reckoning, too.' A glance to her brother. 'Father, is he upstairs?'

'As ever.'

'A moment, Jade. I must see grandfather.'

Without another word, Felicitra climbed the stairs. She heard her father's voice calling as she neared the top. One step before entering his room, she paused. With a hand to her face and a stern thought to scold herself, she donned her mask of control. How long before it would slip? Taking a deep breath to inhale the comforting scents of home, Felicitra stepped into her father's room.

'Felicitra, you've come.'

She nodded, certain if she spoke, he'd notice the tremor. Felicitra gazed at the old man propped up in bed. He appeared so much smaller than her last visit. Withering. She knew he was ill, but his deterioration was stark. With the shutters closed over, a cosy gloom cradled his tidy chamber. Felicitra crossed the floor to open them. Another glance to the neat room, and Felicitra thought it strange. Touran wasn't the type to fuss over a mess.

'Maid?'

Her father smiled. 'One thing about the faithful: reliable.'

She thought of her brother. 'Not always true, father.'

With a weak motion, her father patted the bed. After opening the shutters, Felicitra moved to his side, sitting on the edge, careful not to disturb his old bones. His red bleary eyes looking up to her, he nodded.

'I know,' he said. 'I know what Touran has done.'

'No matter, I am here now.'

'Did I hear horses?'

Felicitra nodded.

Her father brightened. 'There is still time for you.'

'I sent them away. Messengers to Laria.'

Her father sighed, the brief spark of light fading from his eyes. His hand fumbled across the sheets. He was reaching for her. Felicitra moved her hand to his; holding it with care. His once powerful grip struggled to maintain its form. How long did he have?

'Father, why didn't you tell me?'

'Tell?'

'The illness. It is eating you. I could have sent more medicine, more herbs.'

'It happened so quickly.' He smiled. 'I'm thankful. Better to fade fast than linger.'

Her smile involuntary, her laugh bitter and brief, Felicitra shook her head. The irony of her situation was a vicious stab, but she wouldn't share her black humour. Though it appeared her father's intuition hadn't diminished with age.

He said, 'Yes. You've travelled all this way to take me to safety, but my days are already done.' He lifted a finger to point at her. 'You still have legs, Felicitra. I remember how fast you ran as a child. You might make it if you leave now.'

'I've travelled for days and eaten little. An anxious belly refusing food. I think if I ran, I'd be giddy and faint.' She thought about his words. The mention of time. 'Father? I've seen no armies on my travel. No sign of any Kallerye activity. There is time yet for all of us, is there not?'

'My maid?'

'Yes?'

'Faithful.'

Confused, Felicitra shook her head. 'What of it?'

'Faithful to *them*, Felicitra; the old ways. Arrabelle, she lives on the northern edge of the city. Two days past she came to me; said she'd seen her. She'd seen God.'

'She saw *Earth?*'

Her father struggled to nod his head. 'Arrabelle's not one for gossip. A strong woman, like your mother was. As you are. Lived a long life, she's lost more than most. She was out gathering flowers on the northern meadow when she saw her.' Her father paused. 'I don't know what it means, Felicitra, but she's real. And she's already here.'

With affection, she placed his hand on his chest and stood from the bedside. Felicitra moved to the north window and peered out across the streets below. The city, a ghost of itself, appeared calm. Squinting, she sought for any signs. A shiver rattled her body. Leaves were rustling in the wind, but all else was quiet. She thought she saw a lone figure at the distant statue of Arkana, but the foliage obscured her view. The wide northern avenue, flanked by the trees, stretched to the city wall; glimpses of the arches showing between the swaying branches.

'There is nothing,' she said, turning to face her father.

A noise. Distant. A low growl of the earth; the smallest vibration. Desperate for a mundane origin, she said, 'Cannon fire?'

The reply came from her brother, appearing at the bedroom door with Jonna and Jadebloom. 'The Reckoning has begun!'

'Can we watch? Can we watch?' The children, keen to see the spectacle, ran to the window, jostling Felicitra as they passed. They stretched on tip-toes; Jadebloom just tall enough to peek above the frame. 'Father, father, we can't see. Where is Arkana?'

Felicitra stared at her nephew and niece. Jadebloom's pink toes squirming on the floorboards, Jonna's head bobbing up and down. Such excitement. Such a lie. It was murder. Her teeth clenched, she paced to Touran, offering him a whispered rebuke.

'You could have left. All of us; *we* could have left.'

Touran smiled. 'Sister, you will see.'

Another distant rumble brought a fine powder from the ceiling; cracks appearing in the plaster. White dust falling as tears. Felicitra, looking to the window, stepped to her father. She knelt beside him, taking his hand.

'Thank you, father, for all that you gave me. For all that you taught me.'

He nodded, a pained effort showing in the shudder of his head. His gaze moving around the room, he smiled. 'Look at that, Felicitra. I told you one day we'd be a family again.'

A third tremor shook the house. Masonry crumbled from the walls, the ceiling shedding larger flakes. With the dust becoming thicker, her father said, 'From earth, we come.'

A kiss on his forehead, Felicitra replied, 'To earth we return.'

He squinted; his eyes tracking to the window. 'Comfort them.'

Felicitra nodded and moved to the open portal. The children's bright enthusiasm had visibly dimmed. As she knelt between them, her arms embracing their small frames, her father called Touran to his side. Ever the diplomat, always one to mend bridges, his words to her brother were conciliatory.

'Stay with me, Touran. Pray for me. Pray for us.'

The fourth clap of thunder shook the house with violence. The children squealed; Felicitra was quick to hold them tight to her bosom. Soothing words spoken to their crowns. Behind her, Touran's voice was shaking, although his prayer continued. Words to a god Felicitra knew would pay no heed. There was one true power; yet she was not a god. And she had come.

From the cobbled street, now a sheet of fine powder, she appeared. Rising from the ground, her form was exquisite. Distant, but clear to Felicitra's view, the Terrible Queen of Kalleron was magnificent to behold. A graceful and feminine body, as white as marble, as naked as nature; gems of rainbow colours moved across her flawless frame. Eyes, as red as rubies, stared out from a sculpted face. A modest, jagged crown atop her hairless head.

'Is that... *Arkana?*' Jadebloom asked.

Felicitra turned to her brother, his eyes alert to his daughter's words. Felicitra shook her head. The moment was upon them. The thought bringing tears to her eyes. Forgiveness found in the end.

'I'm sorry, Touran. You're a fool, but know that I love you.'

Her brother nodded, a smile for his sister. He had stopped praying.

Felicitra turned to the view, squeezed Jadebloom, and lied. 'Yes, yes, Jade. See; Arkana has come. They will save us.'

From all across the city, Felicitra could hear muffled screams. A thick, choking dust filled the air. Her focus shifting, seeking the horizon, she saw the golden spires were gone. The Seer's Beacon was collapsing; billowing clouds of grey rising in its place. It was one last message to all, far and wide; Arkalla had fallen. Through the growing haze, Felicitra sought the Queen. Saw her. She hadn't moved. The ground rippled beneath her feet. Strange arcs of stone crackled outward; snakes of rock leaping and dancing as lightning.

A terrible stillness overcame the world. All movement ceasing. The dust suspended without motion. Only the awful cries from the shattered city remained. Felicitra squeezed the children tighter; shielding them from the painful sound. Moments passed; nothing further disturbing the eerie calm. The thunder and rumbling were subsiding. Hope daring to rise in her heart, Felicitra hugged the children tighter. Was it over? She stared, leaning forward to better see the Queen. The strange snakes had become inert; motionless as tree roots. The creature appeared at rest. A bitter contradiction; she appeared serene. A movement to break the spell; the Queen raising her arms to the sky. She paused, as though in salutation to the heavens. The rumbling thunder was gone, and Felicitra noticed the birdsong in the powder-coated trees.

'What's happening?' her brother asked.

'I think it's over.'

Felicitra let out a sigh of relief. A smile graced her face as she dreamed of returning to Petra. She squinted as the queen thrust her arms downward. One blink as the earth fractured; a colossal wall of pressure crushing down on them, and in her arms, the children screamed.

Chapter V

The noise had ceased. His people were no longer calling to him, and in smothered darkness, he knelt before Arkana. All was still in the world. Under his cloak, shielded from the worst of the dust, the Seer dared to dream it was over. With the gentlest breeze ruffling the fabric, he understood—he had survived. Pride swelling his heart, he allowed himself a small smile. A tentative laugh. Arkana had come.

He stood, the cloak falling from his face. The dust was thick; an obscuring cloud to deny his view. A futile wave of his hand stirred the white mist. The Seer coughed, the dry powder irritating his lungs. He brought the cloak back to his face, and covering his mouth, he stumbled forward. Step after blind step, he walked along a path he didn't recognise. Under his feet he felt compacted earth. Not cobbles. Perhaps the debris? Layers of dust to smother the street. A strange silence permeated all around. There should be cheering. Where was the jubilation?

'Hello?' he called out. 'Can you hear me?'

Nothing.

Again, he called out. Not even an echo came as a reply. There was an immense emptiness, as though shouting at the wind on a barren plain.

'We are saved. Arkana has spared us. Come from your homes. Rejoice!'

'Who is Arkana?'

A woman's voice. Her words came from all directions, whispers of stone carried in the dust. The Seer turned around, seeking the woman. 'Arkana. Our Lord.'

'I know not, Arkana.'

Her voice was gentle, bereft of fear or joy. He did not know it. He asked, 'Who are you?'

'I am.'

He couldn't see for the dust. Agitated and uncertain, the Seer turned in circles. He called out to the woman. 'Show yourself. Show yourself to me!'

It was the noise of the ocean, of the tide across shingle. As water, the dust fell to earth. The Seer stared. The Rivyn was in the distance; at the shore, it was thick with a grey broth. A blue sky above. Parallel lines of ghostly white trees, some destroyed by fallen masonry, spread out from where he stood. Where was the city? The towers and temples? Irregular mounds of white and grey, as though snowfall across undulating meadows, were all he could see.

'I am,' the voice behind him said.

Spinning to face it, the Seer's stomach convulsed, his heart in his mouth. He fell backwards, landing in a pile of soft chalk. It plumed into the air, only to drop back down as dry rain.

'*You!*'

She stood before him. The Terrible Queen of Kalleron. Behind her, in the distance, the white gave way to green. Forested hills rising from lush pastures, and beyond them, the mountains in the north. Confusion addling his thoughts, the Seer scanned all around. The same sight greeted his eyes. Arkalla was gone. Raised into tombs of white dust. As he watched, he thought the ground moved; the hills fading in scale; the earth was absorbing itself. From under dissolving mounds, structures appeared. Here, a broken and twisted wooden staircase; there, an orphaned wooden wall. In the east, something strange. The pauper district. Innocuous among the white; brown shacks battered by the falling stone debris. Damaged, uninhabitable; yet still, they remained. A glimmer of hope to think that some would have survived. Dashed as the Seer imagined the lacerating splinters of wood as the buildings toppled down on top of them.

The Queen spoke.

The Seer, hearing only noise, stared at her. A beautiful thing. Not a woman; for she was not human, but she had a graceful physique. A jewelled and wonderful creature, she was neither short nor tall. A physicality he found difficult to gauge. She appeared tranquil and at peace; not at all wearing the aura of her name, except perhaps the circlet of glass upon her crown. A doubt settling in his mind. Where was the Kallerye army? Where were the machines that had sent destruction to his city: the cannons? The siege towers?

'Where? Where are they?'

'They?'

'Your army? Your machines of war?'

'I have none.'

The Seer shook his head. 'You must. To wreak such destruction.'

'I do not destroy.'

She spoke with conviction. The Seer, blinking his disbelief, raised his arm to the dust. 'Everything is gone. *Annihilated*.'

She paced forward; the Seer scrambled backwards through the debris. The dust rose but fell back again as though it had weight. Was he dreaming such madness?

'I am dead?'

'Dead?'

He knew he ought to be scared. The cataclysm; perhaps the trauma had brought this heavy fog to his mind. Yet the Queen's behaviour brought a sobering edge to the moment. Her questions, her denial.

'Am I dead?' he repeated.

The Queen stared; her oversized, blood ruby eyes swirled with unknown intelligence. Her finger raised to point; the Seer cowered behind his arm.

'You exist,' she said.

He frowned.

She turned her finger to point at herself. 'I am. You are not. Are you death?'

'I live, I think.'

Lowering her arm to the side, the Queen continued to stare at the Seer. 'Kalle has spared you.'

'Kalle? Blasphemy. Arkana has...' He stopped. Realised what was now lost. Thousands of voices forever silenced in the dead city. Why would God spare just one life? Why not take him with the rest?

The Queen paced forward again. Once more, the Seer scrabbled away. The creature stopped her advance. 'This is... fear?'

He stared. Her questions were nonsensical. What was she?

'You fear me?' she asked.

Across the tombs of dust and debris, beyond fields of ghosts, the Seer saw no other soul. No army. No machines of war. The Queen, impossible as it was to comprehend, had destroyed his city by will. And although she had taken everything, and her deed was unconscionable and evil; she appeared as innocent as a child. Whatever fear he held, it dissolved away.

His courage returning, the Seer rose to his feet. Surveying the destruction with disbelieving eyes, he held his horror in check. It was all gone. His city, his people. And his God? Why had Arkana stayed silent? What was the purpose of this cruelty? He found one sole reason to keep his faith from further dimming.

He said, 'Arkana has spared me; he gives me the strength to face you. I have no fear.'

She spoke her reply. Incredulous, he thought he must have misheard.

'What did you say?'

'You need not fear me; I mean you no harm.'

This creature. This power before him. He laughed in her face; couldn't control the flood of emotion coursing through his soul. The Seer doubled over. His laughter turning to tears, and tears to anger, he rallied and faced his foe.

'You're a murderer! A maniac! A monster!' Infused by hatred, he paced forward, halting in disbelief as the Queen paced backward. Was that fear? He grinned; a power, not as any he had known, gripping his soul. Arkana had come to him to smite the evil heathen. He moved toward her, his tongue cursing the Queen's name.

'Stop.'

Her word. Spoken with softness. What followed was not. The Seer fell to the ground; a pressure upon his body as though an avalanche collapsing upon him. Screaming in agony, contorting in terror, and with darkness seeping into his periphery, he called out.

'Please, stop. No more!'

'I am. I cannot stop.'

'You're killing me!'

In an instant, the pressure was gone. As sudden as it had appeared, everything was once again serene. Curled up and shaking on the dusty ground, the Seer stared up at the Queen.

'I do not kill,' she said.

Tears streaming down his cheeks, the Seer wiped a mess of chalk onto the back of his hand. Deep breaths to control the sobbing, he composed what remained of his shattered sanity.

'You have killed everything.' Tortured by the thought; afraid to say it aloud, the Seer whispered instead. 'You have killed God.'

'I take my own, nothing more.' Her hand pointed to the remnants of his city. 'I am stone. I am Earth. All of this is me. It is not yours to covet.'

He had thought of her as the Queen. But she was so much more. Now he understood. She was the elemental Earth. The impossible was true. Nobody believed Kalle's lies; none thought the self-declared immortal had captured the Earth. But here she stood; the brutal hammer held in Kalleron's devious hand. She was as real as the devastation and death all around.

'Why?' he asked. 'Why kill for him? How can Kalle control you?'

'I am. I cannot be controlled. You are not. He controls you.'

A shake of his head. 'No. He commands you.' The Seer pointed to the rubble. He spoke with passion, shaking as he did. 'He made you do this. You kill for him.'

The Seer expected a reply, but the Queen became still. Moments passed, and the only sound was the wind scouring the streets. He looked around and saw colour. Shades of vibrant green and silvery brown. The trees; the dust had fallen from the leaves and branches. It was life among the stone ruins of Arkalla. He understood; she had claimed it all back. She had come for her own.

'My god,' he said. 'You don't know what you do. Do you?'

Silence.

The Seer rose to his feet. He approached, wary of the unnatural power she wielded without thought. 'You don't know, do you?'

Nothing.

Another step. Another. Where was she? Within reach, she appeared absent from her sublime form. His hand moved to her face, an irresistible urge to touch the countenance of the Old Gods. He said, 'Earth?'

Her head moved to stare at his hand. He froze when she spoke. 'I am curious.'

'Of?' The Seer, his hand still extended, held his nerve.

'You.'

'Me?'

'He takes them all; the humans. Why Kalle has spared you, I do not know.'

The Seer brought his hand to his body. The Queen's ignorance was a disappointment. A weakness in her immortal character. He shook his head. 'Kalle is not my god. He does not control me. He rules his people by fear and sends you to do what he can't.'

'I have seen his truth.'

'No.' The Seer struggled to remain calm. 'He has you fooled. Kalle the Golden is a liar. A manipulator. He is the greatest at doing the very worst that men can do. He deceives to control. And he...' The Seer shook his head, finding it hard to believe his own conviction. 'He controls you.'

The Queen appeared adamant. 'No. I am. He controls you.'

The Seer raised his arms to the side. 'Then let him take me now.'

'What are you doing?'

'Asking Kalle to take my soul. I offer my life to his glorious name.'

The Queen stared. The Seer waited. Grains of the hourglass trickling in time. A Kallerye clock ticking its mechanical chime. With a twitch of impatience in his arms, the Seer dropped them to his sides. A new vision appeared; a clarity of thought, of nothingness and the end.

He said, 'Kalle has no power over me. But you do. You can fix your mistake; what you have failed to finish. Kill me. Kill me now and complete his work.' It wasn't a bluff. His world had been an illusion; the elementals were real. Everything he had known and loved, all his devotion and servitude; it was all for nothing. 'Kill me. Give me peace and send me to my own.'

'Give me your hand.'

With hesitation, the Seer offered it to her; his palm to the sky. Curious, he watched as she held hers to the side. From the ground, shaking itself free of the dust, a shiny black stone appeared. Stark against the white. It ascended toward her fingers, and as though ripe fruit, she plucked it from the air.

'To cease to be; this is your wish?'

He looked at his dead city and nodded. 'Yes. Kill me, as you have the rest.'

'I do not kill.'

Ready to protest her games, the words forming on his lips; the Queen interrupted him.

'My sister is not as I. She will grant what you seek.'

'Sister?'

'Fire. Find her, and she will give you what I cannot.'

The Queen dropped the stone onto his open palm and took a pace backwards. Mesmerised by its simple beauty, he stared at the black gem. Was it Obsidian? Warm to the touch, it was pleasant against his skin. A sound of the ocean distracted him; a wave across the shore. Closing his fingers around the gift, he looked to the Queen. She was gone. Nothing left but dust scouring the empty streets. Resurrected in the breeze, billowing clouds were blowing across the land. Alone in his dead city, the Seer opened his hand and stared at the Queen's offering. She had called her sister by name: *Fire*. The Seer knew of the old texts, but he had dismissed them long ago to choose Arkallon's other faith. With the Queen's gift, the old knowledge returned to his mind. Secrets of Fire, and her other name. *The Great Destroyer*.

Chapter VI

It was the third night in a row, and Petra was standing alone where Felicitra had departed for Gwynerath. Shadow, halfway down the boardwalk, considered his options. Hadn't he told her to give it more time? It had only been a week. She wasn't a bird; he had said she couldn't fly back. Petra hadn't laughed. But she had returned each night; waiting after the last ships had come home to port. He wanted to do something, but with an experienced understanding of Petra's prickly nature, he turned around. Better to walk away and live another day.

At the water's edge, with the moons of Noctyrne and Ambyr bathing the port in hues of ice and fire, Shadow stumbled into Argan. As big as two stacked barrels, and wrapped in a light-coloured fur, the Bruhadian was hard to miss.

'Watch it, big man,' Shadow said, deflecting blame.

'Preoccupied?'

'Huh?'

Argan patted his solid chest. 'You bumped into me.'

'Yeah?'

'I'm not like you. I don't sneak around.'

Shadow appraised the Bruhadian's outlandish stature. He had a point. His finger tapping his temple, he growled. 'I'm out of sorts.' Shadow thumbed toward the end of the dock. 'I've not had a good drink with her ladyship for days. She's been fixating on the water.'

'She's missing Felicitra.'

'We all do. Besides, she's been away before.'

Argan grumbled. A sound as though cattle groaning. The Bruhadian offered nothing else other than his bovine mimicry.

Not averse to the company of Argan, although he could be hard work, Shadow pointed to Honourhome. 'Want to give a degenerate some company?'

Argan released an expansive cloud of white breath into the freezing night air.

'Is that a "yes"?'

A smile on his face, Argan said, 'Degenerate? You?'

Shadow recalled the inglorious term being thrown his way on more than one occasion, although he couldn't recall who had said it. Treating it as a dishonourable yet accomplished achievement, he'd never thought to protest. 'You think I'm not?'

'You're many things. Many annoying things. But no; degenerate you are not.'

High praise from the Bruhadian. Shadow slapped his shoulder. As oak, he was. More than firm, the man appeared immovable.

With a nod to the inn, Shadow repeated the request. 'Want to?'

A gruff murmur given in reply, Argan turned and moved away, climbing the steps to the inn. Glancing back at Petra, Shadow saw her on the pier; a ghost against the darkening sky. Still as stone, her silver hair was flicking in the wind. Felicitra had to return soon. Only she could restore the captain's soul, and then things could get back to normal.

Honourhome, as bustling as ever. Shadow followed Argan to his favoured booth. The Bruhadian liked to observe, preferring to seat himself with his back to the wall. It was a fitting choice; the small alcove was suitable for three. With Argan pride and centre occupying it all, Shadow pulled a chair from a nearby table. He could have squeezed in beside his friend, but thought better of it. Neither was the hugging type. With two fresh ales on the table, Shadow raised his wooden tankard.

Argan frowned. 'To?'

'Anything.'

A grumble and a sip. It seemed to be the noise a Bruhadian made when content. Shadow, fidgeting on the hard seat, yanked a fur from the plush booth. Honourhome, as did most Larian inns, decorated its hard furnishings with an outrageous supply of hides. A modest fire burning against the far wall provided ample warmth, but it was a tradition to supply the furs. Trees were less bountiful on Laria's harsh ground. It was more frugal to trade for fur than to burn through the dwindling forests. Shadow shook his head, resting his rear on the soft pelt.

'Why do people even live here?' he asked.

'In Laria?'

'It's a frozen waste. It's... mostly awful.'

'It is cold. I admit, I prefer the continent.'

Argan hailed from sun-kissed Bruhada; Shadow knew that much, although it was obvious from his stature, darker attributes, and the manner in which he spoke, often choosing his words with care. But the place didn't give the man his identity. It gave Shadow pause for thought. He tried to think what he could ask without breaking the rules of the Melody.

'I'm figuring you were born in Bruhada?'

A frown from Argan. A slow nod.

'You miss the heat?'

A confirming grumble. A sip of ale.

'I've never been.'

Argan placed the tankard down on the table and appeared to take interest. 'I've not seen it for a while. I knew it before the fall. Bronze, copper, and gold. The domes and roofs glinting in the sun. The pillars of the Great Library, the Fortress of Bruhale. The expectation of dusk; watching the sea become ablaze in the setting sun. Nothing cold in Bruhale. Everything afire with a welcome warmth.'

'It sounds... nice.'

Argan smiled. It was wide and genuine. 'I know you believe poetry and culture is beyond your soul, Shadow, but Bruhale would make you think twice.'

A defence from the conversation; Shadow lifted the ale to his lips. He took his attention from Argan and stared into the dark vessel. It was true; he had no love of poetry. The romance and mysticism of a bard's song was anathema to his ears. He despised false empathy; preferring to find the sort of love that lasted a single evening. Words? They were just letters made pretty. But Argan wasn't a romantic fool reciting flowery lines; he was describing a place. An old nation for which Shadow had deep admiration.

'I respect your country a great deal.'

Argan shook his head. 'You said you've not been?'

A thumb to his chest, he said, 'Me? No. But I've heard the tales about what happened all those years ago. The Battle of the Bridge. To see it; to imagine it. Can you even?'

Argan grumbled.

Shadow raised a hand to apologise. 'I know it's against the rules; to needle and prod about history, but I'm just saying: to think of the old Butcher, Te'anor; to see him face to face with Baza'rad. The most legendary of battles.'

Argan said nothing.

Shadow couldn't remain quiet. 'I thought...' A gaze or a glare, he wasn't certain, but the Bruhadian was staring at him. Undeterred, he said, 'I figured: your bulk, your strength,' he leaned forward, 'I mean, come on. You're unfeasibly strong. Quick too.'

Argan shook his head.

'You were Royal Guard, weren't you? Part of the elite?' Shadow knew he was treading on dangerous ground, but he kept plodding. 'Were you there?'

'The rules, Shadow.'

'I'm not asking who you were; just thought you were big and stoic enough to be the King's faithful.' To soften the accidental interrogation, Shadow said, 'Even I was a soldier for a while. There, you know something about me. Tells you nothing, see? It's harmless. Just words.'

'I was not Royal Guard.'

It was disappointing to hear. Shadow wondered if he should tell Petra? He predicted her likely response; she'd probably be pissed that he'd broken the rules. A squint at Argan and he asked, 'Then, like me, once a soldier, surely? I mean, hasn't every man served?'

Another Bruhadian grumble to reply, and to Shadow's surprise, Argan nodded. 'I served for the majesty of Bruhada.'

Shadow raised his tankard. 'To soldiers.'

Argan lifted his drink and brought it to meet Shadow's. The Bruhadian appeared deep in thought, a slow nod of his enormous head hinting at hidden memories. With their tankards touching for longer than Shadow felt comfortable, Argan said, 'To the fallen.'

'To the fallen.'

Not another word was said of Bruhada.

The next morning, Shadow was roaming the deck of the Melody with aimless intent. All the days of graft waiting for Felicitra to return had left little else to do. Argan had tired of pushing his barrels, though he had found another aimless chore. He was standing above the water, hauling up discarded anchors on rusted chains. Shadow shook his head at such unnecessary labour. He turned and stared at the door to Petra's cabin. He hadn't seen her emerge; wondered if she was even on board. The tension was becoming palpable. Other crew members had noticed Petra's off-colour demeanour, and as her closest acquaintance after Felicitra, they had questioned him about her mood. Every reply he gave was the same: to fuck off and mind their own business. None had taken offence at his brusque response. They hadn't come for gossip; they had approached him to show they cared. It was a tiresome irony that they wouldn't bother the captain, yet they would come to him. It was as redundant as asking a pot which soup it preferred.

'Hello there?'

Shadow turned to face the voice that had interrupted his thoughts to see a woman standing on the dockside. Attractive, with tanned skin and brown hair, she wore the garb of a common mercenary. The dark winter cloak, pulled across her shoulders, hid much of her armour, but the leather and chain shirt remained visible. The winter fleece concealed her weapons, with only the pommels obvious, poking against the fabric. Two swords, as Shadow judged it.

He approached the gangplank and frowned a greeting to the woman. 'Morning.'

'This is the Melody of the Sea?'

'Clearly. And you are?'

'I'm Areya. I...' The woman hesitated, dropping her gaze for a moment. 'I must speak with the captain. Is she aboard?'

Shadow shrugged. 'Don't know. What's this about?'

'Are you crew?'

'I'm on board, aren't I? You've a message to deliver?'

Areya nodded. 'She paid me to speak to one person. You're not her. My business is with the captain.'

Before he could ask the mercenary who had paid her, Petra appeared from her stateroom. She seemed alert, though her eyes were dark and tired. She slung her fur over what Shadow guessed was yesterday's clothes and approached.

'I'm the captain of the Melody.' She nodded to the mercenary. 'I'm Petra. What news?'

Areya dropped her gaze; her shoulders slumping. It troubled Shadow. Something had her agitated, and seasoned mercenaries didn't carry such crippling baggage. It wasn't a good omen. Areya took a deep breath and returned her focus to the captain. Her features were grim.

'May I come aboard?'

Beside him, Petra exhaled as though punched in the gut. She turned her head; her gaze searching the sea. Shadow looked to Areya; frowned at her. The mercenary stared back with unknown horrors haunting her face.

'Please, may I board?' Areya asked again.

Her focus on the horizon, Petra whispered the name hovering in Shadow's mind.

A foot on the plank, not yet invited, the mercenary said, 'She sent me.'

'My Felicitra?' Petra shifted her focus onto the woman. 'You've seen her?'

Areya halted. 'I... I saw her.'

'Saw? Where is she? Where is Felicitra? Why has she not returned?'

Shadow peered westward. The fragile mercenary, the message for Petra, and not a whisper of Felicitra. He didn't need to hear the words. The fates had spoken. Shadow turned and noticed the crew mingling on deck. They were watching. Staring as Petra faltered; a crack in her armour prised open by the cheerless messenger. His captain was struggling with the moment, and Shadow had no more patience for Areya's fumbling words.

'Answer the captain; where's Felicitra?'

The mercenary didn't reply. Her body shuddered; her mouth was clenching tight shut. Tears were welling in her eyes.

'No,' Petra said with a feeble breath. 'Not this.' A sad plea to Areya. 'Where is she?'

Areya couldn't speak; her body convulsing in wretched gasps. She collapsed to her knees, almost toppling into the water. Shadow rushed to her side, hauling her to her feet.

'Stand, woman! Stand!'

As if reacting to a scolding parent, Areya stiffened, although her eyes remained lost in grief. Shadow, uneasy with the gathering crowd, helped the mercenary along the ramp. Petra stared at him, her eyes glazed and wide. She trembled as though a lost child. Fearing it might make her appear weak in the eyes of the crew, Shadow gritted his teeth and leaned in close to her ear.

'Get into your cabin, now!'

On any other day, he'd never dream of barking an order at his captain. Enforced shore leave without pay would be the price. That punishment he could take. This display of emotion, he could not. Shadow ushered the mercenary inside, and with Petra following, he understood the revelation to come would be desperate.

Petra paced as Areya sat shivering in the chair. She had been silent for minutes. Shadow had decided it would be best to medicate the woman. Water put on the stove, sedative herbs mixed with the Ouhla tea, she'd be lucid soon enough; at least for a while before she fell into a chemical slumber. With the cup in her hand, Areya stared at the floor. A glance to his captain—he wanted to tell her to stop pacing. It was shredding his patience. Just for once, he thought it would be better to keep his mouth shut. He turned his attention to the mercenary.

'Areya. What can you tell us?'

She nodded, thanked him for the tea. 'Hestra and I were the escort.' She glanced at Petra. 'For Felicitra. We rode from Gwynerath; made good time for Arkalla. The town was... quiet. I thought it was abandoned, but everyone was indoors. Their Seer had persuaded them to stay. It was...'

Petra stopped pacing. 'It was what?'

'Suicide.' Her voice subdued; Areya shook her head. 'Nothing. Nothing could...'

Shadow tried to remain calm as the mercenary stumbled over every sentence. 'Areya. You need to tell Petra what has happened. Where is Felicitra?'

Areya lifted her head. Looking first to Petra, she appeared to change her mind and switched her gaze to Shadow. As though distracted by him, she began her story again, her fingers fidgeting with the handle of her cup. 'Something about the wagon. Gone. A brother, I think.'

'Touran?' Petra said. 'That prick was there?'

Areya shrugged. 'Felicitra sent us away. Sent me to you, Petra.'

'To me? And that's the last you saw? Where is she then? What news of Felicitra?'

Her posture visibly crumpling, the mercenary spoke to the floor. The herbs were taking effect; Areya's tone was becoming monotonous. At least it was better than the outpouring of grief.

'We'd left the city when it began, Hestra and me. The rumbling. Thunder throughout the plains. We stopped, dared not ride the horses, dismounted. That's when we saw it. The dust. There were four, perhaps five, percussions. The world beneath our feet shaking. Each one sending great clouds into the sky. We saw the spires collapsing; the great beacon fall. The noise was terrible. I don't know if I imagined it, but the air was full of screams and crying.' Areya shook her head. 'It must have been a trick of the wind.'

In the pause, Shadow looked at Petra. Motionless. Her face was chalk white; eyes red and sore. His friend was collapsing within. He wanted this over with; needed to move Areya along. 'And Kalleron? Soldiers? The war machines? Where were they?'

Areya shook her head. 'Not one. Not a single cannon. But the city fell. Everything falling to pieces. It was the last that was the worst. A terrible roar of thunder. I swear the earth cracked beneath our feet. Almost lost the horses had Hestra not grabbed the reins. Pulled his arm so hard it did. He's still recovering. Never seen a Bruhadian so scared. I stared at the clouds, couldn't see anything. Then, in a blink, it was gone. No dust. No nothing. Just hills of white where Arkalla used to be.'

'That's not possible,' Shadow said.

Areya nodded. 'I know.' She began bobbing her head. Rocking her body back and forth. 'I know it's not. But I saw it. I did.' She stopped, her eyes staring through him. 'You know what I saw?'

Shadow shook his head.

'I saw the desolation of the Old Gods. I saw it. I saw what they can do.'

Petra took a step forward. She appeared listless. When she spoke, her voice was bereft of warmth. 'The people, Areya, what happened? What happened to Felicitra?'

'Felicitra, yes. A letter, she said she gave you a letter. You must read it; she said you promised you would.'

'Nothing else? She sent no other message?'

The mercenary shook her head.

Neither woman moved. The cataclysm Areya described was horrific; it had traumatised her, and for lambasting her emotional state, Shadow suffered a rare stab of guilt. But there was worse. The lurch in his stomach was a consequence of her account. A truth he had to accept. It was a struggle to believe, but he knew it to be so—the Terrible Queen of Kalleron had delivered Kalle's threat. A witness of her coming, Areya confirmed the power of the creature he had claimed was a deception. He was a fool; he should have known, but as with all monsters, it was easier to be ignorant and pretend they didn't exist.

Petra, moving to her desk, brought his attention back to the room. The words came close to his lips; a blundering and senseless reassurance. He held his tongue. The thought was redundant as the lie it would be: Perhaps Felicitra had survived? No. Areya's description held no room for hope. He watched his captain remove a folded letter from a drawer in her desk, her fingers turning it slowly. Over and over.

Petra appeared to compose herself, her voice steady but hollow. 'Thank you, Areya. You have my gratitude.' She gestured to Shadow to show her out. Taking the mercenary's arm, he walked her to the door.

'I'm sorry, Petra,' Areya said, stepping onto the deck.

Shadow hailed the attention of young Florent. She came to him, eyes wide, expectation written on her face. Shadow shook his head. 'Find Areya a bunk. She needs rest.'

'Aye, sir.'

Florent moved away, guiding the stumbling mercenary to her temporary bed. Shadow turned to the cabin to see Petra holding the letter in her hands; the parchment unfolded. She looked up. An uneasy silence between them; she gave no insight into her emotions. She was hurting inside, probably worse. Yet she refused to show it. It was that emotional fortitude that had attracted him to her. Not as a lover; he had long given up on that conquest. No, it was her supreme strength of will. Someone honest and tough enough to keep him in his place. This silence, though; it was brutal. It was painful to watch her struggle.

'Captain?'

'Thank you, Shadow.' She waved him away. 'Close the door as you leave.'

'Aye, captain.'

He stepped onto the deck, shutting Petra inside. He wanted to walk away. Knew he should, but if she could see him beyond the glass, she might appreciate his presence. Wasn't that what friends were for? He waited a moment, wondering if she had read the letter. Quiet at first, he wasn't certain; it was the faintest sound. The soft noise coming from the cabin was a dagger in his heart. Louder now; it was unbearable. Tearing at his callous heart, it was something he never thought he would hear from Petra. Not just tears. She was bawling; a terrible and mournful wail. Across the deck, Argan was looking his way. Other crew members turning their attention to the desperate sound. Shadow nodded to the Bruhadian and bowed his head. Something dreadful had come to the Melody, and he knew there were dark days ahead.

Chapter VII

Two days had passed since she had opened Felicitra's letter. Written in her neat handwriting, she had pictured Felicitra's red lips shaping every word, her breath carrying them across a gulf to reach her.

My dear love, Petra. I am gone from you now, but forever hold me in your heart, as I shall you, in mine.

The first sentence had buckled her knees; made her dizzy and sick. Petra recalled the moment she had collapsed to the floor. She hadn't wanted to read any further. But she had made a promise to Felicitra. Her mind in turmoil, and through blurred vision, Petra had steadied herself to hear what else Felicitra had written. It had been sobering. The detail of the message was not a tribute to the soul. It was pragmatic and cold; delivered from the hand of an elemental cultist. In her passing, Felicitra had given Petra the key to a secret door. With the letter in hand, her fur wrapped tight, Petra stood at the end of the boardwalk, gazing westward. She waited for the predictable company; knew he would come. Everyone would have learned of Arkallon's demise. They all knew what that meant and who was now lost. It surprised her that Shadow had taken so long to approach. A few paces behind, his tone was subdued.

'Petra?'

'Shadow.'

The boards creaked as he came alongside. She glanced his way. He wore a heavy fur slung around his shoulders. In the rarest of Larian days, with not the slightest breeze, Shadow exhaled in voluminous clouds of vapour. The ships in the harbour had nowhere to go; their sails limp and useless. Not a single sound coming from the hulls; the familiar groaning of wood rolling on the water was notable for its eerie absence. It was as though everything had died.

'First stupid question. How are you?' Shadow asked.

'Empty.'

'Second. Do you... Do you want to...' He struggled to continue, but there was no emotional tangle in his voice. Awkwardness, perhaps. He sighed. 'You want to talk?'

'No. Not of that.'

'Oh, good. That's... good.' His tone was ripe with relief.

Shadow's reluctance to engage in matters of the heart was a boon to Petra. She was accustomed to people assuming she was a damsel in distress; it was her petite build, her pretty looks. It wasn't that she was a woman; there were other female captains, but they had more rugged builds than she. Shadow knew her better, though. They shared a mutual understanding of life and necessity. It wasn't that neither of them cared; it was that neither cared to show it.

He said, 'But you want to talk?'

Petra brought the letter to the fore. He reached for it, but she retracted her hand. 'Not for your eyes.'

'This is what you want to talk about?'

'Yes.'

'But I can't see it?'

'No.' Her emotions were still raw. Bludgeoned into submission. It took effort to say Felicitra's name without a fracture appearing in her voice. 'Before she left. She gave this to me. Told me to read it if... Well. I've read it.'

Shadow blew a breath. 'You said you didn't want to talk about it.'

'I don't. But there was more than... It wasn't a...' What wasn't it? It felt foolish to say such simple words to someone other than Felicitra. 'It wasn't a love note.'

'I'm not following.'

With the letter firm in her hand, she saw the inked parchment in her mind. The intentional and vague instructions from Felicitra. A symbol here, a cypher there. All the riddles within were based on their shared and often intimate knowledge; something a stranger wouldn't understand. The message had been clear, but she wouldn't engage further with it without telling Shadow. Not that she sought his permission or his blessing. It was a courtesy for a friend.

'I trust you,' she said.

'Bit silly, that.'

'You're an idiot, Shadow. But I do trust you. As you trust me.'

He grumbled.

Petra said, 'There's a cult...'

He interrupted. 'No. You can stop right there.'

Seldom a talking point, they had briefly spoken of the cult in the past. Musings of Felicitra's purpose. Petra had curious interest, but Shadow's position was absolute. Things had changed, at least for her. 'I'm taking the ship to Kalleron.'

His reply, delivered with an exaggerated breath, was telling. 'Shit.'

She had expected a stronger rebuke. What she had not wanted to say, she said anyway. 'You don't need to come.'

'Fuck right off with the martyrdom!'

His cutting reply was no surprise, but she couldn't ask for his company. 'I can't assume you'd go along with it.'

'Of course I will. Who else'll keep you on the straight and narrow now?'

A barb, it was piercing. She wondered if he realised what he'd said? Even if he had, she didn't have the energy to fight. Shadow's sudden intake of breath was followed by a quiet curse.

'I didn't mean... Oh shit, Petra. I'm sorry. You know I don't think when I talk.'

Felicitra. More than Shadow; she had been the hand to guide her wayward path. And though Shadow's company was a compliment to her character, it had been Felicitra who had steadied her raging soul. One woman had quelled the anger she had held for so long; a problematic trait even murderous Shadow had once described as unreasonable.

'I'd like your company,' she said.

'You'll have it. But know I'm not happy.'

'I need to finish something.'

'With the cult?'

The message in Felicitra's letter had been practical. And unusual. Once deciphered, it had revealed directions to a house in the Mansion Hills, the western rise overlooking the city. Strange and eccentric instructions to arrange a meeting with a contact known to Felicitra. The steps within seemed theatrical. Petra would have thought it a poor joke had anybody other than Felicitra written it. But there was no doubt it was her hand that had penned the letter.

'I made a promise, Shadow.'

'To join those lunatics?'

'No. To read her letter. And it asks me to do this.'

'To do what?'

Petra paused. She didn't know. The letter was as good as a map. Though a map on its own was not a direction. 'I don't know. All I do is that I'll go to Kalleron and see where, or to what, she has sent me.'

'All right. No decisions then?'

'There are no decisions to make, Shadow. Just this.'

'Well, we're not sailing today. Not even Argan could move the Melody in this lull.'

Petra wanted to leave as soon as possible. Remove herself from the warm memories of Honourhome. In Kalleron, she would feel apart from the pain. Ironic, given she'd be following the path laid out by Felicitra. But to walk it made it feel as though she wasn't gone.

'Is it wrong, Shadow?'

'Wrong?'

'To hope?' She didn't look, but heard him fidgeting. 'I want your honesty. It's what you're best at.'

'And what is it you hope for?' he asked, his tone bristling with cynicism.

'A miracle, perhaps.'

Petra turned, surprised to see him walking away. At first hurt, she realised it was exactly what she needed; something cold and familiar. She shouted after him.

He didn't stop, though he called back to her. 'I'm done with this, Petra. Sort yourself out; you've a ship to captain. A crew to command. I'll be at Honourhome tonight; at sundown.' Shadow stopped, a glance over his shoulder. 'You'll come?'

It was the last thing she wanted. 'Maybe, just for a while.'

Shadow turned and set off. She resisted an urge to face the western horizon, scolding herself. Instead, she focused on her friend. Before Felicitra, he had been an unconventional anchor. Sometimes she could drown in his chaos. As a drug, his company was euphoric and dangerous. It had suited her. But he always kept her safe; never intentionally put her in harm's way. Tonight then, she thought; perhaps some mayhem to bludgeon the pain?

It was sundown outside Honourhome, and Shadow was leaning on the wooden post of a Larian Lamp. Clever things they were. He had often thought them similar to their Kallerye cousins. Petra had told him otherwise. A mineral from the Anastra mountains, *solastrite*, it was useless for heat but burned bright. Cut into rough cubes, when lit with a chemical flare, it emitted a soft white light for hour after hour. Shadow recalled Petra's Larian pride when she had told him about it. He had revelled in the anticipation of her response; teased her and asked what sort of flare was used to ignite the native invention. She had fumed. Her little pouting lips cursing him with choice words. It was Kalleron that first created the chemical flare; an invention from its sorcerer engineers. Smiling to himself, thinking of Petra in better days, it surprised him when she appeared from the gloom.

Clad in her white fur cloak; underneath, she had donned thigh-high boots over sealskin leggings. Over a white blouse, she wore what he thought was a black corset; although, as she approached, Shadow realised it was something far less ordinary.

'Armour? You're wearing an armoured bodice?'

Petra tapped a solid breast. 'Seems so.'

'Why?'

She puffed her breath into his face. It reeked of spirit. Not judging, but irritated she had left him out of an early session, Shadow shook his head. Petra, her hands covering the rounded curves of the hardened leather bodice, looked beyond Shadow to Honourhome.

'I'm nobody's tonight.'

'How drunk are you?'

She held a hand at waist height. 'A little enough to get me here.' She paused, lifting her hand higher. 'But not so much I couldn't get here.'

'A skinful, then?'

She giggled, leaning in. Under the Larian Lamp, he saw the heavy eye make-up applied with shoddy precision. She had smeared theatrical levels of dark powder to her lids. Did Petra think it hid the grief? It didn't. Worse; the excessive charcoal reminded him of the sex-slaves from the Dursch district in Shaddenhyne. Women and effeminate boys, all dosed-up on hard narcotics. That wasn't pleasure. It was a line not even he would cross. Though he was thankful for the repulsive thought; it helped him to focus.

'You look like shit,' he said.

Petra grinned. It was ugly, somehow. Her hands came to his face, and she clawed him to her lips. Shadow pulled away, stupefied by her lustful kiss. She was beautiful to behold; more alluring than almost any woman he had known. But it was Petra, and apart from being blazing drunk; she had made her sexuality clear.

'Do I taste like shit?' she asked.

This was the woman he knew. An impulse of the old chaos flashed inside and it was impossible to control; he slapped her. A soft tap. It was a warning between friends. Her eyes flared under the make-up. Petra swung a wild hook. It had been a while since they had play-fought; his hand open, hers closed. He had controlled those bouts, always making sure Petra felt in charge, never letting on that he pulled every blow. But her reaction to his playful slap was rapid, and the surprise blow struck his face. Landing on his jaw, it felt as though a loose bag of stones.

'Tough guy wants to fight?' she asked.

'No.'

But he knew the drill. With his palm, he jabbed her shoulder with enough effort to stumble her backwards. He hadn't used much force; the alcohol would do most of the work. Petra whooped and yelled; joy was clear in her voice.

'That's better!'

She came at him again, her clumsy attempts to hold her cloak making her appear as though a maid stumbling with flagons of ale. Another wild punch; this time he moved out of its path with ease. He shoved her away, thought an insult might help.

'You fight like a little boy.'

Petra, regaining her balance, stood upright and pointed at his crotch. 'Well, you're hung like one.'

Shadow snorted. He couldn't deny the humour. 'You'll never know.'

'I'll ask any girl in Hoydai to find out.' She squinted, placing her thumb and forefinger on her chin. 'Or pretty boy. Horse. Dog.'

'Enough.' Shadow pointed to the inn. 'More poison?'

'Much more.'

'After you.' With an extended arm, he gestured to the stairs.

Petra curtsied as she passed. 'Why thank you, kind sir.'

Argan frowned.

'Seriously,' Shadow said, once again facing his friend in the booth.

'She passed out?'

Shadow pointed to the padded seats. 'We sat down here. I went to buy the drinks, and when I came back, she was on the floor. Two hairy fishermen were trying to haul her up... no pun intended.'

'And she's back aboard?'

'Aye. Put her to sleep myself. That's when I noticed the bloody dratch. There was a dreg left, so I had a swig. Bloody crazy. Not your regular swill. Powerful as a god's piss. Figured I'd bought the drinks here so...' He pointed to the tankard in Argan's hand.

'Thank you.'

Shadow shrugged. 'I've never seen her this way.'

'It's been a bad few days.'

'I know. But still. I saw a glimmer of the old Petra. The old, old Petra. I don't know, Argan, maybe it's me getting on, but she's better the way she is, or was, with Felicitra.'

The Bruhadian put down his drink, and clasping his hands, he stared at Shadow. There was more than tonight's conversation in his eyes. Shadow could feel it. The news from Arkallon had been grim. Everyone had felt it. But Argan had seemed more troubled than most. Shadow guessed it had brought memories of Bruhada's capitulation.

Argan said, 'Arkallon was the last.'

'Last?'

'Tormelor. Thania. Bruhada. Now Arkallon. All the city-states and nations north of the Rivyn. There's nothing left for Kalleron to take.'

'That's good, right?'

Argan huffed. 'You think he'll stop?'

'Kalle?' Shadow knew of the Golden King and his ambitions. His ignorance of politics didn't prevent popular gossip from finding its way to his ears. Though there was a problem with Argan's weighted question. 'All the rumours say she can't cross it; the Rivyn.'

Argan grumbled. That great big rumble in his chest. It sounded as though secret knowledge was struggling to stay quiet.

'What? What do you know?' Shadow asked.

'There is more to Kalleron than its queen.' Argan appeared doubtful, but he nodded. 'I know it.'

'Well, the Rivyn is one thing. An ocean is something else. I think we're safe here.'

The smile that crept onto Argan's face was unsettling. His raised eyebrow was a prompt Shadow couldn't ignore.

'What, you don't think we're safe?'

Argan shrugged. He brought the tankard to his face and drank. Shadow sighed. He had thought drinking with Petra would have been therapeutic. For both of them. Instead, he had found himself once more in the philosophical company of a quiet giant.

Shadow said, 'Enough talk of the world.'

'Then what?'

'What else? Wars and Wenches.'

Argan frowned.

'Don't worry. It's a game I play with Petra. She loves it. I'll tell you the rules as we go along.'

Chapter VIII

Mount Etherus. A glorious sight under the light of the moons. General Aracyse, peering beyond the tinted pane, looked up at the highest point of the Kulkarrons. The wind howled with relentless fervour as it tore through the narrow twin peaks, although he heard only a muted expression of the raging gale. The glass between him and the exterior was thick, and the walls of his study were a fusion of Larissian timber and metal alloy. Most of the industrial complex was of similar construction; the living areas draped in soft fabrics to shield the workers from the bitter cold that crept through from the exterior. Taking its title from the mountain, they had built Etherus to endure. Its purpose had required the greatest engineering achievement in Kalleron's long history.

A knock on the door drew Aracyse's attention from the view. 'Enter.'

'General.'

It was his senior engineer, a man he considered a friend. 'Franklin. It's late. What brings you at this hour?'

Franklin shook his head. He didn't need to say anything; Aracyse understood. 'Another death?'

'Yes. Unfortunate.' Franklin's expression changed. It was almost cheerful. 'It wasn't a fall from the platform this time.'

'The furnace?'

'No. During yesterday's storm, it seems a guard became disorientated at the gate.'

'What happened?'

Franklin shook his head. 'Man versus nature. His colleague says he wandered off into the blizzard; he alerted the interior guards, and they went to call him back. It was a ferocious gale. Said he could barely stand. He struggled for a while against the elements, but he had to give up, couldn't leave the gate unguarded. Once the storm abated, they sent out a search party. Found his body on the old crumbling access path. You recall we closed it down?'

Aracyse nodded. He would have preferred a simple fall, or a fiery end in the furnace. Guards abandoning posts and losing themselves down old roads did not sit well with his suspicious mind. 'Why was he there?'

Franklin shrugged. 'Snow blind? Partial delirium? Whatever, there had been a serious rockfall. It came down right on top of him. They said he was unrecognisable, some of his body had gone over the edge.'

'His keys?'

The engineer shook his head. 'They didn't recover a full body, and what remains they found were pulverised.'

A glance to the window, Aracyse noted how calm the weather appeared; a myriad of stars sparkling in a cloudless sky. An illusion of safety; he knew the exposure at night would be lethal. Too cold to investigate until the sun came up. 'At first light, I want to see for myself.'

'See?'

'Where this happened.'

'General, it appears quite innocent.'

Decades of battle and years of commanding hardy men and women had taught Aracyse many things. Franklin was an intelligent man. A supremely competent engineer, but his trust was too generous and his suspicion was lacking.

'Franklin, do you know why I'm in charge of Etherus?'

His friend frowned. 'You don't normally ask for accolades, but...'

'I still don't. But this accident is unusual. A rockfall up here? To be expected. But a guard leaving their post? To wander onto a path they would know is treacherous. And to die, the body left, as you say, unrecognisable. Franklin, it sounds like the *perfect* accident. The problem is, in all my long years of service to Kalleron, I've never known of perfection in chaos.'

'I see.' Franklin shuffled. 'You think it suspicious?'

'The gate key. This accident forces us to presume it is gone with the body parts spilled over the edge. Convenient?'

'Well, when you say it like that.'

Aracyse recalled passing through the guarded gatehouse on his arrival many months before. The design and placement of bulkheads created a reasonable buffer from the wind, although he knew the dangers of Etherus could never be completely mitigated. Once through the outer barrier, there was an interior section with a second guarded gate. Four guards in all.

'Did all the guards conduct the initial search?' he asked Franklin.

'I believe so. But the conditions stopped them fairly quickly. At least, by their account.'

'I don't like it, Franklin. Not at all. First light, I'm going outside. For now, you'll speak to the remaining guards. I want to know exactly what they saw, and for how long they left their posts.'

Franklin squinted, his voice cautious. 'You really think...?'

'I do. Lock down the nursery. I don't want anybody in there.'

'Aracyse, you don't believe anyone would be foolish enough to go for the Furies?'

He nodded, glanced as a rogue gale buffeted the walls. 'Not from the vault, but the nursery can be open to the winds. It's where I'd go if I was...' Aracyse stopped, his thoughts trailing to an old conversation with the previous general in charge of the complex. 'They whisper under the wind.'

'Sorry?'

'Something General A'dan said to me.'

Franklin's eyes widened, his grey brows lifting. 'Yes, I recall now. You told me that.'

'The cult. I can't shake the feeling it's the damn cult.' Aracyse strode to the weapons rack hanging on the wall. He snatched his compact war hammer, an excellent tool in confined spaces, and threw on his cloak.

'General?'

'The guards, Franklin. I'm going to the Nursery myself.'

If the cult had infiltrated the complex, Aracyse saw no signs of disturbance. He strode along corridors, where oil lamps maintained a functional gloom, and met the occasional worker who would salute him and go about their business. He had come to Etherus as a decorated and revered soldier, but had been keen to show a more thoughtful side of his character. The engineers of Etherus had warmed to his better nature; they had learned to trust him. Those workers he saw on his way to the Nursery gave him no cause for alarm. Nor did he hear any unusual sounds, although away from the living areas, the wind was louder; the walls trembling in the constant roar. On his approach to the Nursery, he saw a guard stationed at the door. As Aracyse approached, the man saluted.

'General, sir!'

He recognised him, though he was one of the few whose name he didn't know. 'Everything normal?' Aracyse asked.

'Yes, sir.'

'Your name?'

'Arther, General.' The guard paused, shuffled on the spot. 'Is this an inspection?'

Aracyse didn't want to trouble the guard with his suspicions. He gestured to the door. 'Yes, Arther, it is.'

The guard opened it. 'The Nursery is yours, General.'

Not afraid, but cautious, Aracyse poked his head into the room. In the dark, he could see nothing. The only noise he could hear was the rattling of the metal shutters. Pulling back, he looked at the guard.

'Nobody's been in?'

'Not since sun down. As scheduled.'

Aracyse nodded. 'Stay here.'

'Yes, sir!'

Inside, he moved to the interior wall. Aracyse fumbled for the lamp and found the small metal cog, dragging his thumb down on it. Inside a glass bulb, a shower of sparks briefly illuminated a pond of black; a wick rising from the murk. Another grind of the iron wheel, and more sparks danced inside. This time they caught, and a flame sprung from the oil-soaked wick. Moving to each of the six lamps, Aracyse brought illumination to the room. Silver backed screens reflected the glow; an amber warmth revealing the Nursery.

Aracyse grumbled. He had expected treachery, but was relieved to find none. The shelves that held the glass spheres for inspection were empty; the cannonball sized orbs stowed away for the night. On the far wall, the metal shutter rippled against the elements. The gearing used to open it was intact, and there were no obvious signs of sabotage. In the large open space, there was no place to hide. If there was an intruder, he would see them. Aracyse paced around the room, completing a circuit. He sighed. Perhaps his paranoia had been unjustified. Yet he couldn't shake the sense that something was amiss at Etherus. Tomorrow would tell him more.

He moved to the door, stopping at Arther. 'Key?'

Without hesitation, the guard reached to his belt and pulled the iron key from its hook. He handed it to Aracyse. It was cold in his hand as he turned it over, not knowing for what he searched. Something about it, the smallest clue? But the key was tarnished, and the teeth worn. It was as it ought to be.

'Nothing out of the ordinary?' he asked the guard.

'No, sir. Should there be?'

Aracyse smiled. 'No. Everything seems... normal. But I'll take the key, keep it with the other that Franklin holds.'

'Of course, General, whatever you wish.'

Aracyse closed the door and turned the key, satisfied to hear the solid bolts sliding into position. It was a hefty door with a complex lock. One of Anders' creations. Nobody was getting in. With one last nod to the guard, Aracyse left the Nursery and returned to his study.

It was good fortune that the weather had remained stable, and although the wind was wild, there was little to obstruct his view. Aracyse, standing on the very threshold of the Etherus complex, peered down the path. Rock and ice frozen as one; the surface was another hazard, traversable only with the use of iron studs on the soles of the boots. With the guard who had witnessed the disappearance by his side, Aracyse moved away from the safety of the gate, protected from the elements by a thick winter cloak. As though punches from unseen assailants, the wind knocked his body; violent gusts darting in and out of the pass. It caused him to laugh.

'General, what's funny?' the guard, struggling to stay upright, called out.

'Her Lordship is angry. She doesn't want us here.'

'Who?'

Aracyse wanted to salute the Wind, but he thought his arms would act as sails. He imagined his heavy frame being lifted as a rag doll. 'The Wind. She does not welcome us.'

The guard didn't answer; perhaps he hadn't understood the reference? Most of the workers at Etherus were oblivious to its true purpose. They were all told the same thing, that it was a weapons workshop. The explanation given for its hostile location was always the same; to keep it away from enemy eyes. That wasn't a lie. But it wasn't the whole truth. Few were privy to the powers at play in the mountain. Aracyse often wondered if they knew, would they stay?

Unperturbed by the blowing gale, Aracyse trekked onward, following the downward slope away from Etherus. Soon he had come to the old road; a pass cut into the side of the mountain. The ground fell away sharply to the east, leaving a meagre sliver of ground to traverse the path. With countless battles under his belt, it amused him to feel the apprehension rising in his gut. The way forward posed problematic questions: why would a guard choose to come this way, and how would they have navigated such a narrow ledge in a white-out? As Aracyse saw it, the hostile conditions would explain the guard stumbling blind in the storm, but not his precise route. Pushing his body to the wall, he crossed the pass with care. Once he had moved beyond the worst, he beckoned for the guard to follow. Aracyse was thankful the sure-footed soldier made quick work of the ledge.

'How far to the rockfall?'

The guard pointed. 'Around the next outcrop.'

Aracyse turned and continued on. Nearing the destination, he stopped. He scanned the ground, the same mangle of ice and rock as before, although deep blankets of snow lay in drifts along the side. Unable to shake his paranoia, he sought anything that might let slip any plot against Etherus. A footprint, a discarded rag. There was nothing.

'How far did you come down?'

'On the night it happened?'

'Yes.'

The guard thumbed backwards. 'I'm sorry, General, we didn't dare come this way. It would have been unduly reckless; I've seen men swept away by the winds. No, we found Alarsta after the storm; when it was safer to explore.'

'Sensible. Did you know the man?'

The guard shook his head. 'Newcomer. Past few weeks, served a month at most.'

Despite the bitter cold and the buffeting winds, Aracyse felt some tension drain away. A recent recruit with little experience of Etherus? It was tragic, but the mortality rate among new workers was higher. A year alive on Etherus had become an informal badge of honour. With a nod to the guard, Aracyse completed the short walk to the rockfall.

A substantial slip had occurred. The cut of the pass had fallen down, and a great void was obvious in the cliff above. It would have been devastating. One positive thing, Aracyse thought; the wind appeared less agitated, the curve of the path having taken him away from the gale. He turned to the guard, who was staring at the mass of rubble.

Shaking his head, the guard pointed at the boulders. 'That's where he was. We had to move some rocks.' His finger drifted to another pile of debris. 'See those larger flakes? They'd cut right through the poor bastard.'

Aracyse moved to the flat shards of smooth stone. He knelt beside them, moving his gloved hand across the sharp edges. Frozen blood and hard, twisted flesh lay scattered. It was gruesome, although he had seen similar remains on the battlefield. One small mercy; this unfortunate man would have perished in an instant.

'I've seen enough,' he said, standing up.

'Yes, General.'

Aracyse scanned the area one last time. Defeated by the evidence given to his eyes, he sighed. Nothing at all appeared unusual; not for the expected dangers of Etherus. He recalled his conversation with Franklin. *A perfect accident.* Shaking his head, he grumbled and started the treacherous trek back to the Etherus gates.

Chapter IX

Mount Etherus was a hostile environment, but there were rare days when the winds appeared tame. It was such a morning, and Aracyse stared at the technical drawings on his plain desk. A plan for a cage, Anders had worked on the design to provide a shield for the glass rack in the Nursery. Two days had passed since the inspection of the pass, and Aracyse's nerves had settled as much as he would allow. He had puzzled about the vessels they would bring to the Nursery from the furnace. The workers often left the glass spheres without thought of incident, as though the danger was over. It was an obvious lapse in judgement. Every step in the manufacture of a Sprite was fraught with risk. It seemed naïve to let them sit in the Nursery, unguarded from mischief or mayhem while they awaited inspection. His finger tapping on the drawings, he raised his head to the sound of footsteps approaching the open door.

'Good morning Franklin. News?'

'Morning General. Bad, I'm afraid. The first batch was cracked and ejected from the complex. But they began work straight away on new spheres; they should be ready soon.'

'I see.'

Franklin paused. He appeared to be waiting for an invitation. Putting down his carbon stylus, Aracyse sat back in his chair. 'How many times have I said? When my door is open, Franklin, you don't need to wait like a chambermaid.'

The engineer smiled. 'Old habits.'

'In Etherus, we create new habits. We can leave the old ways to die.'

'Seditious words, Aracyse.' Franklin peered at the desk. 'New habits, indeed.'

'The cage?'

'The stylus. Finally done away with ink and quills?'

Aracyse plucked the stylus from his desk. He peered at it, marvelling at its simplicity. 'Quills are for poets and pomposity. This is the future, Franklin.'

The engineer laughed. It was a genuine bellow from his lungs.

'What's so funny?' Aracyse asked.

'You glorify a writing tool when we walk the hallowed halls of the most advanced engineering complex in the world, surrounded by genius and industrialisation.'

Aracyse smiled. 'Proud words, Franklin.' He held up the compact stylus. 'Shall I use this trivial item to record them in the history books?'

Franklin laughed again. When he recovered his composure, he strolled to the faceted circular window. He tapped it; the sound coming back as a deadened thud. 'You know, this window took one year to create.' The engineer traced his fingers across the metal frames into which artisans had housed each pane. 'The alloy is light, but flexible. The glass, flawless; the smoked tint uniform across every shard. Only Kalleron could create this.'

The work had impressed Aracyse when he had first set eyes on it. A spider's web of dark panes; the tint allowed him to view the Kulkarrons without straining his eyes. The clarity of the glass was so precise that sometimes he thought there was none; a rare smudge of oil from his own fingerprints to remind of its presence. Aracyse pushed his chair back and stood up, joining Franklin at the window.

'Still there, I see,' the engineer said.

Aracyse peered to a far peak. 'The temple?'

'Yes. It's a wonder it remains.'

'Perhaps not for long. You can see the recent collapse on the flank.' Aracyse pointed. 'See where the rock is lighter?'

'It's tantalisingly close. Who were they, Aracyse? Who could build up here but us?'

An ancient shrine. Robbers had looted and desecrated most of them centuries ago. Abundant across southerly Shaddenhyne, it was a disaster for Kalleron's elemental scholars that the nation's desire for excess had left scant history behind. To Aracyse's knowledge, what he and Franklin looked upon was an unspoiled and unique relic, possibly the last ever elemental temple. So close, yet so far away.

Aracyse said, 'In our modern world, it's difficult to imagine the hardy folk who climbed that mountain. How many centuries ago? Perhaps millennia?'

'How many attempts have we made?'

Aracyse shook his head. 'A handful, but even that is too much for all the lives lost. She doesn't want us there. That peak isn't anywhere near willing as Etherus to host foreign guests. As much as she howls and blows, our lady of the Kulkarrons has graced us with relative mercy.' Tapping the pane with his fingernail, Aracyse wondered about the provenance of the temple. 'Is that perhaps the house of the Wind?'

'By the gods, Aracyse; that sent a shiver through my soul.'

'As it should, Franklin.' He turned to look at his friend. 'We walk a glorious path here in Etherus; a tribute to the might and majesty of Kalleron. But don't forget who this world really belongs to.'

'Indeed. Well, given how much we agree on our true insignificance, shall we perhaps venture to the Nursery? The new batch should be on its way. Let's see what we've stolen from her sky?'

Aracyse bowed his head and extended his arm. 'Let's hope that today, she graces us with some better luck.'

In the Nursery, Aracyse observed the workers wheeling in small wooden carts covered with plush fabric. Concealed beneath the soft material, each of the three carts carried six glass spheres. The workers handled the skull-sized orbs with great care; lifting them from a velvet-lined, hemispherical depression. From there, they placed them on the viewing rack on the wall opposite the metal shutters. Once all the spheres were resting on the padded wooden shelf, the workers left Aracyse and Franklin alone in the room.

'Are the valves all sealed shut?' Aracyse asked.

'They'd be cracked if they weren't. The blowers performed above expectations on the second batch.'

Aracyse pictured the preparation of the spheres. The most delicate and important operation in all of Etherus, if not the entire world. The immense furnace powered the equally impressive bellows that drew air from between the raging peaks. The artificial lungs sent the captured wind through copper pipes and onward into thicker iron conduits. In the glass factory, the blowers worked in pairs, one shaping the sphere, while the other channelled the captured air into the freshly blown bulb. Once cooled and sealed, they could only hope to have captured a Sprite. That was the name Aracyse preferred. To everyone else, it was called a Fury. So rare was the chance to succeed that in a productive year, they might only create a dozen specimens. Grievous injury was common, often by manner of careless accident. It was by terrible chance that a Sprite had once been involved in such misfortune, with General A'dan's gruesome death revealing the brutal reality of the elemental weapon.

With the internal door closed and the metal shutters down, Aracyse stood in a peaceful gloom. The quietly rattling sun-shield leaked small beams of light into the room. The floor, cushioned with a white fur, picked up the highlights as though the crests of waves. Those little peaks were as far as the morning rays could wander. It was crucial that the glass remained hidden from the sun's touch.

'No matter how much we think we know,' Aracyse said, 'there is more left hidden than we have found.'

Franklin, moving to the shutter mechanism, hummed. 'How so?'

'From Bruhale's library, we learned much of the old ways. Chance made us realise it could be real. The sorcery of the elementals might be more than myth.'

Franklin, groaning with considerable effort as he worked the gearing mechanism, called back. 'This doesn't feel like sorcery to me.'

'We've engineered myth into reality. Fables written by unknown hands have allowed us to create immeasurable power.' Aracyse inhaled. It was sobering to know with what they played; to understand it was no game. 'Do you ever think, Franklin?'

'Frequently, but of what?'

'Those who first worshipped the power of the elementals. What happened to them?'

With the shutters open, and a grin on his face, Franklin said, 'Perhaps they dropped one too many Furies?'

A joke. Perhaps too close to the truth than was comfortable. Aracyse looked at the rack of glass spheres, all now bathing in the sun's rays. They did not have long.

'Let's go, Franklin. Grab your covers.'

He moved to the rack and, careful not to obstruct the light, Aracyse gazed into a sphere. It irked him he had never found a Sprite. Nor had he seen one. Once trapped, they placed the orphans of the Wind into the dark of the vault. It was that which he had alluded to earlier; the light from the sun. How had they learned it was daylight that agitated the Sprite trapped within? What else was waiting to be gleaned from the consequence of more disaster?

'This one is empty,' he said, moving on.

Vessel after vessel, the sound of Franklin's sighs joining with his own, Aracyse was ready to give up. Only two remained, and he and his friend were side by side. They jostled one another, careful not to bump the rack. Moving his frame to better see the spheres in the growing sunlight, Aracyse gasped. He held his breath, tapping Franklin, not knowing where his hand connected. But Franklin was tapping back. They had found two.

A ribbon of red danced within the glass. As though blood swirling in water, it moved around the vessel. Exposed to the sun, more colour appeared, so too, the vibrance increased. He had expected to see the hues of the sky; it was thrilling to see shades of fire.

'It's incredible,' he said.

Franklin sighed his joy.

Mesmerised by the display, Aracyse noted the colours shift as the movement changed. The light, now colder and revealing shades of blue, was pulsing. 'Franklin?' In an instant, the display was over, smothered under a fabric cover.

Franklin tutted. 'Need I remind you of General A'dan?'

A wave of excitement swept through Aracyse. 'Franklin, I never imagined the Sprites would be so beautiful.'

'And in that beauty, my friend, lies great disaster. Remember, Aracyse, it's only you that gives them that delicate name. These are not Sprites. What we have just inches from our delicate and fleshy bodies is the dreadful power of the Wind herself, and I assure you; what lies within is bloody furious.'

They were wise words. He had read all the reports on the progress of Etherus when he had taken charge. The descriptions of his predecessor's demise were vivid. Aracyse had been due to take control of the complex months earlier, but other matters had delayed his retirement from active duty; one last campaign against rebels in the Tormelorian hills. A sobering thought; had he avoided that last mission, perhaps A'dan—a good man—would have escaped the mistakes that had ended his life?

As he pondered the past, Aracyse heard the door opening; it was Franklin calling in the workers. Three men entered the Nursery, two of them pushing carts. Different from the previous trolleys, these had low bases with tall sides. A luxurious and soft bed of pillows sat within a hide frame. Aracyse had questioned the rationale for such an obvious oversight; the same spheres that contained a Sprite after the inspection had already entered the room as an elemental weapon. Why not treat them all the same? Franklin had explained: Too many carts and too much time transporting the spheres had led to rushed behaviours and a frightening number of near misses. His senior engineer had reminded him you could make a process more efficient, but it was harder to improve people. Wise words Aracyse could equate to the theatre of war. Franklin had mentioned another factor. The probability equation; most inspections yielded nothing from the Wind.

Nodding to the cart, Aracyse said, 'I still think we should use those for all transport.'

'General, as I've said—and you need not worry—the other carts are just as safe.' He patted the soft cushions. 'This is almost a courtesy; a nod to *her* graciousness.' Franklin leaned in, his voice a whisper. 'You know? Let her see that we're keeping her children safe.'

Aracyse raised an eyebrow. 'I hope she appreciates our hospitality.'

'I'm sure she does.'

The clatter of the shutters interrupted Aracyse's thoughts as one of the three workers lowered the sun-shield. Franklin had moved away and was speaking to a worker, pointing with excitement at the Sprites. The worker's head bobbed with obedience to every command. Franklin returned to Aracyse and appeared as cheerful as he had ever been.

'This has been an exceptional day, General.'

'Not one, but two Sprites.'

'*Furies*. Remember, they are weapons. You wouldn't give your enemy's weapon a—dare I say it—a romantic name, would you?'

Enthused by the mood, Aracyse nodded. 'I call my hammer Rose.'

Franklin frowned. 'You do?'

A chuckle released with genuine warmth, Aracyse clapped his friend on the shoulder. 'Of course not. I'll consider my words in future. Especially around the workers.'

'General, please don't think I'm nannying you. It's just a reminder of what we hold.'

Aracyse smiled. He valued Franklin's honesty and logical mind. Essential attributes for an engineer, especially on Etherus. 'Franklin, there are few people who would dare. But if it had to be, I would readily accept your scolding words.'

The engineer appeared uncomfortable with his praise. It was a proper response, although Aracyse's words were truth. All good soldiers knew how to motivate their troops; the greatest leaders knew when to take their advice.

Franklin said, 'If you're happy, General, we'll get the spheres to the vault?'

'Of course, Franklin. Make the arrangements.'

With an unnecessary bow, the engineer returned to his men and fussed over the transport of the Sprites. It pleased Aracyse to see the care and attention Franklin gave to man and task. Content with the moment, and elated with the haul, Aracyse walked to the door.

'Franklin?'

'Yes, General?'

'Brief me at sundown. My study.'

Franklin looked up from the cart. 'Brief?'

'A report of today's efforts, and an inventory of the vault.'

With a frown, Franklin tipped his head with an uncertain nod. 'Yes, General.'

Aracyse turned and walked away. His senior engineer and good friend in Etherus deserved a reward for his trials. A fine bottle of Bruhadian Spirit awaited him. Brought to the complex to reward the day he had found his own Sprite, Aracyse thought Franklin would welcome a shared drink. Today had been a good day; what better way to top it off than with a celebration and intelligent conversation between friends?

The wind had returned, and through the dark glass, the Kulkarrons were barely visible. Clouds shrouded the moons; their ambience was nothing but a hint behind the cold veil. Aracyse, staring at the nothingness, thought of the guard who had left his post. He tried to imagine the confusion and fear such a night would bring; it brought a shiver to his spine.

'Can you imagine it, Franklin?'

Seated behind, his friend said, 'What's that?'

'Facing the elements on a night such as this? Brutal.'

'Not considering the elemental herself?'

'Yes. Nature doesn't need them to render life a near impossibility. I've heard tales of the Anastra range in Laria. Even more hostile than here.'

'Is that possible?'

'Could it not be?' Aracyse turned to face his friend. Franklin's cheeks were red; an appreciation of the Bruhadian spirit showing in his relaxed demeanour.

'Well, if we weren't shielded by this magnificent complex, would we not die?'

It was a logical premise. Aracyse nodded. 'Practically a guarantee.'

Franklin brought his glass to his lips. He sipped the spirit and frowned. 'Then how do we measure *more* hostile when we know Etherus kills with ease?'

The point was concise. What could be more hostile than death? With a smile, Aracyse sat on his chair and faced Franklin across his desk. He nodded at him, expressing his agreement. 'The spirit. Do you like it?'

'A little too much, I fear.' Franklin peered into his glass, a fine cut crystal ware from Kalleron's finest boutiques. 'I might need wheeled back to the dormitory on a Fury cart.'

'I could arrange for that.'

Franklin had a grin on his face. 'As a child, I once rode a cart down Greolda Avenue. You know of it?'

Aracyse nodded, although it no longer had that name. The Greolda family had amassed a fortune buying and trading minerals. On Kalle's orders, workers demolished their grand home and created lush gardens, building a statue to honour Kalle on the site of the house. The Greolda's had sold their business and moved to Hoydai to retire in the lush southern city. That was what the people were told. Aracyse knew better; his fellow soldiers had carried out the executions. It was the final purge of Kalleron's elite, decades ago. The Greolda's wealth had become too great a threat for Kalle. Not that they were ambitious people. It was their hubris. Nobody could assume the trappings of royalty other than the king. Not in Kalleron.

'Greolda? It's Sannah now, isn't it?' he said.

'Actually, yes, it is. But... you should have seen me, Aracyse. Flying, I was. Absolutely flying down those cobbles. My arse cheeks were black and blue for weeks.'

Aracyse chuckled, imagining a juvenile Franklin on a cart, no doubt built to exact specifications, careening down one of Kalleron's steepest streets. Lost in the imagery, he noticed Franklin's posture change; straightening up, then leaning his elbows on his knees. He cradled the crystal glass in his hands. His expression was serious.

'The Greolda's were assassinated.'

'I know.'

'Of course, I suppose you would. It wasn't...'

'Me? Not directly. Back then, I was far down the chain of command, but the men who did were in my unit. Does that bother you?'

Franklin's response appeared genuine. Aracyse could read people well, and his friend's posture was relaxed to a greater extent than what the alcohol alone would enable.

'If they sent you to Etherus,' Franklin said, waving his hand at the walls, 'to ensure my loyalty, I trust you know the truth?'

His question was unexpected. Unnecessary. 'Franklin, I have no quarrel with you or with your patriotism. You needn't worry about my thoughts, nor should you consider me one of the king's spies.'

Franklin straightened, his eyes widening. 'I never mentioned the king's spies.'

The engineer's defensive attitude was understandable. Greolda was a lesson to more than just the wealthy: never aspire to be anything other than what you were told to be. Kalle's rule was absolute. That mantra applied to all spheres of life. No matter how valuable you were to Kalleron, you were always its pawn. All human life was expendable under Kalle. Aracyse sought to quell his friend's alarm with a personal tale.

'You recall the last Bruhada campaign?'

'Yes. Gods, that was years ago.'

Aracyse nodded. 'I was tasked by Te'anor to lead it.'

Franklin's eyes widened more, his mouth hanging open. 'Good grief, I never knew.'

'I never led it.'

'Well, yes, the old Butcher did. Wait. I'm confused. Where were you?'

Aracyse was about to confess to seditious behaviour, but he trusted Franklin as much as he could with any loyal soldier, and though his friend was loyal to Kalleron, he was more faithful to Etherus.

'You know I value our work?'

Franklin nodded. 'Your motivation is unmatched, Aracyse.'

'And I can trust my words with you will remain between us?'

A hesitation. 'Yes.'

'Before that campaign, I picked a fight with another captain. I let him pummel me. I received a demotion, and they sent me to the salt mines south of Old Thania as punishment. I served six-months there.'

Franklin was on the edge of his seat. 'Why?'

'Two reasons. First, I was rising through the ranks. A tremendously skilled fighter, but more than that, Franklin.' He tapped his temple. 'I was a thinker. I knew what was going on. I had to slow my progress and appear wayward enough to require further education. Before Greolda, I knew what was happening. I was in a few of those death squads.' Aracyse shook his head. 'That is blood I do not honour, Franklin. But I knew it back then. Hubris would get me killed.'

'And two?'

Aracyse leant back in his chair. He thought of Bruhada before the conquest. A city as no other, except, of course, Kalleron. The Bruhadian capital, Bruhada, under its king Baza'rad, had long thought itself too separate to be a threat, but Kalle's eyes had fallen upon it.

'An informal agreement had endured between the two nations. But Kalle broke it with reckless military incursions.'

'For what reason?'

He offered Franklin a cynical smile. 'Because he could. I fear no man, Franklin, but I understand this: Kalle, no matter what you may think of him, is unmatched in battle. Even in my prime, if I were to face him, I would surely die. There is only one other warrior I view the same way. It would be an honour to face him, but it would be my death.'

'Baza'rad?'

Aracyse nodded.

'But... if an honour, why not take the command Te'anor offered you?'

'I was young then. Not so relaxed about my mortality. I'm sure I would have given a good fight. But imagine if I survived against such a man. Even if I had lost, what legend would they speak of me? The young Kallerye soldier that the great King Baza'rad couldn't kill. It all comes back to my first point. Hubris, Franklin. If Te'anor hadn't died in that battle, I think he would have disappeared, just like the Greolda family.'

Franklin sat back in his chair. 'Why tell me this?'

'I trust you, Franklin, and I ask for yours.'

'You have it, Aracyse.'

Nodding to his friend, Aracyse stood and moved to the window. Unseen, lost in the dark, there was a temple to the elementals beyond his reach. Speaking to Franklin's reflection in the glass, Aracyse said, 'What we do, why we do it. Do you understand?'

'To the glory of Kalleron. We build weapons.'

'Is the Queen not a weapon?'

'Without equal.'

Aracyse faced Franklin. He raised his arms, gestured to the complex. 'Then why do we need this?'

'Oh, I see. Is it not for overseas? Campaigns where we cannot send our Queen?'

It pleased Aracyse that his friend was intuitive enough to repeat what he himself had heard. But this was not the truth. Not at least what he had gleaned from illicit conversations inside Kalleron's fortress.

'It is to do to the Queen. But not her earthly limitations.'

Franklin shook his head. About to place his glass down, he took another sip. 'Then what?'

'She's changing, Franklin. Her behaviours are becoming erratic. It started years ago.'

The engineer's brow furrowed, his eyes narrowing to become slits. He shook his head.

Aracyse said, 'She's creating things inside the fortress. Flowers of stone. Inanimate, and some say, hideous creatures of granite and marble. The creatures may be rumour, but I've seen hints of it myself, spied her garden from the Generals' Tower. There is less stability in her behaviour. We assume some things are eternal.' He gestured to the window and the mountains beyond. 'People think these peaks are static, but we know they shift and move, they change with glacial time.'

'I'm still not sure what this means?'

'Our Sprites, Franklin. The Fury. They are not a supplement to our Queen's power. They exist to replace it.'

Franklin fumbled his glass, almost dropping it onto the rug. 'She's leaving?'

As the wind howled beyond the window, and the room shuddered, Aracyse poured a measure of spirit. He offered another to Franklin, who raised his glass to accept.

'We cannot know that. But there is suspicion.' Aracyse pointed to the east. In his mind's eye, he pictured an inhospitable place not dissimilar to Etherus. 'If that day comes, and Laria discovers our Queen has gone, they will send their leviathans to ravage our city. They may be ancient, but they rule the seas. And now they have a grudge to bear.'

Franklin's gaze dropped to the floor. 'Would they really wage war if she left?'

'I think, yes.'

'But why? Why risk coming to us? What madness would that be?'

A brave runner had delivered a message to Etherus. Addressed to him, and bearing the military seal of Kalleron, he had known what it would be. It was a formal confirmation of the latest annexation. Although Arkalla had not surrendered, neither had it survived.

'Laria's ally, Arkallon. Kalle made good his threat; he sent the Queen.'

Franklin let out a long breath. 'Poor souls.'

'The death squads will look for survivors, but the city is gone. From there, we will move on Gwynerath, and once we control that, Laria's trade will be strangled. It was an unintentional consequence.'

Franklin shuffled in his seat. He rose to his feet and walked to the window. Taking a sip of his spirit, he huffed onto the cold pane; a smudge of vapour spreading out on the glass. Aracyse watched the edges of the mist recede.

'What we've done, Franklin: By proxy, I fear we've declared war on Laria.'

Chapter X

Awake. Had he heard a noise? Aracyse's chamber was dark. The wind was howling in muted gusts beyond the walls. He leapt from his bed. Standing and holding his breath, he tilted his head to hear the smallest anomaly. Decades of service had developed an ability to rouse without stupor. A trait that benefitted survival; it had plagued his rest. There must have been a sound, something other than the constant background judder of Etherus. He tried to recall if it had been part of a dream. Had he heard a scream or the wind? Whichever it was, Aracyse moved to his closet and hauled on his day clothes. One extra garment at hand: his trusted, short-handled war hammer.

He left his chambers, and as he moved through the study, Aracyse glanced at the window. Not a hint of colour outside, there was no sign of light; dawn had still to come. He travelled with caution through the empty corridors. At this hour, Etherus would see minimal activity; only the guards and essential personnel moving around. Apart from the wind, he heard nothing; the absence of noise was what he expected to hear. But as Aracyse moved away from the habitation area, he heard distant shouting. It was a rally of words; a tone he recognised. Cries of anger and confrontation. It was a skirmish. In an instant, he was running; the hammer in his hand was a pendulum to fire his speed. Aracyse paused at the first junction, waiting for the sound to repeat. Etherus could be a maze; he would only find the source if he followed the echoes. A thought; Franklin's chamber was nearby. It would be wise to rouse his friend if he was not already alert to the noise. With haste, Aracyse arrived at Franklin's dormitory. The door was closed over, and Aracyse paused, listening for sounds beyond. None came from within the room. His hand on the latch, Aracyse pushed open the door.

'Awaken! Awaken!' he called to the dark.

In the gloom, there was no response. 'Franklin?'

As Aracyse's eyes adjusted, he saw shapes. Four beds, one of which would be Franklin's, the other three belonging to his senior technicians. The meagre light from the lamps in the corridor offered poor illumination, but Aracyse could see that nothing moved; the indiscernible shapes on the beds lay quiet.

Aracyse said, 'Wake up!'

With no response, his blood chilled. He raced to Franklin's bed, agitated by his friend's deep slumber. He grabbed the man, tried to shake him awake, but he didn't stir. The body was a rag-doll in his hands; slippery hands that were slick with a warm damp.

'Franklin? Gods no!'

Too dark to see the injuries, it was clear Franklin was dead. In the dim light, dark patches patterned the ghostly sheet. It was a shroud. Aracyse stood from the body; his reactions numbed from the shock. Yet there was worse to consider. He looked at the other shapes in their beds; he didn't have to check them. Aracyse knew; Etherus was under attack. He fumbled beside Franklin's bed, moving his hands to the bureau, turning over papers he couldn't read, and disturbing things he couldn't see. He only sought one thing, and it wasn't there. Franklin's key to the vault was missing. With thoughts of treachery flooding his mind, Aracyse roared with rage. His fist clenching tight around the hammer, he pulled the sheet over Franklin's face and sped from the dormitory.

A brief journey brought him to the vault. Seven men were dead on the floor. Beyond them, the great iron door lay open. The chamber where they stored the Furies was dark within; no secrets offered to Aracyse's eyes. A quick glance at the dead, and he saw two were guards. The rest wore furs and heavy cloaks that he didn't recognise; they had come from outside. Not enough time to check for life; he moved to the vault door. Nothing stirred within the chamber. A cursory glance and Aracyse sighed with relief. The inner cage appeared untouched. Behind the bars, the crates that contained the Sprites were intact. He moved into the gloom and rattled the cage door. Locked. Confused, he turned, and his heart sank at what he saw. The Nursery carts. Tucked neat against the wall to the side of the vault door. Aracyse raced over and peered inside. Too dark to see, he moved his hand inside, taking care not to bump the glass. He disregarded his caution when he found nothing; his hand gouging into fabric and wood. It was a desperate search for what wasn't there. The Sprites were gone.

With a roar, he brought his hammer crashing down on the cart. Etherus breached and Franklin murdered. Terrible acts, but they were insignificant compared to this grave treason. But what of the screams he had heard? And where were the Sprites? For a moment, Aracyse thought the infiltration was over; perhaps a Fury had killed the thieves and guards? But the bodies on the floor were intact, and the screams had been of rage. The dead at the vault lay in peace, not pieces; a Fury's wrath was a violent evisceration. The screams he heard would have been terror. No—the bastards were still inside Etherus. Aracyse saluted his dead guards, ruing that he couldn't give them the respect they deserved, and he turned on his heels to speed down the corridor. There was only one place to go; there was only one way out.

He charged through Etherus, happening across panicked workers spilling from their dormitories. Aracyse ordered the startled faces back inside their rooms; instructing them to barricade the doors. On his passage to the exit, two guards joined him. Not fully dressed; it was probable the commotion had awoken them. They queried his haste, but all he could tell them was to keep pace. At the inner gate, Aracyse found more bodies. Three intruders, two guards. It was a spiralling death toll, but there was worse to behold. The inner door was open, the freezing blast blowing snow into the antechamber. Aracyse glared at the fresh powder. There were prints left behind and their direction was clear; they were moving away, fleeing Etherus. The perpetrators had already gone.

'General? We're under attack?'

'The attack is over. But Etherus is not safe.'

'What is your command, General?'

Aracyse looked at the open door. It would be foolish to leave the safety of the complex, but it would be cowardice to remain. He had to find the Sprites. The secrets of Etherus could not be shown to the world. With haste, he stooped, removing one of the intruders' winter cloaks. He slung it over his shoulders, and fastening it as tight as he could, turned to the guards.

'You have the key?'

Both men shook their heads. One said, 'We only grabbed our short-swords.'

A growl from Aracyse; there was no time to waste. He pointed to the dead guards. 'They must have theirs; take them, lock the door behind me.'

'General, there's a storm out; you'll die.'

Aracyse nodded. 'If it must be, it must be. You have your orders. Lock that door.' The guards nodded, although their eyes betrayed their unwilling to follow his command. Aracyse huffed, realising there wasn't time to elicit a guarantee from his directive. 'Nobody comes through!'

With the heavy cloak wrapped around his frame, Aracyse slipped through the portal and entered the outer chamber. The wind was furious; the gale blowing phantoms across his vision. It was dark, but there was a speck of light in the distance. A blue chemical flare moving away. He turned and gave one last order to shut the door, then stormed into the night.

He lifted the heavy cowl of the cloak and plunged into the snow. A thick fleece lined the inside of the hood; it provided some protection from the cold, but Aracyse hadn't dressed for the exterior, and the chill was penetrating. Large snow drifts had covered the icy path, and the distant blue light danced across the white. It was a trail for Aracyse to follow. Head down, he pushed forward at a frenzied pace. Without gloves, his fingers would freeze. He ruffled the cloak, pushing his hands inside; his grip tight on the hammer. The thick fur shielded him from the wind, but the permeating and bitter chill would not spare him for long.

It was ironic. The same obscuring snow blowing all around also illuminated his path; the white surface was the only thing to guide him toward the blue light. In the dark, he would be invisible, and hidden from view, he pushed ever faster toward the foe. There were three figures in a row, all skirting the face of the cliff. One carried the flare at the front, the other two following behind. Aracyse gave thanks for the small mercy that they had not taken the old pass. With his heart pounding in his chest, he pounced on the straggler at the rear. No warning given, Aracyse removed his hand from the cloak and brought his hammer crashing down on the hooded figure. One heavy blow to the crown, and he dispatched the murderous criminal in silence, the body crumpling to the ground. In his rage, Aracyse cursed his foolish impulse. They carried the stolen weapons; he had to be more careful. Onwards, he ploughed, and reaching the next thief, caution forced his hand. He brought his knee up high and thrust his boot into the bastard's back. A woman squealed as he sent her tumbling forward, and she crumpled into the snow. With her cry a brief echo against the storm, the last figure turned as the female scrambled to her feet. Aracyse lifted his hammer, holding it toward them.

He shouted at them; his voice a storm of its own. 'Give back what you've taken!'

Buffeted by the wind, the male thief called back. 'You'll not have these.'

Aracyse couldn't see where they stowed the Sprites, but the assailants hadn't denied their presence. He glanced from man to woman, trying to discern who carried the spheres. It would be wiser to share the load, especially in the hostile mountains. That was his concern. Whatever action he took now, he might cause the release of a Fury.

'This ends here,' Aracyse said. He knew his words were truth; the bitter cold was creeping into his bones. He stepped forward and saw the face of the man revealed in the azure light of the flare. A tattoo above his eyebrow; it was a slavers' mark from Kalleron. He had served the king to earn his freedom. It shouldn't have surprised Aracyse that such a man would find his way to the cult. 'You're a traitor!'

'General? By the gods, Velestra, it's Aracyse Stranghame!'

'Then you know this is over,' he said.

The woman paced backward as Aracyse took another step forward. She turned to her accomplice, saying something lost to the wind. This was his chance; their attention focused on one another. Aracyse lunged, but the woman reacted, shouting at the other.

'Go!' she said, pushing him to the edge of the pass. She brought a sword from her cloak and sidestepped Aracyse's blow. As the woman swung the blade toward him, he parried it with ease.

Again, she cried out. 'Now, Yerin. It'll survive!'

It'll survive?

A moment of confusion, and Aracyse understood. Yerin was about to jump; give his life that the Fury might survive. He reached toward the thief; a gesture, not an action, and Aracyse cried out.

'No!'

It was too late. Yerin lowered his hood; a pale smile illuminated in the blue glow, and he tumbled over the ledge. Aracyse made to lunge toward him, but it was a futile attempt; the dark had already swallowed the thief. The other swung at him, her sword battering into his heavy cloak. Unharmed, Aracyse turned. She withdrew a bundle of fabric from underneath her cloak, and with her weapon in the other hand, she displayed her prize. He stared at the spherical fabric ball, realised it had to be the other Fury. He had lost the advantage.

'We've got one now,' she said. 'This is spare.'

A soldier with dreams of glory would face a dilemma. How to survive that which was not survivable? Aracyse was immune to such problems. Ambition had lost its lustre; it had long departed his weary shores. He had served, and he would one day pay his penance. It was naïve to believe he could disarm the woman and retrieve the Fury. She had already shown her competence by dodging his feint attack, and after such limited time in the hostile grip of the Kulkarrons, a numbness was muddling his movement and grip. He laughed, looking at the woman's gloved hands. How warm they must be.

'The great General Aracyse, laughing?' she said.

'At least you came prepared.' A thought; if he was to die, there was something he wanted to know. 'Who killed my guards and workers? Who took the vault key?'

'That doesn't matter.'

It was a truthful response considering what treason they had committed. But he wanted to know. 'Tell me! A favour before death. Was it you?'

'No.'

'Your role in this?'

She tapped the bundle with her sword. 'Runner, I suppose.'

Aracyse took one step forward, his freezing legs slowing his pace. The woman's sword whipped up, the tip shaking one foot from his face. It was a wraith in the dim light cast from the snow. Aracyse knew if he didn't move now, he would die from the cold. Not a noble death. He raised the hammer, gripping it with as much force as his tingling fingers could muster.

He raised his voice above the blustery gale. 'You'll not win this fight.'

She dropped her sword to the ground and ripped the fabric shell from the Fury. 'No, I wouldn't imagine. But nor will you!'

The woman turned and hurled the glass sphere at the cliff face. Aracyse lost the Fury in the dark, although he thought he heard it smashing against the rock. He brought his arms to his body, expecting the worst; he had read everything there was to read about the weapon. Carnage was certain to follow.

Nothing happened. The wind howled; it sounded as though laughter.

Aracyse recalled the open vault. Had they taken an empty vessel? He focused; the few paces to the woman would be quick. He charged. She was quick, ducking to stoop and retrieve her sword. But she was too late, his hammer swinging down, her parry too slow. Where was the impact? Aracyse's arm flailed in the wind, unseen hands hoisting him into the air, flinging him into darkness. As though hit by tumbling boulders, he smashed into the cliff, landing yards along the icy path. Fortune appeared to be on his side; his return to earth was far from the precipitous drop. What had hit him? Dazed and confused, invigorated by the shock; Aracyse rose on unsteady legs. In the darkness, he heard the woman scream. A piercing and terrible cry cut short with a guttural groan. *The Fury*.

With only the path to guide him, Aracyse turned and stumbled back toward Etherus. Closer and closer he came; the gates emerging from the gloom. Pumping harder with his legs, his strength sapping in the icy chill, his steps hit the air as something lifted him into the sky. Tossed and swirled in nothingness, and with pain lashing his body, Aracyse neither cried out, nor did he fear what was happening. Death came to all men; and what better way to die than by *their* hand? With a brutal thump, he collided hard with the mountain and fell to the ground. Still, he survived. Why?

Uncertain where he was, Aracyse struck out with his hand, pushing against the ice. He crumpled as his arm collapsed under his weight. With a grunt, he forced his body up using the other, and stared at what remained of his bloodied left arm. He couldn't see his hand. Where fingers ought to have been, there was a flow of blood gushing onto the pristine snow. He laughed. Such a surreal sight; the senses numbed by shock and the freezing kiss of the mountain. Aracyse tumbled onto his back and stared up at the sky. It was coming for him.

She was beautiful. Not quite human, the form the elemental had taken was a mimic of what a girl should be. And though she had no flesh, angry wisps of white and blue defined her shape. Chaotic and alive, she was an orphan of the Wind. No longer the harmless Sprite; she was the Fury. It floated above, staring down at Aracyse. Why had it not finished the job? He was done; the blood loss, the cold. Aracyse Stranghame was already dead.

The child of the Wind continued to stare; the noise of the gale becoming ever more furious. Arcs of blue fire ripped across the pass as the child's form unravelled. It was as though daggers were drawing across his skin, but Aracyse would not cry out. This was what men of war deserved. Whether delirium, or guilt; he did not know, but through his pain, Aracyse said, 'For all we have done, I am sorry. This is *your* world.'

In an instant, the storm ceased, and the wind dropped; the last flurries of snow falling gently to the ground. The child, nothing but a voice on the breeze, laughed. A melody for the mountain.

She said, 'This is not my world.'

Darkness covered Aracyse's vision and his senses became a void. One last echo in the end; two words fading in his mind.

I am.

Chapter XI

'Can we talk?' Shadow asked.

Petra shifted her focus from the letter in her hand, lifting her head to greet him. 'Shadow. What is it?'

Framed in the cabin doorway, he appeared agitated, casting furtive glances over his shoulder. It wouldn't have surprised her if he proposed an illicit trade. Perhaps some hard narcotic he might have stowed away after the Hoydai trip.

'Can I come in?'

She gestured to the chair opposite, and Shadow strolled over, plumping his backside down with an extravagant sigh.

'Such drama,' she said.

Shadow pointed to the letter but said nothing. He didn't have to; she understood his silent question. Two days ago, they had left Laria Port as she had planned. They had sailed from the island on an easterly wind, passing the Barge Isles, a chain of small rocky plateaus protected by steep cliffs. Claimed by Laria, they served as offshore trading posts. Each major islet, of which there were five, was defended by Laria's most prized asset—a battleship. Great hulking vessels; naval artisans with forgotten knowledge had constructed them in previous centuries. Those industrious hands had crafted the hulls with Larissian timber, a rare wood derived from the Larian birch. It was stronger than darkwood, lighter than Tormelorian Pine. That tree was now so sparse, and the ships so massive, a decree cast down by successive Larian kings forbade further construction. But they served their purpose well; there was no other nation with a ship as powerful, or as invulnerable. The fleet, rumoured to number a mere dozen, had long protected Laria's interests from all threats.

Looking at the letter in her hand, Petra said, 'Have we not been over this?'

'If by "over", you mean you've told me bugger all, then yes.'

'What more can I tell you, Shadow? We're going to Kalleron, and I'm going to find out why Felicitra left this instruction for me to do so. There really isn't anything else to say.'

Shadow huffed. Petra smiled; his mannerisms often conjured the image of a petulant child. Quick to temper, stubborn, drawn to simple pleasures, and curious to the point of inviting danger, he had few social boundaries.

He said, 'But you'll promise you'll not get involved with the cult?' He sat forward, his face a contorted grimace. 'Look, I know Felicitra was knee deep in all that shit, but,' he pointed back and forward between the two of them, 'that's not really us, is it?'

'Because we're pirates?'

'Because we are.'

She shook her head. 'But we're not just pirates, Shadow. We trade, we sail; we're runners for other people's goods. We've conveyed messages to others, have we not?'

'So?'

Petra sighed. 'So, what harm is it to follow one more message?' She waved the letter. 'And what if this leads to another message? Aren't you curious, Shadow?'

'Nope.'

'You bloody are, you damn tool. If I put a box on my desk,' Petra lifted her finger, tapping it on the wooden top, 'and told you there was nothing in it, you'd not be able to stop looking at it. You'd still want to open it. You'd *need* to know. It's in your nature.' Again, she waved the letter. 'I'm confused why this has you so... irked.'

Shadow stiffened. 'Did you just say "irked"?'

She nodded.

'Who uses that word?' He pointed at the parchment in her hand. 'Is that in there? That's a stupid word.' He paused, a frown forming on his brow. 'What does it mean?'

'Irritated, annoyed.'

Shadow spread his palms to the ceiling. 'Then why not say so? But anyway, I'm not... irked. I'm concerned.'

It was a surprise to hear. Petra raising an eyebrow at his confession. 'You. Concerned?'

He nodded.

'The most I've seen you concerned is when you're served a shoddy pint, or you've found a new rash on your manhood.'

Shadow stared. 'That is a low bar.'

'It's the level you set for yourself.'

Shadow smacked his lips. 'I won't argue. But my concern isn't for my safety. It's for yours.'

Petra thought of the letter; of Felicitra's contacts. She shook her head. 'She wouldn't endanger me.'

Shadow waved an apology, his hands in a flurry. 'Oh, no, no, no. Not like that. Of course she'd not. But the place or the people she's sending you to? Even if it isn't the cult; do you think Kalle doesn't have eyes on it? I mean, it's naïve to think it operates with impunity.'

There was truth to his words. Petra hadn't considered that Kalleron would have spies everywhere. It was a paranoid state; as were all tyrant nations. Her willingness to hold on to Felicitra for just a little longer had clouded her judgement. This would be no stroll to an innocent and quaint house on the hill. She had been foolish, but it wouldn't deter her from following the letter.

'I'm still going.'

'Then let me come with you.'

Petra shook her head. Shadow's words had created an unease, although they had also confirmed her decision. 'If you're right, and you may well be, then it would be stupid to bring anyone else. No, this is something I must do alone.'

'Damn it, Petra. What if something happens to you?'

She smiled and spread her arms. 'Then all of this becomes yours.'

Shadow stared. His eyes narrowed as a silent vowel formed on his lips. 'What?'

'I'm serious. I have no family. This ship is all I treasure, and I know nobody more deserving than you to be shackled with the responsibility of looking after her and her crew.'

'Shackled? The way you say it, sounds like you're looking to offload troubles.'

Petra grinned, tried to imagine Shadow rallying a boisterous crew. 'You'd manage.'

'I could sail to Hoydai. I could sell the ship for...'

She slapped her hand hard on the desk. 'Don't even think about it! That's not funny Shadow.'

He said, 'So, don't let anything happen to you.'

She blew a huff into the air and stared at the ceiling. Caught in a daze, Petra didn't hear Shadow's words. 'What?'

'Seriously. You'd give the ship to me?'

Petra nodded. 'Yes. And I know you'd not sell her; not if I ask you to promise it.'

'What about the others? What about Argan? He's as good as number two around here. For all rank means shit on the Melody—yourself excepted—isn't he mentioned in the will?'

She laughed. 'There's no will, you daft bastard. It's what I say that goes. You know that; they know that. Besides, you've been with me the longest by a nautical mile. I think it'd surprise the others if I had any other decree.'

'I suppose.'

Petra sat upright, and for theatrics she tugged on her blouse, keen to appear serious for her idiot friend. 'Shadow?'

'Uh-huh?'

'Please understand, I have no intention of giving up on this ship, my crew, or our friendship? And as much as I mean what I say, when I tell you that this ship falls to you; I'm not letting go of her without a fight.'

Shadow smiled. 'Good. Then, after your silly business in Kalleron, what's our next business?'

Petra had already made plans. The ship needed specialist treatment; something she could only arrange through a contact in Dreyahyde. The aromatic resin she used to coat the walls of the cargo hold had lost most of its potency. 'I sent a runner from Laria two months back. Darsur should have enough T-resin by now.'

'Darsur? In Dreyahyde? Is it that time of year already?'

Petra nodded. 'Close enough.'

'Can't we get it anywhere else? I mean, it's Tormelorian pine, isn't it? Can't we sail up the Rivyn, get it direct?'

'That'd be much easier, but then we'd have to pay a hefty tax at Tormelor port. That robbery alone is three times what Darsur charges.' A grim thought occurred to Petra. Dark clouds drawing across her mind; images of ash and dust blowing on the wind. 'Besides, we'd need to sail past Arkalla. I don't much feel like seeing it. I've heard enough the past few days.'

'Me and my big mouth.' Shadow grimaced and shook his head.

'It's not your fault. It's just something I need to deal with. And it's difficult. Anyway, we'll sail the northern route, stop off at a few of the smaller ports. Hot sun, golden beaches. Pirate life, eh? Forget all of this shit.'

Shadow stared at her from across the desk. His gaze was intense; as comforting as the thought of those warm beaches, and just as distant. He said, 'It'd do us well to get away from things for a while. Places don't get much farther than Dreyahyde.'

'We could try Drohendrir if we want to stay on the west coast?'

'Well, if we're going to venture that far, how about that little town farther south? What was it called? You know the one.'

Petra delved into her memories; tried to recall which town he meant. It had been a long time since she had sailed so far south on Kalleron's western coast. Those were heady days, full of chaos and mayhem in the time before Felicitra. Days long past when they found pleasure in flesh and fight. How many lovers and casual affairs had Petra enjoyed before she had settled? Those were the days when she ventured south of Drohendrir. The memory brought a warm blush to her cheeks.

'I can't recall much, to be honest. It's a messy soup in my mind. Those days were manic.'

Shadow lifted his hand to his head, scraping his fingers through an unruly mop of black hair. 'I guess we were young. I just remember the energy and the enthusiasm; although, I'm not sure I remember much of what happened in those days. Not the detail, anyway.'

Petra nodded and thought of how reckless they had been. It was as though they were two souls seeking the fastest route to oblivion. Narcotics, alcohol, fighting, and encounters with any woman that dared look her way. Or his. Every day. They hadn't been proud times; perhaps it was better they hadn't returned. Had she stayed, there would never have been the blessed times with Felicitra.

Petra brought her hand to her face and snorted. 'That's where I stabbed you!'

Shadow appeared shocked; his eyes wide. 'Oh, my gods; I'd forgotten all about that.'

'Too much haze?'

'Far too much haze.' He appeared uncomfortable, pulling another grimace of guilt. 'What did I do again, exactly?'

Petra recalled the night. Another chapter of debauchery and drugs. 'I was in bed. Crashed out for the night. Hadn't even undressed. I felt hands on me, trying to get to private places. I can't remember when I knew, but I knew it wasn't a woman. I reached for the dagger in my boot and stuck it into somewhere. You yelled.'

Petra shook her head. The memory, although vague, was an anomaly. She remembered it with fondness. Not for what had happened, but for Shadow's absolute contrition in the following days. What could have triggered terrible memories of her father's mansion, instead, had revealed Shadow's genuine remorse.

He shook his finger. 'It wasn't your bed, I think. It was that bloody tavern; corridors like a fucking maze.' Shadow slapped his head. 'You remember Tavin?'

'Tavin?'

'Harbour worker, she was...'

Petra tried to recall the girl, but her memory was fuzzy. In her mind's eye, she saw long blond hair and delicate features, although she wasn't certain they weren't quite as Shadow remembered. She smiled. 'Tavin was a girl?'

Shadow squinted. 'That was a woman. I'm certain.' Shadow's doubt was plain to see; his finger tapping on the armrest. 'Anyway, they looked lovely; prettier than most ladies. She'd invited me up earlier that night; said to go to her room. I think. You were in the wrong bloody bed, the wrong room. How'd you even get in? I was ready for some carefree fun. I slipped in beside Tavin, but it wasn't them, it was you, and you bloody stabbed me.'

Not only had Shadow shown guilt beyond compare; Petra had expressed shock at her actions. In fairness, she thought in reflection, it would have only been a matter of time before such a confused accident would have occurred. Such was the frequency of their drunken malaise.

'Were they good days, do you think?' she asked.

Shadow grinned as the lovable idiot he was. 'They were definitely some sort of days. I'm amazed we survived it all.'

Petra pointed to his waist, where the dagger had punctured his flesh. 'It never gives you bother, does it?'

He pulled up his cotton shirt, revealing the small scar. One of many on his battle-hardened body. 'We'd had so much excess; I had some fat on me back then. It's all good. Mind, if we did that again...'

'Shadow!'

'I'm only saying: don't go stabbing me there again. It's not fat no more. I'm all man.'

Petra waved her finger at him. 'I still keep a dagger close. If the wrong fingers touch me, they're coming off.'

'It's lucky I leer at you from far away then, isn't it?'

'I'm going to dock your pay if you keep this up.'

'Pah! I'd just nick it from the hold.'

Petra leant forward, her elbows on the desk. 'I know you already do. It's why I pay you less than the others.'

Shadow rose to his feet, assuming a dramatic and exaggerated pose. 'Well, if this is how you're going to treat me, I'm leaving.'

'Close the bloody door when you do.'

With a flourish fitting for a theatre in Hoydai, he bowed at the door and shut it behind him. Petra stared, watching as his silhouette remained at the glass. A

85

smile on her face, she tapped her finger, waiting for the final curtain. Her patience rewarded; the door opened and Shadow peered through the gap.

'All jesting aside, captain. You know I've got your back.'

Petra nodded. 'I'm counting on it.'

After Shadow left the cabin, Petra stopped smiling and looked at the letter on her desk. With Felicitra gone, she could feel the turmoil rising within. That old and problematic trait. It was her defence of brutality against a heartless and violent world. Signs of it had shown in the past few days; behaviours that had raised eyebrows from the crew who had come after Felicitra's arrival. It was a person she didn't want to become. A ghost she thought she had left behind. The letter had offered her a means to find a purpose, and despite what she had said to Shadow, she kept all options open. And though that felt as a betrayal, she was counting on Shadow more than ever. He was the mirror of the past into which she stared; a place and time to which she had no desire to return.

Chapter XII

Petra stood ready with the gangplank as Argan pulled the mooring rope tight, tying it around the iron cleat on the dockside. Once secure, he moved toward Florent who, after years of floating as a butterfly on the Melody, had begun the harder graft of life aboard ship. She struggled with the other rope, although with Argan approaching, she appeared to find her skills and tie it off in time. Petra smiled; Argan stopping in his tracks as Florent threw a gentle insult his way. It was amusing to see the comparisons. Shadow had suggested the young woman's behaviours were mimicking his own.

'Florent, leave Argan alone.'

Florent smiled and waved back, pointing to her handiwork. Petra waited for her to return aboard, praised her, then gave Argan a surreptitious look, nodding for him to check the rope. He yanked on it and gave her a confirming nod. Petra strode to her cabin and stood in front of the door.

She called out to the crew. 'On deck!'

It was a necessity to brief them each time they docked. Every city in every nation had its own rules. There was a jutting anomaly with the city of Kalleron. It had few prohibitions, although it was worse that the laws appeared to be created at will by greedy justices. Transgressors of these arbitrary crimes, whose purses were too light, often found themselves sanctioned with harsh punishments. As the crew assembled, a dozen men and women shuffling on the deck, Shadow came alongside. Regardless of her stance on rank and order—there being none of it on the Melody—she still insisted Shadow act as her right-hand man. After him, Argan, the dedicated helmsman, stood in as ship's captain, and he was the last to join them, taking his usual position at the back.

'Listen up, everyone! If you hadn't noticed, or you didn't care,' Petra gestured to the city, 'we have arrived in Kalleron. Here we have typical continental weather: hot and dry, and we have an atypical continental culture: none.' Laughter rippled across the deck; she knew they understood her opinion of Kalleron's cultural deficit. 'This city is not your friend. Be aware and be wary. Punishments are harsh, and laws are unknown. Gamble with the wrong hand, and you could lose yours.' She looked at Shadow, pausing long enough to ensure that the crew was paying attention. 'Be careful who, or what, you choose to play with. Flesh is expensive here, or worse, it is stolen. There are slavers everywhere, watching for new blood, watching over their wretched hires. I would ask you do not pay for sex in Kalleron.' Petra pointed to the hilltop over-looking the western harbour. 'Unless you pay there. It's the only house in Kalleron that I know doesn't use slaves.'

A hand rose from the crowd. It was Jessika, Florent's partner in mischief. Petra pointed to her. Jessika asked, 'Is it safe to go ashore?'

Petra nodded. 'Stay clear of the eastern and southern docks. The western hills are associated with a higher class. Your only fear there should be of muggers. But don't assume you can handle them; the justices, or worse, the overseers, can come down hard on foreigners.'

Florent raised her hand, and Petra nodded. 'Captain, if it's so dangerous, why are we back here?'

'I have business I must finish. You can stay aboard if you feel safer. We'll have the kitchen stocked, and the ales filled. For those that go ashore, curfew is an hour past sundown. They toll a bell just before then; you'll know when to return.' Once more, turning to stare at Shadow, and with another ripple of laughter among the crew, Petra pointed to the gangplank. 'If you're not aboard by then, you're finding your own lodging.'

Shadow stood forward. 'Unless you're agile as a cat, and can make the jump.'

Petra hauled him back. 'But if you fall in, be aware the sewer outflow passes this dock. You'll have noticed the aroma, I'm sure? Questions?'

The crew mumbled; a dozen heads shaking in unison.

'Then, dismissed!'

Petra watched them moving from the ship, Florent and Jessika holding back. Shadow turned to face her. She said, 'You'll keep an eye?'

'On the girls?'

'Girls? They're women now.'

'Aye, but I've looked after them for years. Since Florent was... well, you know.' Shadow sculpted an hourglass figure with his hands.

'Since they were sand?'

He scowled. 'You know what I mean.'

She did. Florent, the younger of the two, was developing when they had found them. It had been after Thania's collapse almost seven years ago. Shadow glanced at Florent and leaned in close to Petra.

'I don't want to think of them as young ladies. You know I raised them, as far as I'm concerned, they'll stay girls forever.'

Petra frowned. 'You know Florent has...'

'Stop. Seriously, I don't want to hear it.'

It was hilarious; his inability to cope with the girls' maturity—their sexuality. It was a comforting irony that Shadow, for all of his debauchery and lust for life, was averse to the well of vice that was found in younger bodies or captive souls.

Petra said, 'Make sure they're alright, eh?'

'Aye, captain. And you, off to your secret meeting?'

She shook her head. 'Tomorrow. I think I'll need to wait until tomorrow. The message mentioned Kerscher. That is tomorrow, isn't it?'

Shadow hummed. 'We left Laria on Larastra. What's Larastra in Kalleron?'

Petra wasn't certain. She brought her fingers to her face, tapping each digit. Kalleron had an unusual six-day week. Not that it adhered to time as other nations. It didn't match up with Laria's calendar. Kalle, the immortal, had decreed time to be irrelevant. In her lifetime, Petra had known the city to reset the calendar several times. History, she had noted, was not of great importance to a King whose time was eternal. Of course, everybody understood that to be a lie.

'Wait, I think you're right,' Shadow said. 'Kerscher comes after Dorascher, yeah?'

'Uh-huh?'

'Five days since Laria.' Shadow displayed his thumb, followed by each remaining finger on his hand. 'That's Karsta. Pretty sure that matches Larastra. So, we've got Mehstra, Torastra, Ostra, and Strathalla. Is Kerscher the weekend?'

'Shadow, Kallerye weekends don't match those in Laria.'

'Oh, bloody hell.' Shadow turned away, his attention on the dock. 'Hey!'

A fisherwoman, walking past with a sizeable catch in her basket, peered back. Shadow asked, 'What day is it?'

The woman shrugged. 'Dunno, love. Maybe Dora?'

'Dorascher? You think?'

Another shrug. 'As good a guess as any.' She nodded a farewell and set off along the boardwalk.

Shadow sighed, turning around to Petra. 'Fucking useless. But if it is Dorascher, then tomorrow might be Kerscher.'

Petra smiled. 'Get used to it Shadow, remember, and you should bloody know, Kalleron has its own peculiarities. Time, or lack thereof, is meaningless.'

'Then why do they ring the night-time bell?'

She realised it was a strange exception. 'It's a harbour bell. Probably for safety after dark?'

'Makes sense, suppose.'

'Few things do here. Where are you off to, anyway? What haunt will have your pleasure today?'

Shadow lifted his head; Petra thought it might be an attempt at an aristocratic persona. Speaking down to her, he said, 'It certainly shan't be that awful hole of intelligentsia. What do you call it? Tarkin's, is it?'

Petra slapped his shoulder. 'It's not like that at all. But I suppose to someone with your bottom-feeding tastes, it's upper class.'

'Posh bitch.'

'Slum dick.'

Shadow feigned shock. 'Well, I'll catch up after curfew, if you'll have me for one in the cabin?'

'As long as you come back clean. The place is bad enough without whatever stench you're considering getting into.'

With an exaggerated inhalation, Shadow turned and pranced from the Melody. On the dockside, he bowed to her. 'You be careful. And no killing, you hear?'

Petra laughed and waved him off. Today would give her a chance to compose her thoughts. There was much to absorb, more to process. For all Shadow's wonderful distraction, Felicitra's letter was never far from her mind, but until she met the contact, she was certain to keep her nose clean.

Settled on the slopes of the western hills, Tarkin's Inn was a relief from Kalleron's grubby underbelly. Seated under a shaded canopy of woven birch, Petra sipped red wine and picked at dried meats. The view too good to waste, she had opted for the inn's pleasant and fragrant rose garden. Small colourful birds hopped along the old brick wall, often darting under the wooden tables to snaffle crumbs dropped by the relaxed patrons. It was a sanctuary to Petra; removed from the hustle and bustle of the busy port. High in the hills, she held a commanding view of the city and its primary features. Although the Bay of Kings swept in an extensive arc, with a second larger expanse of azure water farther west, the hub of the capital centred around the smaller eastern bay. The jutting outcrop that split the crescent of golden sand was home to the more affluent and well-to-do, although Kalleron's visible wealth appeared modest. The townhouses she had passed on her way to the inn were more reserved than those of Laria Port, or those she had seen in Arkalla.

Situated under the imposing eastern cliff face, the restricted harbour was home to Kalleron's local navy. Smaller vessels and light frigates bobbed gently in the calm waters. There were a few larger warships anchored farther out in the bay. Too distant to discern their names, Petra imagined their size would be impressive to those Kallerye who had never sailed the Larissian Sea. As mighty as these ships appeared in their own harbour, they were insignificant compared to the true leviathans of the sea.

The colossal fortress of Kalleron occupied the plateau above the harbour, where the rocky cliff merged into the imposing marble wall. Petra had always thought it unnecessarily tall, although a friend in Tarkin's had once informed her why it was so. Behind that vast structure, hidden from view of the world, were the elusive inner workings of Kalleron. A city within a city. The fortress was a boundary that reminded the port area of its master, and beyond that inscrutable wall, few knew the truths of the secretive realm. She had been told of a castle, perhaps a sprawling palace. Nobody could say for sure. Only those who had access to the inner sanctum of Kalle would know, but those people were loyal devotees to the King's cause, or they were the servants that lived their entire life in the fortress.

Petra stared at the gleaming white wall; one thing needling her mind. It was a stabbing thought that would not relent. The Terrible Queen of Kalleron, consort to the imposter immortal. Was she inside? Areya's description of Arkalla's demise was difficult to dismiss, no matter how hard she tried. It haunted Petra. The elemental was real, and her power was without compare. She had shown herself to be a murderous and evil creature that was beyond redemption, and although Kalleron was a city of dubious vice and corrupt justice, it appeared ignorant of what terror lay behind that formidable marble barrier.

A shiver rattled her body, when Tarkin's voice distracted her from the view. 'You're not cold, are you?'

From Thania, a refugee before its fall, Tarkin was a pleasant anomaly in Kalleron. He never dabbled in the sex-trade, and his patrons were quiet and reserved. Introduced to the inn by Felicitra, Petra had found the atmosphere serene and therapeutic. Although frequented by local justices, Petra understood that much of the inn's inflated prices went straight to their purses. Tarkin's cheerful face never appeared troubled by the informal tax. It had kept his business clean and free of unwanted scrutiny.

'Just some cold thoughts,' she said.

Tarkin paused, appearing to search the surrounds. 'Felicitra?'

Petra had known he would ask. She had not relished the moment. 'She travelled to Arkalla, Tarkin. She went to get her father. They didn't return.'

Tarkin sat down. He leaned forward, his voice quiet. 'That is dreadful. I heard of the fall. I am so sorry, Petra. But perhaps she...?'

She shook her head. 'It's better that I accept she's gone.'

'Perhaps something survived? No city can truly be destroyed?'

Petra lifted her head and looked into his eyes. He was offering false hope; she thought to remind him of the truth. 'And of Thania, Tarkin? What remained of it?'

He sighed. 'I know. I know. But without hope, what do we have?'

She nodded, looking once more across the bay, peering at the city below. The pretty sprawl of marble and pastel colours; hiding within it a den of illicit desire and powerful vice. Above it, there was a monster lurking behind secretive walls.

'Do you never think to leave?' she asked.

'And go where? I'm in my fiftieth year. I'm too old to rebuild a business.'

'You could retire? Travel away someplace.'

Tarkin laughed. He gestured to the beautiful surrounds. 'There are those whose extravagance is a sign of wealth. For me, Petra, my wealth is this extravagance. You know I pay more than my fair share to keep trouble away.' He pointed to her wineglass. A flawless and delicate piece of crystal. 'I buy the finest wines and serve the best food to bring in those with the most coin. But my profits only keep me fed. I have nothing to retire on.' He waved a hand toward the colourful roses. 'This is where I'll end my days. Perhaps someone will remember me and bury me among the flowers?'

'I never realised, Tarkin. I'm sorry. I thought of you as a man of luxury.'

'Yes, well, there's a clever trick to longevity in this place.'

Petra squinted, keen to hear his wisdom.

'Don't covet wealth. It'll only get you noticed.'

'Noticed?'

Tarkin pointed to the fortress. 'As it says above the main gatehouse, "None shall know glory, for glory is solely his".'

Petra had never paid attention to the motto, although its presence was visible around the city's civic landmarks. 'Just words, surely?'

'In Kalleron, you are welcome to spend your coin. Spend it all, if that is your desire. The city, as you know, caters to many, but consumption is the key.' Tarkin placed a silver coin on the table, his finger pinning it down. 'Kalle encourages excess in order that this finds its way to his glory. Kalleron absorbs wealth, it doesn't allow you to build it. Gambling, eating, drinking; think of all the vice, Petra. All of it is consumption; your wealth evaporates. It is what the city asks of its visitors. But woe betide the fool who builds a mansion in the hills.'

Petra cast her gaze back across the city. The modest stone houses now made sense to her. Nothing was too overt. Everything followed a common theme. Not one structure dared to stand apart from the rest. She'd never thought of it; never stopped to question why the city appeared so uniform. Yet Kalleron allowed consumption in excess. It leeched wealth from the rich; it robbed from business, and it all flowed into the fortress.

'A city of pretty boxes.' Petra waved a finger, directing Tarkin's attention to the hills above his inn. 'But what of the mansions farther up, the older ones?'

'The Mansion Hills?' He shook his head. 'All lie empty. From afar, they look pretty enough, but if you're unwise to wander too close, you'll see the decay.'

'Unwise?' Petra was to find her contact within the old mansion district. She wanted to know what Tarkin knew. 'How so?'

'Stupid tourists. They go there for the atmosphere. Like I said, it looks pretty enough from afar, but there are rough types up there. Prowling, waiting. There are also the justices to worry about; even they're not averse to robbing foreigners. If you're looking to visit, keep your wits about you. Not a safe place; not even for a woman as wily as you.'

'I'll bear that in mind, thank you.'

Tarkin nodded, standing up from the table. 'I'm truly sorry about Felicitra. I'll miss her.'

A glance to Tarkin before drawing away her gaze, Petra nodded. 'I know.'

Petra remained at Tarkin's until the sun's oppressive heat had eased. Not yet dusk; the hill overlooking the city cast its shadow across the bay. Fed and watered, and having endured enough introspection to bore the hardiest bard to death, she strode through the grubby western harbour as she sought a shortcut to the Melody. In the slums, she thought she might appear out of place. In Shadow's words, she had the look of a "poncy" sophisticated pirate. She wore a ruby-coloured corset pulled over her favoured, full length, white cotton dress. A Larian wedding garment, she had altered it to suit her tastes; adding sleeves to cover her arms. Beneath the decorative cuff, her tattoos were visible on the back of her hands. An old family tradition, the elegant and cryptic *Sanhe* script etched forever into her skin. She wore a black silk bandana on her head to prevent her skin from blistering in the heat. Under her dress, she favoured her black, thigh-high, soft-leather boots. It was her preferred armour; it was flexible and tough, and it also enabled her to carry her needle-sharp daggers, one sheathed and hidden in each boot. Strolling through the dust and grime, lifting the hem as best she could, Petra cursed her choice of path.

At a junction of high walls, with crates and barrels lining the gloomy alleys, Petra realised she was lost. She could easily retrace her steps, but she didn't want to travel over the unidentifiable mess through which she had already navigated. There had been rank odours she could only equate with diseased death. It had to be onwards. Indecision hampering her judgement, a noise disturbed Petra's focus. A yelp? The background murmur of the harbour, a muted bustle of conversation and occasional banging, obscured the sound. She listened again; it had sounded as though an animal. There it was; a child in distress? Her stomach churned. Petra knew what rotten things happened in this place. Uncertain from where the sound had come, she moved left. Again, she heard it. The child's whimpers from the other direction. Aware time was precious, and shutting out terrible thoughts of what might be, Petra bolted down the alley.

She emerged into an enclosed space shielded by the high warehouse walls. Broken crates and tattered rags littered the sides, and a single broken lamp stood useless in the centre of the rough square. On the other side, yards from Petra, two men stood at the entrance of a dark alley. Beyond it, Petra heard a faint but chilling sound. A girl's voice speaking above her tears.

'*I don't want to.*'

Dressed in muted fabrics that no doubt concealed their weapons, the men were slavers. They turned to her as she entered the square.

'Whore, begone! This is our contract.' The larger of the two said.

From the alley, a man's impatient voice slithered to her ears. 'I need more time!'

Petra thought she could deceive the deviant bastards; use her guile to get close. They had already assumed her profession; they'd salivate at the anticipation of her flesh. A flash of inner thigh above her boot would distract their feeble attention; allow her to get behind their defences, but she had no time for such measured luxury. With a flurry of her dress, she unsheathed her daggers. No time for fancy words or pompous threat; Petra charged. This time there had been no dratch; this time she would fight as her murderous father had taught her.

'Fuck me!' said the large brute.

He fumbled, struggling to retrieve the weapon hidden behind his jerkin. Petra darted to the side, moving away from the smaller man; speeding up her approach to the other. She was upon him as he pulled out a hatchet; a random thought in her mind—who the hell uses a hatchet? He swung it, but the metal edge sliced air; it was a clumsy weapon if wielded without skill. It was easy to dodge. Her speed was her strength, and Petra used it to drive the tip of her dagger into his belly. He yelled, but he was fat, the padding giving protection from the worst of the attack. He swung his axe again, and she leapt backwards, withdrawing her blade from his gut. With a grimace and a rumble, he marched toward her. Petra glanced to the side; the other man was approaching, swiping the air with a short-sword. She had no time to waste. Her arm raised, hurling her hand forward, Petra released the blade. It spun through the air, missing the intended mark. She had aimed for his eye, instead; it pierced his cheek, lodging deep in his mouth. He screamed and ceased his advance, clutching at his face.

A violent jolt launched Petra into the air. A kick? She tumbled to the floor, rolling to absorb the impact. On her feet in an instant, she grabbed the dagger which had fallen from her hand. The big man was impressive; his bulk belying his speed. He had begun his charge, but she was where she wanted to be. Crouching low as he closed in, Petra leapt forward, her dagger held close. With supreme focus, she aimed for his groin, and as his attack sliced down, her blade plunged deep into soft tissue. His scream was tremendous; a blood-curdling, high-pitched howl. As a tower, he collapsed, and she leapt on top of him, plunging her dagger down and stabbing him in the temple. One down, but the other, blood spouting from his check, was coming at her again.

His injury was severe, and although he had pulled the dagger from his face, the puncture had weakened him. Garbled words and ribbons of blood came from his mouth; something gory about *fucking* and *witch*. He swung his sword. Not even close to the mark; it was a defensive swipe. Petra looked to the alley. All was quiet from within. Time—she had none of it left to waste. She advanced on the grotesque, blood-drooling bastard, avoiding his slicing blade with ease, and with a deft lunge, she stabbed him through the heart. He collapsed dead on buckled knees. Without hesitation, she grabbed her other dagger and ran to the alleyway. Invigorated by the fight, her confidence turned to nausea as she thought of what she might find. What Petra knew for certain was that she would deliver misery to the man who had bought a contract for this depravity.

The dark alley was quiet. Not a sound from child nor man. Cluttered with barrels and crates, it was an ideal place to hide. Petra focused, trying to hear the slightest noise. There was a breath. An attempt to hide? She recognised the shallow and rapid inhalations. A tentative step forward, daggers held out, she moved to confront the sound in the shadows.

'Come out. Your slavers are dead. Show yourself; let the child go and you can leave unharmed.' A lie to lure her prey; she had retribution in mind. A noise ahead. Something disturbing a crate. It wouldn't surprise her to see a child being dragged into the grim light. A hostage to a degenerate wretch. But it was a lone child that stepped into view. A girl, perhaps adolescent. It was hard to tell; her dark hair was a dirty and dishevelled mess obscuring her features. She wore a pale blouse which was open at the neck, the loose and torn fabric evidence of a struggle. A cotton panelled skirt did little to cover the flesh of her legs; the flimsy fabric hanging in unstitched vertical sheets. They had dressed her to be seen. Yet this young girl appeared fierce. A caged beast, her eyes were wild. She pulled something shiny from the ground—a short scrap of metal—and held it out toward Petra.

Her hand shaking, she said, 'Stay back, you hear? I'll have you!'

'Sis?'

A second voice. There was another girl hidden from view. Petra stepped backwards, careful to remain out of range. She'd be a fool to let her come too close. Street girls were notoriously dangerous. With such little hope, they lived on the periphery of constant struggle. Fight or flight aggression was a requirement to survive.

'I'm not here to harm you,' Petra said, putting her daggers back into their sheaths. 'See, I've put them away.' She pointed back at the square. 'The men back there, they can't harm you now. Where is the other one?'

The girl squinted. 'You a justice?'

It was a laughable thought, but Petra knew not to let it show. 'Me? No, child. A sailor.'

'Sis, is it safe?' The hidden girl. Why had she not come out?

Petra stepped back again, keen to show she was no threat, although she kept her focus on the girl with the makeshift dagger.

'Stay there, Thelia,' the girl said.

'Thelia?' Petra looked at the shadows. 'That's a nice name.' A hand to her bosom, she introduced herself. 'I'm Petra. What's your name?'

The girl stared beyond Petra. 'Where's Plank and Oaf?'

'Plank and Oaf?'

'It's what we call 'em. Where are they? You said they'd not harm us no more. What's that mean?'

Petra preferred honesty with children. Good or bad, it prepared them for the reality of life. 'I killed them. I stabbed one in the head, the other in his heart, if he had one.'

The girl's eyes sparkled; the fierceness gone. Was that hope?

'Dead?' she asked.

Petra nodded. She imagined what she couldn't see. 'The other man. Where is he?'

'Sis?' the hidden girl said again.

'Thelia, hush!'

'I can help you,' Petra said. 'But we must leave here. If they find the bodies, it'll be more than a slaver coming for us. We need to go; where is the other one?'

'You'll look after us?'

'Yes. If you'll let me.'

The girl turned to the crates. 'Come on out, Thelia.'

Another child appeared from the gloom. Much smaller, she was far younger. A torn white dress, ripped in ugly places, covered her modesty. Petra winced, said to the girl, 'Where's the man that did that?' She struggled to control it; the old impulse rising to the surface. Rage causing her to tremble.

The young girl, Thelia, perhaps six or seven years-old, held out a silver blade. It was the same size as a butter knife. Petra stared at it; it *was* a butter knife. Thelia shook her head. 'He never touched me, miss, I promise. I didn't want him to... so I...' She showed her the knife, offered it to her. Petra, too far away to take it, saw the crimson edge.

Petra's smile was involuntary. 'You cut him?'

The older girl said, 'She had to. Bad one, he was. Thelia's still proper, not like me. But she didn't mean it. You'll not turn us in, will you?' The older girl held her weapon firm, pointing it with intent. 'I'll not let you turn us in.'

Petra shook her head. 'You did a brave thing. A good thing.' Then to the other, she said, 'But we're in danger. Is the other man still here?'

Shifting her stance, the older girl pointed back to the alley. Petra nodded, careful not to alarm her. 'May I see?'

Without dropping her guard, the girl side-stepped toward Thelia, allowing Petra to pass. She paced to the end of the alley, and in the gloom, she saw a man slumped against the wall. Clutching his bleeding neck, he was fading into unconsciousness.

'Help me!' His breath was a gurgling wheeze.

Petra knelt beside him and leaned in close. She spoke to him in a whisper. 'I'd take your balls and let you live, but you've heard my name, and I'm after no trouble.' She pulled her dagger and pressed it against his chest. 'Look at me.'

His eyelids flickered, and she wasn't sure he saw anything, but Petra stared and slowly pushed the knife into his heart. When it was over, she rose from the body and turned to the girls, expecting them to have fled. They hadn't moved; both stood staring at her, Thelia shielded by the older girl. They appeared so similar.

'Sisters?'

A nod.

'Well, Thelia, you didn't kill him. Just enough to stop him. I killed him; you stay innocent—you understand?'

Thelia nodded, her head poking out from behind her sister.

'And your name?' Petra asked the other. 'If I'm to help you, I'd like to know your name.'

'Thelissa.'

'Thelissa, Thelia; I'm going to make this better. But we have to move fast. Will you help me?'

Thelissa glanced at her sister, whose wide saucer eyes peered back from her bobbing head. The older girl agreed, and Petra explained what they had to do next.

Chapter XIII

Petra arrived at the Melody with a hurried pace. A beautiful and dark blue sky overhead, the brightest stars were already sparkling. Noctyrne and Ambyr were climbing on the northern horizon, and all appeared at peace with the world. A glance to the two girls in tow, and Petra fumed at the vile contrast between the heavens and the city. Kalleron was a sordid kiss from diseased lips. As she approached the gangplank, Argan appeared at the deck rail.

'Petra?' His eyes were on the girls.

'Who's that?' Thelissa said, backtracking from the plank, her hand tight on her sister's.

Petra noticed Thelissa's eyes; wide and wild. 'That's Argan. He's one of my crew. A good man.'

The older girl didn't move, pulling Thelia back and stepping in front of her. 'He's bloody big.'

Petra turned and knelt down. 'And he'll smash anyone that comes after us.' She swivelled her attention to Argan. 'Won't you?'

His eyes tracked onto her blouse. 'Yes, of course. Are you injured?'

She looked at her white sleeves; blood spattered across the arms. 'It's not mine; nor theirs.'

'I promise, little ones, you're safe here,' Argan said.

Petra didn't want to force the girls to come aboard; she couldn't. They had to do so by their own free will, but she had to make the reality clear to them. 'What happened in that alley, what I did to those men; the justices will find them, eventually. People talk and purses are loose; they'll know what they were, what they were doing. They'll be looking for two young girls. Are you known?'

Thelissa frowned. 'Known?'

What could she say? The older sister was a victim of abuse. How could she ask what those men might know? A creak from the plank, and Argan appeared beside her. Thelissa appeared frozen, both her hands pushing Thelia out of view.

Argan said, 'I'll stay ashore tonight if you want the girls on board?'

It felt wrong to accept his offer, but time was of the essence. 'Argan, I can't ask that of you.'

He smiled and walked away. 'You haven't. And I'll only be down here. If anyone comes calling, looking for those two, I'll send them away.'

Thelissa's rigid posture slumped, her eyes focused on Argan walking down the boardwalk. Thelia peeked out from behind, her tiny fingers gripping her sister's waist.

'Ow! Let go,' Thelissa said, swatting Thelia's hands. 'Little claws!'

Thelia, staring at Argan, said, 'He's a good man?'

'One of the best. Actually, there's only one other man I'd trust more.'

'But he's so big,' Thelissa said.

'He's from Bruhada. They're all tall over there.'

'Bru-where?'

'Hundreds of miles west. You've never seen a Bruhadian?'

Thelissa shook her head. 'Do they come here?'

'To Kalleron?'

The girl nodded. 'Never seen the like of him.'

It hadn't occurred to Petra. She thought back to all the times she had visited the city; most of it spent arranging trade or relaxing at Tarkin's. Most folk in Kalleron had tanned skin, the sun-kissed continent blessing all by varying degrees. Even Petra could darken her Larian looks with enough exposure. And although the colour of its people didn't define the nation, Bruhadian's were a shade darker, even without the sun's touch. But it wasn't their skin that set them apart; it was their build. And yet Petra couldn't recall seeing many in the city. If any at all.

'I suppose they don't like it here,' she said.

'I'm sorry we made him go away, but...' Thelissa fell quiet; her head dipping down.

Petra hadn't yet laid hands on the girls, neither to check them for injury, nor to lead them from danger. With care, she brought her hand to Thelissa's chin, and with the gentlest touch from the tip of her finger, she applied the smallest pressure to lift it up.

She brought Thelissa's eyes to meet her own. 'Hey. What you've known is gone. If you come aboard, I can try to work things out. But I promise, Thelissa, I'll not let any harm come to you. Just like in that alley; I'll protect you. Do you believe me?'

Thelissa nodded.

'Before you come on board, understand this,' she pointed down the boardwalk at Argan, who had lowered himself against a post and appeared to be meditating. 'Argan is one of my crew. I need him. Not tonight, but he will come back. All right?'

The smallest nod. 'Tonight though?'

'Tonight, he'll stay guard. Keep the bad people away. You'll be safe here while we figure out what to do.' Petra stood from Thelissa and turned to the gangplank. She gestured to the Melody. 'The captain would love to have you aboard her ship.'

Thelissa's eyes widened. 'Who's she?'

Petra smiled. 'I am.'

'You said you were a sailor?'

'And I spoke of my crew.'

Thelia nodded, said to her sister, 'I heard that, sis. She did.'

The slightest grumble came from Thelissa. She turned to Thelia and said, 'Come on then, trouble.' Her eyes scanning all over, she led her sister across the plank and stepped aboard the Melody of the Sea.

Petra wiped the tears from her eyes, dabbing them away with her handkerchief. Seated at her desk, she waited for the girls to emerge from her washroom. Not the largest space, but enough for a tub and commode; she had given them some spare rags and told them to clean up. Having boiled up enough water for a lukewarm and shallow bath, she had left them alone. At first, it had been hysterical; their voices travelling through the wooden panels. Thelia, her whispers louder than she probably imagined, had asked Thelissa if the tiny tub, which Petra assumed was the toilet, was for her feet, and if so, why was the other tub so big? It was clear from their babbling that neither had known any creature comforts. Perhaps the rivers and streams, or even the ocean, being all they had known for hygiene. But Petra's joy at hearing their innocent chatter had turned to grief to hear Thelissa's words. Nothing said to upset her sister, but inferences of things done. How she couldn't get clean enough, no matter how hard she rubbed away the dirt. The smallest echoes of pain coming through the wall. Thelia had not experienced what her sister had; that much had become clear in Petra's short time with the girls. What Thelissa had known, however, and what brief mentions came from hushed whispers in the washroom, told of too much. Yet it spoke of another truth; Thelissa was a warrior. She had absorbed the worst of everything to protect Thelia.

Thelissa appeared from behind the door. She stepped into the stateroom, wearing a blue cotton dress with a dark cloak slung over her shoulders. Although the dress was too long in the hem, she appeared content with her new outfit.

'Are you crying?' she asked.

Petra wiped her face. 'No. Just tired.'

'Oh, should we leave? Let you rest?'

'No, no. I'm all right.' Petra gestured to Thelissa's new attire. 'We can have that dress fixed so you don't trip up. But I think we'll get some other clothes for you.'

Thelissa's expression changed. Uncertainty clouding her features. 'But, miss, I've got no money to pay for nice things. They don't give me none.'

Another stab of reality. It angered her as she fought back the tears. Confronted by Thelissa's plight, she was struggling to stay in control. Too much emotional wreckage, hers and the girls', and she was floating among the carnage. Petra forced a smile to her face. 'Thelissa, you'll not need to pay. I'll get you some clothes for you and your sister.' She paused, peered at the washroom door. 'Where's your sister?'

On cue, Thelia appeared. She had opted to wrap herself in a red cotton blanket as though ready for bed. It wasn't the most practical choice, but the younger sister appeared happy with her simple outfit.

'Are you buying us clothes?' Thelia asked.

Petra nodded. 'Yes. We'll sort that tomorrow.' She waved over to her bed, then to the chairs at the desk. 'Sit where you please.'

Thelissa glanced at the soft bed and walked straight to the chairs. Thelia strolled to the bed and fell onto it. A warm smile returned to Petra's face as Thelia tossed and turned and fidgeted some more until she lay on her side, propping her head on her little hand.

'Are you a princess?' the girl asked.

'Me?' It amused Petra, but she tried not to laugh.

Thelissa spoke. 'We were talking, me and trouble, and we reckon you're not a captain at all. Think you're a princess. Are you? Cos only princesses have this sort of stuff.'

It wasn't something she'd ever been called, except perhaps as a misplaced expression of desire. She shook her head. 'I'm no princess.' She waved her hands at the cabin. 'This is all from trade. It's what we do aboard the Melody. My father had money, and I had fair claim to some of what he kept hidden aside; just enough to get this ship. Needed work, but it's got me here. No, all of this is hard-earned.'

Thelissa pointed at Petra's blood-stained blouse. 'You took on Plank and Oaf?'
'Plank and...? Oh, yes.'
'By yourself?'
Petra nodded. She looked at her sleeves, at the dark blotches. She frowned. 'Why?'
'They weren't sops. Plank was a tough bastard, real mean.' Thelissa squinted. 'How'd you beat them?'

Why lie? Thelissa deserved truths. Petra reached to the daggers in her boots and pulled them out. She held them clear for both girls to see. 'My father was... well, he was a very complex man. He had to fight to defend what he made for himself. Racked up a lot of enemies through the years. He taught me to fight, and he taught me well; showed me how to use a knife when I was young.' She pointed to Thelia. 'As young as you. By the time I was your age,' now pointing to Thelissa, Petra nodded her head, 'I knew how to kill any man.'

A sigh of wonder came from Thelissa. 'Did you? I mean, have you?'
Petra frowned. 'I did, today. Remember?'
'Yeah, sis,' Thelia called from the bed. 'Remember?'
Thelissa slapped her crown. 'Of course. I was just... your story. Can you tell us more? I don't really know stories. You tell them good.'

Petra smiled, wondering if Thelissa could see how false it was. It took all of her composure not to let slip more tears. Every fresh piece of Thelissa's puzzle was a brutal reminder of how cruel her life had been. To not recall the vivid trauma from hours earlier was abnormal, although Petra had seen that same behaviour in hardier souls. A frightening thing she had encountered after bloody and lethal combat. It was the mind shutting everything out. There was a harsh truth to come. If the older sister was to find some peace in her future; she would have to deal with her past. But not tonight.

'What story would you like to hear?' Petra asked.
'Anything,' Thelissa said, leaning forward in her chair, her eyes fixed on Petra with an intense stare. 'Anything about anywhere, far away from here.'

How long since the harbour bell had chimed? Petra waited on deck, hands on the rail, her focus on the boardwalk. The night was warm and calm, far removed from the wind and chill of Laria. It should have felt pleasant, but everything about the place was unsettling; a growing unease building inside. She had checked on

Shadow's bunk, not surprised to see it lay empty. Would he return tonight, or was he skin deep in an unholy mess? Thelissa's response to Argan had been telling, and although Shadow was morally proper in the presence of children, Petra thought the girl might misread his carefree public persona. Ready to return to her cabin and lock the door for the night, she saw him approaching.

Shadow strolled up, stopping on the boardwalk; a confused frown to greet her. He pointed with his thumb, directing her attention down the dock. 'Why is Argan fishing with his mind?'

'What?'

'He's squat down and meditating; like a priest from... well. Why's he doing that? Why's he down there?' Shadow pointed to the open gap between dock and ship. 'Am I jumping?'

'Curfew was hours past. You're jumping.'

'Fine.'

With uncanny grace, Shadow leapt to the Melody, grabbing the rail and vaulting aboard. Petra smiled. He made it look so easy, yet she had seen others try; and fail. It was usually crew members, either goaded by Shadow, or having had placed a wager against him. She thought of the meditating giant at the end of the dock; Petra had forbidden Argan to try, fearful his grip might damage the rail.

'So, Argan. What's that about?'

How to explain? Petra was aware Shadow might not take kindly to her charity. Having taken Florent and Jessika aboard at Thania, and after much protestation, he had mentored them at her request. Although Petra hadn't yet decided what she was going to do with Thelia and Thelissa, she was certain Shadow's reaction would be negative.

'Remember Thania?'

Shadow pinched his thumb and forefinger together. 'Narrow it down?'

'Florent and Jessika?'

A shrug. 'Uh-huh?' His focus shifted; becoming more alert, his eyes widened. 'They're all right?'

Petra waved a hand to placate his concern. 'They're fine, Shadow. They're aboard.'

'So?'

Petra, still in her bloodied dress, stood and waited. She had kept it on for a reason. Shadow often reacted to non-verbal cues better than he did with words. She folder her arms to bring them closer to his view.

He pointed at them. 'That's not wine.'

'No.'

'Oh, for fuck's sake, Petra. What did I say to you? Didn't I say it? No killing.'

'It couldn't be avoided this time. Come on, let's talk.'

Shadow made to stroll to her cabin, but she stopped him. 'Not in there.'

'What? What about our drinks?'

She pointed to the foredeck steps. 'Sit.'

He stared, eyebrows raised. 'Is that an order?'

She nodded. Shadow huffed and walked over, lowering his rear and sighing as he did.

'I'm not going to like this, am I?'

Petra sat down beside him and relayed the story of her entire day, thinking it best to break him in with boredom. He waved her past the humdrum of Tarkin's Inn, but leaned in when she told him of the slavers. As she described more, and spoke of the girls, his face contorted through various grim expressions. She took her time. When she spoke of Thelissa's trauma, she did so with a deliberate pace to avoid ushering in her own turbulent emotions. When she finished, she gave Shadow a moment to absorb it all. His head shaking from side to side, he leant back into the steps. All he appeared able to do was sigh.

Petra joined him, huffing her breath into the night air. 'It was all I could do.'

'Girl, you done good. Younger one's all right?'

'Not been touched.'

'The other, Thelissa, you said? She's...'

'Very damaged.'

'Fucking bastards.' Shadow bumped the wooden boards with his fist. He looked at her. 'So... we know anyone, anyplace that'll take them in?'

'In Kalleron. No.'

Petra had already decided on the immediate course of action. They would stay aboard; the streets of Kalleron wouldn't be safe once the slavers' bodies were discovered. 'They can't go back out, not yet.'

'Of course not.'

'They'll stay awhile. We can bunk them with Florent and Jessika.'

Shadow shook his head. 'That'd not be fair on the girls. Give me a plump tarp and I'll take wolfy down the cargo hold. I can sleep there; they can have mine for a bit. The resin's not been done, so the fumes shouldn't kill me.'

Petra smiled. 'Put you with the goods?'

'Best do an inventory for each night I'm there.' He peered past her shoulder, looking to the unseen dockside. 'So, what about Argan?'

'That'd be Thelissa. When we came aboard, or were about to, he appeared on deck. Thelissa's not seen a Bruhadian before. At least, not a man.'

Shadow's brow crumpled. 'You kicked him off?'

'Gods no! He volunteered; I'd never consider asking that of him. Of any crew.'

Shadow nodded, puffing a breath from his lips. 'The man's a gentle giant. She'll come around.'

'I told her; if she's staying past tonight, she'll need to accept the crew. All of them. It's why I wanted to speak to you before you met them.'

'What? Why?'

Petra stared at him. 'Seriously?'

'Huh?'

She slapped his shoulder. 'You've got a dirty mouth, and you're not very subtle about your love of vice. I offered the girls a seat on the bed or on the chair. Thelissa practically ran from the bed. When I left them in the cabin, Thelia was playing in the sheets, but Thelissa was dosing off in the hard-back chair. I don't think she considers a bed a place of rest. It's awful. You'll need to...' She pointed between Shadow and herself. 'We'll need to tread lightly for now. She's in need of some mending.'

Shadow stood up, patting down his hemp trousers. He walked to the starboard rail and leant on it. He appeared to focus on nothing in particular, the bay wide and empty. Petra joined him, coming to his right side. She stared at the water, rippling with blue and amber accents, and sighed.

'Why do I attract them?'

Shadow huffed a shallow laugh. 'The tragic?'

'Aye.'

'Broken knows broken, Petra, but we know what's broke can be fixed.'

Troubled thoughts inside her head, reflecting on the evening with the girls, Petra wondered if Thelissa was beyond repair. 'Maybe some things are too far gone?'

He grumbled and shook his head. 'You think of us, Petra. We've all got our secrets, but what we know for certain is that we're all broken. Huh? Now, you think we're beyond fixing? Am *I* beyond repair?'

She shook her head. With Felicitra gone, she needed her friend more than ever. The thought of Shadow not being part of her life was painful. 'I don't consider you broken.'

Shadow turned. His gaze was intense but warm. 'I'm not broken because I've got you to keep me fixed. Like all of us on here. Truth is, I can't think or dream that there's another ship or another captain out there that'd be able to fix me. Fix any of us.'

Such warm words. Unusual for Shadow to be so open. Sparing with compliments, generous with insults; she knew it was a shield for his own dark past. Shades of grim confessed in drunken ramblings that she had never sought to question.

'Then, you think we can help Thelissa?'

Shadow lifted his gaze toward the moons, his skin cast in the glow of Noctyrne and Ambyr. 'If you can fix me, Petra, you can fix this whole fucking world.'

Chapter XIV

I can fix this.
 A voice floating in the ether. All around there was a disturbance, but he couldn't see any of it. A discoloured darkness clouding Aracyse's vision. They were troubling noises, whispered and frightened. What scared his people? Whatever it was, he had to awaken; he had to help them. Aracyse tried to move, but he could not. There was nothing with which to move. His senses were numb; he had no legs, felt no arms. All he could do was endure the nightmare. What wicked dream was this?

Bone saw, fetch me the bone saw. The same voice. *I'll need more Vallacyne. No, much more than that.*

Aracyse's world rocked in the darkness. The clarity of sound faded; a rasping noise to replace the chatter. As rat's teeth gnawing on wood, the sound began as an irritation, but it grew louder, and with it, the dark place tugged at him. Wolves now, canine teeth hacking into flesh and bone; that was the sound. The voices returned. A new anxiety in the void.

Doctor Anders, Doctor Anders?

A final tug in the dark. His body lurched and something fell away.

A jar, I said, put it in a jar. We'll want to study that. The voice shouted, angry in the fog. *Where's that bloody Vallacyne?*

The pain. It was the searing pain that forced his eyes open. His left shoulder was on fire, his vision obscured by a haze. Trying desperately to claw at his arm, Aracyse could only stare at... where was he? Confusion addling his mind, the murk in his eyes blocking his sight. The pain! He cried out, but didn't yell; he couldn't hear his own words. What new horror was this?

Dr Anders? He's awake. General Aracyse is awake!
No, no, no. Too early; he'll not survive. You know what to do.
Vallacyne? But...
He'll die if we don't. Do you want to be responsible for his death?

The voices faded. A wave of ice washing over, the fire extinguished, replaced by a freezing chill. Aracyse knew this sensation; a barren battlefield, somewhere high and cold. He tried to find the place he knew. Tried to fight the numbing ice that had crept into his brain. What about his soldiers? What of them? Had they survived? Where was...

'Dr Anders? I think he's ready.'

'Then best bustle off. Go on, shoo; away with you. He'll not want gawping. He'll need time to adjust.'

The voice. Aracyse knew it. Anders Beriafal: a genius from the fortress of Kalleron. Was that where he was? The fog was frustrating, his vision incomplete. A sensation in his left shoulder of stabbing pins and needles.

Anders? he tried to say. A mumble was all he heard.

'General Aracyse, don't try to talk, do you understand? You're on an exceptionally high dose of medicinal Vallacyne. It's Anders. I've had to operate on you; you've had quite an experience.'

Operate? Vallacyne? That was a lethal toxin. Aracyse tried to think why Kalleron's chief surgeon would try to poison him.

Vallacyne?

'All I'm hearing is vowels, General. Didn't I just say, don't talk? I'm going to put some Yverelyn to your nose. I want you to inhale. This isn't common street trash; it's not Ambyr Dust. This will counter the Vallacyne. You'll regain your vision and some limited control of your muscles.'

Aracyse felt something brush his face. He inhaled.

Anders sounded disappointed. 'That's my sleeve, General. I've not got it yet. Hold on.'

The fog was lifting without the Yverelyn, and although his vision and movement were null, his mind was clearing. His first thought of any real clarity: he'd want to talk to Anders about his bedside manner.

'Here we are,' Anders said. 'Now, inhale, General. Snuff it all up.'

Aracyse inhaled. The effect was instantaneous, as though the chemical had travelled straight to his brain. The ceiling came into view and he recognised the surrounds. The infirmary at Etherus. How many workers had he given a final salute to in this grim room? Aracyse tried to peer to the side, but the movement was not there.

'Yes, General, I said limited. I need you to be still. You'll be able to speak in a moment or two.'

A mumble from his mouth.

'A moment.' Anders' voice was impatient.

It was a strange thought that caused Aracyse to smile; at least, he thought he might be smiling. Anders' manners were not lacking; they were absent. A hazy recollection of his first introduction. The engineer and surgeon, informally known as a sorcerer, had seemed disinterested in the General. That alone had intrigued Aracyse. Anders' disregard for authority and power had alienated him inside the fortress. Yet Kalle had exiled him to Etherus to assist in the operations. Not an easy man to befriend, let alone tolerate, Aracyse considered the man to be indispensable. Although there was a barb in the back of his mind, what had Anders done to his body? What injuries had he incurred in battle?

'Try now,' Anders said.

With effort, Aracyse spoke. 'The others?'

'Others?'

'Why I'm here, the battle?'

Anders' bald head loomed into view; a pale, fleshy moon overhead. His wrinkled countenance staring down, Aracyse thought he appeared gentler than his nature suggested. His large brown eyes squinted. 'There was no battle, General.'

'My injuries?'

'You don't remember? My, my; that's fortunate.'

Aracyse puzzled over Anders' reply. How could he find anything favourable in his incapacitation? 'What happened?'

Anders frowned. Aracyse doubted it was concern. The bald head bobbed out of view, and after a moment, his voice travelled from across the room.

'The Fury, Aracyse, do you not recall?'

'Fury?'

Aracyse stared into the cloud that was his memory. There was nothing to guide him; no hint of what had come before. 'It's all grey. All I can see is... Franklin. Some spirit. Nothing else.'

It occurred to Aracyse that his friend may have visited. Perhaps shooed away earlier? Anders was in charge of the infirmary; he could dismiss who he pleased. His thoughts disorganised, Aracyse recalled what Anders had just said. He had mentioned a Fury.

'Was there an accident?' Aracyse thought of General A'dan and his unfortunate demise. 'Is Franklin involved? Does he have things under control?'

'General, you mustn't be alarmed.' Anders came back into view. So too, did a copper needle; an exquisite surgeon's tool. A delicate glass vial with a plunger, the device injected liquified herbs and drugs through the fragile, rolled-metal tip. Too expensive and rare for use on common folk, physicians reserved it for the King and those he deemed worth saving. Aracyse was one such subject.

'Anders, what's happened?'

The tip of the copper needle dribbled a bead of yellow liquid and then disappeared from view. Anders appeared to focus for a moment. 'There. That should do.'

'Anders?'

'You should rest again, General. You'll need all of your strength for what's to come.'

'Anders!' Aracyse's frustration rose within, although a rush of warmth and relaxation smothered his temper. 'Damn it, man, I order you to tell me. I'll have you jailed.'

Anders leaned closer to Aracyse, a smile on his blurring face to accompany his shaking head. 'No, General, in time, you'll thank me for what I've done. Now rest.'

Aracyse stared straight ahead. Anders was pacing back and forth; for once, the surgeon appeared apprehensive. In the infirmary, Aracyse had ordered everyone out. Seated on the end of his bed, he reflected on what Anders had said to him. Medicated to a lesser degree than before, although still on a high dose, the pain in his arm was excruciating. There was worse to deal with; the growing recollection of Franklin's death and Etherus' infiltration had shaken Aracyse. Greater than all of that, he waited with morbid anticipation for Anders to bring the mirror. Not yet able to turn his head to the left, and with his right arm bandaged, he could neither see nor feel what sorcery his surgeon had performed.

'Explain again, Anders, and bring that bloody mirror.'

Anders moved to the corner of the room. From there, he wheeled out a tall mirror housed in an ornate wooden frame. Aracyse had thought it an odd thing to have in the infirmary, but the surgeon had told him it allowed a better view of the obverse side of operations. Now Aracyse needed it to regard what remained of his arm; or what Anders had done with it.

Anders pushed the mirror across the floor, angling it such that Aracyse couldn't see his own reflection. 'Your arm was shredded. The hand was gone. It's ironic that what should have killed you—the cold—kept you alive. But the arm was a problem. We had no choice but to remove it.'

'I understand that part, Anders. I've served my time on the battlefield; I know all about trauma, and I've been lucky to avoid it until now.' He grumbled, agitated that Anders had once again paused; the plane of glass not aligned to share the view. 'Show me what you've done.'

'It's not yet complete. Still a lot of work to do. You know I wanted to keep you sedated, but your constitution is abnormal. You shouldn't be seeing this part of the process. You're not complete.'

'Anders!'

As the surgeon wheeled the mirror into view, Aracyse felt a ripple of anxiety. His arm was lost; Anders had explained that much, but to what extent would the mutilation affect him? He had seen the disfiguring wounds inflicted on others from blade and hammer. Hidden from the people, the casualties of battle were often disregarded; the homeless or incapable, made so by their service. Aracyse did all that was possible to look after the men and women that fought under him; but he was just one man, and he was not the voice of Kalleron. Was he to become the same? Would this injury end his long and storied career?

The mirror turned, at first revealing his bandaged arm, and as the image reflected his battered torso, he saw the remains. Yet, what the mirror showed was not what he had expected.

'What... is... that?'

Anders pointed to the amber-coloured threads, some glistening with weeping blood, that protruded from the stump of his left shoulder. 'Copper wire, an alloy of it, actually.'

'What is it doing?'

'Ah, the twitching. This is good, Aracyse, all very good.'

He looked at the mess where his arm should be. A mane of metal wire *grew* from his shoulder stump, the gruesome strands occasionally moving. Aracyse recalled seeing his first amputation; delivered by his own hand. It had intrigued him how a man could still move after receiving such grievous injury.

His prolonged and frequent exposure to trauma had rendered him immune to its effect; at least, he had thought so, but seeing what horror moved where a powerful arm once flexed, he wretched. Nothing came forth; his belly was empty from unknown days on the infirmary bed.

'What have you done to me?' He had never imagined he could feel revulsion at his own body, yet he had to remind himself, the golden strands were not of his flesh. Anders had amputated his arm, then mutilated his body. The physician had crossed a terrible line. 'This is monstrous, Anders.'

Anders paced backwards. The surgeon's reaction was ambivalent; the previous hint of anxiety lost to his usual pragmatism.

'You've not fainted. Obviously, this...'

'Anders!' Aracyse tried to shout, but a wince was all he could manage, the pain in his chest too severe.

'General, please, you must understand: you shouldn't be awake, although...' Anders paused. He hummed and stared at the hideous hair of wires. 'Although it may benefit the process, now you have some limited control over your muscles.'

It was madness plunging deeper into insanity. What had he done? No matter what he asked the surgeon, Anders appeared intent on avoiding the answer. It became apparent how the physician's behaviour had resulted in his exile. Never on the receiving end, Aracyse had assumed the effect. Now, he could empathise with it. Aracyse wondered if Anders had ever treated the King, and if so, how had he avoided execution?

'Anders?'

'Yes?'

Another tact. Appeal to the surgeon's intellect. 'What will the wires do?'

Anders' eyes brightened. 'Ah, there's the Aracyse I know: a logical man, not keen to dwell on pity.'

Aracyse was about to react, but realised Anders' words were true. Perhaps the trauma, something he had not experienced to such a degree; or perhaps the doses of Vallacyne and Yverelyn that were circulating in his blood every waking moment? Was it these things drawing away his focus? Anders, who had moved to a wooden infirmary cart and was wheeling it closer, interrupted his thoughts. An assembly of cogs and springs cluttered a wooden tray. It was not those items, common in Kallerye mechanical technology, that caught Aracyse's attention. A larger mass of metal sat among the other parts. Anders hefted it from the cart and showed it to him.

'An arm, General Aracyse. I'm going to give you an arm.'

Aracyse stared. The hinged tubular piece, cast in a silver alloy, didn't look as though an arm, although the length was approximate to that of his own. Visible through intricate patchwork sections, he could see springs and cogs similar to those on the cart.

'A mechanical arm?'

'Indeed.' Anders turned it around, displaying what Aracyse thought would be the upper section of the limb. 'I inserted the wires in your shoulder into your muscles. When you flex what tissue remains...' The surgeon raised his finger. 'It will take some time to learn those movements, but when you do, the arm will respond to basic functions.' Anders examined his work. 'I'll have the artisans work on the aesthetics. But you get the idea.'

Aracyse stared at the mirror. He no longer felt revulsion at the wires poking from his stump, although the constant pain was sapping his energy. Anders' mechanical arm appeared heavy; it brought a thought to the fore.

'The arm; it is attached to the wires?'

'Yes.' Anders' smiled. 'You're not going to control it with your mind; you're not the Queen of Kalleron!' The surgeon laughed at his joke, although Aracyse found the humour lacking.

'Will the arm not pull the wires from the muscle?'

Anders dismissed his question with a wave of his hand. 'General, please, I'm not an imbecile. The arm will attach to a leather harness which you'll be required to wear all the time. There will be issues with that, but we'll overcome them later.'

'Issues?'

'Nothing serious, General, but we'll need to set up a regime such that you can wash your flesh. I'm working on that as we speak. Don't worry, Aracyse; it is in hand.'

He stared at the arm, marvelling at its construction. Not prone to fanciful thoughts, Aracyse reckoned it would be more limited than Anders believed. Wooden prosthetics were common; used across the world, but they were nothing as intricate as this. His focus on the cogs and springs, Aracyse pondered a technical problem.

'A wooden leg requires no impulse. I imagine the springs store the momentum, and the cogs provide the movement. Similar to a Kallerye clock?'

'Yes, General.' Anders nodded his head slowly. 'That is how mechanics work.'

'But we wind those clocks?'

Anders clapped his hands. 'Now you're thinking clearly. Yes. I have something else to show you.' He moved away from Aracyse's limited view. There was a clatter of metal, a curse, and the sound of fabric flapping. Anders returned, wheeling in a larger frame, a sheet thrown over the top. He stood beside the hidden thing and smiled. 'General, are you ready?'

For what? He nodded.

'Only Kalle himself knows anything so grand. He is an exceptional specimen. I doubt there are any other men without his physical strength and constitution that could wear what is under here.' The surgeon smiled, his next words quieter. 'Apart from you, General. This is armour fit for a king.'

Anders pulled the sheet and revealed the incredible. It was a large, mechanically infused chest plate. A silvery-metal alloy crafted with exquisite detail. It was breath-taking. Anders turned the display to reveal an equally well-designed back plate. With the marvel rotated through a full circle, Aracyse stared at the armour. It was beautiful. A glance at the arm on the table, and he deduced it would somehow attach to the larger piece, although he was too distracted to fathom the mechanics of it all.

Anders, a wide grin on his face, bowed beside his creation.

'Behold, General, this is the soul of the machine.'

Chapter XV

'You want me to do what?' Shadow said.

Petra's words had been crystal clear, but given what she'd told him about the girl's reaction to Argan, Shadow thought she'd bumped her head.

'Look after them.'

'The big man had to leave the ship so they could board. I'm a man too, you know. You rescued them, Petra; isn't it your problem? I mean, they feel safe with you, right?'

'They do, but I need to go ashore. I've left them asleep in the cabin, but I wanted to speak with you first. Perhaps get Florent and Jessika to help? They bonded to you.'

'That wasn't the same. These girls are different; you said so.'

There was a muted glow in the hold; the Larian lamp giving a false impression of dim daylight. Petra had come to him, and he had assumed it was sunrise, but the tone of her voice was hushed; she was keen for quiet. Shadow listened to the sounds of the Melody. Few noises disturbed the gentle creaking of the hull.

'What time is it?'

Petra glanced at the opening that led to the deck. 'Not yet dawn.'

He scratched his head. 'When are you leaving?'

'Oh, not for hours yet.'

It was an offence; this rude awakening. What dreams had she disturbed? 'Then why are you down here so early?'

'I was restless. Thelia had the bed; Thelissa joined her at some point. My chair's only comfortable when I'm drunk.'

'So, you thought you'd come down here and annoy me? Wait, they're in your cabin? I said they could have my bunk.' Shadow pointed to the bare walls of the hold. 'I didn't have to sleep here?'

'Not last night, sorry.' Petra sighed. It was clear she understood the predicament of her own creation. She shoved him aside and sat down on the bench. Her gaze focused on the floorboards; she appeared torn. Shadow found it difficult to chastise her.

'Look, I'll help, but how are you going to ease them into my company? I mean, given what you said of the older one. Thelissa, was it?'

Petra's head bobbed, and her gaze fell on the floor. 'They'll need to learn. They'll be with us a few days; at least until we can figure out what to do.'

'What if they don't accept me? If they don't settle?'

Her head lifting to look into his eyes, Petra smiled, although it was a hollow grin. 'You need to ask?' She shook her head. 'I saved them from one moment of harm. How much ruin have we saved each other from? If it doesn't work out, we'll find someplace else for them, and I'll not look back. But if I can, I'll keep them safe. I need them to know that.'

Shadow understood. He owed her his life; her generosity and sanctuary had delivered him from a dark path. It was only natural for her to try the same for others, although her loyalties were obvious. They were honest.

'What's the plan? I mean, if I decide to help you,' he asked.

'I'll wake them. Make sure they're settled, and have the talk.'

'The talk? As in the Melody's rules?'

Petra nodded.

Shadow sat down beside her; giving a nudge in the ribs as he did. 'Then what?'

'Come by the cabin after sunrise. We'll sit down and discuss it. See what they say.'

He put his thumb to his chest, making sure she noticed. 'What I say, you mean? If they're staying, I'm not being pushed around by some little oiks, no matter what their issues. This is the Melody; new start, remember?'

Petra nodded. She bumped his shoulder with her own and slapped his thigh. She stood and looked at him with a fondness few could hope to receive.

She said, 'Sunrise, don't dither.'

With thoughts of Shadow looming large, Petra knelt near to her bed. The two children were asleep, both huffing in contented breaths; they didn't stir. A glance to Thelissa's chair, and she wondered when she had moved across to be with her sister. Perhaps to protect; perhaps for comfort? With a measured gentleness, Petra called out their names.

'Thelissa, Thelia?'

The older sister turned over to face her; surprising Petra to see she was already awake. Brown eyes stared out from a pretty face, but Thelissa's expression was a blank mask. There was a distance in her gaze. Rather than speak, Petra said nothing; instead, she offered Thelissa a smile.

The girl continued to stare. It was a cold thing to see, but her focus shifted, and her eyes scanned the room. Her rigid and emotionless countenance softened, Thelissa's eyes shining with a new brightness. A gentle glow appeared on her face.

'Captain,' she said.

'Morning, Thelissa.'

She wasn't crying, but a tear rolled from the corner of her eye. 'Thank you.'

Keen to maintain the quiet, Petra said, 'You don't have to thank me.'

'Never woken up like this.'

Petra frowned. 'Like what?'

'Safe, miss.'

Thelissa, still lying on her side, moved one hand to her face. It was a strange thing to see; this young girl touching her skin: fingertips tracing her lips, brow, and cheekbones. Petra was curious.

'What is it?'

'Bruises. Cuts. I'm not so useful when I'm ugly.'

Petra's new dawn crashed into her stomach. From a shuddering shock, she found strength. The same spirit that had saved Shadow and the rest. A resolve built from the knowledge that whatever Thelissa had physically endured; she would suffer no more. Although Petra was certain the girl would carry the mental wounds, there would be no more abuse. Not as long as she was with Petra and the crew of the Melody.

'Thelissa?'

'Uh-huh?'

'That's all over now. What you've known.'

Petra heard gentle snoring and realised that Thelia was still in a deep slumber. She beckoned for Thelissa to come out of bed. Thelissa slid from the sheets, still dressed in her cloak and dress, and crept away from Thelia. Petra motioned for her to follow, and the girl obeyed without complaint. She led her to the cabin door, opened it, and stepped through. There, she sat on the top step that led to the deck. Patting it, and sure to leave the cabin door ajar, she asked Thelissa to sit down.

Thelissa, seated on the other side, close but not touching, peered into the cabin. She appeared at ease and nestled into the crook of the step. The sun had not yet ascended the eastern horizon, but the sky was ablaze with the fire of dawn. The awakening murmur of the harbour played on the breeze, and distant shouts spoke of early traders setting up their stalls. Any other place but Kalleron, and it would be a perfect morning.

Thelissa, her focus on the cabin, said, 'Is it gone, then?'

'Gone?'

'What you said. You said it's over: what I've known.'

Petra wanted to hold the child. Give her the comfort and assurance that was normal for most. But she couldn't impose. Thelissa's evasive body language had been as clear as the ocean was deep. Yet what she had said was only true on one condition.

'I can give safety to you and your sister for now. As long as you're aboard the Melody, I can promise what you've known before will be gone.'

'And when we leave?'

'When you leave? That depends on what you leave with. What skills you might have learned, new things to set you on a different course.'

'And if we stay?'

'Stay?'

Thelissa brought her eyes to meet Petra's. It wasn't a pleading gaze or a false flag of sympathy. 'If we stay here, with you. If we did that, what would happen?'

Petra hadn't reckoned on the future. To take the girls away from their horror had been an impulse, and although she hadn't factored in new recruits, she wouldn't leave the girls high and dry.

'If I think you're good for the Melody and know what it means to sail on her, and if you want to stay, you can.'

'And never go back to…'

'Never. On my ship, we do honest work, mostly. I promise.' She pointed to the deck, a forceful prod on the wooden boards. 'Aboard my ship, we treat everyone with respect.'

Thelissa nodded and stared at the open doorway to the cabin. 'Thelia's young. She's not too bright, but she's willing. She'll be good at stuff.' Suddenly animated, she bobbed her head. 'She's real good at stealing, cos she's a small one. If you need things, she can get 'em.'

Petra smiled. Her talk with Shadow appeared ever more appropriate; his name coming from the contribution his skills had provided to the ship's profits. A shadow in the dark; he was an exceptional thief.

Petra said, 'I'll not lie, Thelissa. We're not above parting the wealthy from their trinkets.'

'Say what?'

'Stealing. But only from those who don't deserve to have it.'

Thelissa smiled, her face brightening, although her expression quickly dimmed, her gaze returning to the deck.

'I can thieve a little, but she's better. I'm not so good at other things; I've not been learnt much about other stuff.'

Petra was eager to change Thelissa's grim introspection. 'Everybody who comes aboard learns new skills. We'll teach you how to work the ropes, the rigging, how to mend the boards. There's a lot you can do if you don't mind some hard work.'

'I could try that. I'm stronger than Thelia.'

Talk of duty prompted a question. A curiosity. 'Do you know how old you are?'

Thelissa shook her head. 'I know I'm not old like the other women. I'm still young, it's why they... I don't know what years I've got.' She brought her attention back to Petra and straightened her posture. 'What do you think?'

It was awkward to gauge. It was possible Thelissa had matured faster on account of her ill-treatment, though Petra was careful not to say so. 'I think you look, let's see... maybe past a dozen years? A smidge less, a shade more?'

'Thelia's right young.'

Petra nodded; their physical differences were stark. 'I think she looks about six, maybe seven years-old?'

'Maybe.' Thelissa nodded.

Petra wondered about their history, of what had led to their enslavement. It was obvious they had received no education, and there had been no mention of family. Florent and Jessika had lost theirs in Thania's destruction. They had cried and pleaded for their parents for days upon days. Neither Thelia nor Thelissa had uttered a squeak of such familial bonds, although their closeness was without compare. Aboard the Melody, they would need to learn of family and what it meant.

'Do you remember what I said last night? About Argan?'

Thelissa nodded. 'I'm sorry. I was afraid for Thelia.'

'You don't need to apologise to me. Or Argan. I understand, so does he. The Melody is a very different place to be. This isn't Kalleron.'

'I know. I knew that this morning when I woke. I heard the door open. That was you leaving. I didn't steal nothing, promise, but I got up and had a look around. Clean and fresh it is here. And when I went back to Thelia, I saw her sweet little face, and it was different.'

'Different?'

'She looked proper peaceful, you know. I gave her a shake because she looked too peaceful. But she grumbled like the little tyke she is and started snoring.' Thelissa stared at Petra. This time, the girl's gaze was intense. There was no cold distance; instead, there was warmth. 'I've never seen my sis sleep so long, and she ain't slept so sound neither. It's a magical thing, that.'

'And you, do you feel safe?'

'I can't never feel proper safe, miss; gotta watch out for the tyke, but I don't think you'll do me harm.'

Petra smiled for Thelissa. A hard thing to say next. 'And of Argan, and the men in my crew: you'll need to understand that you're safe around them, too.'

'I know that. Some men are nice. I've seen that.' Thelissa's expression shifted again. To Petra, it appeared the girl had two states of being: a grim introspection, and a wondrous joy, although the latter faltered all too easily. 'A whiles back, a man had given coin for me, but when he saw me, he was proper shocked. I asked if I wasn't pretty enough; he looked ill, disgusted with me, but it wasn't that. He said I was too young.'

'What happened?'

'He tried to get me out. But they beat him. Took his money, and beat me too for not doing my job.' Her face dimmed again. Those two simple states.

'Was it the men that I saw? The ones that beat you?'

Thelissa nodded. 'Plank and Oaf.'

'Nobody on the Melody is like that. Not even close. We don't hurt children, we've helped them. There're two girls, well, I suppose they're women now: Jessika and Florent. Took them aboard nigh on seven years ago. Been with us since.'

Petra thought of the day ahead; what she could plan for the sisters. What she had to ask and with whom they would need to remain. She had faith in Shadow's guidance and guardianship, but Thelissa required care. It would be easier to discuss with breakfast; a pleasant bribe to introduce the Rules of the Melody.

'How about you wake your sister, and I'll make you some tea and get some bread and biscuits?'

Thelissa shook her head. 'I told you. Miss, we ain't got no coin.'

'My treat.'

The young girl beamed. Petra wondered how long the brightness would remain.

It was a silly thing. Shadow's own doubts irritating him. He stood on the deck of the Melody; the sun rising above the bay. It was a beautiful morning; a typical and warm Kallerye breeze bringing the scents of the harbour: smoked fish, herbs, and tobacco. Although there was a constant undercurrent of waste, it somehow added to the charm. It was this dysfunction that agitated him. Why the hell was he nervous? He had spoken with girls before, when Florent and Jessika had boarded. That had turned out well. But this? Petra's tales of abuse and woe had left him with an unease. He didn't want to be judged by a damaged child. Didn't need it. With a grumble, he approached her cabin door and rapped his knuckles on the frame.

'Enter!'

With a sigh to focus his nerves, and not knowing what to expect, he opened the door and stepped inside. All was calm. Petra, seated behind her desk with a cup of tea in hand, smiled at him and tilted her head to the girls sitting on a couple of chairs. The wooden frames seemed larger than he recalled. Nibbling bread and biscuits, the girls paid him no attention. Their sole concern was the food. They had dressed in clothing he recognised as rewards from previous adventures.

Petra waved for Shadow to take a seat, and he almost laughed aloud. The chair she had offered was distant from the desk; a clear divide between man and child. Shadow looked at the wooden seat, and then Petra; an accusation in his eyes. She glared at him; her evil eye was as good as an order. He sat down, trying to remain unnoticed. The smaller girl stopped eating and looked at him. She began tapping her sister's arm. The older girl put her breakfast biscuit down and slowly turned around in her seat.

'Girls,' Petra said. 'This is Shadow.'

Convinced they would pounce on his discomfort, he said, 'Hello.'

The older one stared, swallowing the last of her food. The other bounced uncertain glances between Shadow and her sister.

'You're Shadow?' the older girl said.

'I am. I guess you would be Thelissa?' Shadow pointed to the little one. 'Which makes this squirt, Thelia.'

Thelia grinned, emitting a short, excited giggle.

Thelissa hushed her sister. She looked at Petra, who nodded. Shadow noticed a glimmer of mischief in the captain's eyes. Thelissa returned her attention to him. 'You're a thief?'

'If I need to be.'

'And a fighter?'

'If something needs fought over.'

Thelissa hesitated. Petra urged her on, but it was clear she lacked the conviction to say what he assumed she had been told to say.

Shadow spread his hands to the side. 'You can ask me anything. I swear, I'll be honest. Besides, if the captain's said something, it's probably true.'

'You're a loveable idiot?' Thelia said, spitting flakes of bread.

'Thelia!' Thelissa glared at her sister.

The younger sister shrank into her seat, although her twinkling eyes stared back at Thelissa with affection. She resumed her breakfast, chewing on the hard crust.

'I am,' Shadow said. 'To be fair, that's the nicest thing Petra's said of me all week.'

Thelissa appeared to soften, her shoulders slumping, and her ribs lifting with slower breaths. She said, 'Are you though?'

'Are I what?'

'An idiot?'

Shadow smiled, leaning back in his chair. 'If folks think I'm an idiot, it makes it easier to impress them. Or surprise them. Like fighting and thieving; I'm an idiot when I need to be. It's a damn good life lesson, kid. Smarts might get you far, but they'll get you knocked down. But me, I escape everyone's attention.' He pointed to the ill-fitting dress she wore under her oversized cloak. 'Which means I can steal nice things that you get to wear.'

Thelissa looked at her dress, her fingers moving to feel the fabric. 'You stole this?'

'From a lady that had too many to wear. More dresses than days in a Larian week, she had. That was spare. Now, I guess it's yours.'

Petra shuffled in her seat, attracting his attention. 'I said you'd get some more for them. A better fit.'

Keen to keep the conversation going, aware any silence would be awkward, Shadow said, 'Aye, I'll get pretty fabrics. Some hide leggings, a nice tunic, maybe a blouse.'

Petra nodded at Thelissa. 'You and Thelia can tell Shadow what you'd like. He'll fetch some things for you.'

Thelissa looked at Petra. The girl appeared sheepish. With a finger pointing to the far wall, where Petra had hung her hardened leather chest plate, she said, 'That's pretty.'

Petra, surprise on her face, smiled at Shadow.

He said, 'That's armour, love. It's not a corset.'

'But it's pretty. And it's...' The older sister crossed her arms and cupped her hands across her chest.

Shadow wasn't certain what the girl was thinking. He could imagine what thoughts might have prompted her gesture. It wasn't fashion; it appeared to be for protection. Perhaps a shield to wear close to her skin. 'If you want a breastplate, it'd need to be made to fit. Armour's not like clothes; they have to shape it around the wearer.'

'Oh.'

It seemed an appropriate compromise to consider; at least, it was to Shadow. He said, 'I could get you a corset, and teach you how to use a knife properly?'

'Can you?' Thelissa said without hesitation.

He hadn't expected such enthusiasm, although it pleased Shadow that Thelissa had grasped his suggestion with such excitement. 'I can. I can teach you good.' He glanced at Petra, her expression offering encouragement. It was excellent progress. 'If you want to learn how to handle a blade, I'll show you and Thelia.'

A shake of her head, Thelissa said, 'No, just me.' Reaching her hand out to her sister, she rubbed her head. 'She's not to be anything like me; she's to be different.'

It was the small things in life. When what little was said revealed the most about a person. Thelissa, the martyr. Defender of Thelia. Shadow smiled; his heart warmed by her fortitude.

'I'll make you the best knife-fighter in the whole damn world,' he said.

Thelissa looked at him.

And she smiled.

Chapter XVI

Higher in the hills than Tarkin's Inn, Petra felt as though she was walking among the dead. She had been told of the place, and how it would be dangerous, but strolling among the decay of Kalleron's former elite, she felt nothing but awe. She had learned that the tall and extravagant houses, which were built along a lush avenue, had fallen out of favour decades ago. The hill, once a green expanse of prickly thorns, had been cultivated in past centuries, and now a canopy of deciduous leaves offered shade from the midday sun. Although Kalleron experienced hot days all year round, Mansion Hill picked up the condensation that blew in from the sea. The trees, chosen by wise arborists, had flourished. Yet the same damp air had hastened the deterioration of the houses, their once manicured lawns, and the iron fences that enclosed the grounds. The gardens had become wild and unkempt, the gates, now rusted, squeaked in the ever-blowing ocean breeze. Even on the stillest days, Tarkin had said he could hear the mournful cry of disintegrating ironwork.

Petra saw none of the threats Tarkin had warned about, although she had taken care to wear her armoured bodice over her white blouse. A flowing black skirt with generous splits allowed her thighs a glimpse of the breeze. She wore her usual leather boots and daggers underneath. If danger came her way, she was ready with steel, and should a greedy justice question her motives, her purse was heavy enough to bribe the worst of them.

She had left the note aboard the Melody tucked safely in her drawer. She held no fear of Thelia or Thelissa reading the contents; neither girl was literate. That would be another thing they would learn. A smile formed on her lips; the thought of their education bringing an image of Shadow teaching Thelissa how to wield a knife.

Walking along the street, with the ghosts of hubris whispering in her ear, Petra stared at each mansion; all of them set far back from the cobbled surface. Occasionally, she had to check her step; the roots of trees breaking the surface in places, the earth-coloured stones rattling underfoot as though loose teeth in a giant's mouth.

Petra reached her destination and stopped to regard her surrounds. There were two marble gate posts coloured green with lichen, and atop each block, there was a sculpted form. Weathered and less grand than they would once have been, bronze figures, each holding a chalice to the sky, gave a glimpse of better days. With feminine lines, there were folds of a delicate dress billowing around their legs. It was an old salutation to the Wind. Not an uncommon design from times past. Many houses had idolised the old gods, and in Kalleron, such elemental belief was neither encouraged nor denied.

With her hand on the gate, Petra pushed. It creaked with an angry retort to her effort; the sharp crack sending birds flying from the trees. It moved an inch, then stuck fast; the hinge was a terrible mess of inflamed orange rust. The gate was as tall as she, but Petra had wisely chosen her attire; the split skirt was no hindrance to a quick scramble over the ornate metal bars. Once on the other side, she scanned all around. An expanse of unruly garden lay between her and the house. Thick bushes, overgrown and unkempt, had overgrown the path; the gravel covered with a mulch of autumnal coloured leaves. Petra peered at the way forward. Small signs were obvious to her keen eye. Someone had snagged on the twigs; the fresh breaks were too high for a passing animal. There were slip marks on the occasional leafy debris. Others had come here. The cautionary question in Petra's mind: were they friend or foe?

With care, she moved along the path; steady on her feet and ducking under branches. She arrived at a grand marble staircase leading up to the great darkwood doors. The house, constructed of a granite which contrasted with the white stone steps, appeared as a monolithic sarcophagus. Once shuttered windows were smashed; the jagged and coloured remnants offering a glimpse of former beauty. Beyond the broken glass, the house appeared dark. Yet it was a strange anomaly; the darkwood door was new. Drohendrian timber was resilient, but even it would age under such neglect. Another question: why have doors when the windows were wide open?

Petra looked around, seeking eyes that might be watching. The street beyond the rusted gate was empty, not a sound stirring above the creaking hinges and rustling leaves. With a sigh to blow away her growing nerves, she climbed the steps and knocked on the door. Felicitra's message had been clear. One loud knock, then wait for several moments. Then two knocks, a further wait, then a final rap of her knuckles. She followed the command to the letter. Nothing happened. She waited, listening for any signs of movement from within. Nothing.

The note had mentioned a greeting, but that was to be used on a prompt. Where was the prompt? Had she missed it? She waited without reply, time slipping by as grains through the hourglass. How long since she had made her presence known? Too long. Petra raised her hand to the door; impatient, she would try again. Felicitra's voice floated in her mind. A gentle reminder from cherished lips.

They are quiet ghosts, these people I know. Stepping unseen, they leave no trace, follow no path. They wait, and they wait, and only when time itself has grown bored do they show themselves.

Petra lowered her hand and sat on the steps. She doubted she had Felicitra's patience; how long would this day become?

The shadows had crawled across the garden, and time's hand had created new shapes and patterns among the chaotic foliage. A creak behind, and Petra startled. She rose to her feet and drew her daggers. A swift spin, and she faced the door. It was ajar—an inch, but no more. She moved closer, wary of any sudden movements; it wasn't uncommon for doors to be used as impromptu weapons. A lesson learned from experience; Shadow once teasing her about a bruised face, battered after a drunken fight with a vertical slab of timber.

Petra moved to the side, inhaling the odours released from within. A pleasant smell of flowers and dry wood. Not what she had expected from a dilapidated old mansion. About to call out, she again remembered Felicitra's words. *They wait, and they wait.* Petra had not received the prompt. Once more, she sat on the step. Was this a test? She had not sat long when a voice came to her through the gap.

'Have you travelled far?' It was a man's voice, coming from deep within the house. Gruff, it had an air of wizened age.

Petra visualised Felicitra's letter, speaking the lines from within. 'I have trekked long across the earth to reach this point.'

A pause before the reply came. 'And the weather?'

The second line, the handwriting so clear in Petra's mind. 'The wind has a chill, and I am cold from it. Do you have a fire within?'

Silence followed her reply. Had she made a mistake? Petra waited, erring on the side of caution and patience.

The unseen man said, 'Not for you.'

It was what she had expected. 'Then, if I am to leave, will you fill my flask with water, that I may travel home?'

The response was quick. 'Nor will you have that. This conversation is over.' The door closed.

Petra, following the letter's last instruction, stepped to the door and knocked on it four times. One salute for each elemental. There was a muffled click. Then a creak, and the door opened an inch. In her mind, Felicitra's voice fell silent. The letter had nothing more to say. Petra was alone now; she would need her wits. With her daggers in hand, she pushed the gap wider. A sigh for company, she crept inside the house.

A gloomy corridor ran the length of the house, the light from the back room illuminating the dark timber floor. Petra frowned, her expectations of the interior not matched by reality. Where she thought there would be doors leading to ransacked rooms, there were none. It was a uniform and long hallway with few details to observe. There was the darkwood door behind her, and in front was the room at the far end. With no other options, Petra walked down the corridor. At the end, she peeked around the open doorway, where a man seated at a table greeted her.

'Hello,' he said.

Seated behind the solid timber table, his face bore the signs of a long life lived through violence, craggy wrinkles merging with clean and linear lines. In his chair, he appeared a tall man, and his loose, white cotton shirt contoured a powerful frame suited to someone far younger. A thatch of dusty grey hair capped his rugged features. He gestured to a chair opposite, appearing to take no interest in her daggers.

Petra looked around the room. It was plain except for the intricate frames surrounding the large bay windows. Red and yellow roses in tidy pots decorated the wooden ledge; the scent was pleasant and strong. Panelled walls gave no hint of age, and the floor and ceiling were in pristine condition. Beyond the clear and imperfect glass, trees and leafy foliage blocked the view of the hills.

'Who are you?' she asked.

'Please, sit.'

He delivered his words with a gentle tone, but there was a hidden depth Petra couldn't place. She thought it odd how at ease he appeared; her daggers still in hand.

'My blades don't trouble you?'

He huffed a breath of humour. 'Not in the least.'

'Are you armed?'

'No.' Again, he gestured to the chair.

Petra nodded and sat down, putting her daggers into their sheaths.

'Thank you,' he said. 'Why are you here?'

She sat across from a man she assumed was part of a treasonous cult, but she couldn't be certain of his loyalties. She wouldn't give him Felicitra's name. 'I received instructions from...' Petra wanted to say lover; thought another term was better suited for the moment. 'A friend.'

'A friend?'

She nodded.

'Your friend? They enjoy cryptic messages?'

'Only when telling me how to come here.'

The old man nodded. He huffed. 'Come here to do what? We employ no trades here. You're clearly a seafarer come far ashore. What have you come to offer me?'

'Offer you?'

'Yes. Are you not in my house? Are you not here because of your own free-will? I didn't ask for your presence; so why are you here? It's a simple question, really.'

Petra hadn't known what to expect, but his questions and evasion were an irritant to her patience. She wasn't Felicitra. Yet his queries were valid: why had she come to him? She gave him the truth. 'My friend was my lover. She passed, and I owed her this promise to follow wherever her message took me. Her words brought me here.'

The inquisitor's head tilted to the side. He hummed, then shook his head. 'Then leave.'

'What?'

He offered a smile, a cursory gesture. 'Well done. You solved a silly puzzle and found a house with an old man. You've upheld your promise to your moronic lover and...'

'Excuse me?'

He stared. 'Your lover—she sent you to me with nothing but pretty lashes and a pouting little face. I've no time for such pathetic and entitled indulgence.'

Petra trembled. What had prompted his spite? It was uncalled for; it stirred her anger. She tried to think of Felicitra, tried to quell the emotion, when he spoke again.

'Your lover, I don't know what she saw in you. Look at you.' His voice changed, a mocking tone to emphasise his hatred. 'A simpering little girl come to play vagabonds and pirates. This is pathetic. Your idiot lover must have thought me a simpleton!'

It was an explosion. All Petra could see was the mist; a raging cloud of swirling spite and animosity, all of it focused on the old man. She rose, pulling her daggers from her boots. So swift was her movement that she knocked her chair over, and before it had hit the floor, she leapt at the old bastard. Swinging her right hand out, she aimed for his neck; the blade slicing through the air.

An explosion of pain in her thighs. From where? The table sliding into her. Pushed with such force, she fell against it, thrusting out her left hand to stop her face from smashing against the wood. In an instant, Petra shoved herself away, standing ready for his attack. But he didn't come; instead, he waited for her, patient behind the table. He remained seated. It was as though he hadn't even moved. Not to make the same mistake, and careful not to linger, Petra launched onto the table. Anticipating he would kick it from under her, she leapt toward him. Daggers out, and with one knee forward, she came close to striking him when he rose from his chair, side-stepped her attack, and threw her into the panelled wall. Petra crashed to the floor; heaving breaths from her winded lungs. Who was this stranger? Nobody was that quick. Stunned and vulnerable, she expected the worst. It didn't come. Instead, she heard him pace toward her, a tremendous sigh released from his chest.

He leaned forward, holding out his hand to her. 'She wasn't wrong.'

Through gasps, Petra said, 'What?'

Although he was a formidable foe, and his nature was of the storm, sadness tinged the old man's reply. 'Felicitra. She often spoke of you. Said one day you'd come to my door. I'm sorry Petra, I had to know if it was true.'

'True?' She took his hand. Confused and relieved. The threat was gone, and his insults had been theatre. Petra shook her head. 'What was true?'

He smiled, handed her a dagger she had dropped in the fall. 'That you were a wild witch of chaos, and your heart was fiercer than all. She loved you, spoke so highly of you.'

Shaken, but careful to stay aloof, Petra said, 'Then you know what happened?'

'Yes. It hit hard when I heard the news. Felicitra meant a lot to me; to the cult.'

Petra sheathed her daggers and rubbed her sore body. She stared at him, intrigued by his speed and strength. 'Who are you?'

'Kastane. A servant of the cult of the Queen.' He nodded and smiled. 'Now, I ask again: why have you come to me, Petra?'

Petra looked at the toppled chair. 'May I sit?'

'Please. I think we've finished our introductions.'

She strode to the overturned frame and righted it, sitting down with a wince. A frown on her face, shock and surprise still thudding in her mind, Petra stared at

Kastane, who had seated himself with his arms relaxed on the table. She noted he didn't even tremble; not a sign of what had just occurred.

'When I asked who you are,' she said, 'you gave your name. But that's not who you are.'

'Oh?'

'Felicitra told you about me; things I probably wasn't aware she would say to anyone.' Petra smiled, realising the irony of her lover's cult status. 'I suppose she was a spy?'

'One of my best.' Kastane nodded.

'Then you know of my crew?'

'I do. Please understand, Petra, that you sit here now, in my house, is of great risk to us. Even with the precautions we take, our safety can never be assured. But I'm convinced you offer me no threat, neither by physical, nor political prowess.'

From any other mouth, she would perceive those words as an insult. Kastane appeared to operate on a different level. Yet, her point was not of his knowledge of her crew, rather, she wanted to contrast his capabilities against them.

She said, 'Then, if you know of my world, Felicitra will have spoken of Shadow and Argan?'

'The brawler and the Bruhadian, yes.'

'You're faster than Shadow, and although I doubt you could match Argan's brute strength, your own exceeds what you present.' She gestured to his frame. 'No insult intended. So, when I asked who you are, I meant, how can you fight like that?'

Kastane smiled, his old face cracking into myriad trenches and furrows. He pointed to his features. 'You see my scars? You will infer battle?'

'Yes.'

'Then that is answer enough. Felicitra told me of your ship and what rules it has. Consider those rules apply to me, at least when I sit as the head of this house. Is that fair?'

How could Petra deny him his secrecy when she insisted on it with her crew? She nodded. 'It's fair. But it leaves me with questions.'

Kastane clasped his hands together. 'Then, may I ask again, for you've not yet answered mine: Why have you come to me?'

It had been a simple thing: a promise to keep. Although now she had a deeper understanding of Felicitra's relationship with the cult, she was keen to learn more. Petra assumed Kastane would dismiss her questions unless she offered him something first. Though she had to ask.

With a nod to the wall, she said, 'Before you threw me across the room, I told you I'd come to fulfil a promise. That wasn't a lie. But I've lost Felicitra, and to hear you speak of her with such familiarity... I want to know more.'

Kastane sighed, his hands moving to his chest, arms folding. He shook his head. 'My house is a sacred house, Petra. What I know, what Felicitra knew; these are not things to share with outsiders, and you are an outsider. I understand you want to learn more of Felicitra's life, but to speak further requires a contract. An agreement.'

'Which would be?'

'To join us, and in doing so, your ship, your crew; all of it becomes part of my house. If I wish a trade to happen, you would assist. If I wish transport, you would assist. It is not a trivial thing to enter my home. The price is steep because the reward is great.'

Although Petra would never relinquish the Melody, nor the crew, she was curious. 'What reward?'

The old man shook his head.

'I can't give you my ship,' she said. 'My crew is free; they have no part in this.'

'I understand.'

She wanted to know more about Felicitra and the secrets she kept; it was as though she had lived a hidden life. It was a harsh reality; it *was* a hidden life, and although Petra had known of it, being so close to the truth made it an unbearable shade across the brightness she had brought.

'I can help you,' Petra said. 'Just me. I can...'

Kastane waved his hand, held it with his fingers splayed toward her. Even his palms bore scars; it was a miracle he had survived to such an age. 'Stop. You ought to know one thing. Perhaps it will blunt your heart. You were never a mark; Felicitra's feelings were genuine, unhindered by duty, but the more she knew of you, the more she knew how much of an asset you could be. Your trading routes, your devoted crew. She thought they'd be a perfect cover for us. This isn't about what you,' he gestured to her, 'as one person can do. It's about what you can offer to us.'

Petra tried to push away a dreadful thought, but a grim curiosity urged her on. 'If I had no ship, would Felicitra have suggested my skills to you?'

Kastane's shoulders slumped. 'No.'

Petra couldn't hold his gaze. Her head bowed, she stared at the floor. Had Felicitra used her? Kastane had said she had not. But Petra couldn't push away the sense of deception. She kept her focus on the floor when Kastane spoke again.

'She didn't want to lose you. Alone, you would have been more vulnerable. The ship offered a safer door to our ways. Indirect, unseen. Lone operatives risk much; she didn't want that from you. She was adamant that, despite your considerable abilities, you'd be best suited as a peripheral agent.'

It seemed a poor consolation, but Petra understood the conflict. She wasn't naïve to what happened to those who transgressed against Kalleron. She had known of Felicitra's involvement, although she was unaware to what extent. It appeared she was important to the cult. As was Petra's ship.

Kastane said, 'Don't think less of her, Petra. Felicitra protected you from the worst of it. She could have used you without your knowledge; she never did.' With a long and drawn-out sigh, he sat back in his chair. He gestured to the door. 'You may leave, and peace be with you.'

'I'm dismissed?'

'There is nothing more to say. You know all you need to know, which is all I can tell you.'

Petra felt as though he had chided her in the gentlest of ways. She stood and nodded to Kastane, turned around and set off down the gloomy corridor. Without looking back, she left the mansion, climbed the gate, and walked back through the deserted and decaying streets. She had fulfilled her promise; she had met Felicitra's contact. Then why did she feel an urge to return to the house of the cult? Why did she feel anxious about what she would say to Shadow? Under a hot Kallerye sun, Petra kicked through piles of copper leaves and returned to the Melody.

Chapter XVII

On the deck of the Melody, Shadow faced his opponent. Ready to defend, he held a baton of wood in his right hand. Knees bent, and his body poised; he waited for the attack.

'Like this?' Thelissa asked, holding the stick toward him.

'No, no,' he said, dropping his guard and moving forward to fix her grip.

Thelissa lunged, stabbing the improvised weapon into his belly. 'Got you!'

Shadow looked down at the gnarled twig sticking into his shirt. It hadn't hurt, but it scratched a little. At the side, Thelia giggled. Across the deck, Argan shook with a deep and gruff laugh.

'What was that?' Shadow asked Thelissa.

She pulled the stick away, flakes of bark embedded in the cotton. 'I stabbed you.'

'I wasn't ready.'

Thelissa shrugged. It was hard to deny she had done well. The deception was exactly how he would have fought in her position, although her grip was poor and the lunge was feeble. He knelt in front of her, holding his hand out so she could see his own grip.

'Like this. Firm, wrap your thumb around the handle.'

'But I won?'

Careful to avoid touching her, Shadow pointed to her thumb. 'Wrap it around. That's better.' He sighed, then nodded. 'You sure got me, but that's not how fights work. You've got the idea, mind—hit 'em when they least expect it.'

'Then how do fights work? How do I win? How do I keep us safe?'

Shadow pointed at Thelia. 'You mean your sister and you?'

'Uh-huh.'

'First line of defence is to avoid a fight.' Although they were his words, Shadow was a fraud for speaking them. It was advice he would never follow.

Thelissa frowned. She looked at her stick. 'Then what's the point of this?'

'When your legs can't get you far enough away, and you've got no other options. That's when you fight. At least, that's how it should be with you and Thelia.'

'You mean keep her out of danger?'

Shadow nodded, turning his attention to a familiar sound; Petra's boots tapping across the gangplank. 'Captain on board!'

Petra stared at him. 'And why the announcement?'

He pointed to the girls, keen to show her how far they had come along since morning. 'Getting them trained up. Like you asked.'

'How are they?' Petra turned her attention to the girls, and with her hands on hips, asked, 'How has he been?'

Thelia beamed, and Thelissa shrugged.

It was fair praise. 'See, we're doing good!' He recalled the reason for his baby-sitting duties. 'How'd your day go?'

Petra nodded, but her only reply was a murmur. It was neither a confirmation of success nor a grumble of discontent. Shadow would have preferred a more tangible answer, but in front of the girls, he didn't want to press. He'd do that later; she owed him a drink.

Thelissa said, 'I stabbed Shadow.'

The captain looked at Thelissa and smiled; it was a broad grin. 'So have I.'

'Really?'

Petra laughed and winked at Shadow. He didn't take offence; it was important for the girls to feel a sense of companionship. Though he offered Thelissa a more balanced view.

'Just like how you got me; the captain did it when I wasn't looking.'

Thelissa squinted. 'Why would she...' she turned to Petra. 'Why would you do that?'

Shadow's turn to laugh. It was magnificent to see Petra squirming for a reply. After all, how to explain to the damaged girl that a casual stabbing had rounded off a wild night of drugs, alcohol, and vice? It would take the intervention of the gods to sanitise that story.

'Go on,' he said to Petra. 'Best tell her.'

Petra shook her head. 'Thelissa, some stories are for older ears, and you and your sister's are too young for that one. Ask Shadow in a few years.'

The older girl looked at him with a fierce gaze. She spoke with a tone to match her glare. 'You'll tell us!' She held her stick toward him, and he buckled over with laughter. 'What's so funny?' Thelissa asked, still pointing with her stick.

It was too much; the little bundle of rage and her twig of power. Even Petra snorted in mirth. Through tears, he noticed Thelissa's face soften. Perhaps his idiocy, perhaps the irreverence, but she smiled. On the bench, Thelia giggled. He saw her run to her sister, grab the stick, and come at him with it.

Thelia, giggling, began poking him with the twig, which snapped. 'Don't you laugh...,' she said, followed by more giggles, 'at my sister.'

His ribs were under attack, and at the mercy of a little tyke, Shadow looked up to see Petra's beaming face. At her side, Thelissa's eyes were sparkling, and though she didn't laugh as her sister did, it was clear she was enjoying the moment. Life had finally given her something to smile about. It was what the Melody did best.

Shadow, taking the glass from Petra, leaned back in the chair. In her cabin, all was still; the day's play was over, and his captain appeared lost in thought. The glass to his lips, he inhaled the green liquid.

'What's this?' he asked.

'Huh?'

He lifted the spirit, the verdant colour vivid in the light of a lamp. 'This. Where's it from?'

'Oh.' Petra reached to the desk and picked up the bottle. She looked at it, turning it over in her hands. 'It was one we picked up in Hoydai. I think it's Cyreni. Made with fermented Sky fruit.'

'Sky fruit?' Shadow hadn't heard of it.

Petra shook her head. 'Don't know it's actual name, it's what the locals called it because in strong winds, it falls from the trees.'

Shadow sipped the liquid. It tasted sweet, similar to melon, although there was a hint of bitterness. It would do. 'So, your day?'

'Have you ever seen the mansions in the hills?'

He had; he nodded.

'I found where Felicitra told me to go, climbed the gate, and waited. I followed the instructions she'd left and waited some more.'

'Sounds like a fun trip?'

Petra raised her eyebrows and clicked her tongue. 'Yeah, a lot of waiting.'

'And?'

'After long enough, a door opened, literally, and I went inside. It was odd, Shadow, an old grubby house; inside there was an enclosed corridor leading to a room at the back. The mansion was rundown, but that small area was clean. Fresh.'

Shadow knew of such things. At least, he had heard of them. There were a few among the hills; parts of the older estates made tidy for one or two adventurous souls. A means to live among the old grandeur of Kalleron without upsetting the apple cart. Not worth robbing from; those folks who had chosen that life had little of value. Just a pleasant room with a view.

He said, 'No nasty surprises?'

Petra huffed; it was a stifled laugh. 'I wouldn't say that.'

Shadow leaned in. 'Then what?'

'I met a man, a curious man. He had years on him, but he was fast. And bloody strong. He was definitely military, but he was cagey about that. He also knew Felicitra, knew of me, of the Melody. Knew all of us.'

It was an uncomfortable thing to hear, to know a stranger had eyes on you and your own. Shadow wondered how much his friend would tell him; was she sworn to secrecy now she had dabbled with the cult?

'Who was he?'

'Said his name was Kastane.' Petra frowned, gazed at him. 'You know it?'

'No. Not in any context, at least.'

'Well, I think he's the leader. He told me some truths about Felicitra, and sent me on my way.'

Shadow pulled back from the edge of his seat. 'That's it?'

'Hmm. Mostly.'

It was always what wasn't said that tickled his curiosity. He knew Petra enough to know she was hiding things. Not so much lying, but withholding something on account of how she feared he might respond. It annoyed him.

'Tell me the rest, Petra. What happened?'

She stood up and paced to the cabin door. Shadow watched her staring out onto the deck. Her breath became a brief mist on the cabin glass, the evening air warm enough to dispel the fog. After several audible and deep breaths, she turned around.

'I'm at a crossroads, Shadow. And I don't know where to go.'

He wondered if she read the expression that crept across his face. If she had, she didn't show it, although he thought it would have been obvious. He didn't want to ask what these paths were that caused such a dilemma. Shadow shrugged, declining to respond.

Petra shook her head. 'It's not fair. Not fair on you. The crew. Any of you.'

It was cryptic. He wanted to leave; didn't like where this was heading, but Petra was blocking the door. He had come for drinks after a hard day's schooling. Shadow hadn't asked for a crisis.

Reluctant to push her along, he said, 'It's been a long day, maybe sleep on it? We can talk tomorrow.' He raised his glass. 'Just drink now?'

'I need to know what she did. What she knew. I can't get it out of my mind.'

'Huh?'

'Felicitra. Kastane told me so little. I know she was involved; I want to know more.'

Shadow fidgeted in his seat. The evening wasn't going to plan. Petra's inner conflict was bursting out, and although he didn't relish the direction that the conversation was taking, it was selfish to ignore her needs.

He downed the Cyreni, put the glass on the desk and huffed. 'So what does that mean? You want to know more; it sounds simple. Ask.'

With her back against the cabin door, Petra slumped into the frame. 'I'll only learn more if I return to him. To Kastane.'

'Why is that a problem?'

'I'd need to swear fealty to him, to his house.'

'His house?' Shadow didn't understand. Then it occurred to him what she meant. 'Oh, no. Not that. Join the cult?'

She nodded. It was a solemn confirmation. Shadow thought of Laria when they had shared similar words about the cult and Felicitra. He knew Petra had harboured romantic thoughts about running free with her glamorous spy lover, but that was fantasy. Everybody knew Kalleron hunted spies, and they tortured those they caught. It was why they had created the bastard prison, Seawall; a woeful place to dissuade would be plotters. There was no glory in that.

He said, 'The cult isn't a game, Petra. It's...'

Petra's tone was harsh as she cut him off. 'It's my ship, and that's my damn dilemma. I want to find out where this goes; what she was, Shadow. But I can't, not without offering what I have. Felicitra shielded me from the worst of it. She knew I'd do anything for her. The Melody offers other options for them, and if I help, I might find the truth.'

Shadow couldn't remain quiet. Petra's words were nonsense. 'You're asking us to fight Kalleron on the chance you *might* find something? You'd do that?'

Petra screamed with a howl of frustration. She flung her glass across the cabin and put her hands to her face. Shadow grimaced as she did what he didn't want her to do. Her shoulders heaved, lurching up and down, and although she made only the slightest noise, her sobs were a terrible sound.

'Petra?'

She didn't move. She just cried. It was a thing he wasn't meant to see; something they had never wanted to share. It occurred to him how hurt she must be to break down in front of him; to show her vulnerability. Petra was only human, and he had been selfish. Cold. It was what he thought she had needed him to be. He had an answer to remedy her pain. A truth.

'Oh, fuck it. Whatever you do, Petra, I'll do it with you. You know that. Come on, now. Stop crying.'

Her sobbing, quieter now, continued. Through those wretched sounds, and shielded by her hands, Petra said, 'I never fucking wanted this.'

'I know.'

'But I can't let her go. Not like this.'

'I know that too.' He sighed, thought about what he could say to make things better. Doubtful there was anything, he said, 'Look at me. Petra, look at me!'

She lowered her shaking hands from her face. A fool would believe her weak and timid; Shadow knew otherwise. The judder was rage, the tears were anger. Although there was grief on display, this was not sadness. It was the uncontrollable mist; something she had spoken of in years past. A furious curse that Felicitra had dispelled. With her death, it seemed Petra's demons had returned.

Shadow said, 'I know what she meant to you. I know what she did for you.' He laughed. 'Gods, you were a liability before she appeared.' He patted his old stab wound. 'You were a maniac.'

Petra wiped away her tears. She blew a breath to the ceiling and spoke in a tired voice. 'It's everything, Shadow. It's not just Felicitra. Yesterday I found Thelia and Thelissa.' Petra placed her hand beside her hip, palm down. 'Thelia, she's just a baby. And she was for sale, right here, in Kalleron. Thelissa's blossomed too early. You know why? She's already had a baby, or she's carried a life inside. This is what Kalleron does. It's what it offers, and I despise it. There's an ungodly fucking monster in a palace behind those pristine walls. It kills anything and everything. There's a king who makes people disappear. All the while, the fucking degenerates and morons—like us—we just wander about gawping and pay for what we want to take. Every one of us. We're all involved in the glorification of this rancid city.

'The cult offers a way out. It'll give me an answer, and by the gods, I'm taking that answer, and I'm going to walk that path. I know from the letter that I need to wait another six days. The door to Kastane's house will be shut until then. I'll figure out what I'll say, figure out what I'll do, but I'm following Felicitra. Maybe it'll get me killed, but if I don't do it, Shadow... I'll likely get me killed anyway. You've seen the worst of me. You know I'm speaking the truth.'

Shadow exhaled, realising he had held his breath throughout her tirade. It was a lot to absorb, too much for one evening. He pointed to her captain's chair, and with a fresh glass, he poured her a drink.

'Sit down, please.'

Petra nodded and walked to her seat, taking the glass from his hand with thanks.

Shadow said, 'I know what Kalleron is. It gave birth to me. And it might've been your pretty face that got me here, but you weren't the first hand to bring me from the depths—did you know that?'

Petra shook her head. 'The rules, Shadow. You don't need...'

'Fuck your rules. Just this once. You broke our contract when you broke down in tears, so let's even the scales?'

She appeared stunned, although she nodded.

Shadow said, 'I served Kalleron. I'll not say what I did, but they were awful things; things that broke me. It's why you found me the way you did. You took me from that. But it was another hand that lifted me from a darker place before those days. You'll not have his name, but he came first; it was his intervention that saved my life the first time, and without that, I'd not have been around for you to save. There'd have been no adventures, no wild nights south of Drohendrir. Kalleron chewed me up twice, Petra. I know how bad it is, but because of what I lived through, what I *survived*; that's why I'm the way I am. I'm like a dog beaten by its master; I'll still go back for more, no matter what it does to me. But if you want me to bite, I'll bite for you. You're my handler now.'

Petra stared. A smile appeared on her lips. 'You're my bitch?'

'Must be. Can't be a dog now, can I? I'd probably hump your leg.'

Petra scoffed. She shook her head. 'I've only ever told Felicitra of my past...'

Shadow raised his hand to interrupt. 'Nope. No more.'

'You shared. Don't you want balance?'

He shook his head. 'Petra, I love you. When I thought you liked me, as a man, I *wanted* you. You snuffed out those flames pretty damn quick, but I'll tell you this: I've walked away from far lovelier ladies than you, but I've stuck by you through all your shite. Whatever it is, it's magical to me, and in my life, there ain't never been magic. Apart from those two hands; his, and yours. But I think if I knew about you, what made you special?' Shadow waved his hand in front of his face. 'Nah. Don't spoil your magic, Petra. Don't ever say you're normal like me. Because you're not.'

She bowed her head. 'I'm glad you don't want to hear. But I'm happy I shared it with Felicitra.'

'It's better that way. I'd probably not respond the way you'd want. Sad stories, or whatever it is; they don't work on me. Probably a bloody doll you lost down a well.'

Petra laughed. 'I'm the way I am because of a doll?'

Shadow smiled. 'Yeah. A little hemp sack doll, with crappy button eyes sewed on. A creepy little fucker. You called her Sally, after your maid.'

It was working, Petra chuckling along. 'Please, tell me more,' she said.

'Sally was a buxom lass; you had a right proper fancy on her. It's how you got your woman love. You sewed two thimbles onto Sally-doll's chest to make her more like the real thing. Liked to tug on them, you did. That's why you were so mad when you dropped her down the well.' Shadow winked at her. 'You and your dirty wee Sally doll. What memories she must have, eh?'

Petra erupted into fits of giggles. When she found her composure, wiping her eyes, she said, 'You're a clown, an absolute fool.'

Shadow, content he'd turned a terrible evening around, raised his glass and leaned forward. 'To fools.'

Petra clinked her glass against his. 'Forever fools.'

Chapter XVIII

The days blended into one another, each sunny morning bringing the same sense of dread to Petra. She had made her choice; her focus was clear. She had discussed the plan with Shadow, and although he had offered his loyalty, even he appeared uneasy with what was to come. On this morning, she had asked the crew to assemble in the hold. None of them knew why she had summoned them. None except Shadow, who was on deck with Thelia and Thelissa, teaching them how to tie a hitch knot. Thelia's face was a mask of concentration, a little pink tongue poking out from her lips, while Thelissa's focus shifted between her own efforts and Shadow's demonstration.

The sisters had bonded well with Shadow, and although Thelia would occasionally hug him, his response was to prise her away and feign horror. Petra knew he treasured the affection. His own words to her over evening drinks had said as much. He had been quick to clarify it wasn't that he wanted the attention; it was that it meant Thelia's social skills were normalising and it would give her a better chance at life. Thelissa hadn't shown a tactile side, and Petra admired Shadow for his temperament toward her mentoring. He wasn't one for hugs and overt displays of emotion, and it was that which Petra thought worked well with the older girl. She had asked them, every day, how they were coming along: were they happy aboard the Melody? Thelia was ever-grinning, and in the first few days, Thelissa would offer a shrug. Yesterday, she had smiled, telling Petra that she enjoyed being aboard. It was a momentous step.

Petra wondered if that smile would remain after she had told the crew of today's decision. As though he had read her mind, Shadow glanced at the cabin door. A squint from his eyes as he gazed through the small circle of glass. Petra nodded, tilting her head to suggest he follow the others. With his head bobbing, he put down the ropes and ushered the girls to the hold. With a deep breath, Petra opened her door, strode across the empty deck, and descended into the gloom.

In the hold, the odour of the Tormelorian Resin greeted her nostrils. Although it was pleasant, the scent was weaker than it ought to be. The pungent pine contained chemicals that masked the contraband she often carried, and when fresh, the smell would be overpowering. It served its purpose well, confusing the harbour sniffer dogs at many a port.

Petra squeezed through the crowd; gentle apologies given from the crew as she jostled her way to the front of the hold. Illuminated by the lamp, she faced her day of reckoning. Scanning the faces, certain her expression would give away her nerves, she counted their number. All present and standing to attention, all apart from Argan, who had seated himself on Shadow's makeshift bed. At the front of the group, Shadow stood flanked by Thelia and Thelissa. Petra glanced down, noticing Thelia's hand grasping his trouser leg.

'Relax, all of you,' she said. 'This isn't a naval ship.'

The crew shuffled and sighed, an instant transformation into what she knew. Although they appeared calm in posture, there were many anxious eyes staring back at her. It was to be expected; this morning's meeting was unusual.

'I'll make this as quick as I can, although I'm unsure you'll like what I have to say.'

'What's that?' Florent asked.

Shadow said, 'If you let the captain bloody speak, you'll find out.'

A murmur of laughter spread among the crew. Petra was happy for the distraction. She continued when they settled. 'Losing Felicitra, as crewmate and companion, hasn't been easy on any of us. It has been hard for me. But she left me something, a last message I had promised to read and act upon. I followed those instructions, but they gave me more questions than answers. I'd be lying if I said what I do next is an easy choice. It isn't. It's the hardest thing I've ever had to do. But I can't walk away from what I've seen; I can't let Felicitra down by forgetting what she stood for.'

Petra paused, stealing herself for the hammer blow she was yet to deliver. A movement caught her eye, Argan's hand lifting.

'Argan?'

'Yes.'

Petra was confused. 'Yes?'

'I will follow.'

'I haven't asked anything yet.' Petra stared, shifting her glance to Shadow; had he told him? But Shadow shook his head. She brought her attention back to the crew, a further glance given Argan's way, and said, 'Today, I'll be meeting a contact. If all goes well, in order to follow the path Felicitra has laid out for me, the Melody, and all who sail upon her, will have a new purpose.'

'What's that?' Florent asked.

Shadow said, 'What did I say?'

'Sorry.'

Petra was keen to finish. 'We'll operate under a new guise. What we trade, where we sail, if I understand things properly, we'll be sailing under the wind of another master.'

She had expected a murmur. A grumble of discontent. What she couldn't tell them: that if Kastane accepted her offer, they would work under the cult; she would colour in a different light. 'I will take this journey if it's offered to me. But it will place the ship and the crew closer to harm. We may find new enemies, and the risk of capture will mean imprisonment, or worse.'

'Who is to be our enemy?' Argan asked.

Petra looked at Shadow, who nodded. She said, 'Kalleron.'

Argan stood, his head scraping the ceiling. He raised his arm as far as the space allowed. 'You have my service.'

Florent and Jessika, their arms raised, called out. 'Us too.'

One by one, and with no coercion, the crew all agreed, a chorus of "aye" joining a sea of hands. Petra turned to Shadow, his arms at his side. He glared at her.

'I'm not a bloody marionette; you know my answer.'

Petra held her hand to her mouth as Thelia grabbed the cuff of his shirt sleeve and tried to hoist his arm as a sail. Too short to manage, a miracle occurred. Thelissa stepped in and, reaching for Shadow's wrist, she gave him a nod and lifted his arm with hers.

Thelissa said, 'Where you go, we go.'

Petra smiled. She turned to the crew. 'I thank you all. When I know more, I will tell you what I can. Dismissed.'

The chattering crew left the hold, but aware of company, she turned to see four had remained. Argan, Shadow, and the two young sisters. 'I said dismissed.'

Shadow said, 'This *is* my bunk.'

Petra looked at Argan. Not wishing to seem rude, and conscious of his heritage, she said, 'You wish to say something? Of my decision?'

Argan stepped closer. Apart from his physical stature, he had an aura about him; something she couldn't place. A shadow in the dark, or perhaps better suited to his quiet nature: the eye of some great storm.

He said, 'Bruhale was once the most beautiful city on earth. I had friends, family, and a purpose. I served my country, and though I don't seek another war,

I owe nothing to this place.' A pause, and Argan appeared to consider his words. 'Kalleron took everything from me.' He gestured to the hold; to the Melody. 'This is my purpose now. I give you my strength when you stand tall, and offer my hand, should you fall. That is the promise of Bruhada.'

'Thank you, Argan,' Petra said, humbled by his words.

Without saying more, he moved to the stairs and climbed to the deck.

Shadow said, 'What was that?'

She couldn't be sure. There was an intensity in his tone, an undercurrent of emotion she hadn't seen. She said, 'What we've discussed before. His status, perhaps?'

'Ah. Revenge for what happened to Bruhada?'

'Maybe, and I'd be a fool to lose someone as powerful as him.' She turned to the sisters. 'And you two? You're certain you want to stay. This could be dangerous for all of us.'

Thelissa, bringing Thelia to her side, said, 'This feels like a proper home now. We've known danger, and this isn't it. Besides, Shadow's taught me good with a knife. If you'll keep us, we'll stay?'

Petra nodded. 'You can stay. Now shoo, go above deck while I speak to Shadow.'

Thelissa pulled Thelia away, and the sisters scampered up the steps.

Shadow, heaving a sigh from his chest, said, 'Better than expected?'

'It was.'

He smiled. 'That's because you're an idiot, Petra.'

She wasn't insulted, but she was curious. 'How so?'

'This isn't just a crew. You know that. Every man, woman, and girl aboard this ship knows the truth. Without you, they'd be gone already. All of us; except maybe the big man. We're not servants, Petra, and we're not lackeys. We're family. Your family, and unfortunately for you, we're stupid enough to follow wherever you lead us.'

She was aware of their loyalty, but Petra had never taken them for granted. Shadow's words were a comfort, although they didn't remove all of her anxiety. 'There may be real danger, Shadow. This might not end well.'

In his eyes, she saw a spark. 'In danger, Petra, and with our backs to the wall, you'll find the very best of us.'

In the hills above the city, Petra sat on the chair she had toppled one week earlier. The walk to the mansion, the scramble over the gate, and the ponderous drama to gain entry had all been the same. The voice that had called to her was not. Petra sat opposite a sophisticated and beautiful woman. A Bruhadian, she thought, though her skin was lighter than Argan's. Her sculpted features, raven hair, and dark eyes were a distraction from the uniform that she wore. Over a flimsy white blouse, a lacquered corset, coloured black with red accents, was visible beneath her luxurious black cloak. On her hands, she wore leather gauntlets coloured to match the rest of her attire. Small metal plates reinforced the fingers of the gloves. Beneath the table, unseen by Petra, there would be a red and black panelled skirt, complemented by black knee-high boots. A rapier with a keen sharpness would no doubts be hanging from her belt. It was the attire of an overseer. The masters of Kalleron's judiciary and the formal eyes of Kalle.

The voice had been unexpected; the sight of an overseer was a shock. Petra had concealed her dismay, thought better than to run or make a fuss. She had sat as instructed, and assumed one of two fates: this was a test, or it was a trap. Either way, she would wait for the woman to speak further. She didn't have to endure the anxious silence for long.

'And you are?' the woman asked.

'Petra.'

'Why do you sit here?'

'I spoke with a trader last week.' Petra pointed to where Kastane should be. 'He had offered business, but I had to consult my crew first.'

The Overseer clasped her hands; the metal plates clinking together. 'What business did he offer?'

Petra shrugged; she could offer an honest response. 'He didn't really say. I hadn't offered my services. I had to consult with my crew before deciding.'

'Your crew then. Were they obliging?'

'As ever.'

The Overseer sat back in the chair. She was considering her next question. Petra had a rudimentary understanding of the overseers and their role within the court. Had she taken Kastane's offer, she would be in grave trouble, but she hadn't. She had refused him her service. Petra, the crew and the Melody, were not part of the cult. They were clean. She just had to remain calm.

Petra said, 'If you are here, I assume the man I met last week is already in Seawall? If that's the case, I'm glad you've spared me the trouble of what appears to be a poor trade.'

The Overseer nodded. 'It would have been a terrible decision.' She sighed, then leant forward, her elbows on the table, her chin on her fist. 'Such a protracted means to gain entry, simply to organise a trade. Don't you think?'

'A dear friend gave me the key. I trusted her; why wouldn't I?' Petra thought to deliver a killer blow to the conversation. A truth she could easily convey. 'I'm a sea-farer; I suppose you know that? After all, the court's eyes are everywhere. You'll know then that some goods I trade here may not be so welcome in Laria or Dreyahyde. Ambyr Dust, practically a street currency here, is contraband in Dreyahyde.' Petra nodded, a firm bob of her head. 'I must be careful with whom I trade. This isn't the first time I've had to dance around a simple knock on wood.'

The woman appeared content with the reply, and she sat back once again. She looked around the room, although she appeared to be wasting time. After a pause, she said, 'You seem genuine enough, although this discussion will continue elsewhere.'

Petra was confused. Why must they go elsewhere? About to object to the Overseer, the woman banged her fist hard on the table. On Petra's right, a panel on the wall turned from white to black, a void forming where the board disappeared into darkness. From the opening, four men appeared. Dressed in the black and red attire of the guard, they piled into the room.

'What is this?' Petra said, ready to draw her daggers.

The Overseer stood and pointed at Petra. 'Take her weapons. Take her to the fortress!'

She had a moment to react; this wasn't a test. Four guards from a backwater port she would fight. Not four Kallerye guards and an overseer. Although Petra thought she could flee, what fate would befall the crew if her attempt failed? Other ports had put her in jail, always on spurious charges that bribes would erase. She would need to play that game now. This petty infraction wasn't worthy of Seawall.

Her hands raised, trying to control her anger, Petra said, 'My daggers are in my boots.'

'Remove them,' the Overseer said to her. 'Carefully.'

As instructed, and one at a time, Petra unsheathed her blades and placed them on the table. A tremor in her fingers, she moved her hands from the weapons.

'You will come willingly?' the woman asked.

Petra nodded.

The Overseer said, 'This man you met, can you describe him?'

Although she could, she wouldn't. If she had to, she'd play that card later. Shaking her head, she said, 'He sat with his back to the window. When we met, the sun was high. It framed him. All I saw was his silhouette. He had an athletic build. A measured tone. But I think he positioned himself that way so I couldn't see, although I'd recognise his voice if I heard it again.' Her last sentence was an honest gesture, something to offer from the lie she told.

'That will be helpful.' The Overseer nodded to the guards, who closed in. 'Don't play games.'

'I've no wish to cause trouble. I have nothing to hide from you.'

The Overseer stared at her. 'We shall see. Take her away!'

The rough hands seizing her arms were a violation, but Petra focused on remaining calm. She had done no wrong, and there was much to lose if she showed her true nature. A thought of two dead slavers flashed across her mind. No, it wasn't that. The Overseer wouldn't care about such a trivial loss. This was cult business, and it appeared Kastane's house had fallen. Petra wondered if the man was even alive.

Hoisted to her feet, the guards marched her away toward the mansion door. A voice called out from behind. A recognisable gruffness; it was Kastane. There was a crash from the back room, and the sounds of a violent struggle. In the commotion, the guards released Petra and ran back to the Overseer. Again, Kastane's voice rang out.

'Run, Petra. Run!'

If he knew anything of her nature, he would have known that was a redundant command. To run from a fight; that she could do. But to run from the man who could bring her closer to Felicitra's truth? That wasn't an option. Besides, he had called out her name, a man with whom she professed to have no knowledge. Why would he call to her if they were not in league? Watching as the guards stormed down the hallway to their master, Petra bolted after them.

With a scream, she lunged, driving her heel into the back of one. He released a cry as he tumbled to the floor and fell into the back room. There, Petra saw the Overseer on the ground; Kastane standing over her. She wasn't finished, but she was down and out. Petra glanced at her daggers on the table and rushed to grab them. A miscalculation of timing and a consequence of bad luck; a fist swung into her face, sending her crashing to the floor. There was a sudden pause in the melee, broken by Kastane roaring and flying at a guard. It was bad fortune she had caught a glancing blow, but it was better luck the guards had not yet drawn their swords. Petra sprung to her feet and lunged for the table. Another blow, this time to her body, but it failed to topple her; she swung at the guard, her fist connecting with his blocking arm. With her free hand, she grabbed a dagger and swung it toward his face. A violent jolt rocked her shoulder; a brutal force clamped onto her wrist, cutting her attack short. Her blade hovered an inch from the target. She stared. Shocked to see Kastane's grip tight on her arm.

'Enough!' he said. At once, the guards fell back.

Petra glared at him, struggling to free her arm. 'Let go!'

Softer this time, his piercing blue eyes wide, he said, 'It's over, Petra. It's over.'

She squinted. What was over? What was going on? Kastane loosened his grip. She snatched back her hand and stepped away from him. Petra surveyed the room. The Overseer, who had appeared injured, was getting to her feet and dusting down her cloak. The guard she had downed was standing up and rubbing his back. The others were at ease. The Overseer had a strange smile on her beautiful face.

'What?' Petra said, incredulous. 'A test?'

Kastane nodded.

She raged at him. 'Are you fucking mad? I could have killed someone.'

'Fortunately for us all, you didn't.'

She wanted to lunge for him, although from experience, she knew it would be pointless. A growl in her throat, she simmered; tried to rationalise his stupidity.

The woman said, 'Petra, the eyes of Kalle are everywhere; we had to be sure.'

Petra turned to her, pointing to her attire. 'So, you play dress-up to create theatre?' To Kastane, she repeated her accusation. 'If I'd grabbed a sword from one of your men, I'd have stabbed him in the heart.'

One stepped forward, pulling away his cloak to show his scabbard. He pulled the hilt, revealing a wooden blade.

The woman spoke again, tapping her corset. 'This is not a costume.'

Petra stared. 'What? What do you mean?'

'Kastane is my master. And I am an overseer.' She extended her gloved hand. 'Kallisa.'

Rejecting the gesture, Petra said to Kastane. 'What is all this? Clearly, it's not what it appears to be.' She pointed at the woman, Kallisa, then at him. 'Overseer. You, a cultist. What deviousness is this?'

Kastane paced to the Overseer. He placed a hand on her shoulder. 'Kallisa is not loyal to Kalleron. She and I share a common path.' He gestured to the four guards. 'As do they, although their attire is, as you say, dress-up.'

It was difficult to remain calm with her nerves frayed and her suspicion raised. Could it still be a ruse? Petra turned to the Overseer and Kastane. 'How can I trust anything you say?'

'If you choose to follow me, I will give you proof of where my loyalty lies.'

With reluctance, Petra nodded. She had come too far to walk away, regardless of her doubt.

Kastane dismissed the men, who moved into the void where the panel had been. They descended unseen stairs into the darkness. Kallisa followed the guards. Once again, Petra was alone with Kastane in his peculiar house.

He said, 'If you follow me now, you are choosing Felicitra's path. Do you understand? There is no going back.'

The mention of her name rallied Petra's mood. She nodded her head, and the cultist stepped into the void. With a deep breath, followed by a long sigh, she strode from the bright airy room, and into a new world of darkness and secrets.

Petra travelled in silence through confined tunnels that were hewn through the rock. Worn tooling marks scarred the stone, and long fingers of solidified salts descended from cracks and seams where moisture had penetrated. The odour of dank earth replaced the scent of roses and dry wood. Modern lamps, incongruous with the rough passage, lined the walls. The same mineral flare burned inside as those she knew from Laria. After a continual and shallow descent, the corridor opened into a small chamber from which there were two further exits. Petra followed Kastane and Kallisa as they continued to the right. The guards moved away down the other tunnel. She had expected to enter some grand chamber furnished with tomes of ancient texts with engravings of cryptic symbols. There was no such mystery. With time passing, it seemed the trek might go on forever when a familiar smell greeted her senses. It was the sea air. Curious, she tried to peer beyond the other two, a glow coming from the end of the tunnel. At the front, Kastane slowed and held out his hand, and although they were already silent, he appeared to ask for more. Petra held her breath, watching as he moved to a slit in the wall through which a sharp slice of blinding light penetrated.

'It's clear,' he said.

Kallisa moved to his side, and they pushed and pulled at the wall. A portal opened, and a shaft of widening daylight flooded the corridor.

Kastane signalled to Petra. She came to his side, and shielding her eyes, stepped into the light. What she saw filled her with confusion and utter disappointment. She turned through a full circle to gather her whereabouts. It was a hillside above the arc of a beach. Nearby, lethargic plumes of smoke rose from stone chimneys on thatched cottages. Petra brought her attention to the immediate vicinity. An overgrown shrine surrounded by a small cemetery. There was no chamber, no library of secrets. It was the other slope of the Mansion Hill; the rural backside of Kalleron.

Behind her, the tunnel from which they had come exited into an alcove. The simple shrine, a marble arch set into the hill, was to the elemental Water; the slab at the front lying open to reveal its secret. Kastane pushed it, and the rock slid with a grinding rumble. It moved back into a recess, and Petra realised that once shut, there was no way back. With a final grunt, Kastane sealed the door and stepped away. He inhaled the fresh air and exhaled with a contented grumble.

'Peaceful,' he said.

Petra stared at him. 'I was expecting…'

'Extravagant halls and intrigue?' Kallisa said.

Petra felt foolish. Her expectations were more suited to romantic fantasy. 'Perhaps not something so grand. Maybe a room. A desk and some books.'

Kastane huffed. He directed Petra to a flat slab, a long gravestone propped on two granite blocks. She looked at it, saw the weathered etching on top. It was no longer legible. A once cherished memory lost to time and the elements.

'I'd rather not sit on somebody's grave,' she said.

Kastane moved to another similar stone and sat down. He smiled and gestured to the cemetery. 'Nobody lives here.'

'But the dead.'

He shook his head. 'No. There are none here. This is part of my house. Inherited from the past.'

Petra frowned. 'I don't understand.'

As Kallisa sat beside him, Kastane said, 'Kalleron tore the old cult down decades ago. It kept few secrets.' He patted the granite slab. 'This is one of them. It is an old place, but it was never a home for the dead. They created the graves under Kalleron's nose. What better place to meet than a funeral for Kalle's lies?'

'This is cult land?'

'It is nobody's now,' he said.

Kallisa pointed to the village. 'They live a humble life, invisible to most. They are quiet ghosts.'

Felicitra's words; they were similar. Petra said, 'They're cultists? This is a cult town?'

'No.' Kastane's tone was firm. 'They are elementalists, and they don't covet the power the king wields; they see his actions as dishonest and vulgar. They know what the Queen is; what Kalle hides from everyone's view. But they cannot help her, neither can they stand willingly against Kalleron. They are simple people.

So, as Kallisa said, they remain quiet and patient, and they give welcome, if they must, to us.'

His words were intriguing. 'They revere the Queen?'

'They do,' he said. 'As do I.'

'What?'

Kallisa spoke. 'This will be difficult to hear, especially with what you know of Arkalla and Felicitra, but the truth is not what you believe.'

'I know of one truth; told to me by a mercenary sent by Felicitra herself. A witness to what happened. I lost my love, but the Queen destroyed a nation. Is that not genocide?'

Kastane nodded. 'It would seem so.'

It was frustrating to hear him contradict himself, but there was more; he had an understanding deeper than her own. It made sense, of course; his position within the cult. Regardless, it irritated Petra.

'Genocide,' she said again, in case he had missed her point.

'When you sat down,' he said, 'did you brush the stone for ants?'

Petra smirked. 'Of course not.'

'Why not?'

It was a ludicrous conversation. Petra had thought she was joining the cult; an elusive and secretive cabal of intrigue. They appeared more interested in the affairs of a tiny insect.

'They're just ants,' she said.

Kallisa leaned in. 'This is how the Queen views life. If we are even that to her. It's all she understands us to be.'

'Nonsense.' Petra glared; she switched her focus between the two cultists who had clearly lost their minds. 'She is the weapon of Kalleron and she kills with impunity. How can she not understand?'

Kastane smiled. 'Consider what you know of Arkalla. Is it natural? The destruction?'

'No, it was heinous.'

'Was it a human hand that dealt that blow?' he asked.

Petra, the reply ready on her breath, stopped. She shook her head. 'No, it was Earth.'

Kallisa nodded. 'One of the old gods. An elemental power that is beyond nature. Beyond us.'

It wasn't something she wanted to consider; it was easier to think of the Queen of Kalleron as just that—a queen. But she was no such thing. There was a question, though; a glaring problem.

She said, 'Then why does she do what she does? Why does she serve Kalle?'

Kastane said, 'Whatever you think of Kalleron, and no matter how much you despise its empty soul; at the head of the monster is not Kalle, but a legacy of ingenious deception, elemental knowledge, and barbaric enforcement.' He looked to the sea, appearing to appreciate the view, and nodded to Kallisa.

She said, 'As much as my people in Bruhale are captive, as much as the common folk in Kalleron are captive; so too is the Queen.'

'Captive?' Petra said, leaning so far forward she almost fell from the slab. 'Nobody could capture the Earth. That's preposterous.'

A curious smile on his face, Kastane said, 'It's time you learned the truth about Kalle, his mortal line, and the lie that entrapped the curious and wandering Earth. It's time we opened your eyes to a world to which we don't belong.'

Chapter XIX

'When's she coming back?' Thelissa asked.

'Soon,' Shadow said, although he wasn't certain.

The deck of the Melody was quiet. One week in dock and the regular chores were complete, even the daily tasks were long finished. Under a typical Kallerye sun, most of the crew were lazing around the waterfront: some fishing, some bartering, and others had taken themselves farther ashore. Shadow remained aboard, observing the sisters, who had not left the ship since their arrival. The girls lounged on the steps that climbed to the upper deck above Petra's cabin. The only other crew member who had stayed was Argan, loitering somewhere below deck. Shadow thought his demeanour had changed since Petra's talk, his posture more alert than the relaxed Bruhadian he knew.

The girls had also changed, though theirs was to do with life aboard the Melody. Thelia not so much as her sister, but Thelissa's temperament had softened, and she appeared comfortable aboard the Melody, and speaking with the crew. She had professed her guilt to Shadow about her reaction to Argan on the day Petra had taken them aboard. Every day since, she had greeted the friendly Bruhadian. Argan would give a brief reply and continue his business; a response that Thelissa seemed to appreciate.

Good to his word, Shadow had found new clothes for the sisters. When asked where they were from, he had winked. The girls understood. A selection of cotton blouses, leather and fabric leggings, and a dress for each. To Thelissa, fixated on Petra's body armour, he gave a sturdy black bodice. He had been careful selecting a piece that wasn't sultry or suited to the trades, and Petra had confirmed his choice was a good fit; a button up front, dispensing with frivolous lace, and lacking fine detail. In Petra's words, it was as plain as it was ugly. Thelissa loved it, choosing to wear it every day over her blouse. Today, on the steps, the girls wore their blouses and loose cotton leggings with their bare feet exposed to the breeze.

Shadow peered up, seeking the sun. A few more hours and the city would be in shade as the rays disappeared behind the hills. He cast his eyes that way, looking to the mansions, their upper floors visible through the greenery. A deep breath released as a long sigh; he wondered what news Petra would bring. What fate awaited the Melody? Lost in his thoughts, a distant commotion distracted him. Voices and chatter travelling across the harbour.

'What's that?' Thelissa asked, raising her head to the noise.

Shadow stood from the barrel, which had been his seat, and moved to the rail. On the steps, Thelissa had already settled. She was quick to relax, finding little interest in the world beyond Thelia and her safety. The noise was coming from the dockside, farther to the east. A low rumble of excitement hanging in the air. Shadow noticed Argan appear from below deck. He joined him, looking out across the bay.

The Bruhadian pointed at a ship sailing into port. 'There, that ship.'

Shadow saw it. A rare naval ship; it was a vessel of great prestige. 'A general's frigate.'

Argan grumbled.

Painted black with sails to match, the ship had red accents around the trim. Hoisted on the mainmast, a unique flag fluttered in the breeze. Set against a white background, a flaming red sun with a golden eye at its centre rose behind a black and jagged mountain.

'Is that whose ship I think it is?' Shadow said, doubting it could be what he thought.

'And who is that?'

Shadow continued to stare, scanning the deck of the sleek frigate. He had known Kalleron before Petra had come to him; he had served, and although Petra would not be privy to his darker secrets, there were things that even a common soldier would know.

He said, 'That flag was associated with General Aracyse. I thought he had retired years ago, or at least, he had disappeared. You know of him?'

'Only what legend says.'

Shadow was curious about what Argan would say. A Bruhadian's insight of Kalleron's military was usually clouded by animosity. Shadow was a native; and though he understood his nation's nature, he couldn't empathise with those whose lands the King and his terrible Queen had conquered.

'What does legend say?' he asked.

The Bruhadian stared, and for a moment, Shadow thought he hadn't heard his question, but after a snort of breath, Argan replied. His tone was pensive, a hint of thoughts from a faraway place, as though he was trying to recall an experience once lived.

'I told you I served Bruhale, and though in my time he was a younger man, there were rumours of his prowess. I had thought...' Argan paused, seeming to scold himself with a tut. 'That was the past, and it is gone. But what I understand of Aracyse is he is greater than the legends say. And you? Do the rules stop you from speaking what you know of him?'

Shadow turned to Argan. It was a hard path to walk: the secrecy of the Melody, but it wasn't a cast-iron rule; it was a rite of passage. To be free of what had once been, and to sail forward on a new adventure. The past wasn't forbidden; it was yours alone. Shadow had put much of his past to rest since joining Petra, but there were things he could share with Argan. Perhaps the Bruhadian would open up about his mysterious history?

Shadow said, 'I served under Aracyse.'

It was amusing to see Argan's reaction; his stoic face expressing great surprise. 'You know I was a soldier,' Shadow said. 'We know that much about each other.'

Argan rallied his composure, nodding to Shadow. 'Is it true? His legend.'

Shadow returned his focus to the frigate docking at the naval harbour. 'Kalleron demands that its soldiers are ruthless, and that their commanders and generals are equal to the task. The Butcher was before my time; you'll know of him. Kalle sent Te'anor to Bruhale, and he more than met his match in King Baza'rad. That bastard Te'anor was unkillable, yet Baza'rad did the impossible. Well, so the legend says. Aracyse wasn't the same.' Shadow glanced at Argan, aware his words might be ill-considered, but what he wanted to say was a necessary truth. 'Aracyse was a good man. Wasn't twisted like Te'anor, or Ramhellt. They were nasty sons of bitches, quick as kill their own mother than the foe, so they said. But not General Aracyse; I respected him. Sorry if that offends. I figure you don't like to hear good words spoken about Kalleron.'

'An individual has to be judged on their merit.' Argan leant over the rail. 'If you consider the man had honour, I would accept that.'

'Oh, he had honour. And soul. Don't get me wrong; he was a killer, but he never took glory from it. I'd see him on the battlefield, searching for the fallen, friend or foe, and he'd kneel beside them. Those who were dying, he'd send them off to ease their pain. Sometimes thought I saw him pray.' Shadow recalled an image, thought better than to share it. Atop a hill covered with dead and dying bodies, Aracyse kneeling with the setting sun behind. His helmet held in one hand, war hammer in the other. With his head bowed, and a great black cloak rippling in the wind, it was a sight that had sent shivers down Shadow's spine.

'There's movement,' Argan said, pointing to the ship.

Shadow stared, straining to see. Could it really be? A tingling sensation across his flesh, Shadow held his breath. There were no heroes in his world, but there were people worth dying for. And there he was.

Argan said, 'Is that him?'

Although distant, Shadow was certain it was. 'He's a big old bastard, is Aracyse. Did I mention that?'

'I can see.' Argan seemed impressed. 'How tall is he?'

'Not as tall as you, but not far off. Wears plate as though it's not even there. But he'll be older now. I doubt he's anything like I remember.'

Shadow observed the gigantic figure clad in black moving among his men. A head above the rest, he disappeared from sight. An answer to an earlier question: yes, Aracyse was alive, not yet retired. Though it was strange; experience had taught Shadow the logistics of Kalleron's war machine. It was unusual for a general with Aracyse's renown to come to the city. Kalle preferred his sole place as the resident legend. Whatever had called Aracyse back, it would be nothing trivial.

He voiced his thoughts. 'I'm not sure how Baza'rad treated his military, but Kalle's not one for sharing the glory. To bring Aracyse back means something's up, and not just a bunch of bandits in the Southlands.'

Argan stared down at Shadow, then pointed to the mansions in the hills. 'Let's hope it has nothing to do with that.'

Shadow looked to the hills, thought of Petra wandering alone along those cobbled streets. What trouble would she find there? What intrigue would she discover from the cult?

'Well, whatever's going on, I've got a strange feeling we're about to be pulled into something riskier than trading trinkets.' He offered Argan a smile, something to cheer up the old soldier. 'Better dust down the leathers and sharpen your steel. I think we'll have proper business coming soon.'

Argan smiled. 'We use hammers.'

'Of course you do,' Shadow replied, slapping the Bruhadian's solid shoulder. 'Of course you bloody do.'

The moons were high in a glittering dark sky, and the harbour bell had chimed. Shadow, seated upon the gangplank, faced the shore, his focus drawn to all movement. Petra was late, and although it was her prerogative to do as she pleased, it was out of character. Her clandestine meeting complicated things. It was a worry he could have done without, made worse by the sisters, who refused to go to their bunk without the captain aboard. They sat on the deck, perched on top of two barrels he had pulled closer to the edge. They peered into the gloom, waiting for the boss to come home.

'Why can't we sit on the plank?' Thelissa asked.

'Yeah,' Thelia said. 'Why not?'

For the third time, Shadow said, 'Because you'll fidget.' He pointed at Thelia. 'I know you bloody will, and you'll fall into the soup below. I'm not jumping in there to get you.'

'He's right,' Thelissa said. 'You'll wiggle and wriggle and slip under the ropes.'

'I'll not!'

'Wriggle and wiggle, and you'll go *sploosh*,' Thelissa said, poking her sister.

'Oya! Stop it!'

Shadow smiled at their antics. The playful niggling between the sisters calmed his nerves and served as a distraction from the worry that had grown in his thoughts: Petra's turmoil, and her decision to ally herself with the cult. And now General Aracyse had come to Kalleron. Such a pleasant and calm evening; a cool breeze to stir the warm air. It should feel lovely, but it felt as though a lie. Something Kalleron itself might conjure. He huffed. Even his thoughts were more suited to Petra's erratic moods. It wasn't right.

'There she is,' Thelissa said, pointing to the waterfront.

Shadow tracked her finger and sighted the captain moving along the docks. She appeared in no hurry, walking without hindrance. If she carried an injury, it wasn't serious; if she carried gifts, they were too small. He turned to Thelia, nodding to her.

'Remember what we agreed? I let you stay up late, but you need to do like I said. Or you're grounded.'

'What's that? Grounded?' she asked.

'Like a ship run aground. Grounded. You can't go nowhere.'

Thelissa frowned. 'But we're not, we're docked.'

Shadow puffed a breath. 'It's a bloody figure of speech.' Petra had almost returned. With a whisper to Thelia, he said, 'Get ready.'

As Petra came close, her eyes met his. She appeared tired. Shadow, anticipating her reaction, nodded to Thelia; a silent prompt given to carry out his command.

Thelia, puffing out her little chest, said, 'Oi, what time do you call this?'

She delivered it with perfect timing. Shadow grinned, waiting for Petra to respond. She stopped in her tracks, stared at Thelia, and bowed.

'I am sorry, captain Thelia. My day has been long. I have no excuse for my tardiness.'

'Captain Thelia,' Shadow said. 'You hear that? Promotions already.'

The girl grinned, although she appeared doubtful of the praise. She pointed at Shadow and said, 'He made me say it.'

He raised his hand. 'Guilty as charged.'

'Said he'd throw me in the sewer if I didn't.'

Petra glared at him. Stupefied, he stared back; he hadn't said that at all, protested as much to Petra, who shook her head in mock disgust.

'He didn't really,' Thelissa said. 'Little tyke's only being funny.'

Shadow glanced at the older sister, giving her a nod of thanks.

Petra, at the edge of the plank, and with her hands on her hips, said, 'Everyone aboard?'

'Aye.'

'We should talk.'

Shadow hauled himself to his feet and shooed the sisters away. 'Playtime's over, off to bed. Go, begone.' With giggles and laughter, Thelia and Thelissa pushed and slapped at each other as they danced across the deck and disappeared below. Shadow gestured to Petra's cabin. 'A debrief?'

With a nod and a sigh, Petra strolled past and disappeared inside. Shadow followed behind, a murmur of discontent within. The captain slumped into her chair with extravagant disregard, a sharp creak coming from the frame as she tested its constitution. She kicked her legs up and let them fall onto the desk, crossing them at her ankles. Her split skirt fell away, revealing her boots and thighs. Shadow, happy to gawp at a beautiful woman, waved at her display and grimaced.

'Petra, that's a tease I can't afford,' he said, pointing to her legs as he sat down.

'It's just flesh. We've all got it. Besides, this is my cabin. I could sit here naked if I chose.'

Shadow hummed. 'At least you're wearing your practical knickers.'

Petra pointed to her short bloomers; a ruffle of white hiding all the important parts. 'What did you call these again, when you saw me in them in Hoydai?'

Shadow laughed, recalling his own words. He raised a finger. 'Quite ironic, really, given where you've been. Man-shunners, cos they're damn ugly.'

She laughed and slapped her thigh. 'But they're so comfortable.'

'So, your day? Seriously, you were gone so long; I was sizing up your cabin for a bigger bed.'

'It was... a day.' Petra took a few breaths, long and drawn out. She was composing herself, although Shadow couldn't tell if it was fatigue or intrigue.

He asked, 'So, what can you tell me?'

'I thought I'd need to keep you in the dark; run this thing myself, but that makes no sense. So, I thought I'd tell you whatever I wanted to, then I thought of Kastane. He's a powerful man, Shadow. I didn't want to betray any trust, so I mentioned about bringing you in.'

He raised his hand. 'Nope. I don't want in. I'm here for you. If you're getting into bed with them, then you can get it embroidered into those awful knickers. But I'm not the cult type. Need my freedoms.'

'Are you finished?'

'Aye.'

'Good, because you're not part of it. I am. But what we do, what we're about to do, where we go; you need to know. We treat it as any other voyage or trade. Is that fair?'

He supposed it was. Nodded to confirm it. 'Drinks?'

'I'm not moving. Go get some; you know where it all is.'

Shadow stood up and moved to the cabinet. He opened the ornately hinged door to reveal the liquid treasure. Inside, there was a measure of dratch, some dregs of Cyreni, a dozen bottles of rum, and another spirit he didn't know. Several bottles of red wine had dust on their necks. He held up the bottle he didn't recognise, a label written in a script he hadn't seen.

'This one?'

Petra nodded.

'What is it?' he asked. 'Is it strong?'

She shrugged. 'It might strip the tar from the hull. I picked it up a year ago in Shaddenhyne.'

Shadow sat down and pulled the cork stopper from the top. He sniffed the vapours and winced. 'Tar-stripper it is.' He poured two glasses, took a sip of what seemed to be a potent spirit, and settled into his chair. As the liquid burned the lining of this throat, he said, 'Then, what can you tell me?'

Petra reached for her glass in an ungainly fashion, her fatigue telling in her sluggish and cumbersome movements. With glass in hand, she sniffed the contents, pulling the same expression he had, and sipped.

'God, that's strong,' she said and took another. She relayed her adventures to him, but he was quick to stop her at the mention of the woman.

'Pretty?'

Petra nodded. 'Stunning, I'd say. She'd send all hearts a flutter, loins too.'

'And an overseer? I'm confused.'

'Then let me speak, and you can ask questions after.'

Petra continued her story of what appeared to have been a staged interrogation, a fight of which he was envious, and a journey to a mysterious cemetery on the other side of the hill. Her long walk back explained much of her fatigue. There was detail, but Shadow lost focus on the parts that didn't involve descriptions of the woman, Kallisa, or the fight at the beginning. With his drink finished, and her story over, he stood up, retrieved her glass, and returned to the cabinet. As he poured another, he thought of her story. Elements of it he thought he had missed were bouncing around inside his skull.

'You say they have no base? No secret hideout?'

'No, they meet in plain sight, mostly. Kallisa's role allows her to do many things, although she has to tie her movements to official business.'

Shadow passed Petra her drink before sitting down. 'Clever plan.'

'The court is always looking for some place where they all gather. Kastane knows that would be suicide. So, they operate as small cells, always moving, except for the meetings in the hills, but even then, there is nothing in that house.'

A thought occurred to Shadow. 'They must have plans, records, or at least stolen documents?'

'They memorise all that they can. Burn what paper they use. They have a saying that they are like ghosts, and it fits them well. They've had their problems, but Kastane has organised them into an effective and invisible organisation.'

'And you say they've given you a mission now?'

Petra nodded. 'We sail in two days. To Gwynerath.'

'Gwynerath?' Shadow sat upright. He looked at Petra, tried to see some show of emotion. The coastal port was Arkallon's primary hub. Even in Laria, before they had come to Kalleron, they had heard tales of the refugees. It was where Felicitra had gone to never return.

'Don't worry about me,' Petra said, clearly aware of his concern. 'You're thinking of Felicitra?'

'Aye.'

'All of this brings me closer to the truth of what happened. To who she really was. If I'm settled with this course, then so can you.'

It allayed one concern: that of Petra's wellbeing, but there was another pressing issue. Shadow, not entirely convinced, sat halfway back in the chair.

'There'll be Kallerye ships. Soldiers. Pirates. It'll not be safe.'

'I'm aware, but we're traders. They can board the Melody if they must, they'll find no issue. Our cover is that we're to meet a business contact in the high cliffs. It's a solid ruse; a wealthy man who wants to secure passage away.'

It sounded so easy. Shadow doubted that was the case. 'And then?'

Petra smiled and stifled a yawn. 'Kastane's a careful man. He didn't say. It's a chain of isolated knowledge. When we meet the contact, we'll know what we're doing.'

Shadow fully reclined, slipping his rear to the edge of his chair. They had one day of rest before setting sail. For now, he was content to sip the burning liquid. He thought to ask more of the woman, Kallisa, when Petra dropped her glass to the rug beneath her chair. A glance over, and her head had lolled to the side; a gentle wheeze coming from her mouth. Shadow stared at her. Petra of Laria; this little svelte thing. She was as much of a warrior as he, as much of a leader as Aracyse. He sighed, realising he had not told her of the day's gossip; of the return of a legend. Although, if they had recalled the General to Kalleron, perhaps other places posed less risk. Places such as Gwynerath? With Petra's breathing becoming heavier, Shadow downed the spirit and stood up. He moved around to his captain, sorted her head so she wouldn't wake with a crick in her neck, and looked at her bare thighs laying across the table.

You are a tease, he thought, but it was only because he wanted to look. He didn't linger. Instead, he grabbed a light throw and placed it over her lap. He moved to the cabin door, and with one last glance at his captain, slipped beyond and onto the deck. All was quiet in Kalleron. All was still. But for how much longer?

Chapter XX

Aracyse had become accustomed to the staring. It was to be expected; it was a reasonable response to his armour and the arm. Wrapped in his silk cloak, and accompanied by his personal guard, he had marched through the fortress gate to the Generals' Tower. Every step of his enormous frame had rocked his shoulder with jarring force, and although Anders had reassured him of its meticulous design, Aracyse would occasionally glance at the metal limb to see if his blood was trickling down onto the sculpted fist. He had an unhealthy paranoia that the hefty appendage might fall off. It seemed no better than a cumbersome ornament; having not yet mastered any movement. The Etherus physician told him the healing process would take a while longer, but Aracyse thought that the volume of regenerative herbs he had consumed might have at least shown some effect. Anders' had scolded him with that exquisite lack of respect. "Patience, Aracyse, I am a genius, and you are but the student of my works". He had laughed at Anders' words, found his honest manner to be a refreshing wind in contrast to the sorrows and sympathy others had attempted to hide. From having wanted his head on a plate, Aracyse had doubled down on his appreciation of Anders' dedication. When the King had summoned him to Kalleron, Aracyse promoted Anders to the rank of honorary general. At least then, he thought, the workers wouldn't see his attitude as wilful insubordination.

The Generals' Tower nested into the marble wall of the fortress, and as all other constructs, it did not rise above the battlements. The gargantuan wall, which encircled the inner-sanctum of Kalleron, had taken decades to complete. Begun long before the Queen had become Kalle's weapon, ingenious minds had planned everything about the secretive fortress. Every element helped perpetuate the myth of Kalle. They had left nothing to chance; although, as Aracyse had learned from Etherus, Kalleron would be vulnerable to the same tool that devised its perfection: the human mind. It was an unfortunate reality there were those that would see Kalleron fall, and they too held the same powers of intellect.

From his elevated balcony, Aracyse stared out across the sunken plain. Hewn from the earth, engineers had excavated down to the bedrock in most places. To the south, along the western periphery of the fortress, the Court of the Overseers stood separate from the rest of the grounds. It was dissimilar to the Generals' Tower; the court having its own unique inner-wall. Behind it, a square of elegant mansion houses was the operating base of the visible eyes of Kalle. The common folk regarded the overseers as the iron fist of Kalleron's visible presence. Although they served that purpose, Aracyse knew there was another hand moving unseen within the fortress.

The great expanse of the southern wall housed those that served closest to Kalle. Servants, advisors, and the guards tasked with staging the daily myth of Kalle's immortality. Those select few never left the fortress. Once recruited, they were slaves to the deception, never again to set foot in the outside world. To Aracyse's left, the northern wall hosted another two towers. As with the Generals', they were taller and wider than that found in any other castle or fortress. On the northern perimeter, the foundations met the bedrock ridge of the coastal inlet east of the harbour. When viewed from sea, the illusion of scale gave the impression that the marble face was hundreds of feet high.

The fortress walls encircled a massive area, but most of the land within was barren rock. There were two exceptions. A castle stood in the north-eastern corner. Built on stilts above an artificial inlet, and approached by a curving wooden bridge, it was the curious seat of the King. Constructed of Drohendrian darkwood, Aracyse hadn't known of any other regent live in such an oddity. The other, a squat marble column, which appeared to grow from the very bedrock, stood alone in the centre of the fortress. The Queen's tower was devoid of regal intricacies and architectural flourishes, and without tooling marks or seams showing in the masonry; legend said she raised it from the ground using her will alone. It was a bizarre monument. A puzzle for Aracyse to ponder on every visit. She had no need of a place to live, yet it was where she wandered when not loose upon the world, destroying other nations. When viewed through a sight glass, Aracyse could see the bizarre feature that surrounded her tower in uneven patches. A garden of stone flowers. He had wanted to examine her creation, but to venture near the Queen's tower was a crime punishable by death. A judgement that applied to all, it was one Aracyse was not keen to test.

With the pain in his arm surging, he turned from the view and walked through the arch into the cover of his grand chambers. This was not Etherus, and as much as Aracyse preferred simple things, his living quarters were ostentatious. Gold fittings for the lamps, golden trim around the portraits of Kalle; artisans had crafted everything to glorify the King. A sigh from his travel-weary lungs, and Aracyse moved to the basin and pushed the handle of the silver-plated pump. After several attempts, a surge of fresh water filled the small white bowl. He reached for a golden goblet and dunked it into the water. The bowl drained too fast, and he cursed his one-handed limitation. A murmur of frustration turned to a chuckle as he stared at the emptying basin. A knock on the door drew his attention from the task.

'Enter!' he said. The door opened, and a woman strode in. An overseer; he had met her before. 'Kallisa, please come in.'

'General Aracyse, it is good to…' She stopped after those few words. His arm had drawn her gaze.

'Ah, yes. Stare awhile, if you must.'

'I apologise, General. They told me but I had not expected it to be so… ornate.'

Aracyse smiled. 'Perhaps a wooden stump with a hook would draw less attention?'

Kallisa nodded. 'I see your sense of sarcasm remains intact.'

'If I cannot make light of this misfortune, then I'd be no better than a brooding sop.' He gestured to the basin. 'Though it is useless for this.'

She frowned. 'What do you mean?'

'I can't fill my cup.' Aracyse looked at the basin, pointing at it with his good hand, the goblet still held tight. 'A modern miracle, or at least, to have such waterworks within a lofty tower. Yet I asked on my last visit if would they fit a stopper, that the basin remains full.'

'You have no stopper?' Kallisa appeared amused.

'Alas, I have not.'

Kallisa stepped toward him, and reaching for the cup in hand, asked, 'May I?'

He nodded and stepped to the side, allowing her to fill his goblet. She passed it to him and moved away. Her attention on his arm once more, she failed to hide her grimace.

'It is painful,' he said. 'You don't have to disguise your reaction.'

'What remains of your arm?'

'Nothing at all, but Anders Beriafal created something exceptional, and though I can't yet animate the arm, he said it will have some functional movement.'

'It moves?' Kallisa's tone was elevated, her eyes wide. She pointed. 'He created a moving prosthetic? That's not possible.'

Aracyse smiled. 'You know of Anders?'

'I do.'

He tilted his head to the side and smiled. 'Then you shouldn't dismiss his work so readily.'

Kallisa apologised and shook her head. 'Oh no, I never intended insult. It's just...'

'Remarkable is what it is.'

Kallisa's gaze remained on his arm. She stared at it, although Aracyse did not find it awkward. She appeared deep in thought.

She asked, 'Is it true? The rumours that came from Etherus.'

He knew the Overseer would have some knowledge of the terrible events, but he was unwilling to reveal facts she may not have heard. The Overseers played a critical role in information manipulation; Aracyse thought better than to give Kallisa something she may use against Etherus. Its work was important, but not all within the court valued its contribution.

'Which rumours?'

She pointed to his metal appendage. 'The arm, of course. Some say a Fury was responsible.'

'What else did they say?'

Kallisa smiled. 'General, I would not presume to know Etherus' secrets, and I'm very well aware that you run a complex operation. All I have heard is that a Fury took your arm.' She shook her head. 'Yet you live?'

'I live. It saddens you?'

'No, General, of course not. But we know the power they hold.' Kallisa pointed to herself, her fingers on her chest. 'I am one of few that understand Etherus to be a weapons factory, and that for Kalleron's glory, you try to tame the wind. It is not without mortal risk.'

Aracyse nodded. 'An accident in transport. It's humbling, really. I swore to be more alert than my predecessor.'

'General A'dan?'

'Yes. And I was careful.' Aracyse recalled the events on Etherus. It was to his immense frustration that so much of what had happened was elusive. The guards who had come to his aid had given some illumination to light the deep voids of dark in his memory. But the grim moment itself was a haze. 'They found me in the snow near the gatehouse; it's why I'm alive today. But others were not so fortunate. I lost a friend and some very good workers in that disaster.'

Kallisa sighed. 'I am sorry, General. I truly am. But it shows the Fury is viable. It will be a magnificent weapon for Kalleron.'

Aracyse stared at her. A Bruhadian, she was an unusual choice for an overseer. It was an anomaly. He laughed, trying and failing to hide his humour.

'General?'

It might seem crude to say what was on his mind, but Aracyse couldn't tolerate unnecessary obfuscation; an irony given the company. His good hand gesturing to the Overseer, he said, 'You're a Bruhadian serving in the Kallerye Court. It tickles me, always has.'

'Should I not serve?'

'I know of few… no, I know of no other such as you in the inner-sanctum. As diverse as Kalleron can be, it still puzzles me that a Bruhadian walks these most secret grounds.'

'You don't believe my kind belongs?'

He had spoken of her ethnicity, and Aracyse had expected Kallisa to respond, but he perceived her words as a distraction from his true meaning. 'Don't play games, Kallisa, you know what I mean. You hail from a proud culture that Kalleron destroyed. Everything you knew, gone. I imagine you were a child when it happened, perhaps not yet born, but I've never known a Bruhadian to serve its new master with the zeal of an overseer.'

He would have been naïve to believe she would falter under such words; overseers were not weak-willed idiots. They ascended through the ranks of the justiciary and were loyalists to Kalle. It was a puzzle regardless.

Kallisa stared at him. Her gaze not wavering, she said, 'Would you do me the favour of walking with me?'

'To where?'

She gestured to the balcony. Aracyse nodded. He put down the golden cup and followed behind as she stepped through the open archway. He joined her at the edge, placing his hand on the darkwood railing. Kallisa pointed to the Queen's tower.

'That is your answer.'

It was obvious as she pointed to it, and it was enlightening to hear her words. A truth few would dare to reveal within the fortress walls, and although her words were intriguing, they were also dangerous. Aracyse would need to keep his wits around the Overseer.

'You serve *her*?'

'I serve Kalleron, but my devotion is to the elementals. Which is fortunate, as Kalle is our elemental master.'

Her latter words were a loyal mantra, not what he expected her to say. Aracyse couldn't stop the wry smile spreading across his face.

Kallisa said, 'My devotion, my fealty—it is amusing to you, General?'

'Half of what you said, I empathise with, but the rest?'

Aracyse winced as a searing pain flashed through his shoulder.

'General?' Her concern appeared genuine.

With beads of sweat on his brow, Aracyse gripped the banister with his good hand. Another glace to his metal limb; still there was no blood. Yet the pain was increasing. It occurred to him that Kallisa's arrival had distracted him. The goblet of water was to dissolve the root Anders had given him in Etherus.

'The arm,' he said, an involuntary groan forced from his lungs. 'The surgery was... complex. It is no simple severance. Anders' gave me herbs for the pain. They're inside my chamber.'

Aracyse turned from the Overseer and strode inside. He located his goblet and was relieved to see there was water left within. Across the room, in a medicinal pouch, the crushed Vallacyne would remedy his discomfort. With the noise of Kallisa's boots on the wooden floorboards, he excused himself and mixed his solution. It was a foul concoction, but the effects were rapid. He leant on the varnished stand for a few moments with his eyes tight shut. Flashes of a dark and wintry sky punctured the shield of his lids; a memory of the Fury's attack come back to terrorise him. Liberated by the Vallacyne, he turned to face Kallisa, who had moved to the other side of the room. She was scrutinising his actions.

'Medicinal Vallacyne,' he said.

'The pain is that great?'

He nodded. 'It is tolerable now. Where were we? Ah. Your fealty to the King; your devotion to the Queen. May I ask you something, Kallisa?'

'You may.'

'We both know the Queen is the Earth. Of that, there can be no doubt.'

She nodded a confirmation.

'And of Kalle? Tell me, as a Bruhadian, is he truly immortal?'

He studied the Overseer's expression, searching for a tell in her features. Aracyse wanted to see her mask slip; he doubted her belief in Kalle's immortality and his claim to be the human elemental. He wanted to see her truth, but he was struggling against the Vallacyne. It was exceptional at removing physical pain, but the side-effects were profound. A fog was descending; his vision beginning to blur, and reckless words were being freed from his thoughts. He realised he shouldn't be having this discussion at all.

Kallisa said, 'It's not recorded in the Bruhadian tradition. But I don't doubt his power.' She paused, took a step closer. 'General, your question was weighted. What is your belief?'

He stared at her through a soft mist. The Overseer was on the attack. He wanted to engage in this battle, but the Vallacyne had him at a tremendous disadvantage. With another paltry servant of Kalleron, he would not hesitate. One-armed and high on lethal drugs, he would still beat them with his logic. Not an overseer; their training and their guile for manipulation would be a step too far.

'I believe I need my rest, Overseer.' Aracyse frowned. 'Why did you come to me?'

Kallisa bowed. 'To welcome you home, General, and to ask that at midday tomorrow, you report to the King. He is expecting a debrief of events at Etherus.'

'Of course.'

The Overseer bowed and left the chamber. Aracyse sighed as the door closed. It shut with a soft click. A punctuation of sound to finish their conversation. He had wanted to delve into her mind, see what sympathies a Bruhadian might have with the Queen. She had made her instincts clear, but she had not reacted to his prompts of Kalle's deception. It would be a mistake he wouldn't repeat. He had spent too long in Etherus; had forgotten the simple rules of Kalleron. An old saying in the court, one that he could not abide. *Trust was rarely useful, seldom repaid, and always a trap.*

Kallisa leant on the General's door and heaved a sigh of relief. What had just happened? The General's conversation had taken an awkward turn. It had required focus not to fall for his subversive tone. He had been clear in his reaction; a public rebuke of Kalle's self-declared status. That he was not immortal was obvious. His elemental claim was ludicrous, although it was a lie that had endured for decades. Why had Aracyse, of all people, tried to lure her into a trap? A thought crossed her mind, something too fanciful; perhaps it was not a trap, but a crack in the General's loyal veneer. It took patience and intellect to achieve the rank of general in Kalleron's army. Those men were not fools; they all played along, but none had ever declared a doubt in Kalle's power. Confused and shaken by the turn of the conversation, Kallisa descended the spiral staircase and exited the tower.

Court decree mandated she did not walk across the rocky plateau. To do so would bring her too close to the Queen's tower. There were much discussed rumours of her power, of what could happen in the elemental's presence. Guards had found servants crushed to death, nothing left but a pulp of flesh. They had strayed too close, so the whispers said. Kallisa scoffed at the thought. She knew the elite guard would seize any fool caught venturing nearby. Take them to one of the three towers where they murdered them, and pulverised their bodies with heavy hammers; the remains left in the grounds to be found later. It was a horrific fate to warn away others. A human punishment framed around the Queen's legend.

She paced along the western wall, the bright sun overhead. Basking in the heat, she glanced to the Queen's tower. It was a voluntary prison. As much as it pained Kallisa to think it, she understood the brutal brilliance and execution of Kalle's deception. A ruse so perfect and confident that it had ensnared the wandering Earth and brought her back to Kalleron as a mighty and omnipotent weapon. Lost in thought, a noise startled her; a sound as though waves dragging across shingle. She looked to her left, her heart in her mouth; the shock stumbling her against the wall. It was the Queen, ten paces away. In an instant, she felt a crushing pain, invisible boulders falling on top of her. She slumped to the ground, suffocating under the excruciating pressure. A frightening image appeared in her mind—those crushed bodies. Was it true? She held a hand out to the Earth, tried to speak. A single word came forth, a feeble gasp.

'*Stop!*'

The Queen paced forward. Each step a mountain upon Kallisa. Darkness clouded her vision. '*Please, stop! You're killing me.*'

In an instant, the pressure was gone. It was as if it had never been there, an incredible and terrible thing. Vulnerable on her back, she looked up at the Queen, her aura somehow diminished, and although Kallisa wanted to speak, she found no words to say.

'What are you?' the Queen asked.

Kallisa continued to stare. Had she succumbed to the pain? Had the relief been nothing more than a dream before death?

The Queen spoke again. 'Are you life?'

'Life?'

'I spoke with life in Arkalla when I was reclaiming my own. I am curious, are you as he? Are you life?'

Kallisa nodded, uncertain of what was happening. She glanced at the northern wall. Obscured by the uneven bedrock, she could see two of the massive towers. The general's balcony was in view. Worse, Aracyse stood there, although if he was looking her way, in the vast grounds of the fortress, she would be a speck against the grey. She had to hope he wouldn't see.

The Queen said, 'If you are life, why are you?'

Bringing her focus back to the elemental, Kallisa shook her head. The question made no sense, but the Queen waited for an answer. Her otherworldly beauty mesmerised Kallisa; the form the Earth had taken was without sex, although the graceful curves and slim build were that of a woman. A spiral of gems that sparkled with an inner radiance adorned her marble skin. Her features were attractive, sculpted and soft, although her blood-red eyes appeared too large for a human face, and they swirled with an unknown depth.

'I am,' The Queen said. 'You cannot be. Yet I met a man who was. If you are life, as he claimed to be, why do you exist at all?'

Kallisa focused, trying to absorb the elemental's question. She shook her head. What was happening? She had never known of anything such as this. Ancient texts described her curiosity, but Kalle's grip had suppressed that welcome trait. What had caused it to return? Kallisa was about to reply, but the Queen appeared motionless. A statue apart from itself.

'My Queen?'

There was no response. She stood there as though time was a fabric she wouldn't wear. A vision came to Kallisa of the world ageing, the mountains shifting into rubble, and the oceans drying to dust—after it all, the Queen would remain; as she always had. A conversation with Kastane rattled Kallisa's thoughts. He had said that death, not life, created the impetus to find a purpose. Death hung over them all, to give reason to create something in what little time they had. Without death to fear, was there any meaning at all?

Curious whether the Queen would hear, Kallisa said, 'I was born. My parents gave me life.'

The Queen flinched. 'That gift is Kalle's.'

'No. It's a human gift.'

'Kalle creates life; he has shown me.'

Kallisa shook her head. 'He showed you a lie.'

'No. He proved his power.'

Was she speaking of the devious ruse of Kalle's ancestors? Kallisa felt a surge of energy rippling through her body. She wished Kastane could see her now. What she would say was heresy, but it was a fundamental truth to the cult.

She said, 'You speak of the woman and child? He cut the unborn from her belly. He stole it from her. Robbed her of a child made from love.'

'I do not know love. Love was not there. You are mistaken. Kalle created life. It was proof of his power; he brought forth his element—the human.'

It maddened Kallisa that her grand statement seemed to confirm the Queen's faith in the lie. Kalle had used the old scrolls plundered from the temples. He had sought all the elemental knowledge that was available to him. Everything he learned, he used to deceive the Earth. How magnificently he had deceived her, but Kallisa could not let the lie go unchallenged.

'Then of Kalle; you believe him to be an elemental?'

'Of your kind, yes.'

'And that he is immortal?'

There was no frown, but the Queen appeared confused. 'That he is, as am I.' A slender marble digit pointed down at Kallisa. 'You are not.'

With a smile on her lips, Kallisa spoke in a manner she thought the elemental might better understand. 'If he is, as are you, then he cannot be undone. He cannot... cease to be?'

'Correct. I cannot. Kalle cannot. We are. You are not.'

Kallisa placed her hand on her chest. 'I know you are true. I know you are Earth. But he is not what he claims to be. If you saw that, would you believe? If you saw him bleed, or suffer as I did when you appeared, could you still believe?'

The Queen stared. It was intense, uncomfortable. Kallisa looked away, unable to maintain her focus. She waited for a few moments; hopeful the Queen would respond but there was only silence.

'My Queen?'

'You suffered?'

Confused, Kallisa thought of her own words. 'Yes, when you appeared. It was painful.'

'I caused you that pain?'

Kallisa nodded. Was the Queen unaware of her oppressive aura? This was a new thing to know; another thing she would tell Kastane.

'I do not kill. I do not cause pain.'

It was incredible; an unprovoked display of denial. It was a weakness in the Queen's belief. Something to use against her. Kallisa said, 'You may not mean to my Queen, but you cause a great deal of pain. You...'

'No!' Her reply was instant. 'I reclaim what is mine; Kalle takes back what is his. You have no purpose without his will.' The elemental pointed to her tower. The ground shuddered, and her marble domain rose higher, growing upward and outwards. Clouds of dust billowed into the air. 'This is my will. As you are his.'

Kallisa stared in disbelief as the ground shook again and the tower reverted to its normal form. A realisation came to her, an instinct overwhelming her curiosity. That impossible display of power would bring the elite guard rushing to the fortress grounds. She couldn't risk being caught with the queen. Her status wouldn't save her from the pulverising hammers. Kallisa rose to her feet, and cursing her own lies, said, 'You are correct, my Queen. I have erred, and I apologise. I am nothing without my master. Let me be on my way; I must do his bidding.'

Without another word, Kallisa stumbled away from the Queen. A dreadful thought: would the elemental follow? Glancing over her shoulder, Kallisa saw the Queen hadn't moved. Her stance was unchanged, frozen in time. Her relief was short-lived. High in his tower, General Aracyse, his cloak billowing in the breeze, was looking her way. One slim hope to quieten her nerves; the Vallacyne. Aracyse had taken enough to blind a horse. Kallisa, moving with increasing haste, reached the Court of the Overseers. A small crowd of workers greeted her, an excitable chatter rising among them. They all asked: did you see it? Did you see?

Kallisa nodded and told what lies she could. As they all pointed to the Queen's marble tower, she stared at another. Her only comfort was that Aracyse had earlier displayed a subversive tone; whether a deception or a confession, she couldn't be sure. Whichever it was, she was sure they would have far more to discuss. Whether that was in his tower or shackled within a cell in Seawall, she would have to wait and see.

Chapter XXI

Aracyse had awoken, but the light in his sleeping quarters was a meagre glow. That he had stirred so early was not a surprise; having taken some Yverelyn to counter the Vallacyne, it was a miracle he had slept at all. Aracyse wouldn't have touched the damn stuff, but the wonder he had observed from the balcony, a magnificent and terrible thing to see, had forced his hand. His vision blurred by the medication; he had witnessed a white figure in the grounds. Perhaps the Queen wandering far from her tower? It had given him no cause for concern. But a wave of pressure had washed over him; an unpleasant and unnatural shudder of force. Hindered by the Vallacyne, he had the notion to clear his senses with Anders' Yverelyn stimulant. The price for his clarity of vision had been an explosion of pain, but what he had observed was worth every excruciating stab. He saw a remarkable interaction between the Queen and the Overseer. More impressive was the incredible transformation of the Queen's tower. An unprecedented event, Aracyse couldn't separate the sensation of suffocation from the miraculous expansion of her marble domain. He wanted to know—needed to know—what had happened between Kallisa and the Queen. He hoped his summons reached her before other, less friendly, hands tried to bury the truth.

Aracyse lay recumbent on his bed, propped up on plush pillows covered with expensive fabrics that he imagined were better suited to a pleasure house in Hoydai. The padding was a necessity; the sheer bulk of the metal arm had forced adjustments to more than his daily activities. At first it had troubled his slumber, but he had become accustomed to the new nocturnal routine. He rose and wobbled under the lop-sided weight, and moved to the washbasin. It had amused him to find a ceramic plug in the sleeping chamber. Kalleron with all its wealth could only afford him one. A single plug for the whole quarters. After washing his body and carefully drying his shoulder and the leather binding, he put on his day clothes and moved to the corner of the room. There, within a darkwood frame, suspended from belts and gears, was the mechanical miracle of Ander's creation; the armoured clockwork core. The physician had shown Aracyse how to *dress* himself using the contraption, and although protracted, it was a private moment. He had no need of servants who might fuss and gossip. With a sigh, knowing it would take some time, Aracyse entered the machine, thankful it was not a daily affair.

When he stepped from the frame, his balance restored with the encompassing chest piece in place, the sun's rays had spilled into the room. Had it been an hour? Longer, perhaps. A surge of anticipation rose within as he realised his guest would soon arrive. With renewed purpose, he left the sleeping chamber and moved into the reception hall, where he would await Kallisa's arrival.

He did not have to wait long, and he took reassurance from the rushed tapping on the wood. It was the report of a guilty hand; a measure of confirmation that his vision had not deceived him. He bade the Overseer enter and greeted Kallisa as she strode in.

'General Aracyse,' she said. 'I received your summons late last night. Unusual timing. Does the King...'

He raised his hand to stop her. 'Whatever you've rehearsed, and what strange manipulation you might try; don't bother. I know of your skill and your mental agility. So, let's not play your overseer games?'

Kallisa appeared to take stock of his words. Her response was a disappointment. 'I'm not sure what you mean, General?'

Aracyse smiled, although he offered no joy. 'I see. Very well, Kallisa. When I meet the King later, I will tell him of my suspicion that you were involved in a confrontation with the Queen, and then, at the end of that forbidden conversation, her tower erupted and contracted. I will explain your whereabouts, from what direction you came, and I'm sure your fellow overseers will attest to that being true. Whatever words you say to refute my story, I assure you, will be pointless. Overseer you may be, but your rank is insignificant to the atrocities I have committed in Kalle's name. The blood of our enemies is my truth. It is a blunt and honest statement of loyalty. Your words are flexible; it is the calling of your profession. Who will the King believe, Kallisa? A trained liar, or a soldier who has faced death for his country?'

The Overseer fixed her eyes on his. She was preparing a response. Aracyse was hopeful his warning had fallen on attentive ears. It was not a bluff; he would not play games with the rumour-mongers of the court.

'I was returning to my quarters,' Kallisa said, dropping her gaze and walking to the balcony. Aracyse followed as she continued to speak, Kallisa pointing to where he had seen the incident occur. 'One moment I was alone, the next, I felt a crushing presence; it was dreadful. I pleaded for it to stop, and then it did. And she was there.'

'That pressure. I felt it from here.'

Kallisa didn't appear surprised. Her voice became distant; an honesty revealed in her unmasked tones. 'She has so much power. What Kalleron holds so dear is beyond our imagination.'

Aracyse had her in a bind. She had admitted the contact; that alone was enough to have her head. He nodded. 'I am pleased you see fit to be truthful.'

She turned to face him. 'What will you do now, General?'

'You have spoken with the Queen. You know what should happen.'

The slightest wrinkle appeared on her brow. 'Should?'

Aracyse nodded. 'I wanted to speak of this yesterday. Your culture, those loyal Bruhadian roots, I thought you would be open with me, but you remained stubborn as the overseer you are. Now, you have little choice. I am just a man who seeks to understand more of the elementals.' He smiled at her. 'After all, I work in their domain. You can aid my knowledge. Or you can remain quiet and I turn you over to the guards.'

She nodded. 'I can trust you?'

'I'm not an overseer.'

Kallisa returned her focus to the fortress interior. 'What do you know of it?'

'It?'

'The King's castle on the water.'

Aracyse stared at the distant construction. It had always vexed him: why live above the water in a fortress that was impenetrable? The castle was not defensible. It was an extravagant wooden lodge, not a fortification.

'I've never quite understood the purpose.'

'If I speak openly, General, can you guarantee our confidence?'

He nodded. 'Of course, you have my word.'

'He lives above water because he understands Earth's limits.'

'Limits? She has none.'

The Overseer shook her head. 'Not as we see, but it is their bind. My family preserved what knowledge they could from Bruhale's library. After Baza'rad disappeared, and Kalleron's forces seized control, they ransacked the Great Library. They ordered the soldiers to take everything. My parents passed on what they could. They told me of the elementals' traits and ties.'

Aracyse stared at the wooden castle. 'What are these traits?'

'Observations made over centuries, long before she was the Queen, showed glimpses of strange behaviours. In the ancient temples, there were carvings, but these were desecrated over time by Kalleron's desire to erase knowledge. They sent missions to seek the hidden shrines; to record and destroy what they found. Kalle used that knowledge to build this fortress. It was his genius to create a lie that could imprison an elemental.' Kallisa laughed and shook her head. 'It makes no sense to us.'

'What doesn't?' Aracyse was confused; the Overseer's explanation was rambling.

'Fire, Earth, Wind, and Water. What do we use to douse a fire?'

'Water.'

'Yet the old secrets don't speak of such basic nature. Water does not douse fire; it repels the Earth.' Kallisa pointed to the King's darkwood castle. 'She might step over a stream, but in all measured time, has she ever crossed the Rivyn? General, she's never moved beyond the northern continent. She is bound to her own element; the earth. She must remain in contact with her essence, one foot grounded at all times. And she cannot move through water.' Kallisa nodded to the wooden castle. 'The inlet beneath that darkwood ramp may as well be the ocean.'

It was preposterous, but it made sense. 'She cannot cross?'

'It seems not. She's never walked along that wooden ramp. Never dipped her toes. The old texts spoke the truth.'

'Remarkable.'

'But that is not his defence,' Kallisa said, turning to look at him. Her eyes were twinkling; it was clear she was enjoying the chance to discuss her Bruhadian gods.

'Kallisa, your words make no sense,' Aracyse said, although her twists and turns intrigued him.

She sighed and smiled. 'What I tell you next, General, would have my head on a golden platter. You're certain I may speak freely, and with honesty?'

'Of course.'

Kallisa nodded. 'Then will you offer me a security?'

He nodded.

'I would ask for your knowledge,' she said.

'What could I possibly know that would interest you?'

'Yesterday, you spoke of Kalle. You asked if I believed in his immortality. Why?'

Aracyse recalled. It had been an unusual day. To arrive back in Kalleron, weary and pained. Perhaps it had been the Vallacyne relaxing his tongue. A thought, confused; had he even taken his herbs at that point?

Blowing away his reticence with a forced breath, Aracyse said, 'What good is it to sneak around the world's worst lie? Everybody knows there is no immortal King. I'm damn sure he knows we know it. But what matter is that when, for all intents and purposes, nobody has seen the face behind the mask, and nobody has recorded his death for centuries. A man of such age would suffer the frailty of his impossible years, but Kalle dons his golden armour and strides with youthful grace. Our King is a unifying symbol, not a single person.' Aracyse stared into Kallisa's eyes. As honest an answer as he could ever give, he wondered if she believed him.

The Overseer tipped her head. 'Thank you, General. It takes a weight from my shoulders to hear you say the words we all know. Only the zealots in the southern wall would defy the truth.'

'Fortunately, the Southwallers rarely stray beyond the fortress perimeter, otherwise their rigid ideology would have Kalleron undone in days.' He returned his focus to the darkwood castle and gestured to its strangeness. 'Of Earth, then. What is the truth?'

'My family had particular leanings, and although I don't follow them, they taught me more than most.'

'Leanings? Other than elementalists?'

'They were remnant cultists, General. It was good fortune that Kalleron eradicated that harmful sect. At least, the court dismantled what they could all those decades ago. My parents walked away from the ruins. It kept them safe from further harm.'

Aracyse was curious. As much as her overseer role would be anathema to the cult, her Bruhadian loyalties would embrace it. She was an anomaly, although he understood she had been useful in hindering the development of the new factions.

'You disown the cult?' he asked.

Kallisa took obvious offence. 'Of course. They seek to free the Queen. They have no thought of consequence; they don't consider what damage that might do to her.'

He was astounded to hear such words. 'Damage the Queen?'

'Aracyse, think of it.' Her eyes narrowed, her voice becoming a whisper. 'What would the gods do if they discovered their world was a lie? What revenge might they wreak?'

It was a profound statement, not without merit. Aracyse had already seen instances of change in the Queen's mundane behaviour. As he had explained to Franklin what felt as though months in the past, she was becoming different. Aracyse saw the change as an instability in Kalleron's forward stride. He mulled over Kallisa's words, recalling the origin of the tangential discussion.

'The cult then, what did you learn? You say the castle is not his defence?'

'Yes. The water itself is not to prevent the Queen from moving to the King. It is to show his power, and that power is his knowledge. To recognise the weakness of a god is to be as powerful as a god, is it not?' Kallisa paused, paced away from him, and appeared to stare at nothing of importance. She returned, blowing a sigh from her lungs. 'Do you know the story of his grand deception?'

He did not, although he had often wondered how a mere man had deceived an elemental. With a shake of his head, Aracyse said, 'I have sought such truth, but I fear it is long scored from the pages of history, or lost to our reach.' In his mind, he pictured Etherus and the inaccessible temple high on the mountain.

'The cult knew,' Kallisa said with a firm nod. 'But to speak of it was dangerous. Few lips would dare utter the truth. They would sometimes reveal it to those whose doubts had to be overcome; to recruit vital pawns for the cult's purpose. Those very words are treason; to know the truth of the greatest deception in history. But I will share them, General, so that our relationship may remain in harmony.'

Aracyse nodded. 'My word is my life.'

'Very well. Kalle's predecessors sought all the elemental knowledge they could. Over centuries, they amassed a wealth of it. Scoured from ancient texts stolen from temples and libraries. You know there were nations on earth long before Kalleron?'

He did, and Aracyse longed to know of them; the first elementalists. 'Those who built the temples, yes.'

'Kallerye scholars studied the forgotten lore and mystic scripts. They found many references to her curiosity; it seemed she was searching for something. They understood what we couldn't possibly imagine.'

Intrigued, Aracyse leaned forward. 'What was that?'

'She was alone. In her world, life had appeared, but it was not of her. Things that grew and died. It was unknown to her. The ancient people knew this. They understood how it affected her, and they gave her a name. You won't know it?'

Aracyse shook his head, certain he appeared as though a mesmerised child.

'*Kor'A*. In their tongue, it translated as the *Weight of One*. It reflected her apparent loneliness. That's what Kalle used to his advantage. Everything the scholars and scribes had deciphered pointed to a powerful but lonely creature. Something seeking purpose. So, they devised a plan to find the wandering elemental and prove she wasn't alone. They would give her what she sought. The greatest engineers created his golden armour, an effigy of the perfect human figure. Over-sized, powerful, and concealing every inch of mortal flesh. Within it, there needed to be a man above all men. The King knew he hadn't the strength to wear the suit, so they created a surrogate.'

'Surrogate? Not the King?'

Kallisa smiled at him. 'You said yourself, General, the King is a symbol, not a person. They nurtured a youth, fed him concoctions of herbs and elixirs. They trained him to be stronger than all others, versed him in the ancient elemental ways, and wearing the armour of Kalle, and after decades of searching, he finally found Kor'A. He spoke with her, as had the ancients, and she responded.' Kallisa's face lit up; her expression glorious to behold. 'Can you imagine, Aracyse, what it was to speak with Earth before this lie had tainted her? A peaceful and curious creature. Turned into a monster by Kalle. Well, nobody knows exactly what he said, but the false King showed knowledge no mortal could know. He explained more about the elemental and her sisters, their limits, than she could have believed a mere human could divine. That was just the start of the deception.' Kallisa diverted his attention to the southern wall. 'Over there, those who work closest to the King. Do you know the name the cult gave them?'

Aracyse could only imagine vulgar profanity. He doubted it would be so simple. He shook his head, squinting at the marble walls.

'The Century Sin.'

'I've never heard that term, and I'm no stranger to intrigue.'

Kallisa leant on the darkwood railing and hung her head. She released a long sigh and composed her stature, standing tall and facing him once more.

'Kalle travelled to Kor'A, accompanied by ninety-nine men and one woman. He announced his power, proclaiming himself to be the elemental of humans, and that he controlled life. The Queen would likely not have believed such a statement, but they had planned for this. These martyrs, with guarantees of wealth to their families, had raw Vallacyne buds in their mouths.' She smiled and pointed to his arm. 'Not quite the refined and measured doses you use yourself. Well, Kalle gestured toward the men, a rehearsed and silent command, and ninety-nine souls bit down on the poison and dropped dead. It seems the Queen wasn't so easily convinced, yet what she did next may have sealed her fate.'

'Sealed her fate?' Aracyse stared at the marble tower. He wondered what mistake an immortal with unlimited power could make?

'Perhaps she doubted Kalle, but from the ground, a spike of rock erupted, impaling a dead martyr. The Earth asked Kalle to recreate life, as she could create rock. I wonder if behind that golden mask, his face showed fear? Regardless, he delivered the ultimate piece of his grim theatre. He reached for the woman he had brought. She was with child, carried dangerously close to term. Even now, when I think of it all, it seems so surreal. The risk of his deception was beyond measure. On his secret command, she too bit down on the poisonous bud in her mouth. Kalle cut the child from her dying body and showed it to Earth. A new human life held in his hands, created by his will—it was how he commanded his element. He had proven control of his own and offered the Earth his elemental companionship. A lie we would see through, but what did she know of that? Kor'A, the Weight of One, finally found a measure of purpose. No more need she wander alone.'

'What of her sisters? Of Water, Wind, and Fire? She is not alone,' he said.

'What do we see of them? The ancient texts mention so little. Of them all, we can only be sure that Earth possesses a physical form. A shell beyond the ethereal bounds, and inexplicably, she mimicked our own.'

Aracyse leant on the railing and absorbed the tale. It seemed impossible, but Kalle had captured a Queen, and although the story was as unbelievable as it was implausible, there was no other explanation other than that Kalle himself was an elemental. Something Aracyse was certain to be untrue. Yet there was a glaring flaw in the horrendous story. It was a fundamental problem of logic. He turned to Kallisa and said, 'If that is the truth, and they all died; how can we possibly know of it? Surely, it is just a fanciful tale?'

Her smile was enormous. 'His deception was witnessed, General. The simplest thing undid his grand plan. Chance; the one thing he could never control. One martyr fumbled with the Vallacyne bud, and it dropped from his mouth before he could bite down on it. What else could he do but lie there, pretending death had come? It was there he bore witness to the monstrosity of the infant's birth, and it shattered his fealty to the King. It was the beginning of the cult; this sole survivor with knowledge he understood could mark him for death. My parents told me all of this, and although nobody can prove it, I know in my heart that they wouldn't lie.'

'Who was this man?'

She shook her head. 'He died in the initial purge of the cult scores of years ago. We no longer have eyes on the leaders.'

There was one last thread. Aracyse was fearful to ask. 'And the child?'

Kallisa's smiled faded. 'Every incarnation of Kalle is a monster; they follow the brutality of the first. He had proven his power over life and death, and he knew his new Queen would regard us the same as she regarded a lump of rock. We are without meaning removed from our element. He snapped the newborn's neck and left it lifeless on the ground. It was his blatant disregard for humanity that surely sowed the seeds of her own ignorant genocide. How could she possibly value human life when it served no purpose other than to return to its elemental master? The cult began on the child's death. More than the ninety-nine martyrs, that murder sealed his fate. The mother had been told her child would live a regal life. Lie after lie after lie. Witnessed by one survivor.'

The revelation stunned Aracyse. It was barbaric. It was a relief that even in his darkest imaginings he had not manufactured such a hideous plot.

'Surely they would have gathered the dead?' he asked.

Kallisa nodded. 'I would imagine, and they would have known one was missing.'

Aracyse turned and surveyed the fortress. 'All of this built to maintain that extravagant fraud.'

'Which is why it's important that my conversation with the Queen isn't revealed. You'll hold to your promise?'

He nodded at the Overseer. Aracyse felt sickened inside. It was no mystery that he had served Kalleron with a modicum of pride. Other nations were not so perfect that he was averse to war. But the revelation was murderous. It was a disgrace, and it did not sit well within his heart and soul.

'General, are you alright?'

'After that story, no, I don't think I am.' A thought occurred to him; his meeting with the king later. He said, 'That was generations ago, Kallisa. What King are we with today? What is his line?'

'I don't know. After his grand deception, the Century Sin smothered everything. It's virtually impossible to know anything anymore.' Kallisa hesitated and appeared to fluster. 'General, despite my words and my disgust, please remember I am loyal to Kalleron. It is more than one man, and though he projects an alternate reality; my duty is to the Queen and the people.'

He waved away her concerns. 'I am a soldier Kallisa, I serve those who serve under me. Kings, even immortal ones, come and go. The people continue on.'

Kallisa nodded. 'And of the Queen? What do you feel now?'

Aracyse recalled the Overseer's words from earlier, of her fears about what the cult might bring about. 'I cannot fathom her mind. What thoughts may manifest, but I can't see any good outcome if the cult exposes the lie. The deception has lasted so long.' He looked at Kallisa, searched her eyes for an honest answer. 'How would you feel?'

'That is my fear,' she said with a solemn nod of her head. 'I can think of nothing but anger and fury.'

Chapter XXII

Aracyse travelled eastwards within the superstructure of the northern wall. The Generals' Way, hidden from sight, would take him to the King's darkwood castle. All along the enclosed route, pillars of carved marble flanked the wide avenue. With exquisite designs, and inlaid with gold leaf, they were sights that few would be lucky to see. Kallerye Lamps, a superior version of their Larian cousins, illuminated the route, their chemical fire casting a cold azure hue upon the sparkling walls. It was as though Aracyse was walking among the stars, so spacious and glittering was the scene. Every hundred feet, he passed over a small ornate bridge. Underneath, there was a track running perpendicular to his path. The guards used the unkempt lower route to move prisoners to the infamous Seawall, Kalleron's notorious penal colony. Those being ferried to their ultimate death would look up to see the splendour of the Generals' Way; one last reminder of their insignificance to Kalleron.

Aracyse exited the wall and entered the fringes of the northern plain. The wall continued on his left, although the ground sloped sharply away, leading to a shingle shore beside an artificial inlet. As wide as a hamlet, the water merged with the sea during high tides. Narrow channels bored through the marble wall prevented anything larger than the common Red Winnowfish from slipping through. It had been an unforeseen but amusing consequence that a flourishing habitat for the small creature had developed. Many would refer to the King's Lake in hushed tones, using its other name: Winnow Waters.

Aracyse followed the shoreline until he reached the extravagant and curved darkwood bridge. It was the single entrance to the King's residence. Rising on slender wooden piles, the broad walkway arced its way above the lake, reaching the castle which sat upon a forest of thicker supports. Woodcutters had crafted them from the trunks of the massive Larissian Pine. They held the base of the structure no higher than twenty-feet from the water, although the gap doubled at low tide. Two Southwaller heavy infantry guarded the walkway, and clad in their black plate armour, they were as large as the fabled Bruhadian Royal Guard. They saluted him on arrival and stepped aside.

Striding along the ramp, Aracyse cast glances down at the inlet. His heavy step sent ripples into the water, and clouds of pink fish stirred beneath. Wide and strong enough to carry a cart along its curving route, there was a peculiarity about the design. Not a single guard rail, nor a warding rope lined the edge. With the sun's rays sparkling on the rippling water, it was difficult to see the timber supports. It was as though the walkway floated in the air. Under his weight, Aracyse was certain it swayed, if only a little.

Two more guards flanked the castle's massive arched entrance. As the men on the shore, they were far larger than any regular soldier. Hand-picked by the denizens of the southern wall, they were fierce fighters and unwavering in their loyalty. Outfitted in their red and black patterned plate-armour, and with their heads covered by deep black cowls, they were as menacing in appearance as they would be in battle. Once more, Aracyse received a salute as they ushered him inside. He passed under the grand archway decorated with gargoyles and Kallerye motifs, and began his long trek along the Avenue of the King. Totemic and unknown human figures lined the wide and opulent hallway. Aracyse thought of Kallisa's revelations and counted the pairs whose hands met above his head. The figures, each twenty-feet tall, stared down at him as he passed underneath. From their joined hands hung golden chandeliers that cast an upward blaze of light into the vaulted ceiling. Aracyse had travelled halfway when he smiled; the design was becoming clear. He paused at the end of the great space, looking up at the last pairing. He counted fifty in all. One-hundred figures. But above his head, there was no chandelier. It was the last insult to a sinful secret; one male figure, his arms stretched overhead. Different from the others, his reach did not meet that of another man. In his hands he held a tiny figure—a child. The final effigy on Aracyse's right-hand side, a woman, received the fragile burden. The Century Sin; it was there for all to see. Aracyse shivered and stepped to the massive arched door. He lifted the iron ring and let it fall against the darkwood. A lonely echo sounded throughout the hall. Behind the slab of wood, there was a loud thud, and the doors opened inwards on silent hinges.

Aracyse knew what to expect inside The King's Chamber. The theatre and drama of Kalle's stage was breath-taking. Nothing of his reign was mundane. He was a god among mortals. Aracyse inhaled and prepared himself for the show, stepping forward into the gloom and kneeling with effort just yards from where the throne would appear. In the circular chamber, there were few details to observe. Positioned in concentric rings high above his head, lamps plunged everything but the floor into darkness. Aracyse understood the trickery. He had learned of it through an imprisoned artisan. Of how the shadows behind the King had silenced his genius at creating illusion. He had told Aracyse of the mirrors which channelled the light; how they created a sense of depthless space. They daubed the darkwood walls with a curious black paint that absorbed light. Aracyse had marvelled at the room; it appeared infinite, as vast as the universe within which the stars shone down. Yet it was the coming of the King that sent a shiver down his spine. It was a calculated and extravagant act, but the perfect execution of it confounded the senses.

On his knee, waiting in that illusory void, he heard a chorus of voices rise from nothing, transforming into a whispering wind. On his first summons years before, he hadn't even noticed the words; so ethereal was the noise. It was an opera of near silence; the sounds merging as a river into the ocean, the breeze through the trees. Aracyse could only discern a few words: *He hath come; he is life*, and *you are nothing; he is all.*

The whispers ceased as though sound itself had died. In their place, a solid thud on the darkwood floor. Another. The King approaching. Each step was thunder. Aracyse kept his head down. He knew what Kalle expected of him, and he was careful to obey the decree. Not until spoken to should he raise his head. The King was nearing. The slow hammer of his boots on wood was an unbearable din. Again, there was deathly silence; not an echo to stir the quiet. Aracyse stared at the floor and noticed the darkness recede. When he lifted his head, he knew he would see his King seated upon his massive darkwood throne.

'Arise, General.' The voice was thunder.

Aracyse stood, concealing the effort required to rise encumbered by his heavy armour. He straightened his posture and looked at his King. Seated on the throne, a huge and single piece of Drohendrian timber devoid of the riches one might expect, Kalle stared down at him. His golden armour was exquisite; intricate swirls of symbolic text covered every inch. Artisans had inscribed each phrase with perfection. All the known languages of the world flowing around his armoured shell. In the light, the letters appeared to move, making it difficult to discern the meaning. What Aracyse had divined spoke of gods and men, death and eternity.

The suit mimicked the musculature of a man, and it appeared flexible at the joints. There was more illusion involved, perhaps the use of fabric, or sheets of malleable material used to hide the seams. Kalle's head was covered by a sculpted golden helmet, the face conveying a calm expression; something incongruous with the brutality of his reign. The eyes were golden as the rest of the suit; not open, as with other visors. Aracyse wondered how much the King could see from beneath, and although he had wanted to stare, it was a condition of the summons that his gaze could not linger too long. No mortal could look upon Kalle without fear of going mad. Such was his power; so the common folk whispered. To complete the masquerade of a human god, a cowl, sculpted in a silver-metal alloy, covered the helmet. In the downward light, his face was a beacon staring out from the shadows of the hood.

'Your Majesty,' Aracyse said with a bow.

'General, that I might understand your failings, tell me of the arm. Why do you come to me with an imperfect human body? Did I not create you whole?'

Aracyse hesitated. He reminded himself that everything was an act. The South Wall would have briefed Kalle about the Etherus problem, although the General was uncertain how much the King would know.

'A Fury took my arm during the trouble at Etherus.'

'Trouble? Tell me, General?'

He couldn't risk a lie, and although the truth would be a smear on his record, it was wise to acknowledge the infiltration and accept the blame. Humility was better than hubris.

'Your Majesty, cultists breached Etherus. They murdered some of my best workers and took two of our weapons.'

Kalle, inanimate as a golden statue, said nothing. From beneath his mask, his breathing was inaudible. Not even his chest moved with the unseen breaths. Aracyse knew the man beneath was mortal, but everything he could perceive told his eyes otherwise; it was all part of the myth of Kalle's eternity.

The King said, 'The weapons, what of them?'

'One destroyed. They sent the other over the cliff.' Although shuttered glimpses of that night were returning to his memory, Aracyse couldn't recall the moment with clarity. The fall would have shattered the other Fury. Surely?

'The one that was lost. Did you locate it?'

He shook his head. 'They found nothing. The slopes are hostile and harsh. I doubt the weapon survived.'

'If such a weapon was to survive; if the wrong hands retrieved it, would it cause harm to Kalleron?'

Aracyse paused before giving his reply. The Fury that had taken his arm, and the other that devastated General A'dan; both had been powerful and catastrophic to those caught in their rage, but the Fury had its limitations. No different from other more mundane weapons.

'Just one would seem without purpose, your Majesty.'

'And just one is unaccounted for?'

Aracyse nodded. 'Yes, your Majesty.'

Another pause during which Kalle moved his tremendous frame. He shuffled such that his elbow rested on the arm of the throne, his chin settling on his fist. A staged and pensive moment. Aracyse had witnessed it before, and it was uncanny how the movement was so carefully contrived.

'If the cult is responsible, General, what would their plan be? Can your mortal mind unravel such a thing?'

Despite Kalleron's attempts to neuter the cult, the purpose of the remaining elemental sect was unknown, other than its obsession with the Queen's emancipation. There were theories among those inclined to gossip, although Aracyse preferred to keep a logical mind.

He said, 'It is a sect that worships the Queen in her elemental form. I cannot fathom a need to steal a Fury. Perhaps they feel they can extort, or threaten us, perhaps...'

'Us?' The King's tone was harsh. 'Threaten us?'

Aracyse realised his mistake. It was a slip of the tongue, something he was rare to do. He thought of the Vallacyne. Too many moments where he had experienced a haze worrying his clarity, and now he had suggested the King was vulnerable.

'Your Majesty, I meant myself and the servants of Kalleron. I must apologise for my words; I am heavily medicated with Vallacyne. It has been a cloud obscuring my thoughts.'

'Perhaps you should wean yourself off it? As a privileged servant, your wits must be sharp, should they not? You can surely endure some pain for your King? Perhaps it will heighten your awareness; prevent another disaster?'

'Yes, your Majesty.'

Kalle moved his position; this time mirroring his previous posture. With his golden chin on his other hand, he said, 'What might the cult do with the weapon, if indeed they had one?'

'They idolise the Queen. They...,' Aracyse paused and tried to remedy his previous slip. 'They falsely believe that she should be free. One Fury would do scant damage to the outer wall. An assault on the gate would be suicide on their part. I can't imagine a scenario where a single Fury would trouble the fortress.'

'And the weapon, is it the same as the one that tortured your flesh?'

'It is.'

Kalle paused. He lifted his chin from his hand and rose from the throne. He stepped down from the plinth and paced toward Aracyse. Upright, and in his armour, the King stood another half-foot taller and his frame was wider. The golden armour reflected the lamps above, and he appeared more of a god than a man in a mask. It was an exceptional illusion. Kalle stepped forward. Closer than usual, and Aracyse understood it was a test of his character. As with the Queen, decree forbid all but the most devoted servants to come near to the King. The General stood his ground.

Kalle said, 'I know why they want the weapon, General.'

Aracyse delayed his reply. He had to play to his ego. 'Your insight is far superior to mine, my King. Would you indulge me?'

'They believe the elemental weapon will harm me.'

It was a revelation. How many more surprises would Kalleron have for Aracyse? He couldn't imagine how such a plan would ever come to fruition, let alone know how Kalle had gathered such knowledge.

'Your Majesty, a preposterous plan; it could never work against you.' Aracyse said what the King would want to hear, even though he knew it was a lie. 'A simple Fury raised against you would be as feeble as a child blowing its breath on me. Why would the cult believe in such futility?'

'They believe if they show me vulnerable to harm, then the Queen would believe I was not as she. They think to free their idol, they must attack me.'

It was ingenious. Aracyse summoned all of his composure to prevent his own mask from slipping. To prove the King's deception, the cult had to show him as a mere man. Unmatched in combat, and conditioned to endure all the pain that mortal hands could inflict, Kalle was a fearsome and unrelenting foe to all who opposed him. Some said his armour could defect a cannonball. An assassination was nigh on impossible. How would he fare against a Fury? If it was to be used against Kalle, it would surely dispel his myth, but that plan required the weapon to be brought to the King. That was no small feat.

Aracyse, wise to Kalle's suspicions of doubt, said, 'Your Majesty, their plan is desperate and foolish. The weapon cannot harm you. Only madmen would believe in such a fantasy. Besides, they would need to bring the weapon inside the fortress. That's an impossibility.'

'Indeed. I know the fruits of the Etherus project could not harm me, General.'

Kalle turned away from Aracyse. The slightest gestures he performed were as subtle as that single movement. For a King to turn his back on a subject showed impunity. He would know Aracyse's weapons were on his belt. It displayed supreme confidence. A lesser monarch would be fearful of every backstabbing opportunist. It was an unnecessary test of loyalty, and although Aracyse could see no guards within the room, he was certain heavy Southwallers hid within the illusion of the dark depths. He stood motionless as the King returned to his throne.

Kalle said, 'I have a spy deep within the cult. They are proving themselves highly useful. It was their knowledge that informed me of this futile plot.' He paused. Another shift of his massive frame. 'But, General, let me be clear. You have lost a weapon under your watch, no matter its insignificance to me. You are responsible. Do you understand?'

Aracyse bowed his head. The King's criticism was no surprise. If anything, it was warranted.

'You will make this right. You will discover for certain if the weapon is lost or stolen. I will send my spy to you. They will brief you of what they know, and you will assist in what way you can.'

'Yes, your Majesty.'

The King sat motionless on his darkwood throne and it was impossible for Aracyse to know if he was being scrutinised or ignored. It was one of many routines Kalle used to cause discomfort. Aracyse maintained his stance, careful not to stare at the golden mask; his head forward but his eyes down. Moments passed, and from behind the mask, Kalle spoke again.

'You have been a loyal and effective servant, General. I trust that loyalty will continue, and that you will make right of your problematic lapse. Leave.'

Aracyse bowed and turned, the great doors opening as he approached. He wondered what mechanism was at play, what devices and gears were turning unseen behind the panels. The doors closed behind him, and he was once more alone in the Avenue of the King. He took a moment to stare at the carved figures, wondering why the secret would be so brazenly obvious for all to see. It occurred to him; few would walk this path, and those that did were loyal and unthinking. Aracyse murmured and set off down the hall. He would return to his tower and await the King's spy. Then he could set about fixing this blasted mistake and travel back to Etherus. Saluting the guards as he left, and emerging into the blazing Kallerye sun, a potent thought occurred to Aracyse. For the first time in his long service to Kalleron, he realised a simple truth. The King's theatre was becoming harder to endure; the stability of the state was threatened by the recent changes in the Queen's behaviour. In Etherus, he was relieved of all the intrigue and unease. Up there, amid the cold peaks, he could stare at the lost temple, and wonder of its makers. He could revel in the majesty of the Wind and forget about the sins of kings. In Etherus, he was free.

Chapter XXIII

Petra's spirits had soared when the Melody sailed from Kalleron. There was uncertainty ahead, but her new path would bring her closer to Felicitra and perhaps restore calm to her soul. The young sisters had laughed as the sails billowed in the breeze, and they had rushed to the bow, gazing in wonder as the prow cut waves across the bay. The voyage had taken them along Kalleron's north-eastern peninsula, where the view of Seawall was a sobering reminder of what intrigue she was now an accomplice. Thelissa had asked about the strange square holes spread along the sheer marble face. Petra had stared at the cell blocks exposed to the elements. Seawall; a place they sent people to die. Inescapable, it was a prison from where escape was a vertical drop onto the rocky shore below. Where the tide washed away body and bone. Just decoration, she had said; a rare lie to tell a child.

Two days had passed and a strong northerly blowing in from the Sea of Silence had hastened their passage. The masts had creaked in complaint and although the sisters had appeared anxious of the sound, Petra explained the Melody was a tough old girl, just as her captain. With Gwynerath on approach, she had asked Shadow to join her on the deck. The sun had travelled to the western horizon and evening would soon be upon them. Under a darkening sky, Petra scanned the cliffs as Argan steered the Melody into port. Kastane had given directions to a specific berth on the docks; a safe mooring for the Melody.

'Is that it?' Shadow asked, pointing to the dockside. 'It's tight, but it's free.'

Petra scanned the busy docks. She had been expecting Kallerye vessels, but the number of naval ships surprised her. The harbour was a chaotic mess of masts and prow. More than one vessel displayed a damaged hull; a warning of the disorganised frenzy that cluttered the waters.

'Careful as we go,' she said to Argan.

'Aye. Captain.'

Shadow leaned in. 'I think he can see.'

Petra ignored his quip. 'I've never seen it so busy. It's a mess.'

'Won't deny that.'

'And the harbourside, look at it. It's awful.'

She directed his attention to the throngs of people littering the dock. Arkalla had fallen weeks ago. These would be the refugees from the other towns and villages, those seeking to find a new home across the sea in Laria, or perhaps sail south to the Free Lands. It was a desperate sight. Gwynerath had been a colourful and charming port nestled into the high cliffs. Now it was awash with drab colours, tired and dirty faces, and too many Kallerye soldiers. A thought in her mind, she chastened herself. Felicitra. Could she be among them? And although her eyes briefly darted from face to face, Petra knew she was being foolish. It left a dreadful hollowness in the pit of her stomach. She closed her eyes tight and tried to focus on the mission ahead.

She directed Shadow's attention to the guards milling around the dock. 'They're on our berth.' An unwelcome ripple of doubt disturbed her thoughts. 'What should we do?'

'Do?'

Couldn't he see? 'The guards, Shadow,' she said, pointing again. 'Are you bloody blind?' She waited for his reply, but none came. She felt obliged to face him. He was staring at her. A cold gaze. 'What?'

'I think you need to calm down, missy. And don't ever bark at me like a dog.'

Harsh words, but necessary. Her reaction had been out of sorts. An unusual anxiety brought about by the exceptional circumstances. The guards on the docks weren't a surprise. They were an obligation. It was a certainty they would ask for a fee from all ships that docked in Gwynerath. A tax for their own pockets, possibly more for Kalleron.

'I didn't mean to snap at you,' she said, raising her palms. 'I'm just... This is Gwynerath. It's all so wrong. It was so different before.'

Shadow sighed, lifting his chin and puffing upwards. 'Aye, and now it's changed. I get it; you're on edge, but what's done is done, Petra. We need to focus on the moment.'

His hollow words were pragmatic. Shadow wouldn't dwell on things lost in time. Petra, with a vision of Felicitra in her mind, wondered if he had ever loved as she had? A question she had never dared to ask. For all his faults, most of which she adored, he was a good man. Perhaps one day he would find someone who would change his heart?

Petra said, 'A lot's been building up inside, and mores happened on top. I'm still adjusting to it.'

'Well, adjust quicker. We can't have the captain acting like an emotional bard. You'll be singing mournful songs of love and hate next.' He raised his hand as a mock threat. 'I'll be slapping that shit right out of you. You're Petra; you're way tougher than this.'

She smiled. 'Sing like a bard? When that day comes, you can punch me in the face.'

'I'd not want to smudge your terrible make-up. You'd look like even more of a hag. No, I'd just crack the mandolin over your head.'

She frowned. 'How thoughtful.'

Shadow put a hand to his cotton shirt. 'I am a Kallerye gentleman.'

His irreverent talk helped Petra regain her focus. A memory coming to her of older times; recalling how people often misconstrued their relationship. A passer-by, on overhearing her and Shadow's colourful bickering, had asked if she needed help with the common thug. Petra had laughed, thanked them, and waved the do-gooder away, reassuring Shadow he wasn't a brute. She understood the stranger's concern; she and Shadow had a unique relationship. As though two squabbling, but loving, siblings. There was never any malice, and Petra knew Shadow only responded as she wanted him to. He was a sparring partner to be hit; never the aggressor. On the Melody, she had told the sisters of their strange ways to remind them what was and was not acceptable behaviour. Thelia had nodded. Thelissa had scowled and made clear in her expression that she needed no education on that front. An apology given; Petra never mentioned it again.

Argan brought the Melody as close to the dock as possible, but the adjacent ships allowed little room to manoeuvre. Petra looked starboard and pointed to the winches. She had fitted the Melody with the pulleys years before, and they had proven useful in tight spaces. There were three spaced out along the deck, nestled in between gaps in the rail. With a rope tied to a harbour cleat, she could attach it to the winch and, with some effort, the crew could inch the Melody toward the dock. But she needed to throw the ropes first. Petra waved to the guards, directing their attention to the cleats. They stared back, loitering on the boardwalk. Shadow leaned in close.

'Smart arses. They'll not budge,' he said.

'They'll not get their damn coin. Isn't that what they want?'

'They're Kallerye dock rats. Folks that volunteer for that duty are always bastards. They'll make us wait a while, until we're proper pissed, then they'll ask you to throw the ropes.'

Petra squinted. 'No, look.'

One soldier was pointing to a cleat, his foot planted on top. 'Is this what you want?'

'Aye, tie us in. We'll use the winch.'

She guessed the gap to be a dozen yards. She could throw the guide line with ease, then he'd be able to haul in the main mooring rope. She nodded at him, but the guard shook his head. He pointed to the stern, where Argan stood at the wheel.

'Is he a proper Bruhadian?' he asked.

Petra, rope in hand, glanced at Argan; his reply was a shrug. She called back. 'What of it?'

'My mate thinks he's half-blood.'

Half-blood? She turned to Argan, who was descending the steps from the top deck. Petra shook her head to offer an apology.

'Why're you apologising to him?' Shadow said. 'You didn't throw the insult.'

It was true, but she hadn't heard an insult thrown Argan's way for a long while; if being called a *giant* was even an insult. But to question his heritage; to doubt a Bruhadian's bloodline? The comment had thrown her. Petra turned to face the guard. She needed to dock, and any confrontation would jeopardise the mission before it had even begun. Argan came alongside and spoke.

'I am Bruhadian.'

The guard slapped his colleague on the shoulder. 'See that, Birnham? Man's a pureblood.'

The guard, Birnham, shook his head. 'Nah. Half. Ain't dark enough, that one.'

Beside her, Shadow's posture stiffened. It riled him; he was preparing for a fight. She nudged him in his ribs. 'Calm down. We need to dock.'

He stared at her, that familiar fire in his eyes. 'Before all's over, I'm finding him, and he's done.'

'No need for that,' Argan said, his voice a calm cloud. He called out to the guards. 'Pureblood, half-blood, mixed. We're all the same.'

'But you're pure?' the first guard called back.

'I am.'

The guard nodded at Petra. 'Throw the rope, love.'

His words were infuriating. What could she do other than comply? Petra threw the weighted guide line across the gap. Once he had hauled in the mooring rope, he tied it to the middle of three cleats. She was ready to secure her end and grab the next rope, but the guard held out a hand.

'Just the one.'

'One?' It wasn't possible with one rope. 'You need another.'

The guard shook his head and pointed at Argan. 'If he's pure, he'll be as strong as they say. Let him pull you in.' He pointed to his accomplice. 'Birnham here doesn't believe it.'

Petra turned to reassure Argan. He held out his hand, reaching for the rope. She held it to her chest. 'I'll not let them humiliate you.'

There was a softness in his eyes. A twinkle. 'They'll not.'

She wanted to help. Petra understood Argan would try, it was his way, but he couldn't pull the Melody to dock. It wasn't possible for one man and a single pulley. Not even a Bruhadian. It was a cruel trick to diminish his people's majesty. She turned to Shadow to enlist his support; three hands on the winch might make it turn.

The guard called out. 'Just him, and his bare hands only. No fancy winch.'

'What?' Shadow replied.

It was unfair. It would be even more futile than using the winding gear. She yelled at the guard. 'This isn't a bloody game!'

'No, it's a bet,' replied the first guard. 'Give him the bloody rope.'

Petra shook her head; the red mist was rising, but with bitter reluctance, she passed the rope to Argan.

The guard was full of enthusiasm. 'Come on, big man. I've got money on says you can do it.'

Shadow gently took hold of Petra's arm. Resignation on his face, he said, 'Got to let him at least try. That Birnham prick will get his wager from his stupid friend, then they'll help us dock. I'll kill him later. It'll all end up good.'

He was right. 'I'm sorry, Argan,' she said.

Prepared for the humiliation, Petra watched Argan pulled in the slack. The line lifted from the water until it was near horizontal. He took the strain, and the rope shuddered, casting a spray of fine mist from its weave. Petra darted a scornful glance at the guards. How long would they let him try before allowing them to dock? She was powerless, and it was the sense of helplessness she hated the most.

The ship lurched. Everyone gasped. Everyone except Argan.

A startled voice from the docks called out. 'Fuckin' hell!'

She looked at Shadow who, shaking his head, said, 'Jostled in the waves. That's all.'

Another lurch, and Petra stared in wonder at Argan. Hand over hand, he was pulling the Melody into dock. His enormous frame was straining, and the ship was moving inch by inch. Petra moved in close to Shadow, a whisper in his ear. *'That's not possible.'* So close to him, she could see the hair on Shadow's neck standing on end. For once, he appeared lost for words. Petra couldn't look away, and as the crew came up topside to see the fuss, she was aware in her periphery of a crowd gathering on the dock; their excited chatter was audible above the creaking of the hull. Closer and closer the Melody moved toward its berth. Petra looked at the wide-eyed guards. The first was grinning, ear to ear; an impossible wager won. The other stared in awe.

The smiling guard called on his men to assist, and on his command, his men moved to secure the Melody, asking for the other ropes to be thrown.

As the crew obliged, Petra returned her focus to Argan, who was securing the mooring rope to the winch. Clumsy steps brought her to him. She placed her hand on his arm as he stood from his task.

'Argan, how on earth?'

He offered a smile. One simple word to ward away her question. 'Rules.'

She wanted to know how. But he'd invoked the Melody's contract. She couldn't break it, not even for the impossible feat she had witnessed. Petra nodded. 'Damn rules.'

'I'll secure the rest of the ship, Captain,' he said and moved away, busying himself with the gangplank.

Shadow, alongside her, said, 'I think I just wet myself.'

A shiver ran up her spine. 'Me too.'

With the plank in place, the first guard came aboard. Petra stared at him, anger and wonder tumbling around inside her head. She thought about how Argan might react, but he had already moved below deck.

To the guard, she said, 'That was vulgar and unnecessary.'

He smiled, his gaze on the stairs where Argan had descended. 'But a miracle has made me richer for it. And poor Birnham's purse is lighter.'

She wanted this over with. Hands on hips, she asked, 'How much is your fee, and how much for the berth?'

Petra knew how to play the game, but she despised the situation. Even if she could ignore the insults given to Argan, it was difficult to block out the human tragedy of Arkalla's fall. To add insult to injury, these Kallerye vultures were looting from all and sundry.

'The standard harbour fee is much increased.' He gestured to the dockside. 'As you can see, my men are over-worked.'

She looked along the length of the boardwalk to see other guards loafing around on barrels or sleeping on discarded netting. It took effort to resist a barbed reply to his words. Shadow was agitating by her side; she could sense his energy. Petra turned to him and squinted. A silent command. He had to quieten down;

they hadn't even disembarked, and he was itching for a brawl. He scowled and stepped back. Petra returned her focus to the guard.

'This new fee, then. How much?'

'Oh, it'll cost you the earth.'

'Please, stop playing games, I have…' She frowned at the guard. 'I don't have as much coin as you imagine. We left Kalleron with new sails that cost a pretty fortune. Better to grab the Wind and speed us here over calm Waters.'

The guard's brow wrinkled; his mouth down-turned. 'You'll have Kallerye gold then? Five coins.'

Petra sighed; she thought she had heard a clue in his reference to earth. She was mistaken. With a huff, she said, 'And the rest? Your damn fee?'

'Another five, it'll keep us happy during our rest days roasting meat over a blazing fire.'

Another coded word? Fire? Was it co-incidence? It had to be. Although Kastane had given her no script to follow, she assumed meeting any contact in the cult would be as pedantic as it had been at Mansion Hill. She turned to Shadow. 'Go get the coins from my cabin. I know you know where they are.'

As Shadow left to retrieve the payment, the guard said, 'It's been a difficult time. Hard to remember when such tragedy befell a nation as grand as Arkallon.'

'What?'

He gestured to the crowds of refugees. 'This. It's a disaster.'

Unsure want to say, and certain that his words were leading, she shrugged. 'Yet life goes on.'

He raised an eyebrow. 'A somewhat callous approach, is it not?'

'And you, a Kallerye guard, finding grief in Kalleron's glory? I think you're testing my loyalty. You need not.' Petra pointed to the high cliffs. 'I've business with a wealthy trader; he wishes to leave. If we can speed this along, I'm sure he'll reward you well.'

The guard turned and looked at the top tier of Gwynerath. 'Perhaps I'll go to your rich friend instead. And take all the coin.'

Could it be any worse? Petra clenched her jaw and held her breath. She exhaled through her nostrils and tried to remain calm. With a controlled nod, she said, 'He is to travel to Laria on my ship. There is trust involved, and we made the agreement; he would not barter for another contract. There are pirates and greedy guards on the harbour, and he'll only travel with me.'

The guard stepped in, his hand on the pommel of his sword. 'Greedy?'

It was impossible to suppress. The damn mist blurring all thought of consequence. Shadow was nearby. Argan had moved a ship with his bare hands;

he had already promised his might against Kalleron. They could overpower the guards. Petra, shaking with rage and standing her ground, said, 'Fucking try it, you weasely little shit!'

He stepped back a few paces, bending over with his hands on his knees. What was he doing? His response was confusing; disrupting her anger. She had expected a charge; her hands hovering above her daggers. The guard was laughing. He pushed a hand out to her. No weapon. Just an empty palm.

'Forgive me! Forgive me! I had to see for myself,' he said, straightening.

Petra shook her head. Shadow had returned to her side.

With a frown, he said, 'What the fuck's going on?'

'I don't know.' To the guard, she said, 'See what? What is this nonsense?'

The guard composed himself; a smile on his face. 'Your name? Please, what is your name?'

'No, I'll not give you that.'

He raised his hands again; a show of no ill-will. 'My name is Larimer.' He pointed at her. 'You must be Petra. Yes?'

Her confusion was muddling with the mist. She stared; her balance disturbed with an abrupt jolt. She turned to look. It was Shadow who had nudged her. With wide eyes, he dipped his head to the guard. One last moment of fog dispelled by his prompt.

Petra said, 'Larimer?'

'We have a mutual friend in Kalleron, I think? The man who arranged your trade.'

She had said nothing of the cult. The trade was a legitimate ruse. She nodded. 'Yes, I think we might.'

Larimer sighed. 'This could go on for days, and unlike the fools who run about the Mansion Hills, I don't have that sort of patience. I wanted to test you, Petra; they inferred you had anger issues; warned me not to push too hard. I wanted to see this fiery character for myself, and now I have. Do I need to say more, or can we move this along?'

He had to be her contact; the measures taken to conceal his identity were extreme. Regardless, Petra erred on the side of caution. 'What will move this along?'

'Allow me and my men aboard. We can discuss things away from the dock.'

'How can I trust you?'

The guard frowned. He looked to his left at the other guard, Birnham. He replied with a shrug and a nod. Larimer turned to her and said, 'Kastane sent you. I am to tell you the next step, and where that will take us.'

'Take?'

He pointed to the north, at the high Kulkarron mountains. 'We've to retrieve something; you've to take it back to Kalleron.'

Petra turned to Shadow. 'Can we trust him?'

'Can we afford not to?' he replied.

She turned to Larimer. 'Bring your men aboard. We'll discuss this in the hold.'

He waved to Birnham and a few other men, who nodded and crossed the plank. As Birnham came close, the guard stopped.

He said, 'That nonsense with the Bruhadian, all part of Kastane's cover; he wanted it to be genuine. I have to admit, it felt like a Kallerye thing to do.' He shook his head. 'Never thought that was possible. Regardless, I'd like to apologise to him. If I may?'

Petra sighed; a sudden weight removed from her shoulders. These were the right men. They had to be. She directed Birnham to the hold and turned to Shadow. 'Looks like you'll not be getting your fight.'

'Sure, I will,' he said with a mischievous grin. 'When the first one walked by, I heard him say you had a fat arse.'

In the hold, Petra stood with Shadow at her side. She had decided he would be privy to whatever Kastane had planned. Three others had joined Larimer and Birnham, and they sat on crates against the wall. Argan had shown no interest in being a part of the meeting, but Petra had requested his presence. He stood at the bottom of the steps, his frame keeping the gathering obscured from sight. Argan was as wide as a door, and on shady deals in strange places, he often stood in for one. After his display of strength, she imagined nobody would dare come past. Birnham had said his apologies, but Argan dismissed them with civility; it was clear he had taken no offence from the staged display on the dockside.

'You have an impressive ship,' Larimer said, patting a beam. 'Is it Larissian?'

'Timber?' Petra replied.

He nodded.

She scoffed. 'Gods, no. I inherited wealth, but not that much. The Melody is Larian, but that's as close as she'll come to being made of Larissian. It's a sturdy timber, but it's not anywhere as light or strong.'

Birnham sniffed the air. 'Strange hold. Smells like a forest.'

'I keep a clean ship,' Petra said. 'But enough small-talk; the sooner we can start our business, the quicker we can leave Gwynerath.'

Larimer sighed. 'Used to be that folks couldn't pull themselves away from here. I don't think the north's got anywhere like that now.'

'Kalleron does that to a place,' she said.

'Very well, let's get to it. There are some men in the mountains near Etherus. We've to meet them. It's maybe two or three days; weather depending. Half of it on horseback.'

Shadow, propped against an upright post, stood straight. 'The Smoke?'

'You know of Etherus?'

'Aye. Hard not to know if you've been in Kalleron long.'

Petra squinted and looked at Shadow. 'What do you know of it?'

'Everyone knows it belches smoke, and everyone knows there's sorcerers up there. But nobody knows what they're doing. It makes it risky from the go, doesn't it?'

Larimer hummed and bobbed his head from side to side.

Petra said, 'What do you know?'

'You're not meant to know, but I don't think it's right.'

Confused, Petra shook her head. 'What's not right?'

'May we speak in private?' Larimer said. 'One moment?'

'No. What you say, you say it to the three of us.'

Larimer squinted at her. A darting glance sent the way of the others. Whatever covert message he was trying to convey, she was none the wiser.

'Say it, man,' Petra said.

'Felicitra. I met her.'

How long had it been? It felt as though years had become days, or days had become years. Time had lost all meaning since she had gone. His simple words brought it all back. Butterflies fading in her empty stomach.

'When?'

'More than once. I was her contact here. I saw her before Arkalla.' Larimer nodded. 'I ask again; would you prefer to speak in private?'

Shadow was already moving to the stairs, but she grabbed his arm. She couldn't keep hiding behind her grief. It wasn't healthy, and it was wrong to shut out her closest friend. As Argan was turning to leave, she said, 'Stay, both of you.'

Argan stopped and turned to face her. His frown was a silent question. She nodded her head to direct him to remain, then gestured for Larimer to continue.

'She spoke highly of you, of all of you.' He focused on Petra. 'It's clear how much you meant to her. I think you know that. There were a few times she confessed a sense of guilt for keeping you in the dark.'

'That was my choice, not hers.' She was keen to explain Felicitra hadn't withheld her second life.

'I know. But it troubled her. More than once, she refused a duty to stay with you.' Larimer chuckled. 'I remember Kastane throwing a tantrum; how he said love had no place in his cult. He softened enough, in part because Felicitra was damn good at what she did.'

This was what had pushed Petra over the edge; what thoughts had brought her into the arms of the cult. To seek further meaning about the woman she loved. In time, perhaps she would ask him more, but a pressing question came to mind.

'You said something wasn't right. What was it? Why did it bring you to mention Felicitra?'

'She protected you and the ship from more than one dubious cargo that Kastane had wanted to stow aboard. Usually contraband, or gems, stolen from Kallerye sources. She never allowed him to endanger you or your crew.'

'And now?'

'If we come back to Gwynerath with what we hope to find in the mountains, you ought to know what it is. Kastane said to keep you in the dark, but I'd rather honour Felicitra by being honest with you.'

What could be so bad about running contraband? It was a necessity of the business. She looked at Shadow, a wry grin on his face to match her own. She said, 'We've ran that sort of stuff before. This hold can hide a lot of secrets. We're not virgins of the midnight run.'

Larimer's expression was grim. 'You became part of the cult, yes? You've met Kastane and Kallisa. You know of us, of our secrets?'

'Of course, why?'

'Then you know what you've signed up for? You can't walk away?'

She had no intention of doing so, but his tone was off. An undercurrent of threat in his polite manner. 'Speak, Larimer. I know what I signed up for.'

He looked to his men, and Birnham, who appeared his direct subordinate, nodded.

Larimer said, 'You know of the Fury?'

Petra assumed her blank stare was as good as an answer.

'It's a new weapon. Created in the Etherus complex. I wanted you to know that your cargo to Kalleron will be a weapon.'

Although Larimer appeared to be having doubts about the purpose of her mission, Petra sought to reassure him. With a puzzled glance at Shadow, she said to Larimer, 'We're no stranger to weapons either. Good gods, man. Lighten up.'

He appeared conflicted, about to speak, when Birnham interrupted. 'So, you're happy running contraband or weapons?'

'Yes. I think that's obvious.' Petra pointed to the starboard wall. 'You see that panel?'

Larimer looked, then shook his head. 'Panel?'

Petra smiled and tapped the wooden wall beside her. 'There's no other ship that can carry things as the Melody can. I fitted her to smuggle anything, and nobody would ever know. Most of the space is behind these walls. The visible hold is mostly a decoy. There are a few idiot boxes as well.'

'Idiot box?'

'Hidden compartments that a moron could find. We put gold and silver in whenever we carry contraband. Most times they work; harbour rats leave with full pockets.'

Larimer smiled and nodded 'I'm impressed. It seems Kastane chose his runner well.' He turned back to Birnham, who shrugged. Larimer said to Petra. 'Well, where we're heading is cold. Do you have the right gear?'

She squinted. 'I am Larian.'

He laughed. 'Of course. Perhaps I should borrow some furs from you. Kallisa mentioned this.'

'You know Kallisa too?'

Larimer nodded. 'She's come here once or twice in the past. Some sight she was, striding down the dockside in her courtier robes. Men practically falling in the water, gawping at her.'

'Before Arkalla?'

'Aye. She was trying to find an ear that would listen. Tell the Seer that the Queen would come.' He sighed. 'She tried to warn them, but all she found was stubborn stupidity.'

'Or pride,' Petra said, thinking of Felicitra.

'Perhaps. Well then, how soon can you leave?'

Petra looked at Shadow, who offered a non-committal shrug. 'I just need to organise the crew. Shadow is coming, the rest will stay aboard.'

'Very well. We'll get back on dock and take you to the hills. We'll leave some bodies behind to watch the ship. Nobody will trouble her under a Kallerye guard.'

Petra watched the men leave the hold. Argan nodded and climbed the stairs; he was well-versed with the Melody's routine. If she and Shadow were on land, the elegant lady was in Argan's care.

Shadow nudged Petra, his elbow a sharp poke in her side. 'What?' she asked.

'So, you trust them?'

'We've come this far. I've gone beyond the point of doubt.' She tapped his shoulder. 'It'll be fine. Trust me.'

Shadow grumbled. 'Funny thing: trust. Most folk need to earn it, but some ask for it on blind faith.' He looked at her, an intense gaze.

'You don't trust them?'

He smiled and slapped her shoulder. 'It doesn't matter if I don't trust them. I'm coming along to look after you. You do the trusting; I'll do the *told you soes*.'

'You're an idiot.'

Shadow stepped away and left the hold. For a moment, she paused, considering his words. It was foolish to trust on faith, but Larimer had put her at ease. If it was a trap, they would have sprung it by now. And although she felt reassured, she couldn't shake the thought there was something else at play. Yet she had made a promise to herself to learn more of Felicitra's past. This was the only way to do that. With a sigh and a click of her tongue, Petra returned to her cabin to prepare for the journey ahead.

Chapter XXIV

In the Generals' Tower, Aracyse reclined in the merciful shade of the reception chamber. His time in Etherus had acclimatised him to the cold, and he was prone to suffer Kalleron's warmth. It was worse that the afternoon had brought an unseasonal and ferocious heat. He waited for Kalle's spy, keen to learn of their insight, but having donned his full general's attire for the occasion, he found the heat was a hindrance to his comfort. The archway to the balcony was open, but the slight breeze offered meagre relief.

He had tried to read, but the inconvenience of using one arm had proven too much of a nuisance. Aracyse, once happy to sit in a comfortable chair and scroll through the philosophies of General Dhistine of Old Thania, was having to adjust many of his daily habits. With the sun roasting the bare rock of the fortress, it wasn't a good day for an old dog to learn new tricks. His mind caught in a circle of redundant thought, Aracyse was relieved when the thudding on wood alerted him to his guest.

'Enter!'

The door opened and Kallisa appeared, probably an escort for the spy. Aracyse looked at the opening, waiting for the stranger to make their appearance. The Overseer glanced to her side and smiled. With a deep inhalation, Aracyse realised what a fool he had been. It was obvious.

'Come in, Kallisa,' he said. 'You are, of course, alone?'

'You expected another?'

'I shall blame the narcotics. My mind is not normally so slow to put the pieces together.' He thought of their recent discussions, and of his own knowledge of Kallisa's dealings with the cult. 'It makes sense.'

'What does?'

He shook his head and waved her in, gesturing to the luxurious lounge chair. Kallisa closed the door and strode to the seat. With a polite ruffle of her skirt, she sat down and clasped her hands on her lap.

She appeared prim and proper. A strange outward expression for a woman of her profession and ability. He said, 'You may relax.'

'This is my attentive pose. I'm here to provide you with answers, and to guide you with what questions you ought to be asking.'

'Questions I ought to be asking?'

Kallisa nodded, but her body language belied her outer confidence. She was excellent at creating a front; a master of manipulation, but Aracyse was not some lackey or puppet to be dangled on a string. And although the Vallacyne was playing havoc with his memory, he was astute enough to see the awkwardness of her position.

He said, 'The King has told you what you're allowed to say to me? He's given limits to what I may know?'

'Yes, General.'

He gestured to her posture. 'Then relax. We can keep this formality as informal as possible.'

'Thank you, General.'

The Overseer spread her hands across her skirt, moving the fabric to reveal her skin, and she lay back into the chair. Aracyse wondered how much heat a Bruhadian could handle.

'Too hot, even for you?'

'They say Kalleron has but one season: hot. But today is beyond that.'

'I thought Bruhale was warmer?'

She nodded. 'But there are trees and earth. This fortress is a furnace. All those tricks I mentioned; they removed organic material to make a city of stone, but without green, there is no relief, nor shade. In Bruhale, the ocean provides a cooler breeze. The city is open to the northern sea, the walls face to the south.' Kallisa gestured to the chamber. 'We are shuttered in here like bread baking in a clay oven.'

Aracyse rose from his chair and dunked a crystal glass into the basin. He passed it to Kallisa and remained standing.

'I see you have mastered the water pump,' she said.

'Ah, yes. The damn plug. It serves more purpose in here.'

'Kalle told me what he thinks of the Etherus accident.' The Overseer shook her head. 'I don't consider what happened was a mistake of your making. May I be honest?'

Aracyse smiled. It was an ironic thing to say, given her status as overseer and spy. He chuckled. 'I'm not sure if "may" is the right word. Given what I now know of your profession, Kallisa, perhaps the question is: "can" you be honest?'

Kallisa laughed, but Aracyse was careful to remind himself of her secretive duties. Though, so far, she had exhibited an openness he found refreshing.

'I can be honest, as much as I can be dishonest.' Kallisa sipped from her glass. 'But in your company, General, and knowing what you know of me, and my loyalty to my Queen, I think we can trust each other as much as anybody can in Kalleron. No?'

'I would agree.'

'Then, if I may speak freely; what Kalle considers of your failure at Etherus, I see as a miracle.'

It intrigued him. He wanted to hear her thoughts. 'Miracles are associated with divine outcome. What part of the Etherus disaster do you find to be miraculous?'

The Overseer pointed to his arm. 'That you survived the assault on Etherus. Now I know the truth; what you did, General, is heroic. There is no failure in that.'

'One Fury was destroyed; it almost killed me. The other is lost; presumed free on the Wind. Good men and women died when the cult breached Etherus, Kallisa. I found workers slain in their beds. These were not soldiers; they didn't deserve such a fate.'

Kallisa bowed her head. She drew a deep breath and lifted her gaze to meet his. 'General, if we are at war, we must always accept casualties. Etherus was always a target, and those loyal men and women who died did so for Kalleron's glory. Just as any soldier would. Etherus is part of Kalleron's war machine, is it not? Therefore, is it not an extension of the battlefield?'

With thoughts of Franklin in his mind, he wanted to chastise Kallisa for her words. Franklin and the workers weren't soldiers, although it pained him as he realised her sentiments were precise. Etherus' sole purpose was to create elemental weapons. If there was any doubt about its strategic importance, his abrupt recall to Kalleron to explain his failings had dispelled them.

Aracyse sighed. 'You are correct, of course. I think Etherus has softened me.'

'Perhaps the absence of battle has allowed your humanity to restore itself?'

He stared at the Overseer. A beautiful and complex woman. Aracyse doubted he had met a more enigmatic person in all of his life. Although his thoughts were not lustful, he imagined they would have enjoyed each other's company had the world not thrown them together in the manner it had.

He said, 'War asks that we sacrifice much. It's easier to move on from it without reflection. Etherus gave me that time.' He clapped his good hand on his thigh and said, 'And now circumstance dictates we reflect on other matters. What news has Kalle allowed you to report to me?'

'We know that a Fury is unaccounted for, and the King wishes it to be found, or reported destroyed.'

This was not news. He nodded. 'Yes, go on.'

'I know of a cult ship, sailing to Gwynerath, tasked with returning any viable weapon to these shores.'

'Kallisa, we searched, or at least my workers scoured the lower slopes. They found no Fury. The fall must have destroyed it.'

Kallisa shook her head. 'Those who stole the Fury did so knowing how to handle it. I have sources that told me they protected it in a dense fabric, shielded by an outer shell.' The Overseer leaned forward, placing her elbows on her bare knees. 'Can you remember what you saw? Anything? Perhaps when the Fury took your arm; do you recall how that happened?'

Aracyse had tried and failed to remember the detail. He shook his head and paced to the archway, careful to remain out of the sun's reach. 'No. The visions come and go. I just remember...' He paused, a sense of darkness and chaos. Was that after or before the release? Aracyse couldn't be certain, and about to give up, he recalled a sound, not a vision. 'Words. I think there were words. *It will survive*. Is that what I heard?'

'It will survive?'

Aracyse turned to face her. 'I don't know. It makes sense that I heard it, but perhaps my memories deceive me? I've known trauma to do that; I've seen soldiers filling in the blanks with nonsense.'

The Overseer nodded. 'I said they knew how to handle it. They may have gambled on having to dispose of it, and on the slopes of Etherus, if they protected it well, perhaps it survived? What did your workers search for?'

It hadn't been his decision; he had been oblivious for days, kept unconscious during his treatment by Anders. 'I never organised the initial search, but they would have looked for damage on the flank of the mountain. A recent rock fall; anything that would accompany the release of a Fury.'

'And if it was shielded somehow, undamaged?'

Wrapped in padding, or whatever Kallisa thought the cult had used; no matter what, it would be a speck among fields of snow and ice. If it had fallen into a drift, it would have disappeared beneath yards of powder.

He shook his head. 'If it wasn't destroyed, then surely lost? It would be like trying to find a cannonball fired at sea.' A thought occurred to Aracyse. 'Do we still have people searching for it?'

'We do. A few soldiers and scouts.'

It was a surprise to hear. The King had suggested the mistake was to be rectified, and that would involve an ongoing search, no matter the futility. Aracyse frowned at Kallisa. 'Only a few?'

The Overseer smiled. 'We thought of a better option, and now, with the ship sailing to Gwynerath, our decision seems to have been the correct one.'

'I don't understand. What decision?'

'If the cult is sailing to Gwynerath, to retrieve the Fury, they must believe it is recoverable; they must know something we don't. We've pulled away the larger search party. With a few men left on the flanks, we shouldn't scare away the cultists. We'll have eyes on the port, waiting for them. When they move, we'll know.'

It was an excellent strategy. If Kalleron could not locate the Fury, let those who stole it find it first. There was hope he might redeem himself. With his fist clenched, Aracyse surged with energy. A searing pain jolted his body. He cried out and froze, shutting his eyes tight to block the fire in his shoulder. With a wrenching twist, his body lurched.

Kallisa yelped in fright.

Aracyse opened his eyes to witness a miracle. His metal arm was lowering back down to his side. He had accidentally flexed his shoulder muscles. As Kallisa stared, her mouth open, he repeated what movement he could recall. Once again, the arm thrust forward with a vicious stab of pain.

'By the gods,' Kallisa said. 'It actually works.'

Aracyse stared at the arm. He listened to the soft whirring noises coming from the armour. One more time, but with subdued energy, he flexed his shoulder. The arm moved in a manner he could best describe as a push, not a punch.

'Anders is a bloody genius,' he said.

Kallisa rose from her seat. 'That is beyond genius; it is sorcery.'

Aracyse gazed at his metal limb. He could feel the smile on his face, and he was certain he looked a smug fool. 'This ship, then. What is its name and who captains her?'

The Overseer paced over to him. She reached out and touched Anders' work. As though reading an ancient text, her fingers traced the ornate detail. She stepped back and nodded. 'The Melody of the Sea, a Larian trader. She's captained by a feisty woman with an axe to grind. Petra is her name.'

Aracyse wondered how feisty the woman would be when she returned from Etherus with his Fury on board. 'This is the ship you have eyes on?'

'It is. When she leaves Gwynerath, we'll know. Once it departs, our fastest scouts will ride to Kalleron. We'll have time to arrange the recovery of your Fury, General.'

'You'll allow me the indulgence to be on the docks when she comes in?'

Kallisa smiled. 'If I was in charge, I'd make sure it was you that brings it to the King. I can think of no better reward for your devotion.'

Aracyse tried to contain his pleasure. Not only had the spy brought a means to return the Fury, the mechanical limb had become active. He had salvaged something from the weeks of pain the appendage had brought. There would be further trials ahead, but he could begin his path to mastery. It brought a thought of Etherus and it made him chuckle to consider how it would seem.

'General?' Kallisa said.

'A vision of myself returning to Etherus. Of seeing Anders' face. Like an old student returning with gratitude to the mentor who had taught me so much.'

'You long to return, don't you?'

'Kallisa, I miss my mistress. I miss the Wind. And although she is cold and indifferent, it is humbling to witness her glory.'

She smiled at him. 'You can return to yours, and I will remain with mine.'

'Yes, we'll make sure the cult fails. There will be no threat to Kalle; we'll not give them the chance to give the Queen a reason to doubt his status.'

Kallisa bowed and paced one step backward. 'I'll return when I have news of the Melody's departure from Gwynerath. Then we'll make plans to retrieve the Fury.'

Aracyse tipped his head and watched the Overseer leave the chamber. His attention shifted to his arm and thoughts of returning to the cold peaks. Soon, this distraction in Kalleron would be over.

Chapter XXV

'How far will the horses take us?' Shadow asked, leaning over in his saddle.

Petra shrugged. Larimer and Birnham were leading the way. The other three men followed at the rear. The horses appeared native to the mountains. Shorter, sturdier, and with a luxurious coat, they were well-suited to the environment, although Petra doubted they'd travel beyond the sloping meadows.

'Larimer mentioned a pass. I think we'll get through there, but they'll not tread well on snowy flanks.'

She noticed Shadow held his fur tight around his shoulders with one hand, the other on the reins. They had equipped themselves with excellent Larian furs, although Shadow, having complained earlier about being too hot in the foothills, had placed his heavier coat over the saddle.

'You can put that on, you know,' she said.

Shadow shook his head. 'I'll wait until I'm proper cold. It'll feel so much better.'

'Think the girls will be all right?'

He frowned. 'Why wouldn't they be?'

They had left the sisters onboard the Melody. She had told Argan they couldn't leave the ship, although she knew it would be impossible to stop a couple of reformed street-urchins from slipping out. If Thelia and Thelissa wanted to jump ashore and explore the dangerous port, they would.

'You think they'll stay aboard? Do as they're told?' she asked.

'Argan will keep them in place.'

'You think?' She looked at him, surprised to hear such an obvious lie.

'What else were we meant to do? The entire crew appears happy to stay aboard. I don't think they'll want to leave. Think about it, Petra; the docks are crawling with slavers. They know that.'

It was Thelia's young age that unsettled her. Thelissa would know the risks; but would she be able to persuade her little sister, who was becoming more adventurous? Petra hoped Shadow was right, and that Thelissa's fierce protective instincts would keep Thelia's roving curiosity at bay.

Petra nodded. 'You're probably right. Mind, we'll be away four days, maybe more; they've not known either of us to be gone so long.'

Shadow smiled.

'What?' she said.

'Nothing.'

She couldn't help but grin at his nuisance. Petra leaned toward him. 'What?'

'I've never seen you so... motherly.' He pointed to himself. 'It's like we're parents.' His expression was priceless, a cheeky wink for sensible types.

'Good gods. You think the crew sees us that way?'

He nodded. 'And we don't want that, do we?'

'Can't have that.'

An idiotic grin scuppered Shadow's serious tone. 'When we get back, we'll throw them overboard. Get back to proper pirate business.'

'You're bad!'

He grinned and nodded.

Larimer had dropped back to join them. He said, 'You have children aboard?'

'Not our own,' Petra said. 'Orphans from Kalleron.'

'Oh, I see. Your humour; I thought one of you was a parent.'

Shadow laughed.

'Why is that funny?'

Petra said, 'If you know anything about Shadow,' she paused, gave him a comforting nod. 'As much as he's good with them, he'd be a tragedy of fatherhood.'

Larimer appeared uncertain about her comment. He looked at Shadow, who was nodding.

'She's right. As much as I look after the little bastards, I couldn't be a father. I enjoy too much of life's simple things to show that level of responsibility.'

'Well, I suppose that's a fair point.' Larimer smiled. 'Though, ironically, that's a responsible thing to say.'

His thumb planted into his chest, Shadow said, 'I'm responsible to me. That's it. Any fatherly observations are just me following orders. Just me doing my job.'

Larimer laughed. 'And this journey? Is this duty?'

Shadow pointed to Petra. 'Captain says I get paid.' He nodded. 'It's duty.'

Petra smiled at Larimer. 'He plays the fool. He's anything but.'

About to speak, Larimer hesitated. Petra noticed the shift in his demeanour. It was well-hidden, but something had caught his eye. He pointed to Shadow's side, where his heavy blade was showing beneath his fur.

'That's a Kallerye cleaver?' Larimer said.

'Aye.'

'I served before I came to my senses. You?'

Shadow nodded. 'Long time ago.'

There was a subtle tension between the two men. Petra didn't think it was conflict. Something other. What little she knew of Shadow's past, and the nothing she knew of Larimer, gave her few clues about what was happening. She wouldn't pry.

Shadow did. 'Not your favourite weapon?'

'No, I find it too clumsy for what I do. It's a mighty heft of steel on the battlefield, but the skirmishes I face these days require more speed.'

'Daggers?' Shadow asked.

Larimer pulled back his coat to reveal a standard short-sword. Petra thought it looked ordinary; an unfussy weapon he could've bought in a village market. Too hard to resist, she said, 'It looks... functional.'

The cultist smiled. 'That's the intention. It's tarnished for effect. The blade's sharp as the wind, and she'll slice through mostly anything. It gives me an edge for the first dance. In my line of work, I need everything to appear not as it is.' He pointed to the cleaver on Shadow's belt. 'I know how you'll fight with that lump of metal. What way you'll swing.'

Petra smiled and glanced at Shadow, who was also grinning. She turned to Larimer. 'Few people can predict how this idiot fights. His sword is obvious, but his methods are frankly madness.'

Larimer chuckled. 'Well, now I'm conflicted.'

'How so?'

'I hope these coming days bring no danger.' Larimer gestured to Shadow. 'But I'm curious to see you in action.'

With the horses out to pasture on an alpine plateau, and having climbed higher into the mountains, Petra looked east into the distance. They had come far over the past day and a half, and with the sun looming behind the Kulkarrons, the light would soon fade. She inhaled the cold air and gazed at the exceptional view. A few villages peppered the north-eastern shore, their locations given away by the amber points of light speckling the coastline. Beyond the sea lay her homeland, and as mighty as the Anastra Mountains were, the distance and haze obscured them. Everything appeared serene, as though the world had forgotten its worries.

'A magnificent view,' Larimer said, coming alongside.

'Breath-taking. It's so peaceful up here.' She pointed to the plateau, several hours travel away. 'When I'm too old to sail, I could build a cabin there, live among the mountains and stare at the ocean.'

Shadow scoffed at her remark.

'What's so funny about that?'

Draped in his thicker mountain furs, he put his hands on his hips. 'You, settling down?'

'When I'm old and grey. Maybe.'

'Your hair's already silver, you'd not notice the grey.' He pointed to the alpine meadows. 'And an inn? Do you see an inn?'

She smiled. 'I can't be drinking and brawling all my life. I know that's your dream, Shadow, but one day, perhaps I'd like to slow down a little.'

'Pah! I'll live on the coast. Get myself a little oar boat and terrorise the local fisherfolk. When the Rot come close, they'll take me away and show me the wonders of the ocean.'

Petra gestured to Shadow, keen to emphasise her doubt. 'You think the Rotynians would claim you as one of theirs? They have standards, you know.'

Larimer laughed, but he didn't add to the conversation. Shadow, mock offence on his playful face, said, 'You underestimate my allure. I'm quite the specimen.'

Petra turned to Larimer, waving away Shadow's words. On the mountain slopes, movement caught her eye. She patted the cultist on his shoulder, pointing at the high slopes.

'People ahead?'

'Ours, no need to worry.'

Two figures were coming down the slope. They appeared as black shadows on the white flank, but as they crossed the boundary where the snow met scree and shale, they became invisible. As her eyes adjusted, she saw them again. Two men with haggard and bearded features.

Larimer said, 'Skopia and Dehnar. They've been in the mountains for weeks searching for the weapon.' After a pause, he said, 'They've lost some bloody weight.'

His words reminded Petra that her dream of alpine retirement was folly; the plateau would be a hostile place in the unpredictable mountain weather. Higher up, from where Larimer's two men had come, it would be brutal. Despite their scraggy appearance, and how tired they seemed, both men had enough goodwill to smile at Larimer.

Shadow leaned in, tugging on his dark fur. 'You'd think we'd wear white to remain hidden in the snow. Those two were beacons on the flank.'

Larimer turned in his saddle and said, 'White is excellent cover, but we've bitter experience that is counter-intuitive. The darker furs allow us to find our friends when they fall, or when the mountain sheds it's snow and ice. We've lost people who were just yards away; invisible in the storms that ravage these passes. Besides, dark patches are all over the Kulkarrons, where the wind has exposed the rock. There are two colours up here; black and white.'

Petra looked up at the mountain. It was a stark mosaic of ice and rock. As she scoured the slopes for movement, she thought of the weapon they sought, and from where it had come.

'Is Etherus close?'

Larimer pointed to the large peak under the shadow of which they stood. 'It's hidden behind this, another day of travel. But we're not going that far.' As Skopia and Dehnar approached, Larimer said to Petra, 'They'll let us know what happens next.'

'Larimer!' Skopia said, his arm outstretched.

The cultist greeted his friends and introduced them to Petra and Shadow. After a brief round of awkward handshakes, Larimer enquired of his companions' success.

'What news, Skopia?'

His hand rubbing his grey and orange beard, Skopia shook his head. 'They've almost given up. A few folks left searching on the slopes.'

'Etherus?' Larimer asked.

'No, another unit travelled here from Gwynerath. Five men, least that's what we saw.'

Larimer sighed. 'No luck?'

Dehnar huffed, raised his arms to the sides, and let them fall back again. 'We found Yerin's body; gave him what burial we could, but there was no Fury on him. He'd come down far, tumbled a long way.' Dehnar hesitated, appeared lost in his own thoughts. 'Bloody mess, he was. Figured it was the Fury, but Skopia says otherwise.'

'Those weren't elemental injuries, Dehnar; we know enough that...' Skopia stopped speaking; his words cut off too soon. Petra squinted, noticing Larimer was glaring at his friend. The cold and fatigue from the journey had set in and although she hadn't been paying full attention, the silencing of Skopia had been abrupt.

'Elemental?' she said.

Larimer looked her way; his face was a stony mask.

It dawned on Petra; she made the connection, although it made no sense. 'The weapon: it's elemental?'

'You didn't know?' Larimer asked. His bluff was obvious.

Angered by the obfuscation, she stepped closer to him. 'You didn't tell me.'

Larimer stepped away from her and raised his hands. 'All right, all right. I was under orders from Kastane. You weren't to know what it was; it was enough that I told you it was a weapon.'

Petra thought of the Melody, of transporting such a thing. It occurred to her she didn't even know what it was. 'This... what was it, a Fury? Is it powerful?'

Larimer didn't answer. She turned to Birnham, then Skopia. It was Dehnar that spoke.

'She ought to know. Damn Kastane and his secrecy. We've all seen friends die; it would do well to tell the lady what she carries. At least then she can make it safer for the voyage.'

'Safer?' Petra was stunned. She raged at Larimer; her voice carried high on the wind. 'How dangerous?' Shadow had come to her side. As ever, he appeared keen to face a challenge head on, but Petra held out her hand, and as gentle as her anger would allow, she kept him at bay. 'No, Shadow. Let him speak.'

With a nod and a curse, Larimer relented. 'Etherus creates glass spheres the size of cannonballs. They contain a shred of the Wind; the elemental. They're dormant until the glass is shattered or they're exposed to sunlight.'

From behind, Shadow laughed. 'Nonsense!'

Petra silenced him and turned to Larimer. 'An elemental weapon of the Wind?'

Larimer nodded.

'What does it do?'

'Imagine a barrel of black powder set on fire; except, this is a small sphere, and it erupts without flame or heat.'

Petra didn't know what to say. How to react to the claim. With Shadow muttering behind, she said, 'They have the Queen. Why would Kalleron create such a thing?'

Larimer shrugged. 'I don't know. But they have.'

With a blustering sigh, Petra turned from Larimer and paced to Shadow. She gazed at him, seeking a reaction.

'What?' he said.

'What do we do?'

Shadow looked beyond her shoulder. He spoke to Larimer. 'This magical cannonball, this so-called elemental weapon. Is it safe to transport?'

'We have a Drohendrian casket, padded and secure. It'd take a direct hit from a cannon to damage what's inside.'

His attention returned to Petra, Shadow said, 'We've come this far. We do this, then we take it easy. Sail west to Dreyahyde.' He glanced at the cultists. 'I doubt they'd let us turn back now, and I don't think you want this fight.'

Larimer called over to Petra, but she waved away his interruption. To Shadow, she said, 'I don't want to endanger the crew.'

His laugh was cynical. 'You already have.'

Petra's shoulders slumped; her inner spirit suffering in the moment. Shadow was right. She had already put everyone at risk; wasn't that why she had spoken to them all? She cursed herself, realised how selfish she had been; all to chase her heart and find out more about Felicitra's secretive life. Petra had wanted to follow in her footsteps to become closer to her lover, but that wasn't how she felt now, high on the slopes of the hostile Kulkarrons deliberating on her own fate.

She turned to Larimer, stiffening her posture and certain to display her irritation. 'It's enough that I've had to endure such bloody secrecy, but from now on, you'll tell me what you know. If we find that weapon, it'll only go aboard the Melody if I trust you. And right now, Larimer, that trust isn't there.'

An icy wind buffeted the slope, and the cultist looked to the sky. 'It'll be dark soon. We'll need to set-up camp; we can't search at night.' He scanned the surrounds and pointed. 'There, that outcrop. We can shelter at its base; it'll spare us from the worst of the wind.'

'Larimer,' Petra said. 'You'll tell me?'

He nodded, motioned to his men, and set off for the outcrop. Petra waited for Shadow to reach her side.

He said, 'That went well.'

It was ironic. Her anger. Frustrated by a secret, yet she was captain of a ship where the same thing was sacred. And although she had known the cult wouldn't reveal the mysteries of the world, she had expected to be told what she was taking back to Kalleron.

'Kastane doesn't appear to trust anybody.'

'Sensible that. Look, Petra; we're going to have to spend the night with these part-time bandits. Can you let it go? At least so we can get some kip.'

'That depends, Shadow.'

'On?'

She nodded at Larimer. 'Him, and what he can tell me about Felicitra, and how much she knew about this.'

Larimer's words had given Petra scarce comfort. With Skopia, Dehnar, and Birnham given the first hours of sleep, he had posted his other three guards on the perimeter of the camp. He had told her nothing of Felicitra's world except for the brief periods when she had come to Gwynerath for her instructions. As Petra had thought, Kastane kept one hand over the eyes of the cult, and the other around its mouth. Her anger at Larimer diminished as his own frustrations became apparent. Although distrust was to be expected, the cult leader's paranoia was beyond measure.

Wrapped in their heavy furs, and huddled close under the outcrop, she, Shadow, and Larimer held their hands toward the small fire. Petra had asked Larimer if it was wise to give away their position? He had laughed and told her that much of mountain life defied assumption. It was better to stay alive and fight when discovered, than to freeze to death before the battle had even begun.

'Have you not known such ways in Laria?' he asked.

Petra shook her head. 'The foothills are as far as you can reasonably travel; the bitter easterlies and the fierce cold are bad enough on the plains. It's cold here, but it's not the Anastra.'

'This is cold enough for me. I've no wish to feel the chill you describe. Is it true what they say? Is Laria really so hostile?'

She forced a smile to her freezing face. 'Its people are warm, but the land is dangerous.'

'You prefer it over there?'

She looked at Larimer and nodded. It was an odd question to ask a native.

'What about you?' he said to Shadow. 'Laria or Kalleron?'

Without turning his head, his face bronzed in the glow of the small fire, Shadow said, 'Hoydai.'

Larimer chuckled. 'Hoydai? I've been once. Opened my eyes that did.'

Petra reminisced. Warm memories to keep her comforted on a bitter night; she and Felicitra placing wagers on how many conquests Shadow would proclaim. They rarely visited the southern sanctuary for business. It was a place for the crew to relax; a place away from the struggles of real life. It seemed so distant now.

'We'll go back one day, when this is over.' Petra nudged Shadow. 'Won't we?'

His face turning slowly to meet her gaze, he nodded. 'In my head, I'm already there.'

Petra was about to speak when a shrill whistle pierced the air. As one, the three turned; all seeking the source of the sound. Another whistle rose above the gusts of wind. On her feet, Petra scanned what she could of the mountain. Under the moons, the slope was a strange mixture of warm amber and frosty blue; everything else that was rock was a shade of grey. She moved out from the outcrop and struggled to comprehend what she saw. A boulder rolling unevenly down the shale. One dark shadow moving against another. She focused on it; a jolt in her gut as she realised what she saw. Either Shadow or Larimer came to her side, and she pushed her hand against them, silently pressing them back into cover.

She turned to see Larimer. 'Arrows. One of your men is down.'

He moved forward but remained in cover. Petra watched the slumping figure come to rest a dozen yards away. It was impossible to see the attackers, but the whistling arrows had cleared the outcrop. She pointed north along the slope, perpendicular to the path of the body.

'It had to come from there.' Petra looked back, fearful the archer would notice the fire, but it was already out, kicked into ashes. Now they were in dark shadow. As long as they didn't move, they would remain unseen. In the rush of excitement, she had forgotten about the sleeping men, but Larimer had not. He had left her side and was rousing them from their slumber.

Shadow, whispering in her ear, said, 'I feel like a rolled turtle stuck here.'

'We can't move out.'

'There's two of his people out there. They might be...'

Petra knew why he had fallen silent. Across the slope, perhaps a hundred yards, she saw the glint of silver in the dark. Something moving toward them. She lowered her stance, positioned herself in a crouch. Shadow followed, and soon Larimer and his men were all huddled close. Petra pointed to the approaching figures. They were far away; it was too dark to discern detail.

His voice measured, Larimer said, 'We've no idea how many?'

'Or if your people are alert,' Shadow said. 'Or alive.'

Larimer sighed. He patted Skopia on the shoulder. 'You know the slopes better than any of us. Can you move around the rock without being visible?'

Skopia nodded.

'Take Dehnar and find who's left.'

Without a word, Skopia slid into darkness and disappeared, with Dehnar following close behind. Petra squinted at Larimer, questioning his command. It was too dangerous for any of them to move out from cover.

He said, 'They're not fighters, not like us. They'll stay hidden, find out what's happened.'

Shadow interrupted, pointing to the slopes. 'There. Right there. See?'

Petra focused on the advancing group. Across the snow and rock, they moved as one mass, but drifted apart as they neared. Five of them, perhaps fifty yards away.

Birnham, who had been quiet, came to her side. Petra wasn't sure what he was doing; his attention not on the five but on the lower slope. Concerned he had noticed an unknown threat, she tapped his arm.

'What do you see?'

'An arrow.' He pointed to it.

Petra saw. It seemed a redundant observation.

Birnham nodded and said, 'It's long, too long for a short-bow.' He directed her to the figures on the flank. Now they had separated out, it was easier to see their shapes. 'There's no long bows on their backs; we'd see, even from here.'

He was right. Petra crouched lower, the four of them trying to merge with the earth.

'What do we do then?' Shadow said. 'I'm no coward, but if we move out, we'll be no better than target practice for the archers, wherever they bloody are.'

'We wait,' Larimer said. 'For Skopia and Dehnar.'

Petra looked at him. 'And if they don't return?'

'We fight when circumstances force our hand.'

Shadow shuffled, appeared to make a contented noise. Petra was about to question his behaviour when he spoke. 'They're getting closer.'

He was keen to fight. It didn't surprise her; it was his way, as it was her own. But he was rare to engage in a suicidal melee. She bumped him. 'Are you mad? We can't fight while there are archers watching. You said.'

Shadow turned to her. His eyes were wide; the whites were round orbs in the gloom. 'Once those five come close, the archers won't fire; they'll not risk hitting their own. In this wind, taking a shot would be difficult on a steady target, let alone a moving brawl.'

'He's right,' Larimer said. 'That makes it four against five.' He looked at Petra, a frown on his brow. 'Are they good odds?'

Petra looked at the five figures. She saw no long scabbards, nothing that hinted at a clumsy double-hander. They appeared equipped for the hills. She would have preferred to see over-armoured and ill-equipped buffoons. On this ground, she'd have an advantage. But there was no way to gauge their ability; no way to calculate the odds.

She shrugged. 'Good odds are less exciting.' A nod to Shadow, Petra said, 'We'll take what we're given, eh?'

'Every time.'

A crunching sound of shale and rock, and Petra whipped her head around to see Skopia and Dehnar return. Their expressions were clear; a shaking of heads to inform of the loss of Larimer's other men.

'Damn it!' Larimer said through gritted teeth. 'Did you see the archers?'

Skopia nodded. In that moment, Petra sensed their luck change. At least they would know from where the enemy would threaten, but Skopia thumbed back; the foe was descending toward them.

'They've flanked around.'

'We're trapped between them?' she said.

'We wait,' Larimer said, gesturing to the approaching figures. 'They'll soon be close. Skopia, how many archers?'

'Just two.'

'That's settled then. Birnham, take Skopia and Dehnar; deal with the bowmen.' Larimer turned to Petra. She saw the fire in his eyes. 'We three will take five; more exciting odds, eh?'

Petra nodded, hoping he was adept with his short-sword. He had disclosed his past; he should be capable enough, but this was no common bar brawl. Not the sort she and Shadow would enjoy with brazen abandon. This would be mortal combat, and the loser wouldn't get to slink away with just a black eye and battered pride.

She turned to Shadow. 'You ready?'

No quip from his lips. He nodded.

To Larimer, she said, 'On your command, then?'

'On my command.' He sent the other three away, and they disappeared into the night. She wondered if they would all return; and if they didn't, what calamity would ensue if the archers drew their arrows and brought them into their sights? Petra waited, the sound of her breath loud in her ears; an illusion created by the anticipation of danger.

The five men were less than a dozen yards away. Too close for comfort. With a roar, Larimer charged out from cover. Petra's disappointment to be left behind was fleeting. Her thundering heartbeat rattling her chest, she growled; leaping out behind Shadow as he barrelled toward the foe.

Unencumbered by alcohol, the mainstay of a good bar fight, Petra's senses were on edge. She moved with agile haste, and although she couldn't match the speed of Larimer or Shadow, she was nimble crossing the unstable terrain. The enemy, caught unaware, stumbled in the snow and shale; their hands moving to weapons unseen under their furs. Petra's eyes widened as she saw two of the men reach to their backs. She had been mistaken; of the five, three had drawn hand-and-a-half swords, which they wielded in both hands. The other two had brought thuggish and huge blades to the mountains. On these slopes, moving across uneven ground, Petra would hold the advantage.

She cried out, 'Take the bastards! I'll get the heavy-hitters.'

In the blink of an eye, she was between the two swordsmen. Petra was her father's daughter, and although she had not inherited his strength, she had surpassed his speed. As a fly, she darted between the double pendulum swing of the two giant swords. On the scything steel, flashes of Ambyr and Noctyrne punctured the darkness; the wind roaring as the keen blades sliced the air. In a single, deft movement, Petra drew her daggers. Her foe glanced at her weapons, and she saw their surprise. She wanted to believe they thought her a slip of a girl, a fragile thing armed with toys. Her advantage would be total. But it dismayed her to see both men backing away. They understood what range she needed to attack. As they drew away, she glanced to see Shadow had engaged two others. His wide blade chimed a dull tone as it parried their blows. She had no time to scrutinise Larimer—a glint of blue steel flashing in her periphery.

On instinct, Petra rolled to the ground. Uncertain where she would regain her footing, she knew it would be outside their range. She leapt to her feet as one of her foes swung his sword upward, and with her head down, she charged. Just feet from her target, his boot came up and caught her in the chest. A resounding thud pummelled her bones, and her momentum tumbled her to the side. Down she went, skidding into the scree and shale, losing one dagger as she fell. Grasping for the blade, she retrieved it as a sword smashed into the ground beside her. Flakes of rock erupted into the air. An image of severed fingers pushed from her mind.

This was her chance. Digging her toes into the gravel, she lunged from a low height. The enemy dragged his sword to the side; an attempt to block her charge. But Petra had timed her strike to perfection. The blade pierced his long fur coat, digging deep into his thigh. She thought she felt chain-links among the material, but she couldn't be sure. He yelled and stumbled backward.

With a moment to compose herself, Petra scanned her surrounds. The other one was pressing down toward her, taking clumsy steps across the slope. It was foolish. It was perfect. She skipped to the side, then darted back into his path as he swung his sword. His slicing blade split the air but was far from causing Petra concern. She knew what he would do next, and keeping clear of his boot, waited for his return swing. His body twisted, then released as a coiled spring. Petra lunged upwards and stabbed her blade deep into his armpit. His piercing scream was painful to her ears, but the injury would be far worse to bear. Incapacitated by the blow, he released his sword and it spun, flying free from his hands. It soared through the air, a flashing wheel of orange and silvery blue. Petra cried out to Shadow; it was coming his way.

He turned mid-block; his eyes widening. Petra gasped to see Shadow falling backwards, but it seemed the only thing he could do—the rogue weapon was moving with wicked speed. The sword clattered wide-edge against his foe, and Shadow crashed to the ground in an awkward slump. Petra glanced at the remaining heavy-hitter who was bearing down on her. One more second, she thought, watching Shadow defend from the ground. As his enemy swung down, Shadow whipped his hefty cleaver across its path. The thinner blade smashed apart under the weight of Shadow's blow. She'd seen enough; he'd be fine for now. He had to be; she had run out of time. Instinct again dropping her to her knees, she rolled away to the side as the massive blade swung past. On her feet in a flash, she noticed her foe's laboured steps. The wound to his thigh was slowing his advance.

Petra waited for her moment. She needed him to swing again, but he wasn't so quick to expose his weakness to her speed and agility. There was another tactic she could play. She rotated her position, moving above him on the slope. She was giving away one advantage to gain another. As she had in Kalleron, when she had dispatched the slavers, Petra flicked her wrist and sent the dagger flying. A distraction. The heavy-hitter moved to dodge the projectile. Petra was already on her way. He redirected his focus and repositioned his sword. But she had already launched herself toward him. She knew he would labour to lift the heavy blade; there would be little momentum in his upward slice. Although the blade caught her torso, she was already plunging the dagger into his neck. She let it go, and carried on over his head; a vault assisted by the advantage given from the slope. She struggled to control her landing, but as she slid into the shale, she saw her foe drop dead.

On her feet, she realised Shadow had felled one and remained engaged with the other. His opponent was fatigued; the strikes laboured and wild. Larimer was faring worse. His opponent was savage; his poise and speed undiminished. With haste, Petra retrieved her daggers and moved to the first she had dropped. He lay twitching in the blood-drenched snow. She was ready to end his misery, but his movements became still, an artery finally bleeding out. Sensing Larimer's plight was more fraught than Shadow's, Petra rushed across the slope, keeping low, intending to deliver a stealth attack.

What the hell happened? She was on the ground before she could react, face down in shattered rock. A call came from Larimer, but she couldn't hear his words. Petra pushed herself to her feet, giving a cursory check to her limbs and body. She was unhurt, but she was several yards down the slope from the skirmish.

Larimer's voice became clear. A warning. 'He's a bloody Southwaller.'

Southwaller? She'd never heard the term. Whatever he meant, she had to assume the worst. Careful to keep the mysterious man in her sights, she advanced. His attacks on Larimer were as ferocious as they were fast, and they revealed as much about the cultist as they did about the foe. Although Larimer's efforts were flagging, his skill with a blade was impressive. Petra came close, circling the swordsman. She noticed his eyes, wide and wild. His fur concealed his physique, but the veins on his neck were prominent; his sinew and tendons bulging with unnatural size. He lashed out with his blade, and she struggled to maintain her balance. It was a grim reckoning; Petra realising she wouldn't have lasted long against Larimer's enemy. Perhaps if they survived, she would apologise for taking the easy option. She focused on the moment as the Southwaller pressed down upon them. His hacking blows and ferocious swipes kept them in retreat. Petra sought Shadow, but it was all she could do to maintain her defence against the Southwaller. Doubt crept into her mind. Was she losing the fight? Her strength was sapping, and her steps were becoming erratic. She was stumbling as she evaded the ever-faster blade. It was impossible.

A sound came to her ears. In her confusion it sounded as though a celebratory cheer, followed by a surprised curse. Another swing and she was down on the ground, caught by the blade but protected by the thick fur. Larimer was closing in the periphery, but he stumbled to his knees, dropping his sword to the ground. *Gods! this is the end.* The raging Southwaller loomed above, his slavering grin a glint in the moonlight. Petra gasped to see the strangest thing. A sight so glorious that time appeared to stop; the sands of time suspended in disbelief. Above her attacker, there was a Shadow high in the sky.

The Southwaller's grin contorted in a gruesome splice. His face shearing in half, a shower of brain and blood sent everywhere. Petra rolled to the side as he collapsed; her shaking hands wiping the gory matter from her face. Impulse driving her to her feet, she saw the majesty of battle. Spine tingling, spirits soaring;

her flying Shadow had come to the rescue. Invigorated and elated, Petra couldn't resist a prod.

She pointed to the felled Southwaller, the cleaver lodged between the hemispheres of his skull, and between breaths, said, 'I had him.'

Shadow stared at her, his own exhalations forming dense clouds. 'You know you almost took my head off.'

'What?'

'That bloody sword. Almost got me killed.'

Petra recalled the flying double-hander. 'Oh. Sorry?'

'Pfft!' Shadow pointed at the corpse. He turned to Larimer. 'Is that what I think it is?'

Larimer wiped his face and nodded. 'Southwaller.' He grinned, gestured at the cleaver in the Southwaller's head. 'That'll be how you fight, then?'

'Love me a leaping hatchet job,' Shadow said. A pause, and he appeared pleased with himself. 'Don't often pull it off, mind. That was a lucky shot.'

'Well, bloody glad you did.' Larimer looked at the Southwaller, then flicked his head to the side. 'The others?'

In the melee, Petra had forgotten about his companions. She saw them coming from the outcrop. 'There they are.'

Larimer sighed, doubled over, then straightened. 'They shouldn't have been here.'

'Who were they?' Petra asked. She pointed to the Southwaller. 'And how can someone fight like that? It's not possible.'

Shadow stood on the body and yanked his cleaver free. 'Southwaller's are Kalleron's fanatics. I heard about them during my time. Thought it was fancy talk to scare young recruits. Clearly not.'

'Drugs?' Petra asked.

Larimer sighed. 'Enough to kill a horse; they're practically fed them. Sometimes they take a dose before battle. Makes them faster, and they don't feel pain or fatigue.'

'Sounds like Ambyr Dust,' Shadow said.

Larimer nodded. 'Not far off.'

Petra scanned the slopes, casting her gaze all around to see what other danger might come their way. All seemed still, nothing stirring above the wind. 'What now?'

Larimer pointed to his fallen companion further down the slope. 'We bury our own.'

Petra nodded. 'I'm sorry, Larimer. Once we've paid them a fighter's respect, what next?'

'It's too dark. There's nothing we can do up here but wait until morning. We can hide the bodies now, clean up what we can, so it's not visible from afar. But then, we rest.'

Petra nodded, stealing a glance at Shadow. He appeared pre-occupied with the Southwaller, a permanent scowl on his face. She wanted to ask, but thought better of it. Larimer was already marshalling the others. Now was the time for solemn acts. She would seek answers in the morning.

Chapter XXVI

A thick haze spoiled the view across the Larissian Sea. Dawn had coloured the sky a dark fire, but a mist had rolled in, obscuring the coast. Petra, refreshed from a few hours of sleep following the night's excitement, faced the coming sunrise. Skopia and Dehnar had left to search for signs of another camp. Shadow and Birnham were still chewing on dried meat rations when Larimer came to her side.

'I'd compliment the view, but it's murky,' he said.

'I've seen better.'

'How are you?'

She smiled, wondered if his concern was genuine or a mere pleasantry. 'I'm all right. I slept well enough for what rest we had.'

'About last night. The Southwaller, you've never seen one before?'

'No. I've not.'

'We were lucky it was just one. It could have been worse.' Larimer frowned and huffed a sigh.

She sought to reassure him. 'But it was one, and he's dead.'

He shook his head. 'There're no Southwallers in Etherus, at least, not that we've seen. This one's from Kalleron.'

'Is that a problem?'

'We know they're looking for the Fury. But they'd not need such a skilled hand on these slopes. Trackers maybe, but not someone with the might of what we faced last night.'

'Then why?'

Larimer turned and scanned the mountains. With a shake of his head, he huffed. 'Whatever Kastane has planned, the King must have an idea. Only Kalle, or those that support his myth, would have thought to send a Southwaller. And they'd only do that if they knew something specific.'

Petra didn't understand the context. That she was involved with a seditious cult was of no shock, but Larimer's confusion was disturbing. Perhaps motivated by his caution, she surveyed the slopes, seeking what she didn't understand.

'I'm still not sure why this bothers you so much. The cult stole a weapon—an elemental weapon. Is that not enough reason to send more muscle?'

'Oh, these types aren't muscle. They're the keenest blade at the end of the strongest arm. You don't send a Southwaller out on a search party. If Kalleron has wind of the plan, it would make sense the heavy was here.'

She was curious. 'Do you know it? Kastane's plan?'

The cultist smiled. He had a handsome face; a roguish good look that might break many a romantic heart. But in his eyes burned a flame, and she knew that Larimer's focus was absolute.

He said, 'His exact plans? I don't know, but I live my life for this purpose, perhaps to make amends for what I did as a Kallerye soldier. More than that, there are greater powers in this world than the false king, and he holds one under his deception. The Queen doesn't belong to man. That is our only purpose: to free her.' He paused and stared at Petra. She thought she knew what he would say next; an apology for the Queen's terror and genocide. Larimer nodded; a solemn tip of his head. 'I understand you may not have the sympathies we do for the Queen. Her actions have taken countless lives, but she has no comprehension of what we are; of what life is. She can't be aware of Kalle's deception. This is the crux of Kastane's plan. None of us have been told of it, but we'd be fools not to piece the puzzle together. The Fury, the Southwaller? We know we can't physically free the Queen. Kastane has long held the belief that we can only free the Queen by showing her the truth. The King has to be the target; though how he intends to deliver it to him, I don't know.'

Had she heard right? 'This weapon. They mean to kill the King with it?'

Larimer shrugged. 'I've not been told.'

She stared at him. A numbness inside of her. A tumult of emotion spinning within her soul. Petra closed her eyes and suppressed it all; she had to remain calm. But the feelings would not leave, and she knew there was only one person to blame.

'Petra?' Larimer said.

She opened her eyes and offered him a cynical smile. 'I'm an idiot. I'm a damn puppy chasing impossible dreams.' Petra shook her head and walked away. Larimer called her name, but she waved away his words. 'I'm fine. I just need to think.'

Shadow peered up from his last strand of dried meat. 'Think? That's not your strong point.'

Not willing to argue, she collapsed down beside him, knocking the scrap of food from his hand. She reached for it, plucking it from the ground. A sniff told her enough of its taste, and she handed it back.

'Ta,' he said, chewing on it.

'I'm sorry, Shadow.'

He replied with a mumbled query.

She sighed, kicking out at some shale. 'I've been a fucking fool.'

'Uh-huh.'

Petra laughed. To hear Shadow's unadulterated honesty was as refreshing and cold as the mountain air. 'Couldn't you argue my point? You know, try a bit of empathy? For once?'

Still chewing. 'Nuh-huh.'

She waited until he finished rending the slivers of dried meat. When he finally swallowed it all down, Petra turned to him, her eyes repeating the question.

Shadow said, 'A fucking fool, yes. But explain.'

'The Fury. What we've become involved with. I knew it might be dangerous, but I didn't know what purpose it had. If Larimer's hunch is right, I'm in way over my head. I know our safety wasn't guaranteed, but this is... this is madness.'

He grinned. She pointed to the meat lodged between his teeth. Shadow's finger probed his mouth. Petra shook her head, pointed to the other side. With the leftovers removed and sucked from his fingertip, Shadow cleared his throat.

'The Melody's rules and all aside: you were never a soldier. I mean, clearly, Laria must have height exemptions for conscription, but your short arse still wouldn't pass muster, would it? Anyway, my point is: beyond bar fights and pirate duels, and no matter how good a fighter you are; you've never fought an actual battle, no?'

Petra forced a smile to her face. As a child, she had faced her own battles, perhaps not as Shadow imagined it. And although she had dealt with rapists, murderers and all that came in between, she had never fought on the battlefield.

She said, 'Not as a soldier.'

'Well, when you signed up for this jolly jaunt with the cult, you put yourself in Kalleron's way. More than that, you put your neck on the line. Until this point, you've been in control of your life, and even though we've had our scrapes, nothing's really mattered in the long run. Even the slavers you killed in Kalleron; already forgotten. But this?' He gestured to Larimer, who was staring out across the slopes. 'This is different. You said yourself: we're taking a new path. This one's right twisty. The old one's long gone, washed away in the storms, and we're never going back. I said you'd never fought on the battlefield, yeah?'

She nodded.

All hint of humour dropped from his tone. 'This is your battlefield now. And soon enough,' he pointed to where they had buried the bodies from last night, 'they'll start piling up. You're going to have to deal with that. Life as a pleasure pirate was a game. This isn't.'

Her eyes wandered, the stark reality finally hitting home. Her selfish and romantic thoughts of Felicitra and how she could be closer; it was nothing more than the desperate deception of a grieving lover. Such a fool she had been. Her father would be ashamed.

Shadow said, 'Look at me, Petra.' She brought her eyes to meet his. 'You've sided against Kalleron. You're at war.' His smile returned. 'And yeah, you're a silly fucking bastard, but we've chosen to follow you. So, no matter what—more than these cult crazies—I've got your back. You understand?'

She stared at him. Wanted to hold him; to feel the comfort of his words wrapped around her body. It was ridiculous; she knew he would reciprocate if only they weren't both such stubborn idiots. Instead, the small space between them felt at once a gulf and impossibly close. It was their bizarre bind. But it would do.

'Then we keep on?' she asked.

'We keep on.'

It was comforting, although she knew what was to come would bring more danger to her and the crew. Rueing her selfishness, she was alerted by Larimer's voice calling to them.

Pushing herself up, and hauling Shadow with her, Petra stood and moved to the cultist's side. 'What is it?'

Larimer pointed, and Petra saw Skopia and Dehnar on the slope. They were waving at them; a signal to follow.

Petra said, 'You think they've found a camp?'

'It was what they were looking for, but we'll not know until we see for ourselves. We should grab the supplies and head.'

She nodded and told Shadow to gather up his things. Once they had packed their provisions and ensured the fire pit was cold and smothered, they moved off, following Larimer and Birnham.

They trailed behind the two scouts, and after a scramble over some rubble and rock, they entered a narrow depression sheltered by a jutting outcrop. She stopped in her tracks and stared at it. Jagged, cracked, and crumbling, it appeared ready to fall. She pointed it out to Shadow, who shrugged and continued on. With a wary eye, Petra gazed at the area under the overhang and walked into the camp. An unspoiled firepit, glowing with burning embers, lay in the centre with backpacks and gear scattered around.

'Is it theirs?' she asked.

Skopia nodded. 'It's Kallerye for sure.'

Larimer strode into the middle of the depression, standing close to the dying fire. 'No sign of the Fury?'

Skopia's face lit up, his white teeth incongruous with his dishevelled beard. He pointed to a small hollow at the base of the outcrop. 'I've not opened it, but there's a casket packed back into the rock. They've hidden it, but not well enough that Dehnar couldn't see it.' He gestured to the other scout. 'Excellent find, that was.'

'Let's have a look then,' Larimer said and moved to the hollow.

Petra made to walk forward, but hesitated. The cult operated on levels of secrecy, and she wasn't privy to much of it. Was she to see the cargo they had tasked her to carry? She held Shadow back as he stepped forward. He slapped her hand away with a huff and marched on. Petra stood there, watching the men gather. A simple thought, another deception for herself; perhaps if she didn't look, it wouldn't be so real? Stuck in a maze of indecision, she saw Larimer turn and look at her. A frown wrinkled his brow.

'What you waiting for, Petra? Come see.'

She walked forward, relief lightening her step, and joined him. Gathered around the base of the outcrop, they stared at an innocuous brown box which was long enough to hold a bundle of short swords. If there was a rare weapon within, the exterior appeared a poor choice for what Larimer had described. It was neither darkwood nor Larissian. Why hide something so drab?

'Traps?' Larimer asked.

Skopia shook his head. 'None that I can tell. Just a double buckled hinge.'

A gesture to the plain wooden box, Larimer said, 'Careful then, let's see it.'

The scout crouched near the casket, and after checking the immediate area, kneeled beside the box. With slow and deliberate movements, he loosened one buckle then the next. He paused, sitting back on his haunches, before running his nail around the crack of the opening. He turned to Larimer.

'If there's a trap here, it's damn clever. But I think it's safe.'

Larimer said, 'If there's a Fury inside and anything goes wrong, we'll only have a few moments. Skopia, open it slowly. If you hear a crack, anything like glass breaking, move like lightning, and get away.'

Skopia nodded, a squint and a frown to betray his nerves. Petra thought to warn Shadow of his pranks. It wouldn't surprise her if he did something stupid. She looked at him. He was focusing on the box; not a hint of mischief in his eyes. His concentration added to her curiosity, and she turned to watch Skopia at work.

His hands on the lid, Skopia lifted it with tremendous care. There was a tension among them, but Skopia's fingers never once trembled, and his concentration remained complete. It felt as though an age passed as he lifted the lid to the top.

'Hah!' Skopia cried out. 'Bloody knew it.'

It was a disappointment. Inside the casket was another box, but this one was darkwood.

Larimer pointed to it. 'Can you lift it out?'

'Aye, it's got handles.'

Skopia checked the inner box, and when he appeared satisfied of no immediate danger, he lifted the darkwood container from its outer cover. On the ground, he repeated all his checks, and under instruction from Larimer, he prised open the lid. Again, Petra sensed time slowly ticking by, although Skopia's caution was welcome. When he opened the box, what he revealed inside was an exceptional sight.

A deep bed of red velvet filled the lid and the main compartment. Nestled deep within the plush fabric, there was a glass ball held inside a spherical mould. Skopia's fingers moved across the material. Delicate and purposeful, his touch was hypnotic; he had the hands of an artist. Without touching the glass, he withdrew from the box, and turned to Larimer.

An expression of doubt etched on his features, Skopia said, 'Is that it? Is that the Fury?'

Larimer shook his head. 'I don't know. Never seen one.'

'It looks so fragile,' Petra said. 'How can that be a weapon?'

Larimer pointed to Birnham. 'You've got the knowledge.'

Birnham nodded and knelt beside the box. 'We're in the shade here, but if this is real, and if everything we've learned is truth, then the sunlight will show us the Wind.' He looked at Larimer and grimaced. 'Can we move it into the light?'

'Carefully. Skopia, you're certain it's safe to move?'

Skopia raised an eyebrow. He said, 'Nothing's safe up here, but there's no trap.'

Larimer gestured to Skopia, who closed the lid and enrolled Birnham's help. Together, they lifted the darkwood box and moved across the depression. At the edge, they placed the box on a rock. Skopia fussed with its position until he appeared satisfied it was stable. As a group, they walked to the casket, and

Larimer instructed Skopia to open it. He lifted the lid, and the rays of a low sun, peeking between the high mountain pass, kissed the glass sphere.

Petra didn't know what to expect. She looked at Shadow, but he appeared fixated on the peculiar orb. It was a surreal moment; high in the mountains, she and the men watching the sun glancing off the glass. The light, diffracting through the surface, spread across the velvet, a rainbow of colours cast against the red. It was pretty, but it was inanimate.

'Is it broken?' Skopia said, leaning over.

'We could smash it and see?' Larimer said with a grin.

Shadow stepped forward, and Petra reached for him. He smiled and pointed at her. 'Got you!'

'You're an idiot!'

'But maybe not,' Skopia said with a huff. 'Nothing's... hold on.'

Petra and the men leaned in; Skopia pushing at Dehnar to stop him blocking the light. The sphere hadn't changed, but inside the glass, a strange light was glowing. It was a shade of deep red; an impossible brightness from the colour of blood. It was mesmerising and disturbing. Petra, aware she was holding her breath, tugged at Shadow's furs. In silence, with just the mother Wind calling across the skies, she observed the wonders of the elemental weapon. The colour shifted, and the red split into yellow and green as though the rainbow was trying to free itself. In a rapid pulse, the colours shifted again, this time releasing a cold blue hue that cast the red velvet black. Petra stood back. Her spine tingling, she raised a finger to point as Birnham shut the lid. They stared at one another, then at the box.

Birnham, slowly nodding, said, 'A Fury.'

'What was it doing?' Petra asked.

'What they do in Etherus, we can't be sure, but whatever it is, it taps into knowledge that Kalleron has stolen from the world. The Fury is one such thing, and I imagine there is more going on that we're yet to learn. But what you saw, that swirl of colour; that was the Wind herself, at least, a shred of her power.'

'It was beautiful until it changed,' Larimer said. 'It seemed agitated? Can that be right?'

Birnham nodded. 'As little as we know, the Fury is stable in the dark, or until you break the glass. There are rumours it was one of these that killed old General A'dan; he was the Etherus master until Aracyse took over.'

Shadow said, 'Aracyse sailed to Kalleron, days past.'

'Aye,' Larimer said. 'Called back to his master, likely for his failures.' The cultist pointed to the casket.

'I'd not underestimate Aracyse,' Shadow said. 'He'd want to rectify this.'

Larimer nodded, but Petra sensed a deeper threat hidden in Shadow's words. She wanted to ask more, but Birnham had continued speaking of the Fury.

'We've gathered scraps from our sources about how this works. They say the Fury becomes extremely unstable in sunlight. So much that it can free itself from the glass.' Birnham stared at the group. 'They say if it frees itself, the damage is worse. That's the rumour about A'dan.'

'Then I'm glad you shut the box,' Petra said, pointing to the overhang above their heads. 'If it's as violent as you say, I'd not fancy our chances.' A thought occurred to her, and Birnham appeared the one to ask. 'But why glass? Why so fragile?'

He smiled with a shake of his head. 'We don't truly know. It seems at ease; the Fury, I mean. Unaware it's imprisoned. But I've asked myself that same question: why glass? All I can think of is this—how do you capture air?'

She shook her head.

'Glassblowers do it all the time,' he said with a shrug. 'And we know the Smoke's got bellows and a furnace.'

'But you don't know for certain?'

Another shrug. 'Educated guess.'

Larimer turned to her and nodded. 'Are you ready to go? We have what we came for, and it'll take a few days to return with the casket.'

Petra looked at Skopia and Birnham handling the box. If what they had said was true, the Fury was a dangerous and mysterious creation, but something had settled her anxiety. Perhaps seeing its colours dancing inside the glass. It appeared docile when not disturbed. A pretty trinket; not a fatal weapon.

She asked, 'It'll be safe?'

'On your ship?'

'Aye.'

'It's more stable than black powder.' He leaned in, a wry smile on his handsome face. 'And I'm sure you've dabbled in that before?'

She had, and it brought back memories of Shadow smoking his pipe in the hold. Petra laughed, looking at her friend, who appeared nonplussed. 'I'm ready to go. Let's get this back to the Melody. The sooner I'm rid of it, the better.'

Chapter XXVII

On the deck of his frigate, Aracyse looked east across the bay. The cool breeze was a welcome breath on his face. It had been days since he had first spoken with Kallisa, and the confines of the Generals' Tower had become too great a restriction of his liberty. It was a strange contradiction: in Etherus; he was a prisoner to the elements, with nowhere to wander at will, but in Kalleron, where he was free to roam, he felt invisible walls looming on all sides.

For the past few days, he had spent his time on the docks, becoming familiar with the trade and the people. If Kallisa brought him the news she had promised, he would soon have his hands on his stolen Fury. To charge onto the docks, without his presence being known to the harbour folk, would cause a stir. By meeting the locals, he had settled their nerves. His daily routine had quelled the chatter and intrigue, and Aracyse had enjoyed meeting the hard-working men and woman who risked life at sea to bring home the day's catch. Some faces he thought he recognised from the wars, others, their scars recognisable, he knew on a first name basis. It was a comfort when those war-weary faces saw him. All acknowledged Aracyse with a nod or a bow; a shared expression of respect. There was no way that the captain of the cult ship would know of his presence, not until it was too late. When it arrived back in port, they would see no commotion or fuss.

With the morning sun sparkling on waves stirred by a cooler north-easterly wind, he waited for his spy to come. Lost in the peaceful view, with the rhythmic sound of mast bells chiming, he heard a voice call from behind. It was Makala, the captain of his private guard. He was one of half a dozen hand-picked mercenaries. Fierce and loyal fighters, he would rather have them at his side than an entire regiment.

'Yes, Makala?'

'Overseer Kallisa, sir.'

Without turning, his eyes fixed on the water, Aracyse waved his hand. He listened to the sound of boots crossing the gangplank; a subdued reverberation on the wood. A firmer strike as she approached him; the deck solid under foot. She came to his side, and they exchanged a brief greeting. Aracyse looked at the spy and, though she appeared calm, there was a concern behind her expression.

'Is there a problem?' he asked.

'Our rider returned late yesterday with news from Gwynerath. The Melody has sailed.'

Aracyse, reading her hesitation, knew there was more to be told. 'The Fury?'

Kallisa shook her head. 'We can't be sure; the search party hadn't returned.'

'What does that mean?'

'The weather, the elements; you know how hostile it can be.' The Overseer paused. 'I have another fear—an ambush.'

'Ambush?'

'My people spotted Petra and another crewman being escorted by Kallerye guards. As far as I know, they took them to a house in the cliffs, but they disappeared for days.' She paused and paced away. With a shake of her head, and speaking to the wind, Kallisa said, 'The port is in a state of chaos with the migration of refugees. My contacts didn't have eyes on their return, but we know the Melody set sail, and her return is imminent.'

Aracyse frowned. It wasn't the confirmation he had hoped to hear. It would have been a more confident plan to stride aboard the ship and retrieve his cargo. Although he wasn't one to suffer false pride, it would undermine his status and that of Kalleron if he left the Melody empty-handed. His king would not be pleased. It would be wise to avoid an unnecessary humiliation. Two failures in such a short time would be the end of him.

'I had planned to board that ship,' he said.

Kallisa turned to face him. 'You still can.'

'No. I needed to know if the Fury was aboard. A definitive answer. This remains uncertain. It is not my place to conduct a simple search, and as important as this one might be, if I return empty-handed, it will make the King look foolish. Paranoid, even. I can't allow that.'

The Overseer frowned and cast a glance at the bay. 'Then what would you suggest?'

'I'll send Overseer Tremain. We'll keep eyes on the harbour, and once the Melody returns, we'll conduct a routine search for contraband. If this is to be a worthless endeavour, I'd prefer Tremain to be involved.'

Kallisa smiled. 'You don't approve of Overseer Tremain?'

Aracyse held a high regard for the overseers and their work. Tremain was the rare exception. He was an odious snake that revelled in the power of his position. As far as Aracyse could tell, Tremain had done nothing for Kalleron but extend amnesty to slavers and murderers. And though it was Kalle's will that the city be free of general rule, it was a constant irritant to Aracyse. He longed for a cleaner soul for the city, although he knew all too well that the profits of sleaze furthered the wealth of the state. It paid for military extravagances, such as Etherus and his mechanical arm.

'Etherus,' he said aloud, the thought coming to him without prompt.

'Excuse me?'

Aracyse shook his head, scoffed at his own remark. 'I long to return so much that it calls from my subconscious mind. But of the task at hand; Tremain's minimal skill set is best used for these things.'

'And if he finds the weapon?'

'I'll give him the strictest orders regarding this. It will come to me.'

Kallisa frowned and clasped her hands. But she didn't speak.

'Say what's on your mind, Overseer.'

'I could do this. I have conducted searches for contraband; I've awareness of cult activity.'

'That is your weakness.' He offered an apology expressed by an upturned palm and a slight grimace. 'I mean no offence, and I respect your position, but the more you hamper the cult's activities, as you have done in the past, the more suspicious you become.'

The Overseer returned a thoughtful nod. 'A fair point, General.'

'Yes. Tremain is the perfect blunt tool for this task.'

Kallisa strolled across the deck. She moved with a deliberate stride. It was a cadence he associated with deep thought, as though the processes of intellectual functioning required much of the mind's resources. He waited for her inevitable query.

'If the weapon is on that ship, what will you do once Tremain brings it to you?'

'I will escort it to the King myself.'

'You would show him the Fury?'

It was an odd thing to say. The King would demand to see it. 'Of course. Why do you ask?'

Kallisa looked around, her eyes scanning the deck, then she appeared to search farther afield. She paced closer, coming within a few feet. Her voice a whisper, she said, 'May I speak within the bounds of our trust?'

'Always.'

'Kalle is not entirely convinced of the importance of Etherus. As a man, he sees himself as the true power. We know Etherus is supported by those who know better. But there are factions in the South Wall who falsely believe the Queen will remain forever loyal. I fear Kalle may prove unpredictable around what he perceives as a threat to his dominion, whether that is the Fury or Etherus itself.'

Aracyse recalled the King's reaction during their brief conversation. 'He appeared to be testing my faith in his immortality when we discussed... my failings at Etherus. I would have to agree; I see your point. If he has doubts about the weapon's power, he may become reckless.'

Kallisa nodded. She appeared relieved to hear his thoughts. 'Whether he doubts it or fears it, I cannot know. But if there was no Etherus, there would be no Fury, no threat. And there is no mortal man that is stronger or more powerful than he. Only the elemental powers transcend his own. The weapon is certainly a danger to his status, and he knows that.'

The Overseer's warning was not without merit. It gave Aracyse pause for thought. He glanced up at the fortress walls. They were impervious to the outside world in much the same way that Aracyse found the King's concealed countenance impervious to scrutiny.

'You think I shouldn't bring him the Fury?'

She pointed to his arm. 'Would you risk that again? For your King?'

'You think he'd be so foolish? That he'd smash the glass?'

Kallisa shook her head. Once again, she scanned the surrounds, anxious glances sent this way and that. It compelled him to reassure her.

'Only my personal guard are nearby, Kallisa. You can speak your mind here.'

She nodded. 'Imagine, General, that you were a little younger, and you had even the smallest insecurity of your valour or honour. Think of another soldier strutting through the ranks, seen by others as your successor; seen as worthy of your status. If you were so insecure, would you not consider testing your new foe?'

The notion that the King would destroy a Fury in his own presence was ridiculous. It was a nonsense of logic. In Aracyse's opinion, it was the same as drawing a blade across the neck to test its keen edge. But what Kallisa had said; her inference of insecurity—it defined the King's mindset. Nothing had ever tested his immortality, but what if something could? It was a strong possibility that Kalle would want to know. He would *need* to know.

'The more you say, Kallisa, the more impressed I am with your logic. What I thought was obvious appears not to be. But how would I deny the King his right to see the weapon?'

'You would take it to me. I would deliver it to him. I would take that risk.' Kallisa was offering to martyr herself if her fears came true. 'Why?'

'Faith.'

'Faith?'

The Overseer nodded, a small smile on her lips. 'I told you my parents were cultists. You know my loyalty is first to my Queen, as the Earth. I have studied what I can of the elementals. I believe the orphan of the Wind that is trapped within the glass would see my soul. I believe it would see me.' She tapped her fingers on her chest. 'I honour them.'

It was a whimsical dream, nothing more. A disappointing surprise to hear coming from the pragmatic Overseer. Aracyse also thought of himself as an elementalist, yet he had seen the power of the Fury. About to spoil her idealistic imagery, he recalled Etherus and the night he lost his arm. Just his arm. The elemental weapon had eviscerated General A'dan. It had to be coincidence, but he couldn't deny the attraction. Could the Fury see the soul of a human?

He shook his head. 'I think it is too great a risk, Kallisa, for anyone. But this discussion is futile; the King will call who he wants, and they will go. It might be me; it might be you. Perhaps neither. The only thing I can say for certain is that I'll arrange for Tremain to search that ship. Then, I can decide on my next step.'

Aracyse thought Kallisa might reply, but she nodded her head and stared out across the bay. He followed her gaze, and a stroll toward the deck-rail brought them closer. They shared a comfortable silence for a few moments. He assumed she was enjoying the peace and the pleasant view.

'Shall I send Tremain to see you?' she asked, stepping back from the railing.

'Please. And Kallisa?'

'Yes?'

'Whatever the next few days bring, I will make sure the King knows your service was exemplary.'

The Overseer bowed her head and left the deck. Aracyse returned his focus to the bay, taking in the view and allowing the ripple of waves to relax his soul. In the back of his mind, images of a golden king holding a glass sphere painted a grim picture. With a twitch of his shoulder, he lifted his metal arm to the rail. It was a miracle of engineering. But he did not want another.

Chapter XXVIII

Kallisa moved through the streets, shambling with her foot dragging behind. She had wrapped her body in a simple hooded rag and kept her eyes down, making her way to the lower dockside. Evening had come, and the gloom exaggerated the squalor. With her hair tucked under a woven cap, and her face painted an unhealthy pallor, she had disguised herself as the afflicted. She had one last meeting with Kastane.

She hadn't left the fortress in her pauper's garb; she completed the transformation in one of the cult's safe-houses. A strange and clumsy term. There was nothing secure about those dilapidated huts that were scattered among the worst parts of the city. On more than one occasion, she had entered a hovel to find a dead body or an addict with their eyes glazed over. This evening, the only eyes watching her disrobe were rats which scurried away into the shadows. Kallisa was confident they would keep her secrets safe and her modesty intact.

Shunned by the crowds and happy they did not come close for fear they would see her vibrant eyes, Kallisa found her way to her master. She pushed a hand against the door of a squat stone building and walked into the dark space beyond. Inside, she allowed herself a moment to adapt to the dim light. She knew of the place: an old haunt of sinful pleasure, long since abandoned after rumours spread of disease. Too small to be important, nobody had come forward to claim the dwelling; none cared to clean it. It had become another anonymous haunt to meet Kastane.

Inside, there were rickety tables and chairs powdered grey with dust. It was a small space, somewhere where those with coin would wait for the beds in the back. Shuttered away from the outside, there were no windows to allow leering eyes to gaze in. There was a solitary lamp on the wall. It wasn't a modern Kallerye lamp. Instead, an old oil-burner cast an amber glow; a ghost of black soot climbing the wall above.

The room was empty. Kallisa didn't call out, but she put her hand inside her robe, reaching for her dagger. Before moving to the back rooms, she turned and pulled the wooden beam across the door, locking herself inside with the shadows and the secrets of a sinful past.

Kallisa moved beyond the first room, crouching under a low arch. In a short corridor with two openings on each side, she struggled to see. At the end of the narrow space, there was another oil-burner, although its light was feeble compared to the first. She moved her head from side to side to better see the shapes in the dark. One room had the dimmest glow emanating from within, and with caution, she pressed on. At the second portal on the right, she peered around the edge to see a man lying on a bed. His place of rest was a stone block set against the far wall. There was nothing else in the confined space other than mouldy rags on the floor and the smell of decaying time. She thought of her attire; it seemed appropriate for the occasion.

His hands behind his head, Kastane sat up as she entered. In the dim light of another ancient burner, he directed her to sit beside him. Kallisa shuffled across and took her place. She sniffed the air. 'Pleasant.'

'It is the true stench of Kalleron.'

'Perhaps just once we can meet in an inn?'

He scoffed. 'Perhaps you'd prefer to visit Seawall?'

'I know. I know,' Kallisa said. No matter what disguise she wore; their conversations would bring attention. A purse of coin to be had for any mouth that spilled the secrets of the cult.

Kastane said, 'Is everything in place?'

She nodded, realising he might not notice in the gloom. 'It is.'

'How does that make you feel? I can sense you have feelings for the man.'

She did, and what she would do next would stab a knife in his back. Her cause was greater than one man, though, and even Aracyse was a pawn in that game. 'The General is a good man, Kastane. You surely know that.'

'I do.'

'We've spoken occasionally, and I feel as though I could reach out to him; tell him what it is we do.' There was conflict inside her soul; the secrecy and the loyalty—it was a terrible burden.

'Yet he is Kalleron's greatest living general, Kallisa. Such words would have you in Seawall. There is no trust to be had in these men. They are regimented to obey, even when they understand those orders are anathema to humanity. There is no faith in their dark; you mustn't be weak now.'

Kallisa sighed. She pictured Aracyse smiling when she had spoken of her faith in the elementals. She knew he thought the same, but Kastane was right, and she understood in her heart that even friendly souls on the other side were still the enemy.

She said, 'I have raised my suspicions with the King.'

'And?'

'The man is an enigma behind that mask, but I have to believe that he has fallen for our deception. I'm convinced he has doubts about Etherus and its mission. Kalle can't allow himself to be threatened by the power of the Fury. Aracyse said as much. But I have planted that seed over months, nearly a year; telling the King that Etherus is a ploy to destabilise his hold on Kalleron. First General A'dan, and now Aracyse.'

'This is good, Kallisa. Can we really be so close?'

She nodded. 'I've worked on Aracyse to keep him at bay for now. He's one of few people who can identify the real Fury. I'll ensure the South Wall locks it away until dark; he'll not get close, and without the sun's light, he'll be none the wiser. I've arranged for the zealots to see my truth; I'll destroy the fakes in front of them, leave one for the King's glory. All the pieces are in place. I've used all of my resources to get this far. All we need are the duplicates and casket; are they ready?'

'Yes. Larra and her escort will take the casket to the Melody. She'll swap the box and put the Fury in with our inert glass. But she'll leave it on board; say that I'll come to collect it myself.'

Kallisa thought of the pretty Larian woman Petra. Another pawn in the greater game. There was little chance she would escape the deception, and although Kallisa's choices had sent many to their deaths, she had a strange fondness for the feisty captain.

'Is there no way we can spare the Larian?'

In the gloom, she saw Kastane's reply: a single shake of his head.

Kallisa said, 'Perhaps Larra can warn her? Once she switches the caskets and the spheres are inside. She and her crew can disembark; leave the ship empty with just the cargo aboard?'

Kastane appeared to consider her words, and for a moment, Kallisa thought he might have a plan for her salvation. He said, 'When I took my first tentative steps with the cult, I did all I could to prevent unnecessary harm. In my past, I'd created so much distress and pain; I wanted to remedy my mistakes. I know I'll never atone for what I've done, but I thought perhaps this would be different. Yet

Shadow huffed. 'Do I have to remind you?'

'That I signed us up for this? No. But it's got me rattled more than I thought it would. There's too much at risk.'

He patted her shoulder. 'Once the jitters have subsided, you'll miss the excitement. Bar brawls won't feel the same after the Southwaller fight. Mark my words; you'll be back begging for more.'

She smiled. There was an element of truth to his words. 'Well, wake the crew. We'll be landing soon, and I want to get the Fury off this ship as soon as we can.'

Shadow nodded and moved below deck to rouse the sleeping crew. Petra cast a glance at Argan, who was at the wheel. His focus was on the immediate course. At the helm, he appeared stoic and regal. She wondered how much he understood of all of this. He had promised to aid her, but did he know what that might mean? As much as she knew of his abilities, and since Gwynerath, of his impossible strength; Petra wondered what power he might unleash if pushed to react. He had never shown anger. Never raised a fist. Yet she was sure that when the time came, the quiet man from Bruhale would be at her side. It was a comfort for the uncertainty ahead.

It was past midnight, and the harbour was quiet. Petra had sent Shadow to pay the dockhands, and they had shuffled back to their bunks. Under cover of night, she marshalled Shadow and Argan as they carried the casket across the gangplank. Under the light of the moons, Petra ushered them to follow her, directing them to an old cache. Out of sight of the harbour master's tower, she knelt on the boardwalk and slid her fingers between the narrow gaps.

'It's not there. It's farther up,' Shadow said.

Petra, fumbling for a latch she couldn't find, frowned. 'You're sure?'

'I marked it years back; on the edge, see?'

He pointed to a plank with a crude 'S' scratched into the wood. Petra crawled on her hands and knees to the board and moved her fingers into the gap. Careful not to tear her skin on loose splinters, she searched for the hidden mechanism. As she struggled to find the metal lever, Shadow huffed.

'Maybe they found it?'

'Got it!' she said, flicking the latch and releasing the lock. She lifted the board, and a section of wood a few feet wide opened as a hatch. Underneath, a simple compartment lay empty except for a few scraps of cloth. It was a perfect fit for the casket, a hidey-hole that had survived the test of time. In all of her regular ports, Petra had paid for similar boxes. Thieves had raided most, often the same hands she had employed to keep them secret, but this had stood the test of time. A labour of her own efforts, made over many dark nights.

'Put it in,' she said.

Argan and Shadow lowered the box into the cache, and Petra closed over the hatch. She scanned the boardwalk and directed Shadow to a pile of discarded netting and rope.

'Grab that, throw it on top.'

With the cache locked tight and the debris on top, the Fury would be safe. It would give her enough time to send the crew ashore and remain alone to deal with the cult. Paranoia or not; she didn't want to subject the others to unnecessary risk.

Walking the short distance back to the Melody, she said, 'Shadow, take the girls into the hills, go to Tarkin's.'

'What?'

'I don't want them put in danger. We discussed this.'

'You need me here. What if something goes wrong?'

Petra faced him. 'It's an order, Shadow. Take the girls and go. I've got good credit with Tarkin. He'll put you up.' He was about to protest, but she was quick to silence his dissent, sticking a finger into his chest. 'I trust you to keep them safe, and more: they trust you. When we get back aboard the Melody, you'll take the girls and go. Understood?'

With a petulant scowl on his face, Shadow nodded but said nothing.

Petra resumed her pace, and under an awkward cloud of silence, they boarded the Melody. Shadow stormed across the boards and disappeared below deck. Argan, by her side, shuffled.

'Do you wish me to stay?' he asked.

Recalling Gwynerath, she nodded. 'Please.'

With a confirming grunt, he moved away. Petra turned to her cabin, when a voice called from the boardwalk. She whirled around, surprised to see a beggar on the dockside. Kalleron had its problems, but it was rare for paupers to roam the boards at night. Agitated by the sudden appearance that might bring undue attention, Petra hurried starboard.

'Go, get out of here. I'll have the harbour master lock you away!'

The beggar moved the cowl from her head and pulled the cap away from her crown. Luxurious raven hair fell around her shoulders, and though her face was pale, her striking features were the same.

'Kallisa?'

She nodded, gave a quick glance down the pier. 'We need to speak.'

Petra waved her aboard, dispensing with the pleasantries. 'You've come alone?'

Kallisa frowned. 'Larra, is she here?'

'Larra?' Petra shook her head. 'Who's that?'

'No other cultist has come?'

'No. You're the first. I thought you'd bring more?'

Kallisa exhaled a troubled sigh, mumbling a curse under her breath. She glanced to the dockside. 'Something's not right. Larra should be here with the casket.'

'The casket is safe. I've stowed it on the docks.'

Kallisa's brow crumpled deeper. 'It's not on board?'

'Don't worry, I said it's safe. Stashed in a hidden cache. I wanted it off the Melody. Better for my crew to remain apart from it all. I can show you now?'

The cultist brought her hands together as though praying. She drummed her fingers, nodding her head. After pondering unknown thoughts, Kallisa shook her head. 'No, leave it for now. Kastane's plan was to switch the casket, place the Fury with others; two false spheres.' She squinted. 'Larra's definitely not come?'

Petra shook her head. 'No. Just you.'

Kallisa's countenance became grim. 'We need that switch.' She turned again, paced to the starboard rail and peered down the dockside. As Kallisa searched for Larra, Shadow appeared topside with the girls in tow. His expression said much of his demeanour.

He noticed Kallisa. 'Who the gods is this painted beggar?'

'Kallisa. She's with the cult.'

Thelissa frowned and looked at Petra. 'Shadow said you don't want us onboard.'

Stubborn and selfish. Shadow's moods could be as foul as the weather. Annoyed at him, but keen to hide her anger from Thelissa, Petra said, 'We've got some business right now, and the Melody's not the safest place for you to be. I've asked Shadow to take you to a nice inn. It's got good food, and you'll be able to have a warm bath.'

Thelissa's eyes widened. 'Oh, I'd like that.' She gazed at Shadow. 'That sounds good. Can we?'

Thelia yawned; clear she hadn't fully awoken from her disturbed slumber.

Petra stared at Shadow. She made certain to deliver her instructions with clarity. 'We'll discuss this when you come back. Get going.'

'Aye, Captain.' He gave a cursory glance at Kallisa and, with his head down, escorted the girls across the plank. As the others emerged from below deck, Kallisa came to her side.

'You're sending them all ashore?' the cultist asked.

Watching Shadow leave, Petra replied, 'It's safer this way.'

One by one, the crew left until it was only Argan, Kallisa, and herself that remained aboard. The cultist was frowning and shaking her head, cursing under her breath; her pacing was a ticking clock that rattled Petra's nerves.

'Kallisa, what in the name of the gods is it?'

'This is all wrong.'

'Wrong? I have your casket; it's intact. You can take it away; find this Larra and perform the switch.' She looked at Argan, nodding. 'We've done what you asked of us.'

Kallisa paced to the rail and stared into the distance.

Petra's impatience was wearing thin. She called out. 'This damn Larra woman hasn't come.'

Kallisa turned around. 'She had the other box with the duplicate spheres. It's part of the plan. It should be aboard the ship.'

'I don't understand, Kallisa. What's going on?'

The cultist sighed and struggled to speak. Petra looked at Argan, who shrugged.

'Kallisa, answer me damnit. What's happening?'

Kallisa paced over. Petra required no counsel to see the woman's conflict. The Overseer said, 'Larra was to bring the casket and keep it on board.' She pointed at the deck. 'It was to stay here. That was the plan. It had to be here. An overseer is coming, and he was to find the casket on board. It had to look genuine. It had to be convincing. You had to be caught off-guard.'

Petra shook her head, hoping she misunderstood what Kallisa was trying to say. 'I don't... I'm not sure I understand.'

Argan stepped forward. A grumble came from his lungs. 'I think I do. You were to be martyred, Petra. A small fish in the greater ocean.'

Chilled by his words, Petra stared at Kallisa. 'Is that true?'

With sheepish eyes, the cultist nodded. 'That's why I came. Kastane doesn't know I'm here. I came to warn you. If we had the other casket, and the three spheres were aboard, you'd not need to be caught. There would be time to flee; let Tremain find what he seeks. He's a dumb arse; he'd not care the ship was crewless. Doesn't even know what he's looking for, just that he was to take it away. It would've worked without your sacrifice.'

An impulse she couldn't control, Petra lashed out to slap Kallisa. Her hand never hit the target. She turned to Argan, furious and surprised that he had caught her wrist. About to seethe at his insubordination, he spoke.

'What did you expect?'

She scowled, tried to free her arm, but Argan wouldn't let go. It was humbling, and it was what she feared the most—to be powerless. To be feeble at the hands of men. Men such as Kastane.

Kallisa's hand raised to Argan's arm. 'Please, let her go. She's angry. She has every right to be.'

Argan's grip loosened, and Petra backed away. Shaking, she said to him, 'Get off my fucking ship.'

She thought he might protest, but he didn't. He nodded and stepped across the plank and onto the boardwalk. Petra thought he might walk away, but he didn't go far. He moved to a barrel on the pier and sat down beside it.

'Petra?' Kallisa said, drawing her attention from Argan.

She turned to the lying cultist; thought to slap her face even harder than she had planned, but something softened inside. 'You said you came to warn me?'

'Yes. And it betrays Kastane's command.'

She had no sympathy, but she was curious to know. 'Then why come?'

Kallisa smiled, but the brightness in her eyes dimmed. 'We've all to play our role, Petra. I've played mine for long enough. It'll soon be over for me. But you need not play yours; Kastane has taken his liberties too far.' She stopped smiling. 'But something's gone awry; Larra's not come, but Tremain will. That plan is in motion, and I can't stop it.'

'The plan. You mentioned another casket?'

'Larra was to bring it. I fear the worst has happened to her.'

'You should leave, Kallisa. Find out where she is. See what you can salvage of this stupid plan.'

The cultist appeared hurt. 'What we do isn't stupid.'

'Tell that to the children who I sent away. Tell Shadow he was to be captured for another man's glory. How many others have you betrayed?'

Kallisa blinked and inhaled sharply; a moment's hesitation before she nodded. 'I'm sorry. I'll go. But you must leave while you can. I'll seek Kastane, find out what to do.'

Petra frowned. 'You'll not take the casket?'

With a firm shake of her head, Kallisa said, 'I can't. Not yet. We'll need to return for it. Where did you say?'

'Next pier along, in a cache hidden under old fishing gear.' Petra pointed. 'There's a latch near a board with an "S" carved into it.'

Kallisa looked and nodded.

Petra said, 'I'll gather my things and get away. You can go now.' She ushered Kallisa off the deck. 'Go back to your court, Kallisa. Perhaps you'll find some answers wearing your other face? But I've no wish to see it again.'

The cultist moved into the night, restoring her cap and raising her hood. Petra looked to Argan seated on the boardwalk. Her anger had subsided; the mist gone. To witness his patience and civility was humbling. Contrasted with his impossible strength, it made the experience even more profound. Everything about the man was a riddle. She thought of his unknown past, tried to imagine what he had lived through to make him the light he had become. A notion she couldn't push away; had he reacted the way he had because of Kallisa's bloodline? A defence of all things Bruhadian?

'Argan?'

He looked up, a relaxed countenance to greet her meek call.

'I'm sorry. I overreacted. Will you come aboard?'

Without replying, he stood and walked to the plank. A smile crept onto his face, and he nodded. Petra stood aside as he crossed over.

'I can be a hot-headed fool, you know that?' she said

'It takes a long time to quell all the fires that burn inside. You're still young, Petra, but time will teach you; if you let it.'

She nodded. Wise words from the calm philosopher. 'I'm glad you're here to keep me grounded.'

Argan laughed. 'I doubt I can do that.'

Petra squinted at him. There had been nuance to his words.

He pointed to the hill where Tarkin's modest inn sat among the trees. 'When he comes back down with the girls, go easy on his bruised ego. Shadow's your rock, Petra. Not me.'

As Argan moved to the stairs, about to disappear below deck, she called out. 'Argan, if not a rock, what will you be?'

'When you need me most, I'll be your hammer.'

It was her duty to be last onboard, and with Argan sent to safety, Petra had hauled in the gangplank and pulled canvas tarpaulins over the barrels. Under the light of the moons, everything had appeared calm, and since Kallisa's exit, Petra had allowed herself to relax, if only a little. She had found her diary and read the pages that spoke of Felicitra. Losing herself in those memories, Petra had scolded herself for dithering. Now, on the rail of the Melody, with her cabin locked behind her, she balanced with a rigging rope in hand. Satisfied the majestic lady appeared at rest, as though her crew had taken shore-leave, she swung to the dockside and made her way down the boardwalk. It was dark, but dawn would soon come.

Petra stepped from the wooden planks and onto the stone harbour when she saw figures appear from under the arch of the coastal wall. Beyond it, the city sprawled out, and her immediate freedom lay just minutes away. She glanced around and cursed her luck; there were places to hide, but illuminated under the moons, and standing alone on the waterfront, they would already have seen her. All she could do was keep calm and head toward the arch. It was a port, after all. People came and went at strange hours. It might be nothing. Without breaking her stride, she moved forward. Closer she came and her heart sank; a tightness gripping her stomach. The Kallerye harbour lamps and the glow from Noctyrne and Ambyr illuminated what she didn't want to see. Six men and an overseer. But that wasn't all. Petra strained, peering beyond the approaching men. She saw more figures moving beyond the gate. With flashes of steel hanging from their weapon belts, she understood what was happening. It was a rare time that mobilised the city-guard; perhaps such desperate times as now? Was this why Kallisa had come to her? Was this Tremain come for his Fury?

She walked close to the men, a choice to run her path along theirs. Better to appear unfussed than evasive. With control, she said, 'Good night, Overseer.'

Decked out in his red and black finery, he stopped. On his command, the guard came to a halt; six soldiers decked in half-plate and chain-mail. Petra noted Shadow's favourite weapon hanging from their belts.

'Stop!' the Overseer called.

Could she walk on? Pretend she hadn't heard? Petra cursed herself for such foolish thoughts. She stopped. 'Yes, Overseer?'

'From which ship do you come?'

'The Ocean Light,' she replied. A reasonable lie to give; the crew was mostly female.

'Ah. I see.' The Overseer paused. He turned to look over his shoulder. Petra noticed a rising commotion coming from the arch.

'Is there a problem, Overseer?' Petra asked.

'Hold,' he said, a finger raised to silence her.

She leaned to the side. Tried to see the disturbance coming from the arch. It was more men, one of whom appeared to tower above the rest. His black cloak was a shadow in the moonlight, but his arm glinted silver, amber, and blue. Petra recalled something Shadow had said. She took a pace backward.

'Don't you move, young lady,' the Overseer said.

Petra glanced around, sought a means to escape, but to what end? If she ran, it would prove her guilt. She shuffled on the spot, wondered if Argan had slipped away. He had left with enough time. Petra had to believe her crew was safe.

A colossal figure with impressive armour came to a stop beside the Overseer. Six mercenaries assembled by his side. He wore the robes of a Kallerye general, and there was one she knew to be in the city. Shadow had appeared respectful when speaking his name.

The Overseer spoke to him. 'General, she says she's from The Ocean Light.'

With a frown on his face, the General took a step forward. He stared out across the bay, peering over Petra's head. He smiled to himself and pointed to a naval frigate berthed on the eastern harbour. The General turned to her; the curious smile remaining on his face.

'That is my ship. From its deck, I can see most of the harbour. I know The Ocean Light; a fine vessel. She has the markings of old Thania, yes?'

Petra nodded, although she couldn't suppress the sense of dread that he was toying with her.

'Let me introduce myself, my lady.' He extended his unarmoured arm, reaching out to her. He tipped his head with polite deference. Petra moved her hand to meet his. She couldn't refuse. His shake was firm and brief. She stared, confused by his manners. He said, 'I am General Aracyse. Have you heard my name?'

Petra nodded. There was something in his voice. What was it?

'Good. You know who I am?'

'Yes, General.'

He appeared pleased. 'Excellent. Then, my lady, I understand why you'd lie to an overseer; it's only natural to evade responsibility.' He pointed to his ship. 'I've watched the harbour these past few days, and I've come to meet many of its fine people. Mingled with many a crewmember; including those on the Ocean Light. Good folk, and most I'd recognise again. So, I shall ask you—and I will only ask once—from which ship do you come?'

The General stared at the ships moored on the western harbour. She turned to track his gaze. Her stomach lurched. The Melody lay in his field of view. To lie now would be futile. Reckless.

'The Melody of the Sea, General.'

'You are the captain?'

'Aye, General.'

'A name?'

'Petra.'

Inside, she was shaking. Petra summoned all of her strength to maintain the illusion of calm. The General's demeanour did not strike fear into her heart, but his measured approach was more disarming. It was easy to fight her way out of an argument, but she found it difficult to evade his pleasantries. Behind his stark civility, there lurked a decorated Kallerye General. One whose orders had put many to death. Above all; it was his voice that most unsettled her. Something she couldn't pin down.

'The Melody and her infamous captain. Ah, yes. Will we find it on board?'

Now she could tell the truth. 'There is nothing on board. My crew are...'

'Petra.' There was a warning in his tone.

'It is the truth, General. We sailed from Gwynerath; the port is a mess. We were to transport a wealthy trader, but there was none. My ship is empty, please.' She gestured to the boardwalk, an invitation to go to her ship.

The General's smiled slipped. 'I believe you, but Tremain will search regardless.' Aracyse turned to the Overseer. 'Lock down her ship; search it in the morning at first light. It's pointless to do it in the dark.'

Aracyse strolled to the edge of the stone dock. He stared out across the dark bay before returning.

'You will come with me, Petra. Do you understand?'

She glanced at the men and women around her, tried to picture any means to flee. There was nothing she could do. She thought of Kallisa's confusion when she spoke of the missing girl, Larra. With General Aracyse on the docks, it seemed the cult's plan was unravelling. A niggling thought. Could Kastane's trickery be so easily undone?

Petra nodded at the General.

He waved at one of his men. 'Makala, you know where to take her; and how to treat her?'

The soldier nodded. 'Aye, General.'

Petra stared at the towering legend, a wrench in her gut as he said, 'Then take her away.'

Chapter XXX

Damn it! Shadow panicked on the bed, flailed at the sheets, and tumbled to the side. He landed on the hardwood floor, his head pounding, and for a moment he lay there, uncertain of his surrounds. The patter of little feet came running through; two pairs of bare young legs coming his way. What nightmare was this?

'Shadow?' Thelissa asked.

'Why's he on the floor?' Thelia said.

The girls. Shadow leapt to his feet, wrapping the bed sheet around his waist. 'Oi, no looking!' A wild swing of his head. He looked at the closed shutters. Dawn etched a dim light across the wooden slats. He glanced at the girls in their night dresses; a gift from a tired and grumpy Tarkin.

'Did I fall asleep?'

Thelissa nodded and pointed to the empty bottle beside his bed. Shadow blinked. 'I drank all of that?'

'You were mean,' Thelia said. 'You told us to stay in our room.' She pointed to her end of the suite. Petra's credit with Tarkin had afforded him a modest room with two sleeping chambers. That was as much as he could recall. The younger sister continued. 'You stayed there staring and drinking until you fell asleep.'

He looked at the shuttered panel blocking the view. 'Who closed it?'

'I did,' Thelissa said. 'When you started snoring. Didn't feel so safe.'

Shadow, one hand on his head, gathered his thoughts. Petra, some silly business and him being sent away. It had put him in a foul mood. His behaviour hadn't been fair to the sisters. 'I'm sorry. Last night was... I'm just sorry, all right?'

'We're fine, aren't we sis?' Thelissa said, reaching for Thelia's hand.

Shadow nodded and stumbled on shaking legs to the window. He opened the shutters and squinted, trying to focus on the harbour. The early light was as gentle as he could have hoped, but it compounded the thudding in his brain. Bleary eyes and a dreadful hangover were anathema to his concentration. He rubbed his eyes but couldn't see straight.

'Thelissa, come here.' He waved the older sister over. Shadow pointed to the harbour. 'What can you see? Anything happening?'

'Umm. What should I see?'

'I don't know. Stuff?'

'I see stuff.'

He rubbed his eyes, cursing his vision. 'What stuff?'

'Men.'

'Men?'

'Uh-huh. Sis come 'ere. What's that?'

Thelia moved to the window and propped herself higher on tip-toes. With a squeak of effort, she said, 'Is that the Melody?'

'Uh-huh, think so,' Thelissa replied.

'It's pretty.' She pointed. 'There's lots of men.'

Shadow strained to see. He cursed and moved away from the view, shuffling across the floor to find the basin. He poured some fresh water and immersed his face in the cold depths. Eyes open, he blinked before pulling away from the impromptu soak. Shadow dried himself with a towel adorned with too much frivolous lace and returned to the view. With refreshed eyes, he could see what Thelia had. Too dim and too distant, he couldn't be certain, but it appeared to be guards. There was no sign of Petra among them.

'We need to get close,' he said.

'We're going back down?' Thelissa asked.

He nodded.

'Is it safe?'

Shadow didn't know, but he had many reasons to get down to the Melody, not least to find out what was going on. Besides, he thought, Petra had some aryll in her cabin and he could do with a hangover cure. The guards, though; they might pose a problem. Guards? It was a bolt from the blue, bringing a hollowness to his core—*the casket*. Shadow leaned out to peer at the harbour. He couldn't see enough detail to check the cache; he couldn't even locate it from this new perspective. If there were guards all over the dockside, they were surely still searching?

A tug on the sheet wrapped around his waist, and Shadow peered down to see Thelia's inquisitive face.

'Is Petra going to be all right?'

Why wouldn't she be? There was no sign of her on the Melody, at least, not that he could discern. They'd all left for shore. Hadn't they? An icy chill slivered down his spine. His head pounding, and his thoughts muddled, Shadow couldn't recall what Petra had said. He had stormed off in his huff; something he now regretted.

'Petra?' he said.

'She's safe?'

Shadow shooed them away. 'Get your gear. We need to get down there.' They scurried back to their side of the room and he returned to the window. Something worse than his headache had come wandering into his mind. Where the bloody gods was Petra?

It was foolish and reckless. Shadow, walking through the lower streets and toward the harbour, understood the risk he was taking. As he neared the harbour arch, a hushed whisper came from an alley. He turned to see Argan shaded in the narrow lane. A boulder among pebbles; was he trying to hide? Shadow changed direction and guided the girls to the alley.

'Argan?' Shadow said.

'They're all over the docks. They've been searching the Melody.' The Bruhadian frowned. 'Where's Petra?'

Shadow stared at him, a twitch in his eye.

'I thought she'd gone to Tarkin's to join you?' Argan said.

'No, she didn't. She's not here?'

Argan shook his head. 'I've not seen her, but after you left, the woman, Kallisa, spoke about the plans; they seemed undone. Petra sent her away. We made the ship ready for a long berth. She wanted to make it look genuine. I left first, but she couldn't have been far behind.'

'You didn't see her leave?'

'No.'

'When did the guards come?'

'I awoke to see them. I bunked in the Pier House.' Argan appeared agitated. 'It was quiet for a good hour after I left the Melody. Petra must have left by then. All was calm on the streets, so I meditated.'

Shadow looked overhead; the morning light was filtering into the streets, although the sun hadn't cleared the towering eastern wall. 'Are they blocking the entrance?'

'The guards? No.'

Shadow wanted to get to the ship. He needed to find Petra, or a reassurance she'd left. The guards wouldn't recognise him; they had come for the Melody. They wouldn't know its crew. He looked at Argan; not so much a fly, more of a bat in the ointment.

'You stay here.'

Argan frowned. 'Why?'

'You're almost seven feet tall; you'll draw attention.'

'What are you going to do?'

He hadn't thought that far ahead, but with the girls in tow, he could take on the guise of a father. Take a stroll along the pier. It wasn't so unusual. He was certain the sisters would be happy to help. If he got close enough, he could sense what had happened, sniff around for word of Petra. They had nothing to fear; there was no smuggled weapon aboard. Child's play. What could go wrong?

'I'll take these two along.' He nodded to the girls.

'Where?' Thelissa said.

'We need to find out what's happening. Don't you want to see the captain?'

'Yes, please,' Thelia said.

'Thelissa?' Shadow needed the older sister's consent.

She nodded.

Argan said, 'What exactly do you plan to do?'

Shadow faked a grin; he hoped Argan couldn't see his doubt. 'Just a stroll to the old rowboats; you know the ones.'

The Bruhadian stared at him. 'You'd take the children that close to the Melody? That's too dangerous. I'll go alone.'

'You?'

Argan nodded. Shadow shook his head and pointed to the street. 'You walk out there; worse, if you parade about on the docks, all eyes will be on you. Every guard in Kalleron's going to watch where you go. You'd be a big Bruhadian beacon.'

'Someone's coming,' Thelissa said, her head peeking around the wall. 'From the arch.'

Shadow pulled her back; a gentle tug on her sleeve. All these days together and she had come far, but Thelissa still required care—especially when handled. Shadow ushered them back into the narrow close, moving behind rickety crates and battered barrels. He tried to make Argan less conspicuous. A captain of the guard strode past, flanked by his men. He was laughing with them; speaking of the search. Something about leaving the *arsehole* sweat for a bit while they gathered some lifting hoists for the box in the hold. Shadow saw more guards leaving the docks. None carried the casket.

'What's so heavy they need hoists?' Shadow said, then looked at Argan. 'It's your bloody crate. There's nothing else that heavy; everything else they could've moved.' He paused, squinted at Argan. 'I reckon it's your armour.'

Argan's demeanour transformed. 'They can't take it,' he said, straightening up, and preparing to move. Shadow wanted to hold him back; knew that would be futile. The Bruhadian looked down at him. 'I need to go. Stay here.'

'No chance, Argan. We all go.'

Argan gestured to the sisters. 'It's too dangerous.'

Shadow was having none of it. 'You heard the guards; we've seen most of them leave. I'm coming with, and I'm not leaving these two.'

With a grumble and a shake of his head, Argan moved from the cover of the alley. As he stepped out, Shadow was relieved to see a semblance of normality return. With the guards' numbers diminished, curious faces appeared at the opening shutters, and impatient mariners were making their way to the docks. It would provide enough cover.

With the girls by his side, he followed behind Argan. Thelia held a grip of his pinkie, and Thelissa held her sister's hand. It was a dire situation, and he still had no notion of Petra's whereabouts, but he felt a smile appear on his face. Thelia and Thelissa strolling down the pier with their two awkward fathers.

Argan slowed at the junction of the pier. The next turn would lead to the Melody. Where would he go? Shadow came to his side and peered down the boardwalk. He could see figures milling around the deck, but there was no overseer among them. A child would notice the flashy red and black robes. With nobody of importance left on the dock, all the guards appeared to be onboard.

'He must be below deck,' Shadow said.

'Good,' Argan said, a brisk pace sending him to the Melody.

For a moment, it seemed perfectly normal; Shadow following behind with the girls. He stopped, realised what was happening. He called on Argan, but the Bruhadian kept walking. Shadow glanced around; there were no Kallerye guards or soldiers close enough to cause concern. But they would return. Hesitation an unusual affliction, he felt a squeeze on his pinkie.

'Are we going?' Thelia asked.

Paralysed by rare indecision, he watched Argan board the Melody. He wanted to be there; needed to be with his friend, but he couldn't take the girls, and neither would he leave them.

'Shadow?' Thelissa said.

'Wait.'

He watched with conflicted fascination as Argan brushed through the guards and down into the hold. He observed the moment as though detached from time. Frowned as the men on the deck chased after the Bruhadian. Maids chasing a bull from the dairy. He heard the clatter of feet hammering down wooden steps. There was a muffled sound. A few moments passed, then there was silence from the hold.

'Shadow?' Thelissa asked again, with a tug on his sleeve.

'Come on, quick.'

At the gangplank, Shadow stopped and turned to her. He scanned the length of the boardwalk. Nothing to cause concern. On board, though, there were guards and an overseer, and Argan doing gods knew what to them. It was strange; above the normal bustle of an early Kallerye morning, no sound came from below deck. He should have heard something, but there was nothing. Not even a yelp.

Thelissa nodded at him. 'You go, I'll keep Thelia safe.'

He pointed to the spot where she stood. 'Right here, don't move, all right?'

With a bob of her head, Thelissa accepted the command. Shadow huffed and leapt onto the plank. He raced to the steps of the cargo hold, stopping in his tracks, startled to see Argan appear from below.

'Shadow?'

'The guards?'

Argan looked over his shoulder. His reply was a discontented grumble.

Shadow stared at him; trying not to imagine dead Kallerye soldiers in Petra's hold. 'The Overseer?'

The Bruhadian shook his head.

A terrible squeal pierced the air. It was Thelia. In one swift move, he turned and sprinted toward the girls. Halfway across the deck, the Overseer called out from the boardwalk. Petra's cabin door was ajar. How could he have been so stupid not to check?

'Not another step!'

Shadow froze, skidding across the boards. Wrapped in the Overseer's arm, and hoisted from the ground, he held Thelia tight; a silver blade drawn against her neck. Thelissa was flat on the planks, squirming with her hands to her face.

'What did you fucking do?' he yelled at the Overseer.

'You stupid peasants. How dare you defy Kalleron with your heresy. You'll be joining your captain soon; you'll all rot together in Seawall.'

What had he said? Shadow processed the words, repeating them in his mind. Seawall? Time froze, and he looked from Thelissa, now rising on shaking legs, to the knife pressed too hard against Thelia's throat. Her tears running down her cheeks mirrored the sliver of blood creeping down her neck. One wrong move, and she would be dead. Shadow looked at the fortress wall; his stomach twisting inside out.

'Yes,' the Overseer leered, 'They took her to Seawall before dawn.' Thelia whimpered under his grip. Tipping his head to Shadow, he said, 'Shush, child. You're barely grazed, but if they come one step closer; it'll hurt a lot more.'

Shadow glanced to his left. Argan had appeared alongside. The strongest man he knew; his power was neutered by Thelia's plight. An innocent shield held firm against the approaching storm. He tried to rally his thoughts. Of Petra, of now. The Overseer wasn't bluffing, and he was the gateway to his captain. The bastard had played a killer card; one simple deal, one small child on the table. Shadow could do nothing except fold.

'What do you want?' he asked.

'The casket.'

'I tell you where it is. You give us back our captain. You bring Petra back, and I'll show you where that damn box is.'

The Overseer's eyes widened. 'You'll show me the box first. You're in no position to barter.' His attention shifted further down the boardwalk. 'Ah, this is all perfect. Your childish adventures with this nonsense cult are over. General Aracyse will deal with you now. Surrender.'

Shadow turned, casting his gaze to the far end of the boardwalk. There, flanked by six mercenaries, Aracyse was storming down the pier. Even Argan appeared to slump. A heavy breath expelled from his lungs.

The Bruhadian said, 'We can't risk Thelia.'

'You'd fight Aracyse to escape?'

'I'd fight him for the honour alone. But that's a selfish thing when the cost would be her life. Fate has given us one path, Shadow. We've no choices here.'

Shadow stared at his old mentor. Aracyse was approaching ever closer, his guard in tow. In his periphery, he could see Thelia's feeble struggles and Thelissa sobbing on the boards. It was a wretched sight, and he could do nothing to change it. Not without risking little Thelia. Despair in his soul; he dropped to his knees and hung his head. A sideways glance at the fortress wall, a question already answered. But how? How had they captured his captain? What the hell had happened to Petra?

Chapter XXXI

Darkness. A fetid odour. Petra gagged, moving her hands to her mouth. A sudden and painful jolt. Her wrists slapped with force; her movement restrained. She whipped her head up, opening her eyes. In that fleeting moment, she understood where she was. *Seawall*. Her hands were chained to an anchor, unseen beneath the wooden board that was her seat. Her skin was unencumbered by her dress or armour. A moment of blind panic, and Petra reached to her thighs. Bare flesh, covered by a rag, perhaps a hessian sackcloth. She squirmed and writhed, clutching at herself, reaching to protect her dignity as though she could undo what vile deeds men had done. Her trembling hands quietened in between her legs. Confusion replacing fear. There was no pain; no discomfort but that caused by the chains around her ankles and wrists. The fears of that teenage girl had not become a reality. Her body was whole. It was her own. Yet she was a prisoner of Seawall, and the reckoning fell as tears. Petra called out for attention, repeating her meek call several times without response. She was alone.

Leaning forward, far enough that the chains would allow, she put her head in her hands, fingers clawing at her scalp. She could only think of Felicitra. What would her brave lover think of her now? A silly Larian girl gone to play intrigue and treason with cult and king. All of her emotion turned to rage as she thought of Shadow. He was always there to remind her of her folly, but this time she hadn't heeded his advice. Now, she would pay the price. What of the crew? Petra could only imagine what would become of them and the Melody of the Sea. She pictured the beaming faces of Thelia and Thelissa; of how they skipped and gambolled across the deck as spring lambs in a forever sunny Kalleron. What now? Sent back to the streets to endure the cruel whims of evil desire? And Shadow; what of him? Petra saw her stalwart friend. Vivid in her mind's eye. He would face his fate; his Kallerye cleaver in one hand, a tankard of ale in the other. Shadow would fight the gods to prove a point. He would never relent; not until death touched his shoulder and whispered in his ear: rest my friend, you're already gone.

Brooding in morbid and destructive thought, a noise beyond the door brought Petra's attention to focus. Keys jangling. She had a vague understanding of the prison and how it kept its sorry souls. Visible from the water, the wall was an array of alcoves set high above the rocks. Through a sight-glass she had peered to see the six cells in each open space. Those cells were unguarded; left without thought. She knew why. Behind her door, should she somehow break free, there was one way to escape. A near vertical descent to the jagged rocks one-hundred feet below. The marble wall was flawless; not a single crack wide enough for careful fingers to grasp. No purchase to prevent the fall. Petra doubted if lizards even dared scale the sheer northern face.

A door opened and shut; someone was coming closer. The cell was dark, no light seeping in from beyond. It was still night, perhaps near dawn? She couldn't tell. Immediately in front of her, there was a squeal of metal and a rattle of wood. The cell door slid to the side. Eyes well-attuned to the dark saw a towering figure silhouetted in the ambient light of the moons.

'Petra,' he said. It was General Aracyse. 'Are you unhurt?'

A ridiculous question to ask. She wanted to respond with spite, but there was something in his tone. A familiar cadence. The same as their first meeting. What was it? She tried to place it, but in her confusion, she couldn't.

'I'm in Seawall,' she said with a huff. 'Is that not hurt?'

'My men had orders not to harm you. They say you struggled when they asked you to undress. One had to subdue you. A tap on the head.' He paused and paced out of sight. Petra wondered where he had gone, though he returned moments later. 'I apologise for that. They assured me you were not molested.'

His unusual concerns prompted further confusion. 'Why do you even care?'

'A fair question. Let me ask you: When you look at me, what do you see?'

'A servant of Kalle. What do you want me to see?'

'Do you see an evil man, Petra? Do you see hatred?'

She wanted to, but she didn't. *That tone.* As at the docks, his voice was familiar. It came to her, disarming her in the most brutal manner. The voice of a kind murderer. And though it was not him, Aracyse had the aura of her father.

'I see...' She struggled. Emotions were washing across bare shores; a realisation of her predicament drowning her misplaced sentiment. 'I see a man. Just a man.'

'Not a general?'

'Our titles don't define us.'

Aracyse appeared to consider her reply. 'A wise observation; though our titles dictate our actions. Mine are simple. I protect Kalleron and its people from harm.'

'Then you serve a murderous regime. You serve a liar and his horrendous queen.'

'I know.'

Petra straightened her body as much as the chains would allow. 'You know? Which part?'

The light had shifted; it was the earliest hint of dawn. Petra could see his features now, and she saw Aracyse smile. He said, 'All of it, of course.'

'All?' Although trapped in her cell, she was free to speak. 'A murderous regime? A lying king? A genocidal queen?'

He shook his finger. 'It's not genocide what she does. It is horrendous, but genocide is a human ideal; what the Queen does isn't so.'

Petra listened to his words. They tumbled around inside her mind as she tried to cling to a sense of logic. 'You sound like the cultists. But at least you agree; the King is a liar?'

'Yes.'

'Yet you willingly serve?'

Aracyse gestured to her. 'You're Larian, yes?'

She nodded.

'I imagine you'd happily serve Edramus, or at least you think of him as your king?'

'Edramus is nothing like Kalle.'

'No. But his ships dominate the eastern oceans and he rules those waters with violent impunity. You've seen the battleships?'

She nodded.

'Let me tell you about Edramus. Four years ago, I watched from afar as a lone Rotynian vessel tried to sabotage one of those massive hulks. It was inevitable, of course. They obliterated the little ship; shredding wood, sail, and flesh using the battleship's Windspitters.'

Petra failed to see the relevance of his remark. 'And?'

'Edramus ordered three more battleships to scour the seas, and to destroy every Rotynian vessel, no matter its flag. Your nation probably called it a great defence of Laria. But I know from the wreckage that washed upon Kalleron's shores, that they slaughtered women and children in that brutal campaign. Collateral.' Aracyse inhaled a deep breath. 'I have seen much war, Petra, and I know it's not about right and wrong. It is about which outcome is the least destructive for your own people. My people are Kallerye, and I will defend them in the name of our King.'

She reflected on his words. Petra realised that had not been her point. 'I said the King is a liar; you agreed.'

'About his immortality?'

She nodded, keen to hear his treason.

'Only zealots believe that nonsense. We adhere to it because it brings stability.'

What was she hearing, and why? Kalleron's most respected living general was admitting to a seditious secret. But what did that matter? She was in Seawall, and she understood what that meant. It made her situation even starker. Aracyse was giving his confessional to a woman he had already sentenced.

'May I come back to my earlier remark?' he asked.

Puzzled by his manner and conversation, Petra squinted at him, shaking her head. 'What?'

'Do you consider me an evil man?'

She thought of her father. He had been. Aracyse was not; at least, not in the way of callous morality. The thought made her laugh; a shallow snort of humour. How would her life have developed had her father been the General, and not a devoted homicidal maniac?

'This amuses you?'

Petra shook her head. 'No, General. A thought of what might have been.'

'Hmm. Then, may I assume by your tone that you don't consider me a monster?'

'No. I wouldn't consider you that.'

Aracyse waved a hand toward her; it appeared as a gesture to unlock an awkward question. He said, 'What you brought back from Gwynerath—the cargo on your ship. It is important that I recover it.' The General touched his brow with his human hand. She looked at his other; the huge, clenched metal fist. She couldn't be sure if it was armour. Fixated on the intricate lines illuminated in the growing light, Petra listened as Aracyse spoke. 'Tremain will soon begin his search, if he's not already begun. Will he find it, Petra? Is it stowed aboard your vessel?'

'I don't know of...' she began, but he cut her short.

'This is not the time to play heroes. Your role in this is over. You sailed from Gwynerath with something I need.'

She shook her head, thought to speak the truth. 'There's nothing aboard the Melody.'

'Nothing?'

'Nothing but our own possessions.'

Aracyse leaned forward. He drew a sharp intake of breath and said, 'I don't believe you. At least, I don't believe you returned without the item. Berthing the ship at night? No crew left aboard? It speaks of haste. In these circumstances, of guilt.'

She shook her head again, but Aracyse had confidence in his tone; it was unsettling.

'I'll kill them all, Petra.'

'What?'

'Your crew. One by one. We'll find them; we'll scour the harbour, interrogate anything with eyes and ears. I will find them all. Do you think the locals will risk their own lives to protect a foreign crew? And when that's done, and there's no more blood to be spilled, I'll sink your ship. You'll die here, knowing it happened because you felt it necessary to continue to play by the cult's rules. The retribution I'll reap will grow from the roots of your lies. Do you think I'm bluffing?'

Petra stared, dumbfounded at his turn of tone. 'You said you weren't a monster.'

'Not to my own. I don't have to be to yours.'

She shook her head. Another fleeting glimpse of Felicitra. It would be a betrayal.

'Petra, let me tell you a story.' He placed his human hand on his chest. 'One starry and cold night, I awoke to strange noises. I rose from my slumber, and I shuffled through my house. I sought the source of what had disturbed my gentle dreams. Do you know what I found?'

Petra looked at Aracyse. There was a tremor of anger in his voice. 'What did you find?'

'A good friend. A man who tried to abstain from war; an intellectual, a scholar. Do you know how I found him?'

She frowned. 'No.'

'Murdered in his bed. Along with several others. Murdered while they slept. These same people came to my house and stole the labour of my endeavour. They took what was not theirs, and they left my friend dying in blood-soaked sheets.'

As he recalled the story, the General's emotions appeared palpable. He turned away, a heavy sigh as he did. He paced the short distance to the opposite cell door and roared with rage. Petra startled as his metal arm sprung forward, smashing into the wooden portal. As though made of ice, the door exploded into splinters. The sound was cannon fire; the echo rebounding as god's laughter. Aracyse remained facing away; heavy breaths puffed from powerful lungs. Petra wondered if he was readying himself to strike again. He turned around and paced back to her, lowering his arm; noises coming from within as though a clock being wound.

'Petra, we may think a cause is noble, but the deeds that are done to aid that end are often monstrous, even when the men and women themselves are not. I am no monster, but if you wish to play their game, I will bare my fangs and claws. You and your crew will become a lesson to the world.' He pointed his finger, tapping it in the air. 'I don't imagine you fear death. I see a brave woman before me. A warrior. But I see a loyal woman, and your loyalty is to your crew. This is very simple, Petra. When I carry out the executions of your crew, I will do so to prove a point; I will do so thinking of my friend; murdered as he slept. What I do will not be murder; it will be justice. And when I rest my head down at night, I will sleep soundly. Do you believe me?'

His eyes blazed with passion. There was no bluff. She nodded.

'Then this is your only chance. The more time I waste here, the more I know the cult will scheme to get their hands on my property. One chance Petra; no more obfuscation. The truth now, or I shall turn the gears of Kalleron's extraordinarily efficient killing machine. I'll put in motion processes that will condemn all of your crew, past and present, to a painful death.' He paused, inhaled a deep breath and let it out as a long sigh. 'Where is my Fury?'

Petra couldn't hold his gaze. She let her head hang, and she closed her eyes. In her mind, she pictured a faraway place. In Laria, the Sarellian Plains; she and Felicitra dancing on sheets of ice under the light of the moons. Turning in each other's arms, smiling and laughing and joyous in life. She stared deep into her memory, gazed with longing at Felicitra's eyes. They were better days. Before the Queen had destroyed love, and the cult had shattered her world. She cried, her tears falling to the marble underfoot. On the dirt, they created pools of white. Small but precious jewels of grief.

Aracyse sighed and reached for the cell door. Petra lifted her head.

'Wait!'

Chapter XXXII

Shadow listened to the thunder of the General's boots hammering the planks of the boardwalk. Beside him, Argan stood motionless. Both were prisoner to Thelia's plight; in the blink of an eye, Tremain could slice through her throat. It would also be his death. Shadow's retribution would be brutal, but he had no stomach for that trade. He tried to block the image of reckless possibility; a vision of Thelia on the boards, her feeble hands clutching at her lacerated throat. He removed himself from the horror; focusing on Aracyse. Would the General remember him? Would he recognise the boy he had once saved? Pulled crying from a burning slaver house. This boy he had trained to kill so well. Shadow kept his head down, peering from under his furrowed brow. He realised it would mean nothing if the General recognised him. Their deed was treason; there could be no battlefield reunion of old friends. He felt Thelissa's gaze falling on him, and he nodded to her. And though he knew hope had sailed on a cold sea, he offered a smile, and she replied with her own sad acknowledgement.

'General Aracyse, sir,' Tremain said. He released Thelia. Shadow's muscles loosened as he dropped the bundle to the boards. She ran bawling into her sister's arms. Apart from those sobs, there was silence. Shadow twitched, an involuntary response to charge down Tremain. But his old master had arrived, and he remained on his knees. Aracyse said not a word. Shadow observed it all from beneath his brow; the General moving toward Tremain with a measured pace. What memories were surfacing in Shadow's thoughts? Recollections of a time served under Aracyse. Of how the great man conveyed his presence; he was a storm ready to break.

'General?' Tremain said, his voice uncertain.

Aracyse stared at the Overseer. As a tiger pouncing, the General lunged at Tremain. In a sweeping arc, he released his hammer from his belt and brought it crashing down on Tremain's skull. The Overseer crumpled under the impact; his knees buckling, the brief squeal of surprise stifled. Aracyse was already bringing another blow down; the skull shattering apart in a cloud of red mist. Thelia and Thelissa screamed, but the General was not done. The railing obscured his view, but Shadow saw flurries of movement, heard Aracyse stamping on the Overseer. Another blur of his black cloak, and there was a splash from the water. An old memory returned to Shadow. The grandeur of Aracyse. The wrath he had shown to the men who had tried to burn Shadow as a boy. What he had done to the beasts who had violated his flesh. A beautiful choir of screams ringing in the young boy's ears. It was why Thelia and Thelissa cowered in another man's blood. Argan shuffled beside Shadow, a strange huff blown from his lungs.

The General walked from the edge of the boardwalk, putting his hammer back on its hook. To the sisters quaking at his feet, he smiled. With a nod, Aracyse gestured to the ship.

'Go to your family. You're safe now.'

Thelissa was on her feet, bundling Thelia across the plank. They came to Shadow and collapsed into his embrace; Thelia hugging him, Thelissa's arms around her sister. He kept his head low, fearful Aracyse would recognise him. The General remained on the pier and called to his soldiers. He pointed to a pile of debris; some broken netting and tattered rope. They moved away, and Aracyse crossed the plank. On his knees, Shadow shivered. Had the boat wobbled under the General's stride?

'Stand,' Aracyse said.

Uncertain, but following the command, Shadow rose to his feet, pushing the girls behind his frame.

'Good gods! Is it?' the General said with surprise. 'Lift your head, son.'

With shame in his soul, he looked Aracyse in the eyes.

'Erivoll?'

Shadow nodded. 'Yes, General.' A pause, a shake of his head. 'That's not my name now.'

Aracyse approached. Almost as tall as Argan, but somehow larger in that strange metal suit, General Aracyse was a fortress in his own right. Not a young man. His black hair, slicked back, had grey throughout. Shadow remembered him always being on the cusp of old age. Some had joked he was immortal, the same as the King. The hand of the General came to his chin. Shadow felt his head being tilted left, then right. Aracyse removed his hand.

'Erivoll, what have you got yourself into?'

Shadow hung his head and mumbled to the floor. 'Troubles, sir.'

'Yes. Yes, you have. Still, you have company.' The General paced a step toward Argan. Without hesitation, he said, 'Royal Guard. I recognise that posture; your aura of invincibility. Magnificent.' For a moment, the General bowed his head. 'It is a shame about your King. I... As a young man, I had a rare chance to see him... a chance I never took.' Aracyse chuckled. 'Judging by your stature, he must have been even taller than legend said. Your name?'

'Argan.'

'Of Bruhale, Ballastar...?'

'Of Bruhale.'

Aracyse hummed and turned to the girls hiding behind Shadow. 'Come out, let me see you.' His voice was soft. Soothing.

Shadow felt Thelissa resist, but he moved to the side to abide by Aracyse's command. 'It's okay. He's not a wicked man.'

The General lowered his frame. A metal mountain settling on a wooden plain. On one knee, Aracyse pointed at Thelia. 'I'm sorry you had to see what happened to that man. But this one,' he pointed to Shadow, 'will keep you safe. Keep you from harm, as long as he doesn't meddle.'

Aracyse stood, towering above the girls. He turned his attention to Shadow. 'You'll not meddle, Erivoll, will you?'

Shadow, confused by the question, said, 'I don't understand. Any of this.'

'You knew me as a man of honour, Erivoll; that hasn't changed.' Aracyse nodded, as though confirming a story in his own mind. He paced to the stateroom door, tapped on it with his finger. 'Your captain and I have traded.'

Shadow glanced at the pier. The guards were hauling the casket from the cache. 'Where is she?'

'Petra? She will remain where she is. Though I have given her freedoms. She has a block to herself; the doors are all unlocked. A longer chain around her ankle, that she may glance upon the sea she loves. Clothes for her modesty. Sanitation. But don't hold hope, Erivoll. She will remain in Seawall. You understand what that means. It is the price of treason.'

'*No.*' It was the meekest sound. Shadow thought it had come from Thelia. Disconnected from his senses, he recognised his own voice.

'Yes.' Aracyse shook his head, a stern tone rising. 'You cannot think to kill a king, and return to those whose lives you endangered. Petra confessed; she has given me the Fury and secured your release. Your unwitting part in this fanciful adventure is over.'

'What?'

'You're free, Erivoll. You all are.'

Shadow had no words. Petra's plight had him silenced; his thoughts had collapsed. Behind him, he felt the sisters shaking. Thelia's weak sobs were a pitiful sound.

The General pointed to the bay. 'The warship in the mouth. The Blood Moon; it will fire upon the Melody at first light tomorrow unless she has sailed. Once she leaves port, she is banished from Kalleron, as are all who sail upon her. That is the promise I gave to your captain; the terms of your freedom. Her last order for you is to take them all away.' Aracyse gestured to the deck, casting his arm wide. 'This is your ship now, Erivoll. For the sake of the children, leave Kalleron.'

Aracyse nodded, turned around and crossed the plank, joining his guards, who now carried the casket. He appeared to inspect the outer box but didn't open it. With a wave, he ushered them on and approached the Melody.

'You said you were no longer Erivoll. Your Captain said you went by the name Shadow?'

He nodded. His mind was racing; trying to think of any way to save Petra from her fate. Aracyse's presence was a barrier to his normal thoughts. It was impossible to consider any action against his mentor. So impressive and persuasive was Aracyse that Shadow doubted even Argan would be his match.

'Then, Shadow,' Aracyse said. 'May you sail free, and may I never see you on these shores again.'

The General strode away, Shadow watching as he departed the dock. Thelia and Thelissa started agitating by his side, each wiping damp cheeks and bleary eyes.

'What did he mean?' Thelia asked.

'Where's Petra?' Thelissa said.

He ignored their questions and turned to look at the high fortress wall. He could scramble across the rocks, venture around the headland, and gaze up at the marble face. In one of its many box-cells, Petra would be there. So near, yet so far. The archers would release a hail of arrows on any soul who ventured close. The rocks below, augmented by rusted scraps of iron, had their own name: the *Tenderiser*. Shadow looked at Argan; his face a cloud of doubt and sadness. But there was more beneath his expression. Shadow was certain he saw guilt.

To the girls, he told a lie. 'We'll figure something out. Don't you worry, we'll find a way.' He was about to move to the hold when he remembered the guards. Aracyse hadn't even asked. 'Argan, the guards?'

Stirred from an unusual distraction, Argan nodded. 'Unconscious. I used my fists.'

'Get them off. We need to find the crew.'

Thelissa pulled away from him. 'We can't leave. We can't leave Petra.'

'We won't, but we need to be ready.'

He looked at Argan, but he was already moving below deck. Shadow trembled, doing well to hide it from the sisters. A bitter and furious hollowness threatened his soul; a freezing fire burning deep inside. Long ago, a man with a strong heart had lifted a young boy from a terrible darkness. But salvation is a fickle thing, and old wounds reopened. Yet when Shadow had sought his peace, a petite woman had cut the rope and brought him back to earth. Tied instead to her, he had followed hope wherever she went. Where was hope now?

Shadow stared at the fortress wall, refusing to look anywhere but there. A strange sensation on his cheeks; he wiped away the itch. In the breeze, he felt the cold damp on the back of his hand. The itch returned. Cold and tight on his face.

One at a time, Argan had removed the guards from the hold, putting their limp but living bodies into large grain sacks and, with Shadow's help, placed them with care onto the dockside. Shadow had made sure they moved them far enough up the pier that they wouldn't cause immediate concern. He wasn't certain how long they would remain unconscious, but Argan had reassured him they wouldn't dare come back. What would the men have thought? What did they experience in the hold? Thinking of Argan's strength, Shadow shivered.

It was noon, and he sat with Argan and the sisters for company. Thelia had become quieter, cradled in her sister's arms. The usual chatter of excitement was gone, replaced by a subdued silence. Shadow stared at the broken crate that contained the Bruhadian's prized possession. It was a suitable distraction from his anxiety.

'Is it damaged?' he asked, as Argan kneeled beside the wooden box.

'No.'

'Can I see?'

'No.' Argan, his head not turning, straightened his back. 'I'm sorry, it's personal.'

'I won't lie,' Shadow said. 'The girls stole a peek when we were moving the guards. They saw it.'

'We didn't!' Thelia protested.

Argan grumbled.

Shadow asked, 'So, it's a hammer?'

'Yes.'

'From your time as a Royal Guard? Aracyse said it; not me. But that man's got an eye for battle and if he pinned you as…'

'Yes,' Argan said, interrupting his stream of justification.

'Why not tell me? It's not a crazy thing. It's honourable.'

Argan continued to wrap the weapon in its cover. A fine red fabric embroidered with golden thread. Shadow assumed it was the old Bruhadian royal crest. Argan placed the battered lid of the casket on top and turned around, squatting on the wooden boards.

'Your name, the one Aracyse used; can I ask about that?'

Was Argan offering a trade, or was he invoking the rules of the Melody? Either way, Shadow realised his focus on Argan's past wouldn't solve his problems. He had busied himself these past few hours, shooing away the sisters then bringing them back to give them menial tasks; anything to keep his thoughts from collapsing further down on him.

He raised his hands and said, 'What are we going to do?'

'About Petra?'

'Aye.'

Argan shook his head. 'What can we do, Shadow? When Tremain released Thelia, neither of us moved. He'd given up his only advantage. But Aracyse stole our moment. I saw you twitch; I saw you wanted that fight, but the fight was gone. And to fight when there can be no victory, when the battle is already lost? I've seen that. I've lived it.'

Shadow understood. 'The battle on the bridge?'

Argan nodded.

'You were there?'

A quiet voice. 'Yes.'

'Good gods.' Shadow wanted to ask. Felt the urge to resist, but it was futile. 'What was it like? To see Baza'rad and Te'anor?'

About to reply, Argan stopped, his head tilting to the side. Shadow heard what had alerted him; a noise above deck. People coming aboard.

'Crew?' Shadow said, moving to his feet. He stepped to the door and peered toward the steps. Black boots and a jet-black cloak, tinged with red accents, were descending the stairs. Another overseer? Confident in Aracyse's promise of safety, Shadow stood his ground. It surprised him to the see the cultist Kallisa escorted by an old guardsman.

'You!' he said. 'What do you want?'

Kallisa stepped aside, and the guard came forward. He had a battle-hardened face etched with experience. A tall man with grey hair, he had a remarkable presence.

'My name is Kastane; we must talk.'

The cult leader. Aboard the Melody. Shadow clenched his fists; this was the man responsible for Petra's demise. His plan, and his stupid games.

'You're not welcome here,' Shadow said.

'I understand that, but I need to know what's happened. Too much is at stake. Even your captain's life hangs in the balance. There is much work still to do.'

'I'm not part of your fucking cult.'

Kallisa stepped forward. A beautiful woman, her unpainted skin was flawless. When she spoke, her voice was smooth as silk, and her words were a drug to soothe his anger. 'What has happened can be undone; there is still a chance we can make this right. Kalleron has disturbed our plans, but we may yet save Petra. Will you let us speak?'

He wanted to throw Kastane overboard. Perhaps ask the woman to leave; he would be softer on her. And although he knew the overseers spoke with liars' tongues; Shadow couldn't abandon Petra if there was even the faintest glimmer of hope. With a growl, he ushered them into the hold and followed behind.

Argan had risen to his feet, a quizzical expression on his face. His stance was awkward, hesitant. Shadow stared, uncertain of what had given rise to the Bruhadian's curiosity. Kastane had taken a position near the door, Kallisa moving to his side. Dismissing the strange atmosphere, convinced it was bound to Petra's plight, Shadow gestured to the two cultists.

'They've come for news. They say there is a way to free Petra.'

Kastane scanned the hold. 'The casket? Do you have it?'

'No,' Shadow said. 'General Aracyse took it earlier.'

The cult leader growled. Kallisa tried to placate him. 'That means the King might have them both. It can still work.'

Kastane looked at Shadow. 'Did a woman come here? Larra?'

'No. Not that I know. But you said there was a way to free Petra?'

The old man shook his head. 'No, I didn't.'

Shadow frowned, frustrated at his dismissal, realised it was Kallisa that had said they could save her. 'I don't understand; how can we help Petra?'

'We finish what we started,' Kastane said. 'It's how we finish it all.'

There was a point in his life when Shadow cared nothing for anything. A bleak time; as though swimming in a cold sea, devoid of joy and full of despair. Kastane's words spread out as ripples on that same desolate ocean; the undercurrent of doom was clear. This was no glorious victory. It was a final reckoning to bring Kalleron to its knees. And Shadow understood Petra was just another pawn in Kastane's grand plan.

He said, 'You have no intention of helping.'

'Helping?'

'Petra. In Seawall. You'll see her rot there for your cause. Won't you?'

Kastane stared back. His bright blue eyes were fierce. 'There will be no Seawall when we win. When we free the Queen from her prison, Kalleron will face the world's wrath. This empire will fall, the walls will crumble, and we will rebuild it without elemental power.'

Shadow paced toward him. 'And Petra?'

Kastane released his frustration as a tirade. 'Petra? She's just one woman. How many more do you think we've lost to get this far? So many brave souls giving their lives for a greater cause. What Petra brought to these shores we can use to end this. This is about more than one life.'

Argan spoke, disrupting Shadow's thoughts. 'When you came last night,' he pointed to Kallisa. 'You spoke of the plan; you mentioned why you had come.'

The cult leader turned to Kallisa. 'You came here?'

'I had to warn them, Kastane.'

'You warned her?' His voice was a storm of quiet.

Kallisa held her hands close to her chest. 'What does it matter? They have the Fury. For all that we know, they have the second casket. I can make this work.'

The cult leader stared at his companion. 'You disobeyed me?'

Shadow, disbelieving what he had heard, repeated Kastane's words. 'Warn us of what?'

Kallisa looked at him; an apology in her sad eyes. Her master's scowl gave no hint of remorse.

Shadow said, 'You set us up? You wanted us caught with the damn casket?'

Kastane squinted. He waved his hand and turned his back. 'Every cause has martyrs.'

Shadow had one thought: Petra alone in a cell. Shackled to a fate that she had always avoided with guile and wit. Too brave to fail, and too wise to trip up over her own ambition. The one thing that should have given her hope—Felicitra's letter—had condemned her to hell. Betrayed by the people she had sought. Betrayed by her hopeless loyalty for a lost love.

'You fucking prick!' Shadow said to Kastane's back. 'Turn around.'

Kastane sighed and turned. Shadow launched at him; a straight jab to his face. His strike caught air as the old man moved to the side with uncanny speed. The reply was a clip on the ear; nothing so harsh as a punitive blow. To Shadow, it was worse. It was a patronising chastisement for an unruly child. Frustrated by the touch, and enraged by Kastane's indifference to Petra's plight, he swung his fist back at an angle, catching the cultist off-guard. The crack of the impact was loud, and Shadow turned, expecting to see the man stagger. A blur of movement confused his eyes, and two powerful hands grabbed his shirt and flesh, throwing him to the ground. Shadow smashed into the boards; the wind punched from his lungs. Kastane lunged at him, and Shadow's only response was to raise his arms and shield his face from a hail of punches. The old man's power was immense. It was unnatural. And it was over in the blink of an eye.

The cultist flew into the air, his body hurtling across the hold. Shadow stared up to see Argan; a towering statue of fortitude. His hand came down, and on grasping it, Shadow was on his feet before he could think. He nodded to Argan and, about to go back for more, the Bruhadian pulled him back. A stern glare from his friend, and Shadow remained rooted to the spot.

To Kastane, Argan said, 'It *is* you.'

Kastane rose from a pile of shattered wood; crates crushed under his fall. The cultist, somehow unscathed, brushed himself down and looked at Argan. He didn't respond to the recognition; instead, he stared back, a deep furrow appearing on his battered brow.

Confused, Shadow asked, 'Who is he?'

'Te'anor.'

The Butcher of Bruhale. It was impossible. Yet only moments ago, Shadow had been ready to ask Argan of his past; of the legendary battle. If there was a man who would know the Butcher, it would be one of the Royal Guard; those who had witnessed the fall. How could the fates transpire to be so cruel?

Argan said, 'Full plate conceals a man's sins as much as it covers his face. Your voice, your confidence; the way you move. Te'anor moved as you do. Even the limp you hide so well. From the injury I gave him. I can feel that day as I feel the blood coursing through my veins. Will you deny your name to me? Would you dare deny my honour?'

The hold fell quiet. Shadow glanced at Kallisa, who was shaking, her wide eyes staring at her master. A brutal contradiction; a Bruhadian serving the Butcher; if indeed this impossibility was truth. All the while, Argan remained calm; the eye of his own storm. Shadow paced backwards to the girls who were huddling together in quaking silence.

At last, Kastane nodded. 'I was once Te'anor.' He paused; his face lost in confusion. 'The injury *you* gave me?' He was shaking his head; struggling to say words which appeared trapped at his lips. 'I fought through the Royal Guard but they never...' His words faded on a breath. 'It can't be?'

Argan shuffled. Shadow thought he might release an explosion of anger. Before him stood the Butcher of Bruhale: the merciless killer of his people. There had to be justice for his crimes, and who better to dispense it than the renowned Royal Guard?

Te'anor, the killer wearing the mask of Kastane, whispered a name. Shadow shivered as its weight sank to the depths of his disbelief. A convulsion of astonishment shuddered through his body. He looked at Argan, tried to raise his attention. The Bruhadian stared only at his nemesis, not glancing Shadow's way.

Kallisa, lowering her hands from her trembling mouth, said, 'Is it true? Is this true?' She was fixating on Argan; her eyes weeping, her face contorted in ecstasy and agony.

Te'anor spoke of legend.

'Baza'rad.'

King Baza'rad. Shadow's legs trembled. He did well to stay on his feet. Kallisa's tears flowed, and she crumpled to the ground. Beside him came a quiet squeak from Thelissa.

'Who?'

Kastane knelt and bowed his head. 'King Baza'rad of Bruhada. Lord of Bruhale. I will not fight against you. I accept...'

Argan, who was Baza'rad, interrupted. 'Get on your feet.'

Shadow, watching with fascination, assumed it was a command to face his foe. Kastane rose and with his chest puffed out, he said, 'If you wish to kill Te'anor, I will not resist.'

'You wouldn't be able to if you tried,' Argan said.

Kastane nodded.

There was an awkward silence as neither legend moved. Shadow was certain that Argan would exact his revenge; what man wouldn't? What King would let his nation's death go unpunished? But Argan's stance softened.

'I see but the shell of Te'anor before me. Your death would be meaningless now.'

'Argan?' Shadow said. 'It's the Butcher. You'd let him live?'

The last king of Bruhada nodded. 'I defeated Te'anor on the bridge. I had my victory, and I stopped his army from ravaging what remained of my city. But the day Te'anor fell was the day we both died.'

'Argan?'

The Bruhadian gestured to Kastane. 'There is no honour; no purpose in slaughter. Let him live so that every day he can count his sins; they will cut him deeper than any blade. Bruise more than any hammer. I know it will. This is not the Te'anor of old.' Argan asked Kastane, 'Why do you do this now? Why turn on your old master?'

Kastane shook his head. He growled, bitterness ripe in his tone. 'Everything we believed was a lie. Everything we fought for was an illusion. It hollows a soul to feel faith collapsing. To see gods fall. Now Kalle must fall. We needed the Fury to prove one last lie. It will damage, if not destroy him. When the Queen witnesses the deception, she'll not stay loyal to Kalleron. Without the Queen, Kalleron will be vulnerable. Remember, it was she, not I, that took Bruhale. Just the threat of her very existence. Imagine, Baza'rad; imagine a world where men could fight men, and the elementals would watch with disinterest from afar. This is the world I seek. A human world; where power is fair. Where kings can die.'

Argan exhaled a long breath. 'You truly believe you can do this?'

Kastane pointed to Kallisa. She had composed herself; although her body trembled. 'Kallisa has worked so hard to deceive the King, to deceive the court; it all comes down to this moment. We have set the trap.' Kastane held his hands close to his face; he shook them with a slight tremble. 'They've discovered a few of the pieces, but they can't see the board we're moving them on.'

Kallisa spoke, her eyes darting between the two legends. 'The King has been told the weapons are inert. I have convinced him that Aracyse has played him for a fool; that Etherus is a complex of lies. Larra didn't arrive; they must already have the duplicate spheres. I will prove the Fury is worthless when I smash one. The King's hubris and arrogance is his weakness; he believes in his status. Destroying the real Fury in his presence will be a fatal blow to his myth.'

'You would martyr yourself?' Argan said.

'For my Queen.' She bowed her head. 'And for my King.'

'You're not my subject, and I am no king.'

'But you are Baza'rad,' she said.

Argan shook his head. He turned to Shadow. The Bruhadian's eyes expressed untold regrets. 'I am Argan now. None of us are who we once were. Those lives are gone.'

'But...' Kallisa said.

Kastane spoke, his tone impatient. 'Kallisa, we are being given one last chance. We must leave. You must find the other Fury; finish what you can.' He moved across the hold and stopped in front of Argan. Shadow thought the cultist might offer some ill-equipped apology, but he didn't. He nodded and continued on his way.

'What about Petra?' Shadow said. Kastane didn't reply.

Kallisa stepped to Shadow. 'I will go to her; speak to her before my task. If there was the smallest chance, I would bring her to you, but what I do tonight gives me little hope of seeing tomorrow. If I can at least speak to her, what message would you give?'

Shadow stared at Kallisa, a desperate and cruel realisation that no matter what miracles had occurred within the hold, nothing had changed. His world was in pieces. With the weakest smile on his lips, he said, 'You tell her: I'll come for her. You make sure she knows to look out for me every day. As long as the sun rises, there'll always be a shadow, and there'll always be hope.'

Kallisa nodded. She bowed her head to the sisters and turned to Argan. Would she kneel or curtsy? Would she offer allegiance to her new master? She did neither, and remained upright, a simple smile given to Argan. 'If not for my King, then for Bruhada.'

Argan stared down at Kallisa. 'When you speak to Petra; do not tell her of this.'

She squinted, appearing uneasy at his request, and moved from the hold. Kallisa left the Melody following in the footsteps of two men: one the killer of her own kin, and the other, the saviour of the rest. Shadow stared at Argan; a new awkwardness felt in his presence. Thelia and Thelissa had come to his side, the younger sister clamped tight to his waist.

'Mr Argan,' Thelia said.

The King of Bruhada turned to gaze at the child.

'What do we call you now?'

Argan looked at Shadow. The King's glare was an unspoken command. It was clear what he wanted. With a hand to ruffle Thelia's dark hair, Argan said, 'What you've always called me. There are no kings here.' His expression softened, Shadow noting the lines of his brow relax. Argan smiled at Thelia. 'Just fools and princesses.'

Chapter XXXIII

Another squalid and dank hole. A neglected trader's post. One too many raids from Kallerye overseers and the clientele had grown weary. With the owner long since sent to Seawall, the ramshackle building had become one of the port's many *rufaints*. When Kallisa had come to the city, she had heard the term used occasionally. It was a simple Kallerye slang; a means to describe the sort of dive within which she stood staring at Kastane, who sat in the corner. It had doors; it wasn't crumbling to dust, and it was dry enough. As they said: it's got a *roof, ain't it?* The word had become common parlance and its meaning had altered over the years. It was a place wise folk weren't advised to go.

The debris strewn across the bare stone floor told its own history: rags, old animal bones, and broken pieces of timber. It was a story etched in grime. Kastane's seat was an old stool with one leg attached. He balanced on it, propped up against the walls of his corner. Kallisa stared at him through the gloomy light seeping in through battered shutters. There were no lamps to banish the dark. In the monochrome, his face was a harsh landscape of cracks and fissures. Those piercing blue eyes added no warmth to his legend. Te'anor, the Butcher of Bruhale. He had once come to take her city. Kalle had thought Baza'rad would know the consequence of resistance. The King had thought wrong, and Te'anor had paid a just price.

'Tell me, Kastane,' she said, her arms folded, her body stiff. 'Tell me why?'

His features remained impassive. 'Why? Why did I not tell you? Why did I choose this path? Why do I wish to see Kalleron fall?'

She wanted to know all of it, but there was another mystery. 'Why did you kneel before Baza'rad; why did you invite your death?'

A smile crept upon his face; Kallisa thought it might be humility. Kastane grumbled. 'Why waste my last breath fighting a battle I lost years ago? There is no defeating that man, Kallisa. And that broke me.'

'The battle on the bridge?'

He nodded. 'I, Te'anor, the most ruthless and powerful general in Kalleron's ranks. I pushed through his Royal Guard, and though they slowed me, they couldn't stop me. Not me. A great rumbling command came; I couldn't see the voice through the masses of the guard, but it was Baza'rad calling his men to retreat, and those who hadn't fallen cleared from my path.'

Kastane's eyes appeared to glaze over and Kallisa knew he was reliving the moment. She tightened her folded arms as goosebumps appeared on her skin. She shuddered, hugging herself as Kastane revealed untold history.

'Retreat, he said. Fall back. I thought I'd won.' He stared deep into her eyes. 'Can you imagine that, Kallisa? I thought I'd won. But then he appeared; this hulking, great man. Beautifully crafted plate, silver and bronze glinting in the sun. I can look back now and see how majestic he was. But in those days, I was a fool; a slave to Kalle's myth. I thought it was all real. I had seen Kalle in battle. By the gods, Kallisa, the King is a force of nature. But I saw then—Baza'rad was more.

'I faced him on that bridge, a score of my best men behind me. Heavy armour that could deflect any blade, absorb most any blow, and swords that could cut stone. He faced us alone. Strode forward and unslung his hammer.' Kastane seemed to enjoy the memory as though he was experiencing it through the eyes of Bruhale. It was awe. Nodding to himself, he continued. 'That hammer; the haft must have been five feet long. The block on the end was nothing pretty; just a heft of metal. I sent a dozen men forward. Fast soldiers, years of experience worn on their hearts and souls. They fought Baza'rad, and they danced between swings of that monstrous weapon. The few strikes my men landed appeared to glance off Baza'rad's armour. But they got too close. He was lightning fast, kicking two men from the bridge. Kallisa, these were large men wearing full plate; heavy lumps of soldier and steel. Baza'rad kicked them a dozen feet...' Kastane moved his hand out to the side, imitating a falling motion. 'And they disappeared over the edge. Not even a Northern warhorse could do that. He wiped out that first surge, but I had more waiting behind. Before they moved forward, Baza'rad pointed at me. Called my name.'

Kallisa closed her mouth, realised it had fallen open. The nuance of his story revealed more than history. It revealed the man he had become. She listened to his words, hanging on every thread of emotion.

'I remember that walk. Those paces. I came to within ten feet of the greatest warrior I had ever seen. Greater even than Kalle; I know that now. I wish I'd known it then. With my hands on my sword, I told him, "She will come. You cannot win this." I couldn't see his face behind his helmet. Just a dark chasm where his eyes would be. What response his expression might have told me, I never saw. But it was true; it was never a battle he could have won. Bruhada lost the war when Kalle put his finger on the goddamn map.'

Kastane paused, appearing to dwell on the moment. Kallisa knew him as her master. A butcher since revealed as her nation's enemy. It was a jarring thought. The Bruhada she romanticised; the nation she dreamed of with its elegant towers and proud people was no longer its own country. After the fall, it had become a vassal state of Kalleron. And no matter what ruthless legend they hung around Te'anor's neck, she had always known that he hadn't brought the city's demise. Baza'rad had sealed its fate when he dared to defy Kalleron.

She asked, 'What happened? After your warning?'

With a shrug, Kastane said, 'We fought. I gave as good an account as I could, considering I wasn't facing a normal man. He wore me down, and though he clipped me with that gargantuan hammer, it never struck me full force.' Kastane chuckled and shook his head. 'When he had weakened me enough, the bastard placed his hammer on the bridge. Strange; how careful he was with it, but it was an old bridge, and I think he could've taken us all down with a misplaced swing. He went straight for me with his bare hands. I swung, caught him once or twice, but he smashed me to the ground. It was like fighting an avalanche of stone. But I was on my feet in an instant; leaping at him, thought I'd catch him by surprise. Show him I was no normal soldier. But you forget things in the heat of battle; when your life is on the line. I was fatigued. My armour was weighing me down. Like a fool, I never took the drugs they gave me. Mind, I doubt they'd have helped.' He huffed, shaking his head with a cynical smile. 'So, I lunged at him, never got far from the ground. Bastard knelt low and swung at my knee with his bloody fist. How he fights, Kallisa; it's graceful and brutal. You can't react to what he does. What I'd learned in a lifetime, he somehow knew more. Always one more move in Baza'rad's play. Always one step ahead.

'The pain from that blow was crushing. That's what I remember. But after that, I was crawling through the forests of Bruhale. I don't know if I went over or if he threw me off the bridge. Te'anor died that day, Kallisa. That arrogant son of a bitch met more than his match, and when he woke up, he knew he was on the wrong side of history. To believe you're a part of something invincible, as I had under Kalle, is to be a god among men. We had the Queen, our might. But that day I learned we were no longer gods; we were a lie. Kalle had deceived all of us. For a man of Te'anor's arrogance; that was the killer blow. It was a good day for a general of Kalleron to die.'

Kallisa stared at Kastane. What horrors and atrocities he had committed as Te'anor appeared as though tales from another world. A bedtime story to tell children, something to shepherd them away from mischief and mayhem. But Kastane hadn't denied the truth revealed in the Melody's hold. This was the Kallerye General Te'anor. The man whose march through southern Bruhada had claimed the lives of countless numbers of her people.

She said, 'I don't understand. What you were, who you became. Was it so easy?'

'Easy?' Kastane scoffed. 'At first, I had anger. I raged at what had become of me. I knew there were truths beyond what lies we had been told. Kalleron became my focus. The King, so willing to send his men to death, became my nemesis. But as I found my way back, I learned of the elemental ways. I asked myself: What was it that had made Baza'rad and his people so strong? I learned of them, and from there my admiration grew for the nation I had helped destroy. I realised Bruhada was greater than Kalleron. Well, it would have been.' He threw his hands to the sides, a huff from his lungs. 'There are many threads to this, Kallisa. But there's a simple truth. Kalleron gave Te'anor his funeral, and I was born again.'

She knew Kastane spoke the truth. It was logical that his arrogance would turn to spite, and that the old master would become the new nemesis. Besides, there were few reasons to lie now. Her thoughts drifted to the hold of Petra's ship. A vision of the man who had once been the King. A man who had buried his crown in exile. What would he do if the cult succeeded, and the Queen fled Kalleron?

She said, 'If everything falls in place; if we prove Kalle's vulnerability and the Queen reacts, what next?'

'We hope others will rise.'

Her heart beat faster. 'And Baza'rad, do you believe he will retake his throne? Do you think he will return to Bruhale?'

Kastane's expression faltered. From a semblance of optimism, his features sagged into a glum countenance. 'I had thought that. But the man I saw today is not the same man I saw on the bridge. His strength may be the same; but his spirit is gone. Did you not see that?'

Despite her hopes, Kallisa acknowledged Kastane's words. Her legendary king seemed smaller than she had thought, even though he was a mountain of man. 'Was it his exile?'

Kastane nodded. 'We dream of legends and imagine they bide their time, waiting to reclaim their honour. But legends aren't so because of their physical might. They possess qualities and character that come from a strength of mind, of will. I fought a king. His will was absolute. His purpose was true. Neither of us saw that today. Did the man who called himself Argan appear like a king to you?'

She had wanted to believe, if for only a moment, that Baza'rad had returned. But Argan had not given her hope. Before the revelation, he was just another

Bruhadian. His demeanour was not that of a proud and legendary leader, it was of a simple man. A man who had left his past behind.

'I wanted to see him, noble and strong. But when I called him my King, I swear I saw remorse in his eyes. Why would I see that?'

'We can repeat this over and over, but Baza'rad was doomed from the moment Kalle turned his sights to Bruhada. That's what got me, Kallisa; that's where my newfound animosity was born. Kalleron was no military match for the Bruhadian armies, but we fought well; we fought above our position. Yet, despite our efforts, Kalle sent us as an ultimate message. We were expendable. I'd never seen that before; men sent to die for no purpose. At least, not on that scale. Baza'rad's own truth was that he couldn't win. A man free from pride would have surrendered to Kalleron's will. The meadows and fields would be green and bountiful; instead, because of Baza'rad's own arrogance, they became charred and blackened. The rivers ran red with his people's blood because he dared to defy the inevitability of Kalleron's power. The Queen would come. But he had to prove his point, and that point of pride cost his nation thousands of lives. That is why there is shame in his eyes. The irony is, his people expected him to fight. I'm sure he wanted to. But, just like me, he faced an impossible task.' Kastane scoffed. It was out of place with the sombre mood. Shaking his head, he said, 'Perhaps my legend had become too much for Kalle. Perhaps he sent me to Bruhale to die?'

Kastane became still, dropping his gaze to the murky floor. His story was over. Kallisa unfolded her arms and clasped her hands. 'Today has been... a revelation, but it's not over yet. Larra's disappearance can't be a coincidence; we have to assume she's been taken by the court, if not the South Wall. If it were simple street thugs, I'd know by now—I've asked my contacts. She's vanished.'

Kastane raised his head. 'And if Kalle has seized the duplicates?'

'All the better; it strengthens our hand.' Kallisa paused, thought of the cultist who had disappeared from sight. 'As long as Larra stays true to our cause, it should still work.'

'Larra is strong. Whatever happens, I know she wouldn't betray the cause.'

Kallisa nodded. Had she heard disappointment in his voice? She shook it off and focused on the immediate plan. 'If they have them, they'll take the spheres to the South Wall; they wouldn't go directly to the King—even they understand the risk, though they'd never admit it. It will give me a chance to fortify my argument that the Fury is a trick.'

'And Kalle?'

'With the South Wall's backing, I should be able to bring the Fury to him; to prove its part in Etherus' lie. It just has to make its way to the grand chamber.'

Kastane nodded. His features wrinkled. 'And you, Kallisa?'

'I know my fate.'

He shook his head. 'No, can you survive it? Can you escape the Fury?'

She had thought of it. Kallisa was a patriot; a loyal cultist, but she wasn't a fool. If she could get away from the terror within the glass, she would, although she doubted that was possible.

'The King's chamber, as much as it appears without depth, isn't that large. The damage in that space will be considerable. I would have to escape the room, and that would appear suspicious, don't you think?'

Kastane murmured. 'Can you be certain it will be his chamber?'

She nodded. 'Kalle doesn't roam the fortress. I have never known him to conduct counsel anywhere other than the chamber. The lighting and theatre are there to impress and impose. I imagine, if this goes to plan, he might even gather an audience to prove his might.'

'His military men?'

Kallisa didn't know. She shrugged and sighed. 'It won't matter. What they see is insignificant to the effect this would have on the Queen.' She paused. There was one glaring problem with the plan. Years of dedication to the cause could not control the most vital element. The Queen herself. 'Do you really think it will work?'

Kastane frowned. 'Work?'

She said, 'The Queen; she'll leave Kalleron?'

'She's been an accomplice to a lie she doesn't understand. When she finds out she's been deceived, I doubt she'd honour any future with Kalle.'

'And if it angers her?' Kallisa tried to imagine what cataclysm might unfold should the Queen react with rage and wrath. 'Kalleron could be at risk. The people.'

Her old master nodded and offered a cursory smile. 'Would it not be just?'

It would be devastating. Kallisa had heard the tales of Arkalla. And Kalleron was still rebuilding New Thania after the Queen had decimated the old city. If the Queen's reaction was wrath, there would be a horrendous reckoning. She thought of an anomaly. Her recent experience of the elemental.

'There's one thing she has never shown. What sets her apart from us. Even the scriptures speak of it.'

Kastane raised an eyebrow. 'Empathy? Emotion?'

'Yes.'

'She's not human. We can't know what she feels. Even now, we call her "she". But the Queen is neither human, nor a woman. Yet it's easier to label her with terms we understand. By any measure, we can't predict what she'll feel once she knows the truth. But there's one thing I know—the King will lose his dominion over her.'

Kallisa nodded. She noted the light was dimming. The afternoon was passing and evening drew near. Time was running out. 'If this is to work, I must leave now.'

Kastane bowed his head. 'I'm sorry you had to learn of my truth. Today of all days.'

'I learned of two. And at least now, I know there is another power in our world. Perhaps he will find his way, perhaps Baza'rad will return?'

With a smile, Kastane extended his arms to her. She stepped into his embrace and held him as he whispered in her ear. 'Be brave, be strong. And if you can—get out.'

She stood there, savouring one last moment of security and honesty. It was a bitter farewell; she had already said goodbye. Kallisa broke away and stared at the man she had only ever known as Kastane. In those eyes, she saw no hint of the monster Te'anor. Just as when she had gazed at Argan, she had seen no hint of the legendary King Baza'rad. She recalled words Kastane had once said. "Beware of legends, Kallisa, they're just romanticised paintings we make of above average lives."

As she left Kastane, she glanced back and wondered what would have become of the young boy had he put down his father's dagger and picked up his mother's brush.

Chapter XXXIV

It was madness. Petra stood in the open alcove of the cellblock. The northern sky was darkening, and the ocean sparkled with the fire of the setting sun. Her cell, cleaned out and made dignified, still wore the scent of morbid years; a background odour that lingered, whispering she was not free. The metal bracelet on her ankle, not so much a shackle, was a reminder of what she had done, and what deal she had struck with Aracyse. All she had asked for was the safety of her crew. The General had agreed without hesitation, and for her apparent loyalty to those she had captained, Aracyse had given her freedoms she had not requested; but gifts that she savoured. That was the madness. What sort of man was he? Tied to duty but ruled by a morality she would never have expected from a Kallerye agent. It was the bitterest pleasure to walk free from her cell. And though she knew her life would end at Seawall, for his civility and humanity, Petra was grateful.

'In your cell!' It was a guard calling; a curt interruption of her dreams of freedom. She turned to the main door, peered at the face behind the vertical iron bars.

'General Aracyse gave me this freedom. What right have you to take it away?'

'You have a visitor.' The guard grumbled, appearing to talk to someone behind before calling an instruction to Petra. 'Step back; move to the edge.'

She stepped away, a glance to the open end of the cell block. One stumble and she could topple over. The shackle around her ankle would halt her fall. The force would snap her bones. She peered out over the edge, curious about the drop. Paranoia seeping in: how tight was the iron shackle? Might it slip loose and let her body smash on the rocks below? She was a mariner, not a bloody mountaineer. Leaning away from the outer edge, ensuring her feet were firm on the marble, Petra faced the door. A jangle of metal keys. A solid thud. The door swung open, and Kallisa stepped into the cell. Petra's heart thumped with anticipation—had the cultist come to free her?

'Close the door, get back to your station,' the Overseer said to the guard.

A huff and he moved away, Petra listening to the fading footsteps. Another door slammed shut farther back in the wall.

'Kallisa!' she said with expectation.

The Overseer lowered her eyes; not a response to bolster Petra's confidence. Kallisa shook her head. 'I'm sorry Petra, I thought to help you, but the guards on the Generals' Way are on high alert. There is great excitement within the fortress. There's no way I can move you without raising suspicion.'

Petra tried to hide her disappointment. 'I see. Then, news?'

Kallisa nodded. She gestured to the ledge. 'Won't you please step away? It's making me nervous.'

Moving closer to Kallisa, Petra said, 'You, nervous?'

'I have much to do and even more has happened today. I need all my faculties.'

'My crew. Has Aracyse fulfilled his promise?'

'Promise?' Kallisa appeared distracted.

'Our trade. I gave him what he wanted; he gave me what I wished. My crew's freedom.'

'It was you? You gave him the Fury?'

Petra nodded. She had no remorse. 'For my crew. Are they safe?'

Kallisa hesitated. Was she judging her? A sigh, accompanied by the slightest smile, and the Overseer nodded. 'When I arrived; your crew was onboard... without shackles or iron.'

Relief. A small thing to feel, but in her cell, that sliver of goodwill from the General was a branch of hope; something she could cling to while her days passed away into nothingness.

'They'll need to sail by tomorrow,' Petra said, glancing over her shoulder at the ocean. 'Aracyse was fair, but he was absolute. He has banished the Melody from Kalleron. When dawn comes, I'll watch the sunrise from here, but it means everything that they'll go free.'

'Petra, I'm truly sorry. But I'm confused; how did they capture you? I warned you. You had time to leave.'

The cabin. Those memories of Felicitra. How many minutes had ebbed in wick and wax? Her foolish longing had deceived her own purpose. Perhaps she had not really cared. She shook her head and offered Kallisa a cynical smile.

'It's an irony. Or is it just dumb fate? Felicitra brought me to this path. She wanted me to see what she had seen; to live what she had lived.' Petra gestured to Kallisa. 'You know all of this. But I didn't follow because I believed in her cause or the cult. I stepped where she walked because I thought it might bring me closer to her. And it has.'

'It has?'

Petra's arms straightened, her hands sweeping the air as she waved at the cell block. 'This is where it ends. In a room where I'll die, and I know death will find me here. Felicitra must have known her fate once her brother made escape from Arkalla impossible.' She paced to the wall and sat down against the marble, her gaze drifting to the ocean. 'I wake at nights with Felicitra in my dreams. I see the towers of Arkalla; the Seer's beacon aflame on top of Sinder's Temple. My heart races, and I feel sick to my stomach. I see her; the Queen. I imagine how it must have been.' Petra turned her head to look at Kallisa, noticing she had not moved. 'I'm closer to her now because she's gone, and soon, I will follow. No more dreams of death. No more white witches to haunt my nightmares.'

Petra couldn't read what emotions might swirl beneath Kallisa's sublime features. An overseer, a spy. A beautiful liar. The cultist hung her head, then said, 'It is the King who...'

'Damn your King, Kallisa. Damn your fucking cult.'

There was an uncomfortable pause before Kallisa spoke again. 'The Bruhadian?'

'Argan?'

'Do you know?'

Games of questions were not Petra's favoured pastime. She gave a curt response. 'What am I meant to know?'

Kallisa squinted. Something on her mind? Whatever it was, she appeared hesitant to say it. 'He is very loyal to you.'

Petra assumed her words were a distraction. 'You know that of all my crew; what makes you curious of Argan?'

The cultist rallied her composure. She shook her head, blowing away the question with a sigh. 'I miss my people. That's all. Whenever I find myself among them, I hearken back to old times; days I was too young to remember.' Kallisa gestured to herself. 'Before any of this subterfuge. To see a Bruhadian with such devotion to another; I envy that.'

It was misdirection, but it didn't matter; whatever had elicited her curiosity, it served no purpose now. Though it was a boon to her hopes that Shadow and Argan would sail away to better days.

'You saw Shadow,' Petra said. 'Were the sisters there? The young ones?'

Kallisa smiled. In contrast to her previous words, her expression seemed honest. 'Two girls. A little squeak, and an older one. They appeared well enough.'

It was a relief. There was a balance in life; not one she felt she could ever cheat. For many years, Petra had enjoyed an uneven and good fortune. How many times had she and Shadow scraped through some misadventure? Too many to tempt the hands of fate that steadied those scales.

'Do you believe in balance?' she asked.

Kallisa frowned. 'In what way?'

A shrug from her shoulders, Petra said, 'I don't know. Are we kept in check? Are our deeds measured by a higher power?' Petra reached for the chain that tied her to a new destiny. 'I've avoided this for long enough. It's easier to sit here knowing that in some ways, I deserve it. But my friends, what I consider family, are safe. Balance.'

The cultist shook her head. 'I can't believe in balance. There is no fate dire enough for Kalle to weigh against his monstrous sins. Tonight, if all goes to plan, he may well die. That will be just, but it won't balance the scales, as you say. And should the Queen leave; should she once more become free? Even that will not counter what has happened in Kalleron. All the lives lost across the land. I don't see any equilibrium.'

'Perhaps on the small scale then.' Petra forced a smile. 'I see balance.'

Another pause from Kallisa. Petra stared into the Bruhadian's dark eyes. She differed from Felicitra in almost every superficial way: skin, hair, eyes and voice, but it was clear the two women had a synchronous sense of will. Was it that which had brought them to the cult?

'Shadow wanted to give you a message.' The cultist pointed to the open space, to the sea beyond. 'He said not to give up hope, and that as long as there's a sun in the sky...'

Petra interrupted. 'There will always be a shadow.' She laughed to see Kallisa's surprise. 'Do you know when he first said that to me?'

'No.' Kallisa frowned, a sliver of a smile raised on her lips.

'I had seen him at some squalid dive in Shaddenhyne; well, he had seen me. We didn't know each other back then, but he swaggered up to me, said something along those lines.' Another laugh as Petra recalled the moment. 'I told him to fuck off, and he went to the next girl. So much cheek; she was sitting right beside me. He said the same thing, word for word. I think she slapped him.'

Kallisa shared the humour, a gentle laugh of appreciation. 'Men.'

Petra's thoughts darkened. She turned to face the sea; didn't want to show the emotions that accompanied those early memories. Days after his unwelcome introduction, she had been walking in the forest. A sudden noise had startled her; a sharp crack, creaking and gasping. She had sought the source, and straying from the trail, she found it. Witness to a terrible sight; it was one she'd never forget. Legs swinging, twitching. There were no shadows under the shade of the trees but the one hanging from a branch. Petra shuttered away the vision. Tried to compose herself.

With a deep breath and a sigh to blow away the haunting memory, she turned to Kallisa. 'When he joined me on the Melody, he said it again, but this time he said he'd never say it to another woman. It was just for me. A gift, he said.'

Kallisa nodded. 'A rare man.'

'One of the best. If not, the best.'

'What you've done for them, Petra, it is noble.'

'You don't think I betrayed the cult?'

'By giving Aracyse the Fury?'

She nodded.

Kallisa shook her head. 'Kastane wanted it to look genuine.' She gestured to the cell. 'I think this makes that case. We betrayed you. You've betrayed nobody. What you did was what good people do. Decisions that protect people, not the purpose. It's what makes us human.' Kallisa's expression faltered, and there was no hiding it. 'If we were all the same as Kastane, the cult would have achieved its mission years ago. But where would our humanity be?'

'Yet still you follow?'

'I must.' Kallisa paced to Petra. 'Stand, please.'

Uncertain why it was necessary, but content to rise, Petra rose to her feet. She squinted at Kallisa.

The cultist, far taller than she, held her shoulders, leaned in and kissed her forehead. 'Petra, for all that it matters, I wish the blessings of Bruhada on you. May the earth guide you, that you find a place for your roots to take. May the wind carry your breath, the water cleanse your body, and may you find fire, and be warm but never afraid.'

'An elemental message?'

Kallisa stared. In her eyes, there was a spark of life flickering against the dark. She said, 'It is what we say when we know we are saying farewell. Your days will continue, Petra. Perhaps after tonight, something will change. But I saw my last sunrise this morning. My heart is at peace.'

Petra wanted to say something to encourage Kallisa. But there was no poetry to be said; no words of comfort to deny what had to be. She thought of Laria, perhaps not as expressive as Bruhada's ways. There was one thing she could say; a trade of cultures.

Petra took Kallisa's hand, stood on her tip-toes, and kissed her cheek. 'In Laria, we tell you that the cold will no longer chill your bones, and that you will finally know warmth.'

Kallisa nodded and walked to the cell door. She offered a smile and closed the iron barrier behind her. Petra listened as her footsteps echoed down the corridor. Soon, the only sound was the chorus of the sea: the birds calling to roost, and the waves crashing on the shore below. Petra sat back down again. Her thoughts drifting to the Melody, she saw Shadow on the deck, mustering the crew and bossing the girls around. Under a blazing sun, skipping across crystal waves, the Melody's journey would continue. And when Petra's tears fell, they were not selfish and remorseful; they were joyous and grateful that everything she had built, and everyone she had saved, would live on. And though tonight the world might change forever, tomorrow, for some, it would begin again.

Chapter XXXV

There was a sickness in his gut. A nausea; a thing to play on his nerves and hasten the beat of his heart. In Shaddenhyne he had experienced narcotic delusions, one too many concoctions of herbs he had never known. Keen to explore the mind, he had felt as he did now; his racing heart accompanied by a constant jitter that caused his patience to fray at the edges. With the crew returning to the Melody of their own accord, most having said they had witnessed events from afar, he had tasked Argan with briefing them on arrival. Shadow had sent the sisters to their cabin, noting how quickly Thelissa had agreed, hurrying Thelia below deck. The older girl's experiences had given her a keen eye for grim moods, and his was tumbling down into despair. She'd have seen the darkness seeping from his soul.

Seated in Petra's cabin, although not upon her chair, he watched Argan stooping under the door frame and enter.

'All aboard?' he asked.

Argan shook his head. 'As always, Florent and Jessika. I sent Bellingham to get them. He knew where they'd gone.'

Shadow nodded and pointed to a chair. 'A seat, Argan. Please.'

Once he had manoeuvred his massive frame into what seemed a compass point of comfort, the Bruhadian huffed. It was clear he knew what Shadow was about to ask. He grimaced.

'The rules, Shadow.'

Shadow stared at Argan, who was also Baza'rad. 'I'm not sure the rules apply anymore, my friend. At least, not between ourselves. You know my past with Aracyse; you've heard my old name. I know yours. What fucking point is there in silence?'

Argan raised his eyebrows. 'You want to reminisce?'

'Of course not.'

'Then what is there to say?'

'That you're Baza'rad. By the gods; don't you understand? This isn't me we're talking about; a washed-out soldier from Aracyse's death squads. My past is dark, but there's no history to my deeds, none that's worth recording in a fusty old book. But you? You were a king.'

'I was also a husband, a father, a friend, and a soldier to those I cared for. If you could speak to their ghosts and ask them who was more important: Baza'rad the man, or Baza'rad the King, you would find the same answer.'

Shadow scoffed. 'What, that you're just a man?'

'I am.'

He scratched his head. The Bruhadian's reluctance to dwell on his legend was a further stimulant to his fractious state of mind. Shadow realised there would be no discussion of the past. For every peek he wanted at Argan's regal tapestry, he knew all too well the Bruhadian would poke at his own shabby scrawl of life.

Throwing his hands in the air, Shadow said, 'It's an impossible fucking joke.'

'What is?'

'You, for starters.' Argan appeared riled. Shadow apologised. 'You're not the joke, that's not what I meant. But here you are, Kalleron's proper greatest King, not that other fucking fraud, and Petra's stuck in Seawall. That's the joke; you're a living legend, but there's nothing we can do. Not a thing. Is there?'

Argan shook his head and inhaled a deep breath. He exhaled, and after a long pause, he said, 'If there was no elemental power behind that wall, I would walk up to the gates and smash them down. But within that fortress is a sublime power that makes the mightiest warriors appear as insignificant as ants.' Argan shuffled in his seat, his thighs so large the chair moved with him. He leaned forward, elbows on his knees, and clasped his hands. 'Shadow, I'll fight any man, even Kalle, if the lives of my friends were in the balance, but what lies beyond those walls isn't something we can comprehend. If the cult takes that power from Kalleron, then yes, we could do something.'

It was a bitter irony; a contradiction of the fates. Here they were; soon to be exiled from Kalleron with their captain in Seawall. There for her crimes against the King. She had delivered a weapon that could well destroy the immortal Kalle, and that might give her a chance of freedom. Yet the Melody had to leave before dawn. Time was not an ally in this battle, and knowing the ship would have to set sail, he had chosen his path.

'Argan?'

'Hmm?'

'I'm not leaving.'

Argan sat up, placed his hands on his thighs. 'We're not? I think Aracyse is a man of his word. The Melody won't survive the sunrise if she's still moored.'

Shadow nodded. 'Yes, I know. But she'll be gone by dawn.'

The Bruhadian frowned for a moment. His eyes widened, and he flinched. 'No, Shadow. You can't.'

'I'm not leaving her. I'll figure a way. But you'll be in charge.'

Argan raised his hands. 'I once led a nation. I lead no more.'

It was the response Shadow had expected, but he had come prepared. 'I'm the captain now, and I'm passing command to you. Just for a while. Before dawn you'll sail. Before those cannons rip the hull apart; you'll take the Melody. Nobody steers her better than you. The wheel belongs in your hands.'

The Bruhadian was shaking his head, yet Shadow saw the reluctant acceptance of the offer. Perhaps it was too much humility on Argan's part? Shadow couldn't believe there was no hint of the King inside that enormous frame.

Argan said, 'Take her to safety, and wait for you?'

Shadow nodded, although that was a lie. He had no intention of returning to the Melody without Petra.

'And Thelia and Thelissa?'

'Take care of them while I'm away,' Shadow said. 'I'll tell them what I'm doing. They want the captain back as much as I do, but there's no way they can stay with me; not for this.'

Argan nodded.

'So, you agree?'

'We'll sail to the Barge Isles. We'll wait there; you'll find us.'

Shadow smiled. 'I'll catch up.' He stared at his friend, and in his eyes, he saw the recognition of a conversation without merit. They had spoken words to one another. Exchanges of trust in name alone. Might as well be two drunks at the bar. Shadow could see that Argan didn't believe him; he was playing the role that was required. It was how he preferred to say goodbye. To pretend it wasn't a farewell.

With Thelia's tears and Thelissa's grievous huff fresh in his mind, Shadow paced along the dockside. He had glanced to the spot where he and Argan had placed the guards. The sacks remained, but the contents had vanished. Curious thoughts entered his mind. A notion that perhaps they hadn't even reported their beating. It would be an insult to Kalleron that a single, unarmed man had incapacitated them all. But if they had known the truth of who that man was, would they any sooner come back? As a soldier, Shadow was familiar with the sentiment of the rank and file. Around campfires they would jostle and jest, tell stories to one another. Tales of legends would often grace the profanity littered conversation. It pleased Shadow to think that if the guards knew what had happened, they might just return to stare in awe, swords limp in their scabbards.

The sky was dark overhead, and the moons were in ascension over the northern horizon. The bay, calm in another lazy Kalleron night, rippled with the ice and fire of Noctyrne and Ambyr. Shadow stopped pacing and looked out across the bay. A fine Larian trader had set sail, her canvas filled by the gentle breeze. Nary a sound came from the rigging as she slid into the night. At the helm was a giant of a man, and at his side were two young girls. Not so far away that they would lose sight of him on the docks, Shadow held up his hand. From the top deck, the two sisters ran to the rail. One small little creature jumping and waving, the other more stoic in her goodbye. Mirroring his arm, she held her hand up high. And although the helmsman didn't wave, Shadow knew he was looking his way.

Shadow lowered his hand as the Melody turned, showing him her stern. It sailed past the warship that Aracyse had promised would deliver his word. The Blood Moon, a brute compared to the Melody, sat patiently on the water. It didn't turn to trail the Larian ship. The General's word was written in stone; it took a fool to break that contract. Soon the darkness had swallowed the Melody, and Shadow felt a great weight lift from his shoulders. He shook his head, realising he had no plan, no grand scheme to free Petra. He began walking, heading toward the western wall. If he was careful, he could sneak past the military district, use the boulders and scrub that littered the foundations. From there, he would make his way to the rounded corner beyond which the great northern flank of Seawall would become visible. He'd not be able to get close. The tide would be in, and the rubble and twisted metal at the base of the prison would tear his flesh to pieces. A drainage culvert would offer shelter for the night; even Kalleron had its mundane practicalities. In the morning he would clamber across barnacle encrusted rocks, slipping and sliding on fields of seaweed. And once he was near enough to see, but far enough away that the archers wouldn't agitate, he would look for Petra. That would be enough. He had to hold her in his eyes; had to let her know he was there, waiting for her. A plan would come; he just had to think. And if he had to, he would think for day after day, month after month; until his bones withered, his eyes finally shut, and his body moved at peace with the tide. Until he had breathed his last breath, he would never leave Petra.

Chapter XXXVI

Under the last vestiges of dusk, Noctyrne and Ambyr set the Queen's citadel ablaze in a glorious azure fire. At nights, with a perfect lunar light, Aracyse had thought the marble tower appeared to move, shimmering as though it was never really there. He gazed out across the expanse of stone, seeking an answer to a question he dared not ask. Although there were more guards on patrol, the fortress was calm, as it always was. Aracyse had never known disquiet in the grounds of Kalleron's hidden realm. But there was an unsettled anxiety in his gut. He had returned with the casket, only for the Southwallers to take it from him at the fortress gate. They had dismissed Aracyse with false civility; their unease was all too clear. Devious words spoken from behind their bronze masks. They had said they would send for him. For what purpose? That question had answers he would surely learn. But the question was grim; why was he being pushed aside when he had returned with Etherus' prize?

The knock on his chamber door brought him from the balcony. Aracyse grabbed his cloak and, having become proficient in its one-handed use, swung it around his shoulders.

'Come!'

The door opened, revealing Overseer Duhl. It was a disappointment; he had hoped it might be Overseer Kallisa. Aracyse knew few details of Duhl, although what little he had come by painted a picture of efficiency. Neither brash nor timid, he was a constant, if not distant, feature in the workings of the fortress.

'General Aracyse, will you follow me, please?'

It was an unusually curt introduction, Aracyse hesitating before he accepted with a single nod. Overseer Duhl gave him no time to delay and was already turning away from the door. Aracyse frowned, the smallest grumble rumbling in his throat. He followed his escort, surprised to see a Southwaller guard with the Overseer. The presence of the soldier wearing full plate armour was a token gesture. A message not lost on Aracyse; an appeal to his military obligations.

'Overseer Duhl,' he said. 'Is the Fury intact?'

Duhl did not respond, but continued on his way along the inner wall. Aracyse recognised the route: it would take them along the western edge of the fortress. Less grand than the Generals' Way, orderlies used the tunnel for moving supplies back and forth. Wide enough for a cart, and lit by Kallerye lamps, it provided space for Aracyse to walk alongside the Overseer.

'Overseer Duhl, I asked a question.'

'They have instructed me not to answer questions relating to the Fury.'

Aracyse, disheartened to hear his words, hid his surprise. 'For what reason?'

'There is much suspicion within the court. The cult brought a weapon to our city; a weapon from Etherus. I am to speak to nobody about these matters.'

Aracyse was about to ask on whose orders, the question already on the tip of his tongue, when Duhl said, 'Orders of the King. General, I am to speak to nobody until we have gathered in the South Wall.'

The secrecy was troubling. Aracyse was doubtful the King had given any such command. Without other options, he followed Duhl through the western supply tunnel. He distracted himself from the pressing concerns by observing the details of the route. There was a steady and slight incline as the path made its way above the western gate, followed by a decline to mark the passage over. He passed recessed doors and regular openings. Some of which led to spiral stairs that ascended to the concealed battlements. Other places he had never seen. What secrets lay beyond?

The journey to the South Wall was not arduous, but it felt as though an age had passed. Small talk was meaningless, and the oppressive weight of silence was a burden on Aracyse's mind. On arriving at the annexe that formed the internal workings of Kalle's rule, Overseer Duhl stopped at a large, arched doorway. He turned to face Aracyse, peering up at the General.

'I can go no further, General,' he bowed and walked away, leaving the Southwaller with Aracyse. The guard stepped forward and knocked on the darkwood door. It opened inwards, revealing a grand, vaulted chamber. He gestured for Aracyse to continue, and with a nod to the guard, he passed under the arch and into the realm of the South Wall.

Aracyse had few reasons to visit the annexe, but when rare circumstance brought him there, the design and scale always impressed him. He cast his gaze all around to absorb the details of a spacious hall. With dimensions similar to that of a modest temple, it lay enclosed within the solid wall of the fortress. Six pairs of intricate marble pillars supported the vaulted ceiling. Carvings of elemental inscriptions patterned the white rock, blending with designs of geometry and nature. Shadows enhanced the artistry. In the absence of windows, the wall-mounted Kallerye lamps exaggerated the patterns of light and dark. Without the sun to inform the passing of the day, the inner space appeared separate from time. It would always look the same; never changing. A salute to Kalle. An elegant chamber; it had no apparent purpose. On the far end of the rectangular space, there was another arched darkwood door. Apart from the grandeur of the hall, there was nothing else of note other than the two guards who flanked the entrance from where he had come.

'General Aracyse,' one said, his voice reverberating behind his black visor. He pointed across the room. 'They have requested your presence.'

Aracyse nodded, expecting the guards to follow, but as he paced across the chamber, his boots were the only noise. Everything about the summons was wrong. From Duhl's quiet, to the Southwaller guard. He listened to his own footsteps bouncing against pillar and wall. A hollow rumble; it was a march into the unknown.

At the door, he raised his fist to knock, startling as his knuckles swiped empty air. The two darkwood panels swinging inward on silent hinges. The light spilling from the pillared hall encroached into a dark void. The path ahead was lit by what lay behind; the marble floor was bright at his feet, but faded to black as the shadow swallowed the light. Without a command to follow, he understood what they expected of him. With a deep breath, Aracyse paced into the room, and with an ominous silence, the doors closed behind, plunging him into darkness.

Kallisa hadn't asked for theatre, but it was an integral part of the cabal's secret manner. Concealed in Southwaller attire: the white hooded robe and bronze faceless mask; she waited in the same darkness that Aracyse had entered. She had thought to accuse him without obfuscation, but the will of South Wall insisted she discard her overseer skin and don a new flesh. They had said that the General would not know his accuser. The faceplate, with its engineered acoustics, would distort her voice. It was the way of the South Wall; to be anonymous, to be a part of the whole. It had brought relief to Kallisa, and although she knew it was cowardice, she was thankful for the mask she now wore.

They had summoned her shortly after she had arrived at the Court of the Overseers. On entering their den of secrecy, they had shown her two caskets. One she recognised as the duplicate box—what Larra had carried. The other must have come from Petra's Gwynerath run. Wise to a baited trap, she had asked if Aracyse had retrieved both caskets. Through all of her intrigue, and cat and mouse with cult and court, Kallisa had maintained her suspicion. She could not trust the South Wall. Nor could she ask them about any missing girl. She had rolled with their play, nodding and agreeing to all that they said. It had puzzled her; they didn't mention Larra during her time examining the boxes. All they told her was that they had recovered a second casket distant from Petra's ship.

Kallisa had been the architect of doubt in Etherus. Her study of the South Wall's devotion and psychology had pointed to an eagerness to reject all other power. Etherus was a bane to their belief in Kalle. To some, it was a monstrous entity. She had spun a web of deceit to portray the complex as a plot to undermine the King's omnipotence. Having received the caskets, they had opened them and asked what she knew of the weapons. She found it curious that none of the Southwallers appeared to lead, and none were subservient. The secretive commune was driven by a single unifying ideology: they were all one under their immortal master.

On their command, she had inspected the weapons. Exhilarated by the moment, Kallisa had fought hard to stop her hands from shaking when she handled the glass spheres. The cult's glassblowers had created perfect copies, right down to the small sealed valve. They were almost too perfect. Kallisa had struggled to discern the minute details that separated threat and theatre, and the Fury from her flesh. Although she assumed the Fury would rest inside Petra's casket, Kallisa couldn't be certain. They could have switched them. It was a test. Her confidence in her role had all come down to weight. The cult had created the duplicates with an intentional and uneven thickness. It was imperceptible to the eye, but the cult spheres rolled with the faintest imbalance. When she handled the genuine Fury, it sat steady on her palm, weighted to perfection.

The South Wall had wanted to see the proof of her claim; that Etherus was a front for an ideological cause. They had asked that she destroy one; to prove the weapon was nothing more than an engineered trick—a pyrotechnic. Kallisa had offered a different strategy. One that would put Aracyse in Seawall and shut down the blasphemous cult of the Wind. And now her chance had come.

A flash illuminated the room. A single lamp pushing back the darkness. In the glow of that lone light, Kallisa saw the bulk of a man standing central. His frame and features became more solid as each bright globe spluttered into life. General Aracyse. A proud and powerful figure standing in the middle of the room. She observed him for a moment; stealing herself for the betrayal she was about to perform. Many had died for the cult to reach this endgame, and Kallisa struggled to balance the scales against one man. But Aracyse had shown himself to be different. Not a pawn, or a willing martyr; he was an enigma.

On the east side of a square room with a domed ceiling, Kallisa stood behind a stone altar. There was a single open box on top, within which the Southwallers had carefully nested the three glass spheres in a cushioned bed of blue velvet. On the southern wall, there was a grand fireplace recessed into the marble. Black soot discoloured the white; a recent burn to test the draw of the flue. A shallow pit surrounded the hearth; the tooling marks were sharp, the exposed marble bright and clean. Between the altar and the General, the two-dozen feet of space was bare. On the other side of the room, two heavy guards flanked the arched door.

Kallisa turned to the robed Southwallers, two on each side of the box. They nodded, and she inhaled a deep breath to face Aracyse.

'General, you know what these are?' she asked, displaying the Furies. Her voice, altered and deepened inside the ingenuous harmonic mask, was a surprise to her own ears.

Aracyse appeared to ponder the question, staring at the spheres. 'Considering today's events, I assume one of these is the Etherus Fury?'

'One?'

'Two were stolen from Etherus. One was destroyed; the other lost. I ask again, is one of these from the Melody? Is it what I reclaimed today?'

Kallisa spoke, cautious to avoid any reference to the General and their relationship. 'We recovered another casket.' She gestured to the box. 'The one you recovered must have been the second. As you can see, we have reclaimed three of Etherus' fabled weapons.'

Aracyse frowned and shook his head.

'Is there something wrong, General?'

'One Fury was unaccounted for. Just one.'

Kallisa beckoned him to come forward. 'Then, can you tell us which one that is?'

Aracyse approached the altar, stopping one yard from it. Wrinkles furrowed his brow, his eyes tracking over each of the orbs. His hesitation was high praise of the cult's ingenuity at creating such perfect copies.

'General, if you say only one was taken, which is it?'

Gesturing to the spheres, he growled. 'This is not how we test for an elemental presence.'

'Ah, yes. I have heard of the process. Sunlight?'

Aracyse nodded. 'Yes. If exposed, it will show itself within the glass. Without daylight, I can't tell which is which.' He raised his head and his eyes widened. 'Have you checked already?'

'Alas, General, we have not.'

He leaned closer, shaking his head. 'The other two spheres, why have you put them with a Fury?'

'Are they not also Furies?'

Aracyse lifted his head. He stared at her. Under the mask, Kallisa felt vulnerable, as though he might see through her disguise. Yet she understood what truths the eyes spoke, and the General showed no hint of recognition. His confusion was stark, shown by his searching questions.

'Were they taken from the cult?'

Kallisa couldn't respond. She knew they had been, although she had not been privy to the exact circumstances. She turned to her masked and unwitting conspirators. One nodded, and when they spoke, the words came forth as a man's voice. Although with the distortion, Kallisa couldn't be certain.

'A woman. She confessed to being part of the cult. She admitted her heresy, and that the spheres she carried had come from Etherus.'

Finally. A mention of Larra. Kallisa hid her recognition, although she feared what they might reveal of her fate.

Aracyse stepped back. He shook his head with confident denial. 'That's not possible.'

'More,' the Southwaller said. 'She told us they were as harmless as the rest.'

'What?'

Kallisa said, 'We have believed for some time that Etherus does not create weapons. We believe it only creates deception. It is why you are here, General.'

The General stared. There was a turmoil in his eyes, a stupefied expression on his face.

She continued. 'We wished to bring you here to prove to ourselves that there can be no power but Kalle. We wish to see for ourselves what we have long believed: that Etherus, and therefore you, General, are an affront to the King.'

'This is outrageous,' Aracyse said, his voice a wakening storm. 'I demand to speak to the King.'

The Southwaller tipped his head to the General. 'It is with the King's blessing that you are here. We would not trouble our master without first seeing with our own eyes the fraud of the Fury.'

Aracyse stepped toward the altar. Kallisa wondered what he might do: would the great General Aracyse Stranghame lose his temper in the south wall? It would be a mistake. A dozen heavy guards lay in wait beyond the door behind her back. Even Aracyse would struggle against such an augmented and brutal foe.

It shouldn't have surprised her that Aracyse rallied his composure. He pointed to the orbs spread before him. 'There is trickery here. And it is not from my hand. Without the light of the sun, there is no way to tell which of these is the real Fury. Indeed, if they have deceived us, perhaps the cult never brought the Fury to the city? Perhaps it lies elsewhere, waiting to be used?'

Kallisa said, 'General, we have worked to infiltrate the cult at every level. Those that brought us this information have our trust.'

Aracyse smiled a sickly grin. 'Well then, I am glad you hold my decades of service to Kalleron in such high regard.'

'Sarcasm will not win friends here,' the Southwaller said. 'We are certain we know what is happening, and we shall prove it to you, before we prove it to the King.' He raised his arm, relaying the instruction for Kallisa to begin.

'General,' she said, walking around the altar and picking up a sphere. She couldn't be certain if it was the Fury or a fraud. The Southwallers had dismissed her while they created their aesthetic display; no doubts another chance to test her faith. Kallisa handled the first orb with care and was thankful for the mask. It concealed her absolute concentration. Placed on her palms, she held the first sphere to Aracyse. By chance, it was the Fury. Kallisa summoned all of her focus to steady her hand. With control, she asked, 'Is this your weapon?'

'I told you; I cannot tell without sunlight. Whatever this trickery is, we should wait until tomorrow.'

With an unseen smile, Kallisa placed the Fury back in the nest. She picked up another, relieved to be holding a sculpture of inert glass, and displayed it to the General. 'What about this one?'

Aracyse scowled. A huff of breath blown through his nose. He refused to answer.

'Very well, General. I see no point in delaying the inevitable. Let us see this Fury.'

Kallisa stepped toward the fireplace and the pit. It was shallow, only a few feet deep; a precaution planned well in advance. The cult spheres would explode with a fiery display, but there would be no elemental carnage. It was that effect she had pressed upon the cabal of the South Wall; the only thing Etherus was master of was light and sound. To heighten the drama, she looked over her shoulder at Aracyse, whose eyes were wild and wide.

'We do not fear Etherus,' she said, and threw the sphere into the pit.

With a flash of white light and a ball of flame, the glass shattered with a surprising concussion. The power of the blast caught her, and she stumbled away from it. Kallisa looked at the broken shards—her heart thumping. Had she destroyed the wrong sphere? Seconds passed. There was silence in the room; no further alarm. Nothing more than a moment of fright. The tension was palpable, and as she turned away from the pit, she noted how rigid her audience had become.

Caught in her throat, she stifled a laugh. An impulse of relief. Kallisa composed herself and gestured to the pit. 'This is your Fury, General?'

He pointed. 'That was no Fury. A clever trick, but it is not of Etherus.'

Kallisa didn't respond, instead she returned to the box and removed the other duplicate. She turned and thrust it toward his face. She had expected him to flinch, but he didn't. The General was standing his ground, a glare of ice sent from his grey eyes. It was something to use against him; his fortitude and bravery.

'You don't appear frightened of the very weapon you say is... devastating.'

'Generals don't cower.'

Kallisa smiled, impressed by his iron will. 'Very well.' She turned to the Southwallers and held out her hand. An offer to test the Fury of Etherus.

The speaker came forward and took the sphere. He paced to the pit and turned. 'Etherus is nothing.' Maintaining his focus on Aracyse, he tossed the orb to the stone. He walked away, the sphere exploding behind him in another harmless display of light and sound. Returning to the box, he appeared to linger, staring at the last sphere. The true Fury.

Kallisa said, 'Can you not see, General? Three spheres, none of which you could say was your weapon; two of which, at random, we destroyed. Do you see your problem? Where is this Fury?'

He pointed to the box. 'If that is the weapon from Etherus, I would not continue this theatre.'

'And we shall not,' the Southwaller said. 'We have all the proof we need of this seditious betrayal.' He motioned to the guards at the far door. 'Take Aracyse to the King.'

Aracyse bowed his head. He appeared stoic, although his empire at Etherus was collapsing. She had twisted the knife in his back; yet the blade sliced through her own soul. A proud and good man brought down. But it was for a greater cause. As they led Aracyse away, all that remained of her task was to bring the Fury to the King. He could prove his power over Etherus. If he chose not to, she could destroy the orb in his presence. The immortal age of Kalle would soon be over.

Chapter XXXVII

Aracyse knelt before the King's throne. This summons was different; he had been out-manoeuvred by a plot he had never seen coming. The South Wall had taken profound umbrage at his work and deemed Etherus a fraud, although for what purpose Aracyse could not fathom. He awaited his King, and as the whispers began clamouring for their master, and the thunderous footsteps approached, he thought his favour with the court was finally over. It shouldn't have been a surprise; few generals reached his age without notice. His respect reached far and wide. Perhaps he should have died in a glorious battle to avoid whatever betrayal was coming his way.

'Arise, General,' the King said.

Aracyse steadied his mood and pushed on his knee to stand. He preferred dignity, and standing tall, he broke protocol, gazing at the emotionless mask of Kalle. If he was to face his death, he would look his judge in the eyes.

The King's voice boomed. 'We have a traitor among us.'

He stared at Kalle as the echo of a false god reverberated around the chamber. Aracyse expected him to repeat the absurd claim of the South Wall. But the King's head lifted, directing his attention to the grand arched door.

'Bring her in!'

Confused, Aracyse turned. Two Southwaller heavies entered. Between them, they dragged Overseer Kallisa. Not in her court attire, she wore a white robe; the clothing of the South Wall. The guards threw her to the floor, and she fell at his feet. A revelation; it all came together in his mind; the day's strange events, the drama with the smashed spheres. The grand gestures and accusations. It had been Kallisa all along. Incredible. It was hard not to respect her guile. Such a well-executed and devious play, although he was relieved it was her, and not him, on the floor. She moved at his feet, an effort to stand, but the King spoke.

'Stay where you belong, traitor.'

Aracyse looked from Kallisa to the King, another noise bringing his focus back to the door. Four more guards entered, two boxes carried between them. They placed them in front of the throne and retreated into the shadows.

Kalle pointed to the larger of the two caskets. An unexceptional trunk hinged with iron, and sealed by leather buckles; it was incongruous with the grand theatre.

'Overseer, open the casket.'

Aracyse suffered a stab of empathy as Kallisa glanced up. In her eyes, he saw confusion, and he was certain she saw the same in his. His lips formed a silent query; his brow crumpling ever deeper. Why had she done it? The Overseer shook her head and looked at the King.

'Your Majesty? I don't understand.'

'The box. Open it.'

Kallisa nodded with hesitation. Aracyse leaned forward, his curiosity getting the better of him. What was in the box? The other contained the Fury; it was the same casket from the treachery in the South Wall. He held his breath in anticipation. Kallisa unbuckled the straps and paused. Her eyes came to meet his, and in them he saw defeat.

'Open it,' Kalle said.

With her fingers trembling, and her hands fumbling with the lid, Kallisa pushed it open. She shrieked and fell backwards, pushing herself away from the horror. There was a body inside. A pretty but bloodied face peering out with glassy eyes. No bigger than a child's coffin, the casket was too small for an adult. Somehow, they had made her fit. Aracyse stared with morbid fascination. The torture would have been extreme; he knew Kalleron was capable of such monstrosity, and although he had vowed to never use it, his masters were quick to employ sadistic means to seek the truth. They had snapped her limbs; new joints created to fold her into the space. It would have been brutal. Aracyse winced. He hoped the poor girl had succumbed to her injuries before being crammed into her bastard coffin. He stepped back and looked from Kallisa to the King.

'She told us everything,' Kalle said, descending from his throne. He paced around the boxes and stood above Kallisa. 'How you have betrayed me. Such foolishness. I give life and this is how you repay your master? It is impossible to deny my power, yet your insignificant cult believes it can threaten me. It supposes to plot and deceive; to make me appear vulnerable.' The King reached down, and with one hand, he grabbed the Overseer by the throat. He plucked her from the darkwood floor, lifting her into the air as though she were a doll made of rags. 'It is not I who is vulnerable.'

Kallisa flailed, trying to grapple with his arm; her hands grasping at the golden metal wrist, her legs kicking in space. Awed as he was by Kalle's strength, Aracyse did not savour the scene; it was unjust. Kallisa fought hard, her eyes wide and panicked, but Kalle stood firm and the Overseer's frantic struggle weakened.

'Your Majesty?' Aracyse said, keen to summon reason.

'General?' the King replied without releasing the Overseer.

'We can learn even more if you allow her to live.'

'Yes.'

Kallisa fell to the ground. She reached to her throat, coughing and rasping. Her eyes were red, weeping and stricken with fear. A grimace on her face; she was struggling to breathe.

'Guards, remove her; throw her in Seawall.' The King turned to Aracyse. 'Tomorrow you will find out what you can, then I shall reclaim her soul.'

Conflicted thoughts troubled his mind as he watched the two Southwallers dragging Kallisa away. Kalle had spared her for now, but the command was clear to the General. His would be the hand that would end her life. At least he could do so with mercy.

'General,' the King said, drawing Aracyse's attention from the closing doors. 'Open the other box.'

Aracyse nodded and knelt beside the casket. As he released the latches, Kalle continued to speak of the cult plot.

'The girl resisted for a while. She did well for a human. Perhaps I should make all of my subjects as robust as she proved to be. Her deceit was strong, but as we broke her limbs and twisted them for every lie she uttered, she soon found the truth and relinquished the words that delivered Overseer Kallisa's treason. Her honesty flowed as clear as a mountain spring. She named another. Kastane. Their leader; a soldier from our own ranks. She spoke of a house in the hills. I will crush this cult, General. It will all be over, and this degenerate fascination with my eternity will be complete.'

Aracyse lifted the lid of the box. He sighed with relief; a great exhalation to blow away his anxiety. There, sitting content and calm, was the Fury. He allowed himself a chuckle.

'General?' the King asked.

With a grin he thought might appear childish on his face, Aracyse pointed to the sphere. 'This might well be a fraud. Earlier, the South Wall seemed intent on proving that.'

The King peered down at him. 'Oh, but it is.'

'Your Majesty?'

'Do not fear, General; your loyalty is not in question—that was the initial plot. But the girl told us everything. The cult took the real Fury, and this remains a problem that you will solve. The girl's last words came with her final breaths; she told us the weapon remains at large, gone with her master, the man named Kastane. That bauble is nothing but silverspar and glass. The same as the trickery Kallisa used to deceive you.'

Aracyse stared at the Fury. Could it be true? Kallisa's reaction; her resignation when accused of treason was proof of her complicity. If the girl in the box had given that information, then it would follow she spoke the truth of the Fury's switch. But something didn't fit. There was a splinter in his mind. A red swirl in the dark. He had retrieved the casket from the hidden cache. Petra's words had seemed genuine; her part in the cult was that of a simple runner, not a trained spy. Had she also lied? Aracyse grappled with the dilemma. It was possible the girl had given half-truths. There was no way to know until the light of day. It was the only logical course.

'My King?' he said.

Kalle had ascended the throne. He nodded.

Aracyse pointed to what he thought might still be the Fury. 'If the girl lied. If...'

'I spoke to her. I broke her. She would not lie. Every word we eased from her lips has proven to be true. Now, complete her confession; destroy the glass.'

In his mind, Aracyse stood in darkness on the shore of a vast ocean. He could sense the tide coming, although he couldn't see it. It was a suffocating and desperate sensation. Soon, it would overwhelm him. Kalle believed in his perfection; his invulnerability, and Aracyse couldn't question it. He closed the lid of the casket.

'General?'

'Your Majesty, it is best that I test this in daylight. Only then...'

The King interrupted. 'Perhaps your head is full of confusion? We bled the truth from the mortal girl on a promise that we would keep her alive. Do you know what mortals will do to keep living? To clutch at breath? General, if I say she spoke the truth, it becomes my truth.' Kalle stood from his throne. Aracyse had never seen the King so animated. 'Do you doubt my word?'

What could Aracyse say? If he pressed his resistance any further, the King would react with impunity. Kalle couldn't allow a mortal to question his will. But if Aracyse destroyed the Fury, and it was real, there would be carnage. He gazed at the darkness collapsing in around him. There was one chance. If he threw it to the far wall, wherever that might be, it would pose less risk. At least he could run for the door. The King would have the same chance to escape.

'Very well,' Aracyse said, opening the casket. He scooped his hand under the glass and removed the sphere, holding it in his palm. Strange thoughts of General A'dan came to his mind. Stranger that his own misfortune at Etherus was a secondary concern. With concentration, he stood, lifting his frame and heavy armour without the aid of his human arm, and though his thighs trembled, he faced the King with the Fury in hand. 'In the south wall, there was a concussive blast. It may damage my mortal shell. Where shall I throw this?'

The King gestured to the darkness that enveloped the chamber. Aracyse peered into the gloom. It seemed such an infinite depth. He glanced over his shoulder, estimating the time it would take to run for the door. About to hurl the sphere, he heard shuffling.

'Your Majesty, there are men there?'

'General, my guards can endure some silverspar. Prove my truth.'

It was madness. Aracyse looked at the sphere. Perhaps it was paranoia? The girl had given up Kallisa. Torture elicited truth from the weak and lies from the brave. But never had he known it to speak the language of both. With a sigh, and a glimmer of hope in his King's supreme confidence, Aracyse hurled the sphere across the room.

He misjudged the depth, having assumed Kalle had stationed his men against the wall. The sound of glass shattering took a moment longer to manifest. It did not bode well; there was no flash of light, nor was there a blast. It was the simple chime of a crystal vase crashing upon wood. Silence followed, broken by the shuffle of feet. Confused, the reality dawned on Aracyse—it was not a cult sphere. There had been no trickery of light and sound.

'See, General,' the King said. 'It was all a ruse.'

'Where was the silverspar?' he replied, stepping away.

Aracyse peered into the gloom. The King, assured of his truth, remained standing beside his throne when something monstrous giggled in the darkness. Aracyse's blood froze and his spine shuddered. The Fury had awoken.

'Your Majesty, flee! Flee now!' Aracyse said, and ran for the door.

Dragged from the King's chamber, and with her hair falling across her face, the floor passing beneath had become a blur. Where Kallisa had felt the smooth darkwood boards, the bare stone now bruised her knees and shins. One last attempt at dignity. She fought the frustration and despair rising within.

'I can walk. Let me walk.'

The guards said nothing. In near silence, the progress toward the northern wall, to Seawall, remained a steady torment. Confusion replaced her fear. Her body plunging to the ground. They had released her, although they had held her arms so tight, she could still feel the pressure on her flesh. She pushed up on her hands, looking for an answer; careful not to stand in case her captors pummelled her back down to the ground. But the guards had paced away, moving a few steps toward the King's castle. Kallisa heard a strange sound, a muffled thunder and the crackle of lightning, but there was no storm. What had she missed? What would distract the Southwallers? A flurry of movement caught her attention; a figure appearing from the Avenue of the King. Aracyse? Fearful the guards would react, she remained low on the bare rock. They moved farther away, reaching the darkwood walkway from where the General was now coming. He was running, a remarkable feat for a man in such heavy armour. Glinting in the moons, a suit of gold appeared. It was the King. Kallisa's heart soared. The thunder crackled again, and now she saw the glory of Etherus. Splinters of wood were erupting from the Avenue of the King; spears of shrapnel flying into the night. As Aracyse's flight reached halfway across the timber bridge, a tremendous vortex of wind and debris spiralled from the mouth of the grand arch. It was a terrible gale; a howling and angry scream that seemed to rip the air from itself. Eyes wide, Kallisa saw the King wobble on the boardwalk; beneath his feet, the wood was shaking in the Fury's grip. Her elation turned to despair as the power of the Wind dissipated; its energy spent, and its freedom achieved. Aracyse approached, continuing his flight down the ramp, but she stared in horror as the King steadied himself on the darkwood causeway. The General's thundering footfall came to a halt at the shore as he stepped onto the rock. His glance came her way when, over the soft popping sounds of wood falling into the water, Kallisa heard a mighty creak. Kalle stumbled as the walkway lurched. Her smile returned; the Fury had damaged the bridge; it was unstable, teetering on its supports. The Southwaller guards launched themselves along it to save their King. Aracyse screamed at them to fall back.

'Stop! The supports; they're weakened!'

They didn't heed his words. And as other guards appeared, stumbling and staggering from the damaged castle, some dragging limbless shells with them, the King's hand raised to stop them all.

His voice loud above the chaos, he cried out, 'Wait!' Kalle's booming call echoed across the fortress plain. He called again as the injured men moved closer to him. 'Stop! You fools. Stop moving!'

With a terrific creak, and a crack of thunder, the darkwood walkway beneath Kalle's feet collapsed. Kallisa rose from the ground and backed away, keen to stay clear of Aracyse; his focus now on his doomed King. She moved quietly, watching with glee as the King's golden armour fell with the shattered causeway, splashing with chaotic energy into the dark water. An explosion of amber and azure erupted from the impact; the mass of men and darkwood displacing a tumultuous wave of water. A wonderful silence followed, and Kallisa made good her careful escape, watching the water's edge. Could Kalle have survived? Would he rise as an immortal from the depths? The sand of the hourglass trickled by, and as the inlet settled, Kallisa turned to run.

She screamed, falling backward as the white ghost appeared. The Queen. Come to see the chaos. Her aura, although oppressive, was not as it had been, and with her senses intact, Kallisa scrambled away, rising quickly to her feet. She swivelled, surprised to see Aracyse coming her way. He was calling. Calling to his Queen.

'Your Majesty! Treachery. Treason.'

The Queen stared at Aracyse, the General halting his advance yards away. She moved her attention to the inlet, her red eyes observing the ruined walkway and the few men marooned on what remained upright.

'Where is the King?' the elemental asked.

Aracyse pointed to the water. His voice was impatient. 'He fell with the bridge. He has time.'

'Time?'

'Save him!'

'Save?'

Did he know what he had just done? Kallisa's heart soared; Aracyse had shown his lack of faith in Kalle to the elemental. Another voice of truth, no less that of a general of Kalleron, to shatter the immortal myth. Kallisa stared, wondering what she would do next.

The Queen paced toward the inlet. Kallisa followed, keeping an assured distance from Aracyse. She could still flee, but he appeared uninterested in her plight; his attention switching between the Queen and the dark waters. The Southwaller guards who had run to their King were wading into the inlet. It was fascinating; they appeared intent on saving their King, although in their metal armour, they would surely join him in death.

'Guards, wait!' Aracyse called.

They turned, stumbling as they saw their Queen approach.

'Where is the King?' she asked.

Aracyse pointed to the water. His face flushed, and his posture uncertain; he lowered himself on one knee. 'He fell, your Majesty. He fell into the water.'

'Stand,' she said, and Aracyse obeyed. The Queen switched her attention; her gaze falling on Kallisa. 'You said the King was as you are: mortal, insignificant. Watch, and understand your error.'

Aracyse groaned; it was frustration. It was a beautiful irony. Kallisa cast a glance his way, and he nodded. With a growl, he said, 'Well done, Overseer. You've achieved the impossible; but you'll not escape the fortress.' He motioned to the Southwallers wading from the water. 'Seize her!'

'No,' the Queen said.

Aracyse frowned. 'No? Your Majesty?'

'When Kalle emerges, he will choose her fate. He is the human elemental, not you.'

Doubt? Kallisa flinched. If the Queen was certain of her belief, there was no reason to delay the General's order. There would be no pause; they would haul her away to Seawall. To hold still and observe revealed the immortal's curiosity. A human trait; the same vulnerability that had brought her under the spell of the first incarnation of Kalle all those years ago.

'What if?' Kallisa said to her.

'What if what?'

'The King does not return?'

'He will.'

Kallisa stared at the water. Ripples from the Larissian supports, twitching under the weight of the stranded darkwood castle, were the only movement. No bubbles to show life. No golden King rising from the dark.

'He does not come, my Queen,' Kallisa said.

She waited. No response given to her prompt. Kallisa glanced at Aracyse and saw the recognition in his eyes. His shaking head was confirmation of her own understanding. The King was dead. A heap of lifeless gold, unseen in the dark depths. The image in her mind conjured an idea.

Kallisa said, 'Your boundary is water. Is it ours? We drown in your sister's presence. What would she do to the human elemental? What is his boundary?'

The Queen turned her red eyes on Kallisa. Had it been the gaze of a human, she thought it might be a chastising glare; a reprimand for her insolence. But there was no rebuke. Instead, the Queen moved to the water's edge.

She said, 'You cannot understand. You are not. I am.'

With those words, she raised her arms. Kallisa gasped, stumbling backwards as the inlet split in two; a great channel appearing under the castle. In the light of the moons, the vertical walls of the inlet glittered orange and blue. At the edge, floating beams of wood fell dozens of feet to the exposed bed. Unseen in the dark, they clattered on rock and armour. It was an impossible sight to behold, Kallisa struggling with reality to comprehend what she saw.

'There!' Aracyse said, pointing to a faint glimmer of colour on the lakebed. He looked at the Queen who stood at the edge. The guards, sworn to duty, moved into the void.

The Queen called to them. 'Stop. You are not welcome in our domain.'

They hesitated, but they continued on, marching into the gulf and passing the remains of swaying darkwood supports. From the sheer and rippling wall of water, drops cascaded horizontally. Sparkling amber and azure, an impossible rain fell on the guards. They appeared unfazed, continuing on with their march. Halfway to the King, the shower became a deluge, and Kallisa struggled to see the men. As quick as the rain had come, it abated. The guards were gone.

'What the...?' Aracyse said.

'I am; they are not,' replied the Queen.

The elemental strode into the void, passing into a realm Kallisa, and centuries of knowledge, had thought forbidden. Earth was moving in Water's domain. It should not be, yet it was.

'Incredible,' Aracyse said.

'She is beyond us, General, and you'll see what I have done is just.'

He turned to her. Words appeared ready on his lips, but the General squinted and huffed, and turned back to the inlet. From the depths of darkness, a white figure stooped and lifted a golden prize. The Queen returned, pacing with regal beauty and elegance. Behind her, the elemental walls collapsed, and the waves came crashing ashore. The force knocked Kallisa to the ground, pushing her backward, tossing and turning her with Water's powerful kiss. She coughed the liquid from her lungs and rose to her feet, righting her balance and seeking the Queen. She hadn't moved. Kallisa's blood ran as cold as ice to see the water return to the inlet. It coursed around the Queen, never touching her marble skin. Beside her, Aracyse was rising, composing his stance after being knocked over. A terrible and cataclysmic sound punctured the air. It was the castle, crumpling on its damaged supports and falling into the depths. Kallisa stared in awe as the emblem of the King's knowledge and omnipotence slipped beneath the waves. As though a wooden iceberg; an awkward angle of darkwood poked above the surface as a new tide washed across the shore. Planting her feet firm, Kallisa stared at Aracyse. Eyes wide, mouth agape; he appeared awestruck.

With her heart thumping as though horses galloping across the plains, Kallisa walked toward the Queen. Kalle was lifeless in her arms. The sight amazed and terrified her; the Queen had grown taller than Aracyse, proportioned to better fit her King. A thought occurred to Kallisa. Was there a limit to her earthly guise?

'My Queen,' Kallisa said. 'Do you see? He has drowned.'

The King fell to the rock with a crash, Kallisa startling at the abruptness of the Queen's response. To her horror, a spluttering cough came ringing from the mask of Kalle. His body convulsed and water poured from his helmet.

'He lives!' Aracyse said.

Motionless, the Queen observed Kalle's struggle. 'My King?'

Kallisa gazed at the impassive monarch standing above Kalle. Beneath the Queen, the golden armour continued to writhe. He moved, an arm placed in position, readying to push from the ground. He was trying to stand. But he buckled, once more consumed by a wretched cough and violent spasms.

'My King?' the Queen repeated. 'What is this?'

Again, Kalle moved. This time, he brought a knee underneath his frame. Was he about to stand? Kallisa drew her hands to her face; it was horror. It was impossible. No man could have survived the exposure he had endured. Yet still, Kalle lived. It couldn't be true. It couldn't. But he collapsed, his body once more convulsing.

'I am,' the Queen said, and cast her gaze at Kallisa. 'This is not.'

She shrieked as the King erupted into the air; his golden body hoisted upon a marble spike that rose high above their heads. Impaled, Kalle cried out; his groans were a terrible and pained sound. The King of Kalleron released a feeble wheeze as his body became limp. As quickly as it had appeared, the marble executioner retracted, and the King's body clattered to earth, motionless and silent.

The Queen stared at the lifeless golden husk inside which a mortal man had died. She brought her gaze to Aracyse, then to Kallisa. 'He is as you are. Insignificant.'

Kallisa lowered herself to her knee. 'My Queen.'

'I am not your Queen. It is insignificant.'

With uncertainty, Kallisa rose to her feet. She gestured to the King's body. 'The lie, exposed.'

'Yes.'

'I am sorry.'

'Sorry?' The Queen paced to Kallisa, stopping within a breath from her face. Her presence was overpowering. Kallisa stepped away from those swirling and depthless ruby eyes.

'For what has happened to you. For the lie.' The realisation was stark. Kallisa was awakening from a nightmare to see the bright rays of a new dawn. She smiled. 'You are free. You are no longer controlled.' A thought came to her; an old word to better fit the elemental. 'Kor'A?'

The white face remained impassive. 'Kor'A?'

'A name given to you long ago.'

'I am. I am not a name.'

Kallisa struggled with her devotion to the elementals. She knew her heart wanted passion and poetry, but the creature standing before her was no bard or wistful soul. It was the power of Earth, a demigod utterly removed from humanity. Yet still, Kallisa could not let go of her faith.

'But you have followed us. You have observed us. You are curious of what we are, of what we do when we live.' She gestured to her own body. 'You copy our form. Do you not wish for a name? Do you not wish to belong?'

The elemental paced one step back. Her stature diminished, and as though a shadow fading in the light, she became smaller again. No taller than Kallisa.

'Kor'A?' the elemental said, a fan of white digits spread to her chest.

Kallisa nodded. Her vision blurred as tears came. She blinked them away, smiling at the elemental. 'Yes, Kor'A. You are not the Queen of man anymore.'

Kor'A gazed around the fortress. 'This place. What will I do?'

'Leave,' Kallisa said, aware Aracyse had approached. 'Leave before men try to deceive you again.'

'Yes.' Aracyse called over. 'Leave Kalleron. Be free of us, that we may be free of you.'

Kallisa was stunned by the bluntness of his words.

Kor'A turned to the General. 'I have known you. I observed you where I have walked; when I have reclaimed my own. Are you also deceived by this?' Kor'A pointed to the golden armour of Kalle. 'Does he deceive all?'

Kallisa stared at Aracyse, waiting with anticipation for his response.

Aracyse bowed his head. 'He did not deceive me. I served.'

'Is this the power of mortals?' Kor'A asked.

Aracyse shook his head. His glance came to Kallisa, and she thought she understood the elemental's query.

'Yes,' she said. 'We deceive; we furnish our world with lies. It is how the few controls the many. It is how Kalle controlled you.'

The elemental paced away, walking to the shore. She didn't turn to face Kallisa, but the wind carried her words, the air carrying the tremor of stone. 'Those mortals that he reclaimed, and the life he delivered from the woman shell; that was a deception?'

Kallisa, confused by the question, realised she was speaking of Kalle's original lie. The Century Sin. 'Yes. They were all poisoned; all promised glory that was never given. He murdered a child to make you believe.'

Kor'A turned to face her. 'Why do you destroy one another? The abstraction you call time measures your insignificance. Why does your element seek to destroy that which is certain to become nothing? Why end what is already not?'

Kallisa shook her head. Why did humanity struggle against itself? What was it that drove nations to war? What else but power and glory? Transient things that men and women savoured above all. How could she explain such a trivial thing to an omnipotent immortal? Kor'A was a creature that appeared free from the failings of pride.

Kor'A said, 'What the King asked of me, when I reclaimed my own. Did this bring an end to existence? When rock became one with stone, and dust was blown on the wind. What Kalle did not reclaim.' She paused, peered at the lifeless body at her feet. 'Did I... kill?'

Kallisa couldn't answer; she wouldn't say the words she thought might be harmful.

Aracyse said, 'Yes. You have killed tens of thousands of men, women and children. Kalle never reclaimed a soul; his lies had you fooled. Death lies in your past, but it is not of your will.'

'I understand now,' she said. 'The man in the southern city. His words. Are they true? What I am, is this to be a monster?'

Southern city? Kallisa understood it to be Arkalla. But what man had she spoken to? She recalled the Queen's previous words when she had confronted her at the Fortress wall. Kallisa hadn't absorbed them at first, but now she tried to think who it could be; who could have survived the destruction the scouts and traders had described in such terrible detail?

She was keen to refute the words. 'You are not a monster. Kalle deceived you. But this man you saw. Who was he?'

'He thought himself important. I had destroyed his city and his god.'

His god? There could be only one person. 'The Seer?'

'I do not know. But he sought death, and...' Kor'A paused. She gazed at the King; a cannonball sized hole punctured through his chest plate. 'I do not... I do not mean this. I sent him away to find what he sought.'

'Away?' Kallisa struggled with the conversation. She had noticed the legions of guards approaching from the distant south wall. What would Kor'A do? Her thoughts turned to herself, what would happen to her? The guards would arrive in minutes.

The elemental appeared enlightened, and although her tone carried no emotion, there was a vibrance in her voice. 'I sent him to find my sister. Fire is anathema to all; she dwells away from sight. But he will find her; I helped him. You are correct, I am no monster.'

Fire? Kallisa, stunned by the bizarre revelation, knew that time was slipping away. And although she desired to question Kor'A, she wished her to be free of Kalleron. With a tentative step away from the General, she gauged her chances of escape.

'Kor'A, these men will try to punish me for showing you the truth.' She pointed to the guards. 'Will you stop them?'

'I will not.'

'They'll kill me. If you don't help, my life is over.'

Aracyse spoke. 'They will kill us both for what we've witnessed. I saw Kalle die. I can't admit to that. There is time for us both.' The General looked at Kor'A. 'What will you do with us?'

The elemental turned to Kallisa. 'You warned me of this. You did not deceive as he did. I will trust your words. What shall I do?'

Staggered by the platitude and grace, Kallisa could think of nothing but the opposite of what Kor'A, as Queen, had brought to all those lost cities. 'No more death. Leave this place.'

'What will I do when I leave?'

Kallisa fumbled with her own thoughts. To be asked by a god to find a purpose for its existence was a challenge too unfathomable. She shook her head, tried to clear the confusion, when a stone flower appeared in her mind's eye. The answer was already happening.

Holding her hand to the elemental, Kallisa said, 'You must create. Never destroy.'

Kor'A vanished without a word. As the castle had slipped beneath the waves, so too, Kor'A dissolved into her earth. Kallisa stared at the ground where she had stood, then looked at Aracyse.

'This isn't over,' he said. 'I will find you. And you'll answer for what you have done.'

She nodded, knowing he spoke the truth, although his tone lacked the severity she expected. 'Yes, General. But understand, it's not just the Queen who is free. You are.'

Aracyse stared as she backed away. Kallisa turned, and with her head down, she bolted to the northern wall and away from the chaos and fear she knew would come.

Chapter XXXVIII

Petra hadn't slept. How could she? Seated in the open block, her attention and thoughts were on the beautiful ghost sitting on the calm sea. Noctyrne and Ambyr painted the sails a canvas of azure and orange, and the ocean sparkled under her hull. For what reason she didn't know, the Melody of the Sea had dropped anchor out of port. It was a bitter gift of happiness; to see the freedom she had granted her crew. The cost was not so high that she felt cheated and glum, although she knew those days would come when the Melody finally set sail from Kalleron. That time, pushed far from her thoughts to enjoy the moment, would bring pain. In the calm of night, with the ripple of an unseen storm whispering on the wind, Petra's thoughts turned to Shadow. She hoped he would be on the ship, although doubts pestered her mind. Had she thought him a puppy? Too devoted to obey an order to leave? It had been a selfish thought, but it had been an honest one. If she were in his shoes, she thought she might stay behind. So obvious was their connection; so strong was their bond. Perhaps it was why the Melody sat square in her view. Was the new captain staring out from the deck, searching for his friend? Petra shook her head and sighed. She thought to scold herself; to remain strong. But there was no need to be the woman they had known. With what time Aracyse had given her, she would make every moment count. Kalleron wouldn't take her last hours; she would live them upon the waves, conjured in hazy dreams and beloved memories.

The sound of a latch wrenched her from the dream. Damn guards, sullying her proud mental fortitude. Perhaps Aracyse had come for another chat; he had seemed to enjoy their brief conversation, his expressions mixing between frown and grin, scowl and surprise. Petra wouldn't mind his company. His voice and tone brought the strangest sense of familiarity with a past she couldn't savour, but neither would she abandon. She looked at the door, considered standing, but erred on the side of caution. Better to be humble in chains, not defiant on her feet. The time to fight had passed.

The door opened, and a robed figure appeared. Dishevelled and visibly shaking, Kallisa stood in the shadows. Her expression was wild, her eyes wide.

Her voice strained and coarse, she said, 'It's done.'

'Done?' Petra rose to her feet. 'The King?'

Kallisa's rapid nod was accompanied by a manic grin.

'The King is dead?' Petra asked.

The Overseer tipped her head, and her hands came to her face. 'We're free.' She looked around the cell block, eyes darting without focus. 'But not for long. Everything will be in disarray; there's not much time.'

Petra stared, dumbfounded. What was this emotion she felt? Relief? It was not so simple a thing. Disbelief? She turned and glanced over her shoulder. The Melody was a calm sight to quell her rising elation. It brought focus.

'Kallisa, my chains?'

The cultist stared. 'A key!'

'Have you one?'

Kallisa hesitated, then turned to the door. From the iron ring left in the lock, she plucked a sliver of metal. She held it to Petra, tilting her head and offering the key. Her hands were trembling as leaves in the wind.

'I'll not manage,' Kallisa said.

Petra took the key and dropped to her knees. She removed the shackles and stared at them as they lay on the floor. An unwanted sensation of remorse flickered in her mind; they had been Aracyse's gift. She laughed at herself for contemplating the chains as anything other than the end of freedom. What was she thinking? Petra stood and grabbed Kallisa by the shoulders. The cultist wasn't the woman she had been. Confused and agitated; she needed to concentrate.

'Kallisa, how do we get out? The guards?'

The cultist stared into her eyes. In her turmoil, Kallisa possessed a chaotic beauty. 'The Southwaller's will have mobilised, all gone to the King's aid.'

'You said he was dead?'

She sighed and smiled. 'Yes. But their beliefs are not so black and white.'

How could dead not be dead? Petra shook her head. 'I don't understand.'

'I'll tell you when we've time, but we need to leave, and there may be other guards elsewhere.'

'Weapons?' Petra said, thinking of her daggers. 'My gear?'

Kallisa nodded. 'Not far. But after that, we'll need our wits.' The Overseer had shaken her wild countenance. 'Our time is short; are you ready?'

'Always.'

'Follow me, stay close.'

Kallisa turned and moved along the inner corridor. Petra didn't heed her surrounds; excitement and jubilation clouding her focus. The tunnels could have been five-feet or fifty yards, but all she could see was the cultist's robes, and she followed the ghost as she moved through the northern wall. Kallisa paused at an opening on her left and signalled for Petra to stay quiet. A wash of light spilled into the tunnel from an open arch. It couldn't be daylight. A room perhaps? Kallisa moved through the space, and Petra followed. Her focus on stealth, she didn't speak or make a noise, but the grand tunnel they passed under was majestic and opulent. It was a beautiful thing inside a deranged prison. A walkway spanned overhead; the marble bridge decorated with intricate and ornate carvings. Underfoot, Petra felt the roughness of gravel and dirt, but above their grubby path, everything was shining and glorious.

Through the next arch, Kallisa pointed further down the corridor. 'There, that's the armoury. Your gear will be in there. Time's on your side; tomorrow, they'll empty it.'

'No guards?'

Kallisa nodded with a frown. 'Inside, but they'll not be heavies.'

Petra gestured for Kallisa to move forward and followed close behind. At the door, the Overseer warded her away, a tilt of the head directing her to stay out of view. Kallisa knocked on the wood, and from within, a solid clunk of metal heralded a bolt being slid across iron. Creaking hinges preceded a gentle glow cast on the cultist's face. Kallisa's expression took on a serious veneer.

'Did you not hear the noise?' she asked. A pause followed the Overseer's question. 'Don't gawp, man: the noise, did you hear it?'

'Sorry, Overseer, I didn't recognise you without the black.' It was a man's voice.

'Where is the other?'

'It's just me.'

Kallisa moved into the room. Petra assumed that was her signal to follow; to overpower the guard and retrieve her gear. With stealth, she edged to the door and peered in. A lone guard, his hands on his neck, was slumping to the stone floor. Kallisa turned, and in her palm was a sliver of a blade, no longer or wider than a finger.

A glance at the knife, Kallisa said, 'A Drohendrian Fang.'

Petra frowned, not at the knife but at the dead guard. 'We could have overpowered him; subdued him.'

'We saved him a dire fate.' Kallisa pointed to the room. A small circular chamber, there were stacks of wooden cubes with alcoves built within. It appeared similar to a dressing room, not at all how Petra thought it would be. Kallisa asked, 'Do you see your clothes, weapons?'

Petra nodded. There were a few occupied alcoves, and her leather boots were poking out from a recess. She moved across, disrobing as she did, and pulled on her blouse, then her tunic. As the fabric slid across her skin, Petra smiled; it was as though bathing in pure waters. The soft leather was cleansing, rubbing away the dirt of captivity. She savoured the texture of her armoured bodice, her boots, and the daggers held within; it felt as though she was being resurrected.

As Petra dressed, Kallisa said, 'The South Wall will cleanse the fortress. They'll purge anyone not aligned with their deviant ideology.' She pointed to the body on the floor. 'You think they'd spare him? A guard who can't guard is no use to Kalleron.'

Leaning against a shelf, Petra pulled on her boots. 'What of the Queen? Has she left?'

Kallisa's face glowed with joy, her eyes wide and sparkling. 'I think, yes. She knows the deception, it is...' She hesitated; her focus drawn back to serious matters. 'But no matter, the South Wall will rally. There is more than one King of Kalleron.'

Petra stared, pausing with her second boot flopping over her ankle. 'What? What do you mean?'

'There are those who wait in line to become the new King. It is the bastard secret of the South Wall—a reincarnation of their god. They will quickly rebuild.' Kallisa sighed, a sound of wondrous revelation. 'I saw his castle fall into the water. His emblems destroyed. The King dead at my feet, and a Queen who is Queen no more. But Petra, they will rebuild it all behind these blasted secretive walls. Kalleron will not know what has happened. But it is weaker for it. It will not be the power it was; not without the Queen.'

With her boots on, Petra stood. 'When does this rebuild begin?'

'Right now. Somewhere on the other side of this fortress, a brute of a man will be sworn into his role and encased in new golden armour.'

Petra squinted. It was awful. Such calamity, such a victory, but it appeared nothing would change, not at least to the world. 'How will they know Kalle is dead?'

Kallisa smiled, but shook her head. 'They won't. But that was never the plan. You can't destroy faith, Petra. But you can prove a lie; as we did for Kor'A.'

'Who?'

'The Queen's old name.' Kallisa waved a finger. 'Make no mistake, she is Queen no more.'

There was much Petra wanted to know, too much to consider while she and Kallisa discussed treason in a Kallerye guardroom. 'We must go.'

Kallisa nodded. 'Keep your knives ready, we may need them.'

After the guardroom, the journey had been fraught with tension but void of threat. As she travelled behind Kallisa at a pace hindered by stealth, Petra feared it might take hours to find their way out of the fortress wall. In her mind's eye, she had pictured the main gate; tried to imagine what she would face. Distracted by her thoughts, she bumped into Kallisa who had stopped at an iron door set inside an alcove. The cultist grabbed the handle, flicked a latch, and pulled it to the side. On wheels, the door slid across a wooden track set into the floor. It reminded Petra of the cult's secret passageway, where Kastane had brought her into the hills beyond the harbour. As she passed the barrier, Kallisa gestured for her to close it shut. Petra looked for a handle and found a notch in the metal. She pressed against it, and with effort, slid the door across, the metal coming to rest with a soft click. Her hands felt the smooth surface, and Petra realised there was no latch on their side.

'We're trapped?'

In the dimmest light cast by a distant lamp, Kallisa said, 'It's one way. Even fortresses need escape routes.'

'Where does this lead?' Petra tried to imagine where she was, at what compass point they would appear, but the tunnels and chambers confounded her senses.

Kallisa came close. Her voice was hushed. 'The west wall, above the harbour.'

Petra pictured the port. She tugged Kallisa's robe as she turned away. 'The military district?'

Kallisa offered a redundant expression; her shrug suggested there was no other option. She nodded. 'They built it long ago to evacuate the generals. Where else would it lead?'

It made sense. Petra thought of bards' romantic tales where princesses and outcast knights eloped from their evil masters, escaping into lush meadows under blue skies. Her escape would not be so pretty.

'Is it safe? Will it be safe?'

'Better than here, don't you think?'

Kallisa set off down the dark tunnel. It was wide, and somebody had taken pride in its creation. An escape route it may have been, but it was fit for a king, not just a general. After dozens of yards following a steady decline, Kallisa's pace slowed. Her white robes came to a halt, and Petra moved to her side. Ahead, a blank face of dark blocked their way. It was another one-way door.

Kallisa brought her lips close to Petra's ear; her voice was a breeze away from inaudible. 'This is it. The door's damn heavy; I'll need your strength, but we must be quiet.'

Petra grasped the handle, her grip beside Kallisa's. 'Why did you risk it? Why come back for me?'

The Overseer smiled. 'Perhaps I need a friend to take me away from these shores. Perhaps I thought a crew as loyal as yours needs their captain.'

Whichever was the truth, Petra nodded and pulled on the handle. With all her might and focus, she inched the door open. Kallisa levered herself into the widening gap, and pressed against the edge. She held it there, and with her head, directed Petra to slip through. The space was narrow, but Petra squeezed between Kallisa and the door, grabbing the edge once she was on the other side. The Overseer angled away from the sliding mechanism, and with care, they let the iron barrier slide back into place. Petra had expected to see the moons and stars in a clear night sky. Instead, she stood in another dark tunnel.

Kallisa, her voice a whisper, pointed toward a funnel of light a dozen yards from where they stood. 'A culvert. One more grate until freedom.'

Petra followed Kallisa to the massive lattice of metalwork which blocked the way. Beyond it, she saw the sweeping arc of the bay and the scattered twinkle of lights. The ships moored in the harbour were a peaceful and calming sight. Kallisa moved to one side and pointed to the hinge. Petra looked to see what was of importance, shaking her head in the Overseer's direction.

'Push down that bolt; it locks the hinge from within.'

Petra studied the hinge, locating the ingenuous mechanism that held the grate fast. It was inaccessible from the exterior. With the bolt depressed, Kallisa opened the latch on her side. She nodded, and Petra, heeding the warning, moved her hands from the hinge. With a dull creak, the grate swung open.

Kallisa startled with a shriek. Petra saw the source of her fright. A shape rising from the tunnel floor. A guard; one last foe to sour their escape. He stood tall, blocking the path. Petra thought she could take him. A lone guard should be easy. The skirmish, though, it might alert any others beyond. To hell with them—she had come too far. With a growl, she pushed past Kallisa and drew her daggers from her boots.

Not shouting to alert his companions; the guard raised his hand, his voice a surprised whisper. 'What the... Petra?'

Petra juddered to a halt. How could it be? A smile; it didn't matter. It could only be one man. For only he would disobey a direct order from his captain. 'Shadow!'

He stood there, motionless but for the slightest tremble in his hand. His eyes were a sparkle of light in the dim tunnel. Petra stared, lost in the surreal moment. Tears on her face, and discarding her stoicism for the simplest of joys, she dropped her knives and charged forward into his arms. He embraced her, tighter than she'd ever known. She buried her face in his chest, and she felt him nuzzle into her neck.

A whisper distorted by ragged breaths, he said, 'Thought I'd lost you.'

She didn't reply; hugged him harder.

'I had to come. I had to.'

She nodded, her cheek rubbing against his leathers. Exhaling a sigh of ages, she pulled away. Petra clenched her fist and punched him in the chest. In the dark, she couldn't see much of his face, but she knew there was a grin.

'Ah, still got the power of a crippled child,' he said.

'That's for disobeying orders.'

'Well, I'll hit you later; when you're not looking.' The euphoria lingering, Shadow turned his attention to Kallisa, who had stooped to retrieve the dropped daggers. Petra stared at him. This perfect reunion couldn't last. Neither of them would let it, as much as she knew they both treasured it. Shadow duly restored the theatre of indifference that disguised their beautiful bond. 'Who are you?'

'You met her, Shadow, on the Melody. Kallisa.'

His tone became terse. 'You? Again?'

Petra moved her hand to his chest to placate him. 'She freed me, Shadow.' A glance to Kallisa. Petra smiled. 'The King is dead. The Queen knows.'

Shadow fidgeted under her hand. 'It's over?'

'For now,' Kallisa said. 'But we must leave here. Your ship, is it still berthed?'

He shook his head. 'No, set sail. Argan's taking it to the Barge Isles.'

'Not yet, he hasn't,' Petra said, recalling the magnificent view from her cell. 'It's anchored out beyond the bay.'

'Sly bugger.' Shadow raised his finger to Kallisa. 'What about her?'

'What about me?' Kallisa said, her bristling spirit intact.

'I said she saved me, Shadow.' Petra turned to the Overseer. A thought. Overseer no more. She was a traitor to Kalleron. 'What happened here; can you stay?'

She shook her head. 'Not on these shores. I've burned every bridge I had.'

Petra nodded, pressing her hand firmer against shadow's chest. 'You come with us. At least for now. You came to warn me of Kastane's deceit; you risked all to free me from Seawall. No matter what came before, you've earned my gratitude for that.'

Shadow agitated, but he kept quiet.

Kallisa nodded. 'I'd like that. If we can get beyond the Mansion Hills, I can get a sailboat. We can go to your ship.'

'Then it's settled. Shadow, is it safe to travel out?'

'Few guards, mostly drunk.' He stared; a frown visible on the vague highlight on his brow. 'If the King's dead, why's it seem so normal out? Shouldn't they all be running about with their bloomers in a twist?'

Kallisa said, 'It is the way of Kalleron; why the fortress walls are so high and impenetrable. Everything within is a secret. Dawn will bring no change to the people. But the Queen will be gone, of that, I am sure.'

Petra looked from Kallisa to Shadow. 'You take the lead? Get us over the hill?'

He turned his head, and in the light from the mouth of the tunnel, a subtle amber hue illuminated his face. Shadow nodded, placing his hand on hers, which was still resting on his chest. He held it for a moment, and she felt his fingers tremble and his chest rising. One last moment of a shared and beautiful truth before their stubborn game of lies resumed.

Shadow, prising her fingers away, said, 'If you get your grubby Larian paws off me, I'll take you anywhere you want.'

'Then home, Shadow, take us home.'

Epilogue
The Bruhsa

I sail to Laria on a ship captained by a woman whose heart is deeper than the ocean. From betrayal she discovered trust, and from that trust, I hope to find salvation. She calls her swift Larian trader, the Melody of the Sea, and upon her deck, walks a crew of familiar strangers. Once sworn to the rules, our pasts are locked away; there is no grim history among us, but a shared future of hope. Yet my bloodline calls my name, and my heart cannot stifle the truth of my people. Among the crew there is a Bruhadian man. His nature is calm and his heart is gentle, but the Bruhsa must know: Our great King lives, and Baza'rad sails from Kalleron on a journey to a world that is soon to awaken.

The Golden King is dead, of that I am certain. His Queen is gone, of that I know. But as Kalleron rouses to a new dawn, the world will notice no change. And though the destruction of Kalle was such magnificent justice, it will not be the end of the King. The South Wall will scheme and obfuscate, and another man beyond all men will don a new suit of immortal armour. Tomorrow, Kalle will rise again. They will rebuild his castle; craft it which such detail that an ant crawling across the cracks would be none the wiser. The perfect lie will continue.

Yet, without his elemental weapon, the new Kalle will be vulnerable. Kalleron rules by deception and fear, and as I write these words, I think of the proud man at the helm of this elegant ship. His people, my country; we were not defeated by sword and steel. We bowed to the inevitability of what would come. But what would come to others is now gone. The Terrible Queen of Kalleron is no more; Kor'A has returned to the world. Today, I can dream of a time when the lies of the South Wall become so burdensome that the house of Kalle will crumble under the hammer of a mortal man.

To Laria, then. I sail to a new home and a new truth, guided by a bright star. Where it goes, I will follow. When it dims, I will weep. But until my duty is done, and my bones rest with the earth, I shall call my shining light Petra.

About Author

After graduating from university, James D. McEwan worked in fitness for 27-years. He left his career to write the stories that have cluttered his imagination for a decade. He aspires to be a successful author, and to further explore Canada's beautiful Pacific coast. When not writing, he pretends to be a wildlife photographer. If you're out in nature, and you concentrate, you might hear his angry cries when the mischievous creatures cause his camera to lose focus. After a hard day swearing at animals, he enjoys a craft beer or two.

Visit **jamesdmcewan.com** for more information.

Or follow on Instagram **@fictionwriterjames**

Also By
James D. McEwan

Kalleron Series

The Trilogy of Tears:
– **Tears & Eternity, Kalleron Book II**
– **Blood & Fury, Kalleron Book III**

– **Hammer & Glass, Kalleron Book IV**

Other titles not in the Kalleron series:
– **M7RRORS**

Visit **jamesdmcewan.com** for more info.

Printed in Great Britain
by Amazon